Buying the Farm

By Kimberly Conn

Grateful acknowledgement is made for permission to print an excerpt from "Black Water" by the Doobie Brothers. Copyright © 1974 Patrick Simmons (renewed) WB Music Corp. and Landsdowne Music Publishers. All rights reserved. Used by permission of Alfred Music Publishing Co., Inc.

Cover design by Radoslaw Krawczyk via 99 designs

I dedicate this to my family.
Thank you for always wanting to hear my stories.

"You don't choose your family. They are God's gift to you, as you are to them."

—Desmond Tutu

CHAPTER ONE

Someone light a fire under me. I need to get moving. I have responsibilities, obligations, places to go and people to see. I loathe my responsibilities, however, and have no desire to go anywhere or see anyone, so here I remain, in my bed. My alarm went off an hour ago, but I cannot bring myself to get up. I am just not ready to face this day and all it has in store.

I may possibly be the world's worst procrastinator. I think it stems from a total lack of motivation, but at any rate I put everything off—from tasks at work to my very own laundry—and get around to completing them only when my idiot boss is yelling at me or I am down to one pair of clean underwear. Come to think of it, those are two of the reasons I am still in my bed right now. I am procrastinating getting dressed because I have almost nothing clean to wear, and I am procrastinating going to work because I hate my job. *Hate* it. It brings me no fulfillment whatsoever, I can't stand the people I work with or for with one major exception, and I hate that I spend so much time there that it keeps me from doing what I really want to do with my life . . . not that I know what that is yet, but I'm hoping to figure it out. Soon.

I'm not exactly sure what my issue with laundry is. I love having clean clothes to put on, things that smell of Tide and dryer sheets. It's just that the prospect of schlepping down to the dark, creepy, mildew-smelling basement laundry room of my apartment building to hang out for two hours is completely unappealing. My best friend has advised me to put a load in the washer, go back up to my apartment, return when said load is done, and repeat with the

1

dryer. Easy enough in theory, but the last time I tried that I ended up getting robbed of a load of wet clothes. Did I mention my apartment building isn't that nice? It is, however, within walking distance of work, and while insanely expensive by my standards it's still cheaper than most, so I stay.

I continue to lie here, thinking about getting out of bed but not making any move to. I pull my covers over my head and inhale deeply. My sheets smell stale. I try to remember when the last time I washed *them* was. My best estimate is a couple of months ago. I mean, when faced with a choice between clean clothes or clean sheets—God forbid I run two loads at once, plus I never have enough quarters—you pick clean clothes every time. Nobody but me ever sleeps here anyway, so who's to know?

As I seriously consider calling in sick to work, my phone rings. I look at Caller ID and groan. It is my mother. I am not going to answer it. I wait to hear her sultry southern accent fill the room as she leaves a message but, uncharacteristically, she does not. Thank goodness.

The phone rings again. The woman is nothing if not persistent. I pull the covers back over my face like a shield. I should buy the kind of answering machine that does not project sound at ninety decibels across the room, but rather contains the message silently in some alternate universe until I am good and ready to listen to it. Or forever. But that procrastination thing rears its ugly head again, so I am left with an old, loud, in your face, can't-avoid-the-voice-if-your-life-depended-on-it machine. This time though, when the machine picks up, it isn't my mother after all. A shrill, ridiculously cheerful voice comes blaring through the speaker.

"Happy Birthday to you, Happy Birthday to you, Happy *Birthday,* dear Missi, Happy Birthday to you! I know you're there. Pick up the phone!"

I suppress the urge to either vomit or cry, and pick up the phone, trying to sound somewhat less depressed than I feel.

"Hi, Maggie. Thanks for the serenade. You really shouldn't have."

"Well unless you want an encore, quit sulking. It's your birthday!" she crows. "A day without which I would not have my best friend. And what would I do without you?"

"Heaven only knows," I say sarcastically. Maggie is the one person at work that I like. Come to think of it, she is the only person *in my life* that I truly love. She is energetic beyond comprehension, always happy, and can carry on a conversation with anybody with a pulse. She is the front desk receptionist at the law firm where I work, which is perfect for her. She can make people she's never met before feel as though they are talking to an old friend. I think Maggie should be taking depositions because she could squeeze just about anyone of their deepest, darkest secrets. She is that rare, wonderful person who makes me happy after spending just five minutes in her presence. She does have one minor flaw, however. Maggie is, to put it mildly, unattractive.

She has stringy, wild orange hair—not red, but seriously *orange*. She is so skinny you'd call her downright bony, although the quality and quantity of food she eats would blow you away. Maggie is known to frequently put away three McDonald's Quarter Pounders with Cheese and a super-sized fry in one sitting. Her eyes are so large compared to her tiny head that they seem to bulge out at you, and then there is the problem with her teeth. They are enormous, they are crooked, and they rival her eyes as being the first and only thing you can focus on when you look at her.

Last fall Maggie and I took the Amtrak to New York City to do our Christmas shopping, and a woman mistook Maggie for the actress who played Hugh Grant's sister in *Notting Hill*. She is equally bubbly and good-natured, but unfortunately just as strange looking. She is also without question the best friend I have ever had.

"So, are you coming to work today or not?" Maggie asks impatiently.

I push back the covers, make a mental note to wash them before the Fourth of July, and look down at my rumpled t-shirt and pajama bottoms. I roll off my bed, stand, and look at myself in the mirror that hangs over my dresser. My hair is a tangled mess, my eyes have dark circles under them, and I count at least three new wrinkles on my face since yesterday.

"I guess so," I reply glumly. "As a birthday gift to myself I promise to avoid all conflict with Richard."

"Good idea," she laughs, "and as my gift to you, I'll lie to him about why you're late. Let's go out to lunch. I'll treat you to Bangkok Bistro." Maggie's favorite restaurant is in a basement near DuPont Circle, and she goes there at least once a week to order the Beef Ka Prow, which I call Beef *"Ka Pow."* The one time she convinced me to try it I had to drink three glasses of water to put out the fire in my mouth, and still had a sore throat for two days.

"I wish I could," I say, really meaning it, knowing that having lunch with Maggie would be the best part of my day. Unfortunately, I have already committed myself to something that borders on punishment. I inhale deeply and sigh, "I'm meeting my mother for lunch at The Palm."

Did I mention I'm thirty-three today?

After throwing my hair into a messy ponytail and trying to overcompensate for the hairstyle by wearing my best pair of gray slacks and a crisp, white blouse that has miraculously been ironed, I grab my purse and head for the door, but think twice about my gray suede flats and decide to trade up for black heels. I never wear heels—mostly because I am not graceful enough to pull them off, but also because I am a solid six feet tall, and tower over most people, even when wearing flats. This is precisely why I changed my mind. My boss, Richard, is only five-six, and I'm going for the intimidation factor today.

I take the dank stairs from my third floor apartment to the pitiful lobby, pass the horrid floral couch that resides there—though I cannot fathom that anyone would actually contemplate sitting on it—and walk out into the beautiful June morning. It occurs to me that if I'd known how gorgeous it was outside, I would have gotten out of bed earlier, but I quickly dismiss the thought. I wish I were the type to get up early, go for a run in the fresh air, drink my coffee while reading the Post, shower, and still be at work by eight—I actually know people who do all of the above—but I am a procrastinator. So I set my alarm for seven and still manage to be an hour late without a shower.

Since I am already late and it is my birthday, I decide to stop at Starbucks for a latte a few blocks from work. I love how Starbucks smells, and that when you leave, your whole outfit smells like coffee for at least an hour. I wait in line, admiring all the people standing in front of me. There are several businesspeople in expensive-looking suits, a guy who looks like a college student wearing ratty jeans and carrying an old navy blue Patagonia backpack, and a very cute soccer mom type with a double stroller and a Kate Spade diaper bag. When it is her turn, Soccer Mom orders a "tall chai latte with soy milk" and two kid-size soy milks, swipes her debit card, and gracefully maneuvers her double-wide over to a corner where two other cute moms and assorted children wait, sipping their own soy beverages. I feel a pang of envy, not just because they are so well dressed, well-accessorized, clearly married with children, and look even younger than me, but because they clearly do not have to go to work today, or probably ever.

When it is finally my turn, I decide to order my latte with soymilk, just to see what I am missing out on. Perhaps after drinking it I will appear healthier, more youthful, and cuter, like those moms.

4

I breeze out the door onto Connecticut Avenue and take a sip. It's disgusting and extremely hot. Soymilk, as it turns out, has a strange texture, because immediately there is some sort of film on my tongue, not to mention that my coffee tastes completely watered-down. Great. I can hardly afford to waste five dollars on anything, let alone shitty coffee, but I manage to anyway.

Oh, well. At the very least I will look cool and professional walking into my office building carrying a cup of expensive coffee. Nobody else has to know it tastes like crap. I saunter down the sidewalk thinking that perhaps I should be more concerned about my appearance. If I *look* like I've got it together, then people might actually believe that I do. Perhaps I can even convince my mother of it. I focus on walking with more confidence than I feel, and it actually works. An attractive man, who would ordinarily not be the type to notice me, makes eye contact and smiles. I think he even says hello, but in an attempt to maintain my air of coolness I raise my Starbucks cup, take a sip, and proceed to gasp and choke down the hot, tasteless liquid. There goes the smooth, confident exterior I had been going for.

I continue toward my office trying to maintain a positive outlook, but when I am about three steps from the door of the building where Franklin, Franklin and Lewis, Attorneys at Law, is housed, the heel of my shoe gets wedged into a crack in the sidewalk. In slow motion I watch my coffee go flying, and I lurch forward to try and recover it. My fingertips graze the bottom of the cup, knocking it even further ahead of me, and my five-dollar debacle hits the plate glass window outside the lobby. The lid to the cup comes off, sending scalding, grayish-brown liquid in every direction, including all over the window and the front of my white blouse. Not only do I no longer have a cool accessory to carry into work, but to top it off I look down at my wet blouse and see that the damp fabric of my lavender bra is clearly showing through. Apparently my neutral-colored bras are all at the bottom of the huge pile of dirty laundry in my closet.

Pride and soy latte gone, I stagger through the doors into the lobby, where Demetrius, the security guard, stands at his daily post. I can tell he is trying not to laugh, but as I pass him on my way to the elevators I hear a definite snicker. He obviously saw everything through the window. I cover my chest with my purse, push the up button, and wish I were back in bed.

As the elevator door opens at the eighth floor, I cautiously poke my head out to survey the reception area. Richard doesn't usually grace the public areas of the office with his presence, but the way my

5

day is going, I can't be too careful. Maggie is at her desk with her headset on, assuring someone on the phone that she would "pass the information on to the partners," and that "Aunt Ella's death will not go uninvestigated."

I stand in front of her desk as she holds up a finger and hits the intercom button. "Mr. Lewis," she says sweetly, "we've got another corpse at Shady Orchards."

She hangs up and looks at me. "Dear God, what happened to you?"

"Please," I whine, "just help me." I move my purse from its strategic position in front of my right breast.

Maggie gasps and reaches behind her chair to retrieve a fluorescent lime green cardigan. She throws it at me and tells me to put it on. Knowing I must look even worse than I thought if Maggie is so concerned, I shove an arm into one sleeve of the sweater. It reaches to just past my elbow. Maggie is barely five feet tall and doesn't weigh a hundred pounds. If my six foot, one hundred-fifty pound frame can somehow manage to squeeze itself into that cardigan, I am fairly certain I will spend the rest of the day looking like a day-glow sausage.

We decide to tie it around my shoulders using the knotted sleeves to cover the transparent spot on my blouse. It's not perfect, but it will have to do, since through the double doors to one side of the reception area comes Richard, my despicable boss.

"Where the *hell* have you *been*?" he snaps at me. "We're about to file four of the most lucrative wrongful death suits this fucking firm has ever seen, and you're taking your own sweet time getting your ass to work? What the fuck is wrong with you? Do you not *like* being able to pay your electricity bill?"

Since I barely make rent each month I nearly chuckle out loud, but in the spirit of not getting canned on my birthday, I just bite my lip.

"I would fire you right now if I didn't have so much fucking work for you to do," Richard spits, not coming up for air. "So get in your *fucking* cube and work!"

"Please, Richard . . . chill," says Maggie curtly. I gasp, thinking that in coming to my defense, Maggie is about to get *herself* fired on my birthday, which would be the only thing worse than my own unemployment.

"What did you say to me?" he yells at Maggie, whirling around to face her. His tongue hangs from the corner of his mouth, and his lips are moist and shiny with saliva.

"I just mean that if you let the woman explain herself, you might understand and even *appreciate* why she's been out of the office this morning." Maggie looks at me. I panic.

"Um, uh, um," I stammer, and instinctively begin to fidget. I pull the sleeves of Maggie's sweater tighter around my shoulders and then untie them, forgetting why I have it on to begin with.

Richard's beady eyes drop from my face to my chest and a sleazy smile spreads across his face. "Are you lactating, Jennings?"

Maggie, thankfully in control of the situation, gets up from her desk and walks around it to position herself between Richard and me. We both look at her, equally curious as to what she has to say.

"Mr. Lewis," she begins respectfully, to soften him up, "Missi has just been to Shady Orchards herself. Her grandmother isn't doing well, and she's looking into assisted living options in the area."

My mouth gapes open, shocked at how efficiently and beautifully she was able to concoct such a story. I quickly close my mouth and smile, waiting to hear how my alleged visit to Shady Orchards went.

"While the issues now facing Shady Orchards make it an unlikely candidate for Missi's grandmother, she wanted to see for herself what kind of facility it is, to rule it out on her own. As a matter of fact," she continues smoothly, "she was just about to tell me about the tour she went on."

I suppress the urge to applaud her performance, and look over her head at Richard. He looks smug, perhaps because he does not buy the story for a second. Panic sets in again, but suddenly I am saved by his greed and narcissism.

"This is fucking fantastic," he spews. "I want you in my office at twelve o'clock sharp to tell me what you saw. Anything at all we might be able to use in our case against Shady Orchards. Didn't happen to see anyone slap a patient around or smother one with a pillow, did you?"

Shocked by his inhumanity and having nothing to tell him, never actually having been to Shady Orchards—I don't even have a grandmother—I find myself momentarily speechless. I recover quickly, however, with an actual excuse. "I can't. I'm meeting my mother for lunch."

"It's her birthday," Maggie pipes up, still standing between us.

"Oh. Well. Not a problem. We wouldn't want to inconvenience the Diva of Democracy, would we? I've got a meeting with a client at three, so tomorrow, then. First thing in the morning—or in case you don't know when that is, eight o'clock . . . *a.m.*"

"I'll be there," I say cheerfully, making a mental note to go to my desk immediately and make an appointment to drop by Shady Orchards this evening after work. Then at least I'll have some legitimate information to pass along, even if it isn't criminal in nature.

Richard spins around twice before rushing toward the door to the back office. Just as he reaches the door, he turns and says sweetly, "Wish your mother Happy Birthday for me."

I feel an arm around my waist and look down at Maggie. "He thinks it's *her* birthday," I say incredulously.

"That man is like a dog chasing its tail," she sighs, "but did you see him fold the minute you mentioned her? It's like he knows there is only one person in this world scarier than he is. Your mother."

When I finally get to my cube I am reminded of how late I am. File folders are piled a foot high on either side of my computer, which when turned on informs me that I have twenty-six emails to read. I scroll through my inbox, but they are all boring and work-related. I don't read any of them.

Just then the chime sounds indicating another message in my mailbox. I almost ignore it, but the sender's address catches my eye—joshuamartin@dcmail.com. The message title reads *Happy Bday to you!* I open the message and smile despite myself.

Josh was, at one time, the man I thought I would marry. We dated for over two years, every day of which was wonderful. He was . . . *is* . . . the smartest, kindest, and most fun person I have ever known. I learned far more from Josh than I ever have from anyone, most importantly about the kind of person I want to be. When Josh and I were together, I was the best version of myself. I `was motivated, or at least more motivated than usual, thin, because Josh is vegan and as a supportive girlfriend I abstained from all animal products—at least in his presence—and above all, I was *happy*.

Unfortunately for me, Josh turned out to be gay. He apparently even knew he was gay while we were dating, but couldn't bring himself to tell his parents. I should be flattered by the fact that he kept up the charade for as long as he did—at least he could stand me—but I also should have paid more attention to the signs. He loved to paint my toenails, loved to go shopping with me, and goes to New York City every September, which always just happens to coincide with Fashion Week. I dismissed all of it as just "being in touch with his feminine side." It turns out that the *only* side he has is feminine. I haven't dated anyone since, and Josh has been out of the closet for almost a year and a half. The version of me that I was so proud of went *in* the closet, I think.

I read the email. *Hope you have a great day. Know that you are thought of. P.S. Steer clear of that mother of yours, so you can keep the "Happy" in Happy Birthday.* I snort and smile, and save the email just so I have one personal message among all the others.

I turn back finally to the stacks of folders on my desk. They are depositions pertaining to our cases against Shady Orchards. My job as a paralegal is to summarize them before turning them over to the attorneys, and to research past cases that might pertain to the ruling we want. As of today there have been five deaths in five months at Shady Orchards, all sudden and unexpected despite the age of the residents in question. They all also occurred between the hours of eleven p.m. and five a.m., so the families are jumping on the wrongful death bandwagon.

Not that any of them need money. From what I've read, Shady Orchards runs around five thousand dollars a month, although if these families are losing out on inheritances because the money is going to care for Grandma, maybe that's where the desperation to blame someone else comes from. My mind begins to wander, kicking around the idea that perhaps the *families* are somehow responsible. All that inheritance money is getting pissed away by the month, so if they no longer have to pay for the nursing home, more will come their way when Granny buys the farm.

My conspiracy theory is about to take wings when the phone on my desk rings. I snap back to reality, realizing that the piles in front of me aren't getting magically smaller. I pick up the phone and feign cheerfulness as I say, "Franklin, Franklin and Lewis, Missi Jennings speaking."

"Hello, *darling,*" my mother drawls. My mother presents herself as a true southern woman, which is a bit of a masquerade considering she hasn't set foot south of Alexandria, Virginia in my lifetime except to go to Miami a couple of times, which doesn't count. I give her credit, though, because she sure does know how to use her accent to her advantage. I wouldn't think someone so coarse could sound so demure, but she can, and it apparently tricks people into thinking she's much nicer than she really is.

"Mother. Hi. How are you?" I ask, knowing that this is a loaded question when asked of my mother.

"Dreadful, " she responds dramatically, immediately launching into a five-minute rant about the meeting she just finished with her producer.

9

My mother, known in DC culture as the "Diva of Democracy," is a household name among people who follow politics. She started out as an intern at the Republican National Committee during her winter and summer breaks from Georgetown—which, by the way, she had to drop out of when I was born. She later landed a paid position at the RNC, and spent the next couple of decades clawing her way to becoming what she is today, a political commentator and the host of a nationally syndicated radio talk show called *Conscience or Consequence*.

Nina Jennings is a staunch conservative in most areas. Raised in the South, she is a Baptist, though I can count on one hand the number of times we went to church when I was growing up. She thinks anyone who wants a gun should be able to carry one in her purse, supports capital punishment, is vehemently against gay marriage, opposes stem cell research, and wants serious immigration reform. The one area in which Nina shocks the right wing is that she is outwardly and unapologetically pro-choice.

As her only child, it makes me incredibly uncomfortable to hear her fiercely support women who choose to terminate pregnancies for any reason, whether it is due to rape, the inability to support a child financially, or just plain bad decision-making, which I believe is the category I happen to fall into. It doesn't take much listening for me to deduce that my conception was a mistake that kept her from finishing college, and that if she could have a do-over, she would graciously take it.

She is my mother, yet I know virtually nothing personal about her. Her parents died in an accident when she was in her early twenties, and she never speaks of them or her childhood. My father flew the coop as soon as he found out Nina was pregnant, which means that Nina is the only family I have. This seems completely unfair to me considering that I would love a huge family full of brothers and sisters to look forward to seeing on those major holidays that seem so awkward when it's just you and your mother sitting at one of the few restaurants in town that happen to be open. Add to it the fact that my mother wishes she'd never had a child in the first place, and you quickly go from awkward to grim. I hate holidays.

We live nine miles from each other as the crow flies, but I probably see my mother only once every six or eight weeks. Nina has never married, and even when I was dating Josh I never felt that I could leave her alone on the obligatory family holidays. What I would have given to spend a cozy Christmas by a blazing fire in upstate New York with Josh's large Catholic family, drinking hot chocolate and opening presents like scarves and gloves knit by his eighty year-old grandmother who lives in the basement of their family home in Schenectady.

I must give Nina credit for attendance, though. It would never occur to her to *not* spend an awkward, uncomfortable afternoon at a Ritz Carlton buffet with me. Any show of familial affection or celebration, however, is completely lost on her. She looks proud as I open my gift purchased from somewhere like Coach or Tiffany, knowing that her assistant, Nancy, has chosen something truly wonderful, and then takes the wind straight from my sails when she opens her gift from me.

"What a nice blouse. What color would you say it is? Mauve? Ooh," she says, refolding the blouse neatly and tucking it away, "Laura says I really shouldn't wear mauve with my hair color. But thank you so much anyway."

"It's pink, Mother. *Pink*," I say, deflated, because not only did I consult her stylist, Laura, on the purchase, but Laura told me when I called that she was trying to soften my mother's look by adding shades of pink to her wardrobe *despite* her auburn hair. I also spent entirely more than I could afford to on the blouse at Barney's when Maggie and I went to New York, and ended up late with my rent. Ugh, holidays.

When my mother finally finishes her tirade about the morning spent surrounded by idiots who don't agree with her, she slowly remembers why she called. In the meantime, I have folded a yellow sticky note into the smallest square possible.

"So, we're having lunch today," she states, sounding anything but excited about it.

I have little to no patience when it comes to Nina. "Well, I just cancelled a meeting with Richard so I can be there, but if you're too busy we can certainly do it another time." Maybe I can take Maggie up on lunch after all.

Forever the martyr, Nina sighs and says, "I am *not* too busy to have lunch with you, and anyway . . . it's your birthday." She must have just glanced at her datebook. It's not as though we do this sort of thing just for fun.

"Why don't you meet me at The Palm, and I'll drive you back to work afterwards," she offers.

This is highly unusual coming from my mother, but I'm not about to take public transportation if I don't have to. "Fine," I tell her. "I'll see you at twelve."

Feeling drained already, I pick up my cell phone and dial Shady Orchards. A sweet receptionist named Rita informs me that they would love for me to stop by this evening when it's convenient for me, and that perhaps I'd like to observe the water aerobics class at six-thirty. Old people in bathing suits appeal to me only slightly more than lunch with my mother, so I tell her regretfully that I have a late meeting that will prevent me from being there prior to seven. Rita pencils me in and tells me that the night manager, Felicia, will look forward to my arrival.

I work for a while, head to Maggie's desk for a pep talk, and stop by the ladies' room in the lobby to freshen up. I have no lipstick or gloss in my purse, so I swipe some cherry flavored ChapStick across my lips, sneak through the lobby past Demetrius in an attempt to save face, and head out into the sunshine.

CHAPTER TWO

The Palm is on 19th Street near DuPont Circle, which is too far to walk from my office, so as much as I loathe it, I head for the McPherson Square Metro station. I loathe buses even more than the Metro, and I can't afford a taxi.

There are surprisingly few people at the station, which is nice, because one of the things I hate most about the Metro is the sheer number of people that you come into physical contact with while waiting for, getting on, and riding it. I am not a fan of being touched by strangers. To be honest, I am not a touchy-feely person in any situation. My mother and I do not hug—ever—or even do that touch-on-the-arm-while-speaking-to-each-other thing. I think even Maggie senses that I am not comfortable being embraced, because she is extremely touchy with others, and yet only hugs me when completely necessary, like this morning. I can still feel her bony arm around my waist.

When I was with Josh, though, we touched. A lot. And it never, ever bothered me.

I arrive at the Palm at 12:04, and am escorted to the table by a friendly hostess.

"You're late," she mouths, frowning, then returns to her conversation.

I sit and look around at the comical faces of celebrities covering the walls, wondering if there is one of Nina here. Would the artist have painted her smiling like the others, or with her perpetual pucker? I pick up my menu and order a glass of wine from

13

the waiter. It's my birthday after all, and I will be far more tolerant of my mother if I can take the edge off.

"So," she says, finally sliding her phone into her purse. "Are you having a nice birthday?"

"Yes," I quickly respond, choosing not to get into the pitfalls of my job with Nina. She would much rather me be a lawyer than a paralegal, but is equally quick to remind me that my grades were not remotely close to law school caliber. She seems to forget that her own education ended up just short of a bachelor's degree.

The waiter reappears with my wine, which I intercept before it hits the table. I take a lengthy sip under the watchful eye of my tee-totaling mother and order the crab cakes and a side of creamed spinach. In the interest of expediting our lunch, I also inform the waiter that for dessert I will be interested in a slice of their amazing cheesecake.

My mother, who is very health-conscious and still has the body of a much younger woman, orders broiled fish, substitutes steamed vegetables for the mashed potatoes, and asks for more Pellegrino. She then proceeds to ask if I am going to the gym after work today.

"Actually, I have an appointment to tour a nursing home this evening," I say importantly.

Nina scowls. "That's a bit premature, don't you think?"

"It's for a case we're working on, but it sounds worthy of you from what I've heard. Pretty swanky place to live out someone's golden years."

"Good Lord, Missi," she says dryly. "There's nothing *golden* about being old. Your health declines, your skin gets three sizes too large for your body, and the only redeeming factor is that you probably won't remember how miserable you are from one day to the next."

I would add to her rant that you also get mean and crotchety, but that happened to Nina a long time ago. Instead I drain my glass of wine and signal the waiter for another.

"Sorry," I say snidely, "I didn't realize you had such opinions about aging. Why, then, do you care so much about prescription drug plans for the elderly?" I grin, proud that I actually know her platform on the subject, but my triumph is short-lived.

"Because people can make their own decisions to live however long they want. Personally, I would rather die suddenly in my prime and never know what hit me, than be an adult in diapers with an affordable prescription drug plan." Her cheeks are flushed as she sips from her water glass. I am at a loss for words, and grateful when our food arrives.

14

We eat quietly for a while, which is better than our version of conversation.

"I suppose this would be an opportune time to give you your birthday gift," Nina says finally, reaching for her bag. She pulls out a small white envelope and passes it across the table to me. I briefly—and selfishly—feel disappointed that it's not a package encased in that pretty, trademark-blue Tiffany box, but quickly brighten to think that it's a gift card that I can use to pick out something for myself. I am partially correct.

I open the envelope and slide out a thick, embossed gift certificate . . . for 20 sessions with Max, my mother's personal trainer.

"Is this a hint?" I snort, trying to sound amused rather than defensive. I reach for my wine glass and take a long swallow.

"Not at all," she says dryly. "I just thought you might enjoy it. You know it gets harder to stay trim the older you are, and Max is wonderful. Very good-looking, too, I might add."

The wine nearly comes through my nose as I start laughing out loud. I cannot contain myself, and find it hard to stop cackling as I imagine myself with Max, a walking advertisement for performance enhancing drugs.

"Oh, Mother, you are a riot," I gasp, forcing myself to settle down. People at neighboring tables are looking at us, which bothers me. I am definitely not one to call attention to myself, and I also realize that I am probably not doing my mother any favors by making a scene.

Nina, evidently, has had enough. She ends our lunch abruptly by making an excuse about having to meet with her producer before her show goes on-air at four o'clock. She flags the waiter down, demands the check, and I walk out of the Palm with my cheesecake in a to-go box.

The valet pulls my mother's shiny silver Mercedes to the curb in front of the restaurant, and she immediately walks around to the passenger side.

"I have a headache," she says sharply. "You drive."

This is not a good idea, considering I do not currently own a car, have not driven one in at least six months, have no business being behind the wheel of a Mercedes in the first place, and have consumed two glasses of wine in the past forty-five minutes. I climb in anyway, thinking that driving a bigger wedge between Nina and me on this, of all days, is probably not in my best interest.

Again there is silence as I carefully maneuver the car through the streets of Washington, DC. It is not, in my opinion, an easy city to drive in, which is why I live close enough to work to walk, and use the Metro to get pretty much anywhere else. I haven't left the city limits in almost a year, except to go very occasionally to meet my mother in Old Town Alexandria where her house is, and where I can also go by Metro.

Nina finally breaks the quiet by resorting to her tried and true habit of criticizing me. "You know, I'm just trying to help," she says curtly. "You should take better care of yourself. I really do want what's best for you, whether you believe it or not. You're in your thirties now, not as thin as you used to be, and still single. You even have lines around your eyes, which I didn't have until I was much older than you."

I accelerate, trying to get back to my office as quickly as possible, but she continues. "You aren't even dating anyone now, spending all your time at your dead-end job or with that unattractive Maggie girl."

Now she has done it. She can insult me all she wants and get away with it most of the time, but she is in forbidden territory now.

"Don't you dare call her ugly!" I cry out, making a right-hand turn, jumping the curb, and nearly taking out a light post in the process. "Maggie is the best thing I have going for me, and she is the *only* person who cares about me unconditionally." I am on the verge of tears, but know better than to cry. My mother does not tolerate it, and never has. I swallow the lump in my throat and decide to embrace my anger and stand up to her, something I have been putting off for years.

"You are the most selfish person I have ever met, and you don't love anyone, least of all me!" I shout, shocked by my own audacity, but empowered by my ire. "Every person I have ever had a healthy relationship with, you've found fault with, yet you have no freaking idea that my most dysfunctional relationship is with you!"

"Seriously, Missi," she says tersely. "You absolutely cannot be talking about Joshua. You can't possibly count dating a homosexual for two years healthy."

I head up 12th Street, then turn left through a very yellow light onto I Street, which is the one-way street where my office building is located. I can't stand another minute of this bullshit with Nina, and I will never be happier to see my desk and the mountains of files sitting on it if it means getting the hell out of this car.

"That's ripe," I seethe, as I jerk to a stop at the curb. "All this coming from a woman who to my knowledge has never had a proper relationship of *any* kind . . . *ever!*"

My mother turns and glares at me. "Don't you act for one second like you have any idea what I've put myself through for you—"

But I am not about to listen, and cut her off before she can finish. "Oh, please!" I shout. "Just save it, will you?"

"Missi, you're an ass," my mother says, and in one fluid motion she opens the car door and swings her legs out toward the street. I lean forward and press my forehead against the steering wheel. As I contemplate getting out so that my mother can get in the driver's seat and drive far away from me, I hear the roar of an engine followed immediately by the hydraulic squeal of brakes as the entire car jerks to one side. I turn toward the passenger side door, but my mother is no longer there. The door of the car, too, is gone. I throw open the door on my side and climb out.

I run to the other side of the car, almost expecting to find Mother hiding there, some kind of a sick joke in retaliation for my saying such hateful things to her. The door through which she exited the car, however, is bent completely forward, crumpled, and dangling. Her Louis Vuitton purse is on the street next to the car, an open compact lying beside it on the pavement. I hold my breath and pick up the purse, clutching it to my chest, but leave the compact, noting that the mirror is broken and she'll want a new one anyway.

I hear screaming and run toward the sound, thinking that it must be Nina, but soon realize I am running in a circle. I am the one screaming. All I can wrap my brain around is the pungent smell of diesel fuel, and the absence of my mother.

The transit bus has pulled over to the curb half a block down, and people are slowly getting off. A heavy man of about fifty climbs down the steps onto the street and his blue striped shirt with the bus company's logo on the chest tells me that he is the driver.

"Where is she?" I shriek, running toward the man at full speed. He seems completely dazed, and does not answer me.

"Where is my mother?" I scream again, and I look around at the people getting off the bus. "Someone please help me! "

I am faced with a dozen blank stares and complete silence. I head back toward the car, looking for some clue as to where my mother is. There is nothing, so I turn back towards the bus, which by now has almost completely unloaded. The driver and several others are gathered in front of the bus, and I watch a man in faded jeans kneel on the asphalt and look under the front bumper. He groans, turns his head away and vomits on the pavement. The bus driver sinks to his knees and begins to sob.

I cannot seem to make my legs move any longer. I am rooted to the street, willing myself to walk back to the bus. I feel a hand on my shoulder, and Demetrius is there beside me. He must have seen the commotion from the lobby, and for once I am glad he was watching. Together we finally walk slowly toward the bus, and as we approach I hear sad, scared murmurs from the people standing around, so many of them now that I cannot tell bus passengers from bystanders.

One of the men who had been standing with the bus driver comes forward. He is wearing pleated khaki pants, a white golf shirt and a Seattle Mariners cap. "Are you hurt?" he asks, with a look of deep concern on his face.

"No, I just . . . I need to help my mother. She must be badly hurt." I know that she is not simply hurt, but I'm not sure what else to say. I lean down and forward, and see a cloud of auburn hair just in front of the left front tire of the bus. I suck in my breath as the man from Seattle quickly gets between the bus and me, gently pushing me back a few steps. I think to myself that his vacation to the Nation's Capital has just been ruined.

"The police will be here soon," he says, holding his hands out to keep me at a distance from the carnage.

A woman in a lavender velour warm-up suit hovers behind Seattle, her chubby hand wrapped around a brown plastic bottle. "Honey, do you think she wants a Valium?" she asks, and I realize she must be his wife. "I have some left for the flight home."

Without taking his eyes off me, Seattle shakes his head. "I'm not sure Valium's going to help her right now."

Demetrius has been talking quietly on his cell phone, all the while never breaking physical contact with me. The next thing I know, Maggie is running out of the doors of our building. She takes my hand and squeezes it hard. She does not say anything, for which I am grateful.

I begin to hear sirens getting closer, and although this is Washington, DC and sirens are a constant part of the city sounds, I know they are coming here. They are coming to me and to where my mother lies dead under a bus on I Street.

CHAPTER THREE

The police are efficient. Surely this isn't the first death by transit bus they have ever dealt with, and based on my statement along with those of some passengers and pedestrians there is little doubt that this was purely an accident.

The bus driver has been taken to George Washington Hospital for observation after experiencing chest pains, and one other woman from the bus apparently broke her ankle falling down the bus stairs after the accident. Everyone else seems to be okay, relatively speaking, despite the gruesome nature of the scene.

Firefighters work to untangle my mother from the undercarriage of the bus. It seems that after she was hit, she was dragged underneath it until it stopped a hundred yards away.

I am asked by several police officers if I am injured, but nothing hurts. I can't feel anything at all, and I no longer hear the sounds around me. My eyes focus on the front of that bus and the events occurring there.

Maggie is still at my side and has spoken only to ask if I need water or for her to call anyone. I know I should call Nancy, my mother's assistant, or Phillip, her producer, and at least let them know she will not be able to do her show today or ever again. As I contemplate what, exactly, I would say to them, I suddenly hear a noise. Not the sound of the hydraulic lifts moving the bus and not the commotion of emergency rescue workers, but music . . . coming from my heart.

I look down and realize that I am still holding my mother's purse to my chest. The music is coming from inside the bag. I open it, and see Nina's cell phone, the screen lit up to indicate an incoming call. Without hesitation, I take the phone out and answer it.

"Hello?" I say, my voice hoarse and unrecognizable.

"Nina, where are you?" I know the voice belongs to Nancy, my mother's right hand and one of the nicest people I have ever met, which has always made me wonder why she has chosen to put up with Nina for almost ten years.

"It's Missi, Nancy. There's been an accident."

"Missi? Are you okay? I knew something was wrong. Nina is never late, and there's a ton of material she has to read before the program . . ."

"Nancy," I say calmly, "she's not okay." I numbly end the call and drop the phone back in the bag. It immediately begins ringing again.

Maggie gently takes the purse from me and answers the phone. She takes a few steps away from me while she quietly informs Nancy that my mother is dead.

I return my attention to the firefighters, who are now extracting a body from under the wreckage of the bus. For a moment I am relieved, because it is not Nina. It looks nothing like her. The person's hair is a gnarled mess, and there is limpness to the body that just doesn't exist where my mother is concerned; Nina is about as tight as they come.

One of the workers brushes the hair away from the victim's face, and I begin to shake uncontrollably. Amidst the mess of hair and blood, I can see that her emerald green eyes are open, and even now they stare straight at me with the same disdain and disappointment they had across the lunch table.

As the rescue workers gently set her body on a stretcher, I notice that she is wearing a pink blouse. It is streaked with blood, dirt, and grease, but it is definitely a pink blouse—*the* pink blouse. How on earth did I sit across a table from her for an hour and not recognize that she was wearing the blouse I gave her for Christmas? How could I have been so obtuse? I was so absorbed by my anger toward her—hate, almost—that I didn't notice something as simple as that. I wonder what else I missed.

The cloud of guilt that a moment ago had been floating above me now descends and rests firmly on my shoulders. I feel another hand on my back. I turn to face whomever it is trying to comfort me; everyone on the scene has been so good about that, despite the fact that I have never felt more uncomfortable in my life. When I turn, though, there isn't a person there at all. It's Richard, and I suddenly feel more molested than comforted.

"Please, Richard," I say wearily. "Don't say anything."

"I cancelled my meeting this afternoon, so if you need anything at all . . ." he trails off, almost sounding sad. I feel myself soften a little. If my mother can wear the pink blouse, then anything is possible. Maybe Richard is human after all.

"Thanks," I reply, "but I don't know what I need right now."

"I do," he starts in. "You need a good lawyer. This is at a minimum vehicular manslaughter, and maybe even negligent homicide. The transit authority will have no choice but to settle out of court to avoid the media circus, and you'll be set up for life."

I am rigid again, but don't have the energy to tell two people in one day how despicable I think they are. The first time it didn't turn out very well.

The doors to the ambulance close with a thud, the paramedics climb into the front, and it slowly drives away. I begin to wonder how long I will stand in this place before someone will make me leave, so that traffic flow can resume in time for rush hour. Thankfully, one of the officers I had spoken to previously approaches.

"I can give you a ride to the station, if you need one," he offers. "The body is going to the morgue, and you'll need to come in and answer some questions."

"Questions? Why?" I ask, wondering why there would be any question at all about what happened here.

"An autopsy can check blood alcohol levels."

"She doesn't drink," I inform him sharply.

"We still need to figure out exactly what occurred."

"She got hit by a bus," I snap.

"Is there any reason to think this was premeditated?"

"Why would he hit her on purpose?" I ask

"Not premeditated by the driver," the officer says carefully, "but by your mother."

I feel nauseous. "Like a suicide? No. Never. I can't believe you would even suggest such a thing. She was angry with me and got out of the car without looking. If anything, this is my fault," I say, but as the words come out, I think about what Nina said just a little while ago at the table inside the Palm—*"I would rather die suddenly and never know what hit me . . ."*

I suppose she got what she wished for.

CHAPTER FOUR

The good thing is that funerals do not take long to plan and execute—three days, to be exact— particularly when Nancy is involved. I don't know the first thing to do, don't know what Nina would have wanted, don't know who to notify of the arrangements, since I do not have a single living relative in the world and can count my mother's real friends on one hand.

Nancy knows exactly what to do. Knows which church should be reserved, what flowers need to be ordered, and that should there be a single carnation in the lot Nina may rise from the dead and haunt her forever. She knows that musicians need hiring, that hundreds of movers and shakers in D.C. will want to attend my mother's funeral services, and that cremation is totally against my mother's mixed bag of religious beliefs.

I suggest cremation strictly based on the condition of Nina's body after the accident. She would not have wanted people to see her battered and broken. Nancy, however, knowing her better than I, explains gently that according to Nina's Baptist upbringing, resurrection requires a physical body and therefore a closed casket service will be far more appropriate.

I decide right at that moment that I am going to be cremated.

At the funeral I sit in the front row and cannot possibly feel like a bigger fraud—the heartbroken daughter, whose loving mother has been taken from her by a tragic accident.

In the pew with me are Nancy and her husband, Ed. I've never met him before today, but he seems nice, and appropriately sad without being insincere. For my own sanity and moral support, Maggie is directly beside me. She is the closest thing to family that I have, and without her I am swimming in a sea of strangers.

The service begins, and it is truly beautiful. The flowers are stunning, especially the swag of magnolia in full bloom that is draped over Nina's casket—a true symbol of the South, which is exactly the image she would have wanted to perpetuate.

The string quartet, also, is perfect. I actually do know that my mother couldn't stand organ music, which was one of the excuses she used in recent years to avoid church. She said it gave her migraines.

As I observe the crowd gathered here, I am amazed by the incredible respect that my mother commands, even after her death. There are politicians, dignitaries, television journalists, and other well-known figures, many of whom I recognize, but none of whom I have ever met. The Vice President of the United States is here paying his respects as well, even though as a Democrat there isn't much he and my mother saw eye-to-eye on.

As the service continues, I expect a eulogy of some sort, but it never materializes. A couple of days ago Nancy asked me if I would like to read one, but I refused, knowing immediately that I would be ill-equipped to do it. There is nothing I felt I could conjure up that would be heartfelt or even intelligent, and apparently I wasn't the only one who felt that way.

In lieu of a eulogy, additional passages from the Bible are read, ones that reflect on the occasion of death and whatever comes next. The people reading them are all familiar faces and voices, people I recognize from the little bit of news I ever watch or read, but none of which I would say was a *friend* of my mother's. I realize, not for the first time, that I can't actually name a single person I would classify as a friend of Nina's. Her life was her job, and her job was telling anyone who would listen the way she thought things ought to be.

I have never been to a funeral before today. Nobody close to me has ever died. Growing up, my friends had a few occasions to attend funerals, which was something I certainly did not envy at the time, but I now see that in a way a funeral is a measure of how connected to other people the deceased person was. My only familial connection in this entire world is twenty feet away in a mahogany box, and I do not even feel sad. What I feel is empty and very, very alone.

The string quartet begins to play again. The music is beautiful, yet appropriately somber, and seems at once to draw emotion from the crowd. Without looking directly at anyone, I can tell that several people around me have started to cry. I wonder whether they are truly sad, or just doing what people are supposed to do at a funeral. I

23

wonder if they expect me to cry along with them, but as much as I would like to, I cannot cry. I never cry. My mother taught me that.

As the funeral concludes, Maggie and Nancy walk me out of the church. A few people stop to give their condolences, and I am grateful that this group isn't touchy-feely in nature. There are very few who surpass the requisite handshake to attempt a hug, and not one who requires conversation. I take an opportunity to thank Nancy for arranging such a lovely service, and agree to meet her on Thursday to go through some of my mother's things.

Nina's burial will not be a public affair. Her body will be interred at the Mount Comfort Cemetery sometime next week, and Nancy and I will be the only ones present. I suppose this is why, as Maggie and I finally reach her car, I feel some relief.

Relief is temporary, however, because as I reach for the handle to open the passenger side door, a voice from the past speaks to me.

"Missi." The sound is sympathetic and sweet, and rocks me to my core. One word, and I am suddenly the closest I have come to crying during this whole ordeal.

I turn slowly on unsteady legs, expecting that my imagination is playing cruel tricks on me, but there stands Josh. Though we exchange an occasional email, I have not seen him face to face in several months. Josh has always been great about wanting to remain friends, and he does so beautifully, but it's a little harder for me. Despite his proclamation of gayness, I have never really stopped loving him or hoping that at some point he will return to the figurative closet where I wait quietly in the dark.

My chest hurts, which I think is due to the fact that I have been holding my breath since I heard him say my name. I exhale, and lace my fingers together, afraid that if I let go of my own hands, I will grab Josh and hold on for dear life. I don't know what behavior is appropriate for this situation, but Josh does, as he always has, and steps forward to wrap his arms around me.

"I am so, so sorry," he says, breathing into the hair falling over my shoulders.

"You were right," I choke, swallowing the enormous lump in my throat. "I read your email that day. You told me to stay away from her."

Josh shakes his head and takes a step back, keeping his hands firmly on my shoulders. "You know this wasn't your fault. There was no way to prevent this . . ."

"I should have listened," I interrupt. "I should never have gone. Nothing good was ever going to come out of having lunch with her. It never did." It pains me to break the physical contact with Josh, but

I do, and turn back toward the car, where I see Maggie watching me carefully, as surprised by and unsure of this exchange as I am.

Before I can get the door open to slide inside, Josh touches me again. "She was your mother, Missi. And the one thing you've always known whether you realize it or not, is that you had to take the good with the bad. Even *I* knew there was never a possibility that you two wouldn't be together that day."

I sink into the seat, numb again, and know that Josh is right. Love her or hate her, Nina was my mother, and as unpleasant as our gatherings could be, they were our own dysfunctional way of trying to keep our family ties from unraveling.

Now I sit, waiting desperately for Maggie's car to move, to propel me forward to some point in time where I am no longer an errant shoelace flapping in the breeze.

CHAPTER FIVE

Four weeks after my mother's death, I sit at a conference table at a law firm downtown. It is an intensely familiar environment, though I no longer work at a law firm myself. I quit three weeks ago after repeated efforts by Richard to pursue a lawsuit against both the transit authority and the driver of the bus that killed Nina. I made it clear that I had no intention of making a bad situation worse for anyone, nor did I care to profit financially from such a horrible accident. It was, after all, an *accident*. The police found no fault, and issued no tickets.

Richard nearly had a coronary as I gathered up my personal belongings and carried them out in a garbage bag, but it was surprisingly easy to leave. Maggie held the door for me as I walked out of Franklin, Franklin, and Lewis for the last time. I stopped briefly in the lobby to say goodbye to Demetrius, and continued out the door onto I Street, where just a few days prior, my mother was killed. I prepared myself for some unbearable flood of emotion, but it never came.

Today I sit at a different law firm—not as an employee, but as my mother's daughter and beneficiary. I have been putting this off for a couple of weeks, but Nancy, fed up by my procrastinating ways, informed me in no uncertain terms that this meeting would take place today, with or without me. Nancy arranged the meeting, and sits beside me now with a three ring binder representing every facet of Nina's life and a large Starbucks cup in front of her. I want to ask her if she's a soymilk woman, but decide it might be inappropriate under the circumstances. Plus, she doesn't strike me as the soymilk type. My guess is it's just plain old black coffee. I would give my left arm for a cup of Starbucks right now, but my finances were strained enough *before* I quit my job. Starbucks will have to wait until I am gainfully employed again.

My focus is redirected as three men walk into the conference room and join us at the table. I know one of them to be my mother's lawyer, Thomas Anderson, whom I've met twice—once at a dinner party hosted by my mother at which my presence was required only to make certain everyone's wine glass stayed full, and once when we ran into Thomas and his wife at the Four Seasons' Christmas brunch.

The other men, I am informed, are Nina's accountants, Harry Kerr and Nick McMahon. Harry is a large, red-faced, older man who breathes heavily as he shakes my hand and sits down. Nick McMahon, on the other hand, must be a junior associate of Harry's because he is roughly my age, ridiculously good-looking, and—I sneak a peek at his left hand—married.

I remove my gaze from the shiny wedding band on Nick's hand and decide to focus on Harry, as he is clearly the more senior accountant at the table.

Thomas quickly gets the meeting started, stating that our purpose is to make decisions regarding my mother's estate, which includes her house in Alexandria and everything in it, her bank accounts, stock holdings, et cetera. I am told that all decisions regarding the estate will be made by me, at which point I must have a look of sheer horror on my face, because Thomas continues by saying that I will have the input and advisement of the other four people at the table to aid in my decision-making process.

Holding true to my reputation as a procrastinator, I tell them that I would like some time to think things over before I have to decide about anything. What I really mean is that I'd like to sweep all of this under the rug for a while and just not think about it. Nancy, Thomas, Harry, and Nick, however, clearly have other goals, which mean wrapping this up as quickly as possible.

Nancy rolls her chair a little closer to me and puts her hand over mine, which I realize is clenched into a fist. I resist the urge to pull away, and instead allow my hand to relax and my ears to listen.

Thomas suggests that I keep my mother's house for a while since it is paid for, and Nancy points out that it would save me quite a bit of money to live there, rent-free. Nina's house is a beautiful townhouse that is over a hundred years old, impeccably renovated, and located just a few blocks from the Potomac River in Old Town Alexandria. Her street is quiet and serene, but two streets over are upscale shops, great restaurants, and bars that fill up every night. She has only lived there for seven years, after selling the tiny house in Chevy Chase, Maryland, where I grew up.

I think for a minute about my abysmal financial situation. I have somewhere around thirteen hundred dollars in my savings account and spend far more a month on my crappy apartment than it's worth, just because it's close to work. I decide that it might not be a bad idea to stay at Nina's, but I'm not ready to commit just yet.

Next comes the matter of all that is inside the house. The furniture will stay as long as I remain there, and Nancy has graciously agreed to consign or donate her clothes and accessories. Even if I weren't six feet compared to my mother's five foot four, I still wouldn't want her clothes. Her entire wardrobe is very dressy, very tailored, and *very* conservative.

It is now the accountants' turn to speak, and as I pretend to listen, all I can do is stare at Nick. Surprisingly, he is the one doing most of the talking, which allows me to take in his big blue eyes, strong jaw, and perfectly straight teeth without seeming like a total psycho. At one point I catch myself with my mouth gaping open and realize he is no longer talking.

Everyone is looking at me expectantly, clearly waiting for me to respond in some way, and I have no clue what I missed. Nancy, again, comes to my rescue.

"You're speechless," she says.

I wonder for a minute if I just had a bomb dropped on me, but recognize a trace of a smile on Nancy's face, so I am compelled to ask Nick to please repeat what he just said.

My inattentiveness is misinterpreted as shock, and Nick looks back down at the papers in front of him.

"Your mother's total holdings, which include her bank accounts, stock portfolio, and real estate, at this time total over four-point-eight million dollars." He looks pleased, and folds his hands over the papers.

Now I am speechless for real. I heard what Nick said and just cannot believe it. My mother was a millionaire? I mean . . . I knew that she was making a lot of money, but I never really thought about what that would mean in the long run.

"Wow," I barely get out. "I had no idea."

Nancy quickly fills me in. "Well, she did very well for herself and made some incredibly wise investments. She actually paid off her mortgage last year and was starting to talk about cutting back at work. I think she wanted to travel."

My mother? Cutting back on work? To *travel*?

"Wow. I really didn't know her at all," I accidentally say out loud. Nancy, who I am sure knows everything about my relationship with Nina, pats my hand again.

"She didn't let people in," Nancy says quietly. "It wasn't anything you did."

As I attempt to digest all of this, Harry cuts in. "All of your mother's assets are to go to you, and it's pretty straight-forward. Her house is paid for, and the rest of her holdings are either cash or stock. There are some inheritance taxes that will need to be paid, but there will still be quite a lot of money. The only outstanding matter, then, would be her monthly expenditures, some of which will need your authorization to continue paying."

"You mean her bills? Power, water, and all that?" I ask. Certainly they know I'm responsible enough to pay those.

Harry flips through some papers and continues. "Yes, but there's also a Rosa Velasquez, a Max Rockwell, and a Charles Jenner who receive monthly payments from Nina's account."

I think for a moment, and it registers that there are people other than Nancy who will have lost their incomes because of my mother's death.

"Rosa is her housekeeper," I inform them, "and Max is her trainer. What should I do?"

Thomas helpfully suggests that I continue paying Rosa until she finds another full-time job, and that a personal trainer probably has a large enough client base that losing one won't be the end of the world. Max was present at Nina's funeral, so I know he won't show up for a session this week. I think about the gift certificate my mother gave me and how there's no way I will ever call him to work out, and suddenly realize that everyone is staring at me again.

"What? I'm sorry . . . I'm just trying to absorb all of this." I look at each of them, wondering which one was just talking to me.

Nancy speaks first. "What about Charles Jenner? What would you like to do about him?"

"Um," I say searching my mind for some connection. "I don't know who that is. Is he the gardener? Or maybe her stockbroker?" Nick, Harry, and Thomas are all looking at me expectantly, and Nancy just looks sad.

"Missi," she says gently, "Charles Jenner is Nina's father."

CHAPTER SIX

An hour later I am still sitting at the conference table. Harry and Nick left a while ago, and Thomas sticks his head in the door every now and then to see if I need anything. Nancy hasn't left my side, and is trying to fill in some blanks, but there are still many that remain. Nancy doesn't know much about my grandfather, but the fact that she knows anything at all puts her way ahead of me.

I specifically remember my first day of second grade, when my teacher went around the class, asking how we'd spent the summer. Several kids in my class said they'd gone to spend weeks at a time with their grandparents . . . in Florida, in New Jersey, even in South Dakota. I went home that afternoon and asked my mother why I never got to go see my grandparents. She told me matter-of-factly that I didn't have any. She *told* me that they died before I was born. Why would she do that?

What I know at the end of this painstaking hour is that my grandfather does not appear to be deceased, and that Nina has been sending him a check every month for as long as her financial records go back. I also know that the checks are addressed to a Post Office Box in a town called Pritchard, Mississippi, which is presumably where he lives.

My first instinct is to get on a plane to Mississippi, but it's a ridiculous idea. I can name a hundred different countries on a world map, but I couldn't pick out Pritchard, Mississippi without a tour guide. I also don't know if my grandfather will want to see me, since by all accounts my mother has had no contact with him in decades, other than to send money. Suddenly a thought hits me—if I didn't know he existed, does he have any clue that I do? I am at a total loss, and Nancy and Thomas can't help with this.

As I leave the lobby of Laughlin, Anderson, and McKenzie I am temporarily blinded by the sunlight. It is oppressively hot and extraordinarily humid today, and the fact that Washington was built on a swamp doesn't escape me. Just the same, I find a bench at a bus stop of all places to sit down and gather my thoughts.

I have a key to Nina's house in the pocket of my pants. Nina's house is *my* house now. I have a house. I have a housekeeper. And I have a grandfather.

All my life, all I've ever wanted was a family that went beyond Nina and me, and now the thought of it is more than I can bear. I should feel exuberant. I should be packing my bags for Mississippi right at this moment. I should be anticipating a heartfelt reunion with my long, lost grandfather. But I am more afraid than I can ever remember being. What if he doesn't want to meet me? What if he's so hurt by whatever happened with Nina in the past that he can't bear to be around her daughter?

I ponder the possible reasons why they haven't spoken in over thirty years, and wonder if my mother isn't completely to blame. What if he did something to drive her away? Maybe he's exactly like Nina—bossy, controlling, and stubborn. Maybe he's a horrible human being.

As I try to sort through the swarm of thoughts running through my head, I make a decision to go home to my own apartment and go from there. My apartment may not be nice, but it's familiar and maybe being somewhere familiar will help me find my bearings again. My life as it stands now is completely foreign to me.

Besides, my apartment is closer, it's air conditioned, and I feel like I am melting.

By the time I reach my apartment and walk up three flights of stairs I am ready to pass out. I have never been so hot in my life. I shut the door behind me, kick off my shoes, and flop down on my couch. It smells like dog. I'm not really sure why since I don't have a dog, but my couch smells like dog.

I peel myself off the couch and slink the seven steps into my bedroom so I can crawl into my bed. I lay for a few short moments before I remember that my bed doesn't smell much better than my couch. Goddamn laundry. I look at my closet door, which is gaping open. I have washed one emergency load of undergarments since Nina died, but there are still so many dirty clothes littering the floor of my closet that I physically can't get the door to close.

Suddenly, I am struck by the thought that with the money I have inherited from my mother, I could just bag up all the dirty crap, drag it downstairs to the dumpster, and start over. I could go shopping! My clothes aren't anything to write home about anyway. Same goes for the canine couch—I could call someone to haul it off and get a new one. Maybe if I get some really nice things, I'll learn to take better care of them.

Then, just as suddenly, I begin to wonder if this whole day has been a dream. I will wake up again on my birthday, realize I am still wearing my pajamas, and am just now waking up from a long, strange nightmare. As I roll over expecting to see my pajama-clad self, I feel something sharp digging into my right hip. Instinctively, I grab at the pain, and my fingers close on the source. It is Nina's key in the pocket of my brown pants.

I fish the key out and hold it in the palm of my hand. It is shiny brass and says *Yale* on both sides. I am taken back many years to a heated argument my mother and I had when I was applying to colleges. I wanted to stay close to D.C., where my friends from high school were applying. I wanted to be a teacher, and the University of Maryland has a great program. Nina had different ideas and subsequently dragged me all up and down the East Coast to every single Ivy League school in existence, Yale included. She spent thousands of dollars in application fees, and I spent many uncomfortable hours dressed in skirts and blouses being interviewed by uptight academics that were only seeing me as a favor to my mother. I didn't get into a single one and ended up at Maryland anyway.

Nina still refused to allow me to major in education, saying she would not pay my tuition unless I went Pre-Med or Pre-Law. Since the sight of blood or vomit makes me gag, I chose Pre-Law and spent the next four years struggling. I didn't score well on the LSATs, didn't get into law school, and ended up working a series of mundane jobs before being hired by Richard. Nina never got over the disappointment—and "public humiliation"—she claims I caused. I have always found this ironic coming from a woman who never even got her degree.

I sigh deeply and realize I have been squeezing the key so hard my knuckles have turned white. When I open my hand again, there is an imprint of the key on my palm. I stare at it for a long time. It really happened. Nina is gone, and she left me all of her stuff. Her house, her money and, apparently, her father.

My life has, in one afternoon, changed completely. Everything is different than it was just a few hours ago. I decide that something—even something small—needs to stay the same. Otherwise, I might lose my grip on reality completely. I head for my galley kitchen, pull a box of garbage bags from under the sink, and return to my closet. I manage to squeeze all my dirty laundry into three bags, and haul them one at a time down the three flights of stairs to the entryway. I set them down next to the ugly floral couch, which incidentally also smells like dog, and head out the door to the street.

I spend the next several minutes trying to hail a taxi, and when I finally do, I run back into my building to grab my bags of clothes. I am not going to incinerate them, and would never donate three bags full of dirty laundry. I am taking a taxi, which I can now afford, to my mother's house, which is now *my* house, to do laundry. If the landscape of life as I knew it is going to change this dramatically, then the least I can do is wear the same shitty clothes. Besides, I bet Nina has a kick-ass washer and dryer.

Two hours later I have dumped my clothes in three mountainous piles on Nina's kitchen floor, but have yet to figure out how to use her high-tech machines. The door to what I believe is the washer is on the side rather than the top, which confounds me. I have tried to shove my clothes in, but before I can slam the door shut, stuff falls out. Forget even trying to pour detergent in. I've read the label on the bottle of slimy blue liquid that claims to be "high efficiency." I have no idea what that means. I should wear a label that says "low efficiency."

I think about calling Rosa, who is surely the only person who has ever actually operated this thing, but I don't want to bother her at home. She has a husband and children, and better things to do than help a moron like me do my laundry. I also don't have her telephone number, so I couldn't bother her if I wanted to. Completely out of resources, I call the only person in the world I know I can count on to bail me out of a jam.

I have been wandering the house for a while, opening closets and drawers, and basically just surveying the place. It is, in a word, immaculate. Rosa has apparently been here recently, because the refrigerator and pantry have been cleared out. Beyond that, though, I find total organization in every room. I have actually only been to this house a handful of times—Nina and I usually relegated our dinners and holidays to public forums where one of us making a scene was less likely—and on the rare occasions I was here I never paid attention to how neat and obsessively tidy everything was. Even Nina's home office is impeccable. There are no stacks of papers lying around, her books and files are perfectly lined up, and there isn't a superfluous item to be found on the desktop. No photos, no pens, no coffee cup . . . it is the complete opposite of my old desk at work. I wonder how on earth I can share genes with this woman.

I sigh deeply and sink into a kitchen chair just as the doorbell rings. I run for the front door, hurdling piles of clothes and nearly breaking my neck as I trip over the fringes of the Oriental rug in the living room. Out of breath, I fling the door open, shouting, "What took you so long?"

"Um, sorry. We've been swamped tonight." It's the pizza delivery guy, who is not the person I called to help me with laundry, but whom I am almost equally glad to see.

"Oh, I didn't mean to yell at you. I'm waiting for a friend. To help me . . . " I trail off, not wanting to admit to a pizza guy that I can't do my own laundry.

"Um, eat the pizza?" he helpfully finishes.

Grateful, I smile at him. It's the first time I've smiled in a long time, and it feels strange.

"Yes, to help me eat the pizza," I say. I hand the guy some money, tell him to keep the change, and stand in the doorway holding two large pizzas as he gets into his double-parked car and drives away. I inhale the scent of cheese and sausage, and realize that I am starving.

I turn around and kick the door closed with my foot.

"Ouch!" squeals a muffled voice from the other side of the door. "That's what a girl gets for coming to the aid of a domestic disaster?"

I set the pizzas down on an antique console table and open the door again. Maggie is there, wide-eyed as ever, rubbing her nose.

"Sorry!" I apologize, dragging her into the house. She looks around the foyer, as though taking in the grandeur of the place, and her eyes come to rest on the pizza boxes.

"Oh my God, what have you *done*?" she screams, running to lift the boxes from the console.

"Oops," I say, running my hand over the cloudy mark the hot pizza boxes have left on the wood. "That was probably really expensive, and I really need to take better care of . . ."

"I cannot *believe* you only ordered two pizzas! Are you on a *diet* or something?" She spins her tiny self around and heads for the kitchen.

I smile at her retreating figure, and this time smiling feels more good than strange. Everything is going to be okay, I think.

By eleven o'clock that night, four loads of laundry have been washed, dried and folded, the mountains of clothes in the kitchen have dwindled to three color-coordinated piles that I am now surely

34

capable of laundering without Maggie's supervision, and there are exactly two slices of pizza remaining.

Maggie and I are stretched out with our heads at opposite ends of Nina's overly firm, white living room couch. My feet reach all the way to where Maggie's head rests on a silk throw pillow with elaborate red braiding around the edges, but Maggie's feet barely reach my ribs. I feel like an Amazon.

As if she has read my thoughts, Maggie remarks, "Nina wasn't very tall, right? You've got to figure your father is or was a pretty big guy."

I shift a little, feeling self-conscious. Even though Maggie is my dearest friend, we've never really ventured into this territory. I don't speak, waiting to see if she continues, which of course she does.

"I mean, you're so *tall* for a woman. And you clearly did not inherit your height from your mother. Have you ever thought about that?"

I open my mouth to answer, but my voice catches and sounds all scratchy. I clear my throat, and trying not to sound defensive say, "Of course I've thought about it. I've spent the better part of thirty years feeling like I couldn't be more different from my mother, but I learned early not to ask. You want to talk about a sensitive subject? I mean, he didn't even qualify for space on my birth certificate."

"Okay, so Nina made it clear she didn't want to discuss your father with you, which for the record I think is criminal. I mean, good, bad, or indifferent, he's your father." She hesitates briefly, but then adds, "You're right, though, that you and Nina couldn't have been more different, so maybe you're *just like him*."

I think for a moment of the few conversations I ever had with my mother regarding my father. Her answer was always that he was a selfish man who couldn't make a commitment and chose to have nothing to do with us. When I got old enough to pursue the subject on my own, I remained true to my nature and put it off for so long that I eventually lost the drive to pursue it at all.

I shake my head, trying to shake the thoughts out of my mind. Maggie sits very still at her end of the couch, patiently waiting for me to respond. I know her well enough to understand that this is going to be an all-nighter. Maggie is like Dr. Phil. She can talk to anyone about anything, and although she's never pressed me for information about my father before, I can tell she's not going home until this is all out on the table. I decide to be honest with her, and with myself, for once.

"I suppose," I begin, "that I never really pushed Nina very hard for information about my father. She always cut me off, telling me it was his choice, and I let it go at that. When I was in third grade we had *Doughnuts for Dads* day at school, and I asked Nina if we could call him and see if he could come. She gave me the same answer then, and I never argued."

I realize that I am remembering that day, almost twenty-five years ago, like it was yesterday. I remember the purple corduroys and white cable knit sweater I was wearing when I went into the den where Nina worked when she was at home. I remember my mother looking over the top of her glasses at me, never really lifting her head, and her explanation that it just wasn't important. That he didn't want a family. And probably didn't like doughnuts, anyway.

I remember wondering what kind of person wouldn't want a family, wouldn't want a beautiful, smart woman like my mother as their wife, wouldn't want an adoring daughter like me. That's how I used to think of Nina and I, but then I grew up. I decided a long time ago that we weren't the type of family most people would want.

I had spent the entirety of *Doughnuts for Dads* in the nurse's office with a phony stomachache, and after that, conversations about my father occurred less and less frequently, until even Father's Day came and went without a peep from me.

Maggie looks at me sympathetically, but thankfully not condescendingly. "But you made it your life's mission to argue with Nina about everything imaginable. What made you accept her explanation about *this*?"

I yawn, more mentally than physically tired. "Oh, I don't know—"

"Yes you do," Maggie says sternly.

I dig deep, trying to put words to a fear I've harbored for my entire life. "I was afraid, I guess. Afraid to go through all the trouble of investing the time and emotion, only to find out that she was right all along. That my father didn't want us."

"That he didn't want *you*," Maggie corrects, sitting up straighter and pulling her legs to her chest."

My eyes well up with tears, but I will not cry. I nod, and as pathetic as I feel, there is some relief in actually having admitted this to someone.

"What about now?" Maggie's eyebrows are raised, her beady brown eyes seeming to wait for me to make some life-altering decision at this exact moment.

I almost laugh out loud, but end up choking on the sound. "What do you mean, 'What about now?'" I ask, incredulous.

Maggie throws her legs over my feet and gets up off the couch. She walks over to the fireplace and runs her hand along the ornately carved mantel. Then she turns to look at me, and begins to pace back and forth.

"Well, not to sound disrespectful or anything, but I think we can agree that Nina wasn't the easiest person to be around." I nod, as Maggie continues. "She was at best hard to please and extremely critical."

"Mm hm," I concur, not knowing where she's going with her train of thought.

She stops pacing and looks right at me. "Maybe it wasn't *you* he didn't want. Maybe he just couldn't live with her. God knows she sets her standards pretty high; it's entirely possible that he couldn't live up to them and gave up. On her, not on you."

I feel like I am in a psychiatrist's office, laying on a sofa while someone much smarter than me tries to figure out my life.

"Isn't it the same thing, though?" I ask. "Giving up on her meant not giving me a chance."

"Not necessarily," Maggie says, as she starts pacing again. "Maybe he didn't have a choice. At any rate, there's only one way to find out."

I look at her curiously. "How?"

"You have to find him and ask him yourself," she says triumphantly, as if the mystery has finally been solved.

Suddenly impatient, I cover my face with my hands and start massaging my forehead. "Except for one minor problem, Maggie. I don't know who he is. I don't know his name, where he lives, or the first thing about him."

"That, my friend, is where good old Grandpa comes in." Maggie is smiling like the Cheshire cat, crooked teeth flashing and eyes popping out at me. "Missi Jennings, your family tree has precisely one limb on it right now. I say you go out on it and find out where it leads, no matter how precarious it sounds."

CHAPTER SEVEN

I suddenly feel motivated for the first time in, well, possibly ever, to find out just where I came from, and who my family is . . . or what remains of them, anyway. I am dying to know why I have always felt like an alien around my mother. Is it because I am genetically predisposed to be just like my father?

And if I am, perhaps we will make an instant connection upon meeting, and he'll look at me and see himself, and how could he not want to have a relationship with me after that? I am smart, regardless of what Nina may have thought, have a great sense of humor, and will be the daughter he never knew he's always wanted.

I have clear visions of my introduction to my father. Or would it be a reunion? I wonder for the first time if he's ever even laid eyes on me. My mother got pregnant while in college at Georgetown, then dropped out, but stayed in the area. If my father was a college boyfriend, then it's entirely possible that they've never spoken again. Maybe that's why my father didn't want a family. He was young and ambitious as well, and not ready to settle down. Maybe she never even told him.

But why, then, would my brazenly pro-choice mother have chosen to keep me? So much of this still isn't making sense. Nina was never the type to sacrifice her own needs and aspirations for others.

Then it dawns on me. At some point in her Southern Baptist life she had been pro-life. She would never have had an abortion, no matter what—she was raised to believe that human life was sacred from the moment of conception. It was *me* that changed all of that for her. She found out afterwards what having a baby at 20, with no college degree and no husband, would do to her lofty aspirations. Yes, she was extremely successful, but imagine what she could have been without me tying her down. For all I know, she was headed for the White House until I came along.

Maggie left 20 minutes ago, but I call her cell phone and share my latest thoughts with her. She is quiet for a minute, and I think I've lost the connection, but then she starts talking again.

"There's a bit of a problem, then. Your grandfather seems like he'd be a pretty easy guy to find, since we have an address on him."

"Well, a Post Office Box," I interrupt.

Ever the plotter, Maggie quickly responds, "You could easily stake out a P.O. Box, Magnum P.I. If he gets a check every month, at some point he'll stop in to pick it up."

"Then what's the problem?"

"Well," Maggie says, "if your father went to college with your mother at Georgetown, there's a chance that your grandfather didn't know him, or even know who he was. It's not as if the guy stuck around, and it doesn't sound as though Nina was very close with your grandfather. She told you he was *dead*."

"You're right," I say, suddenly feeling tired and unmotivated again. "My grandfather probably doesn't know anything."

"Didn't your mother tell you her parents died together in a car accident?"

"Yes, but that's clearly not the case . . . " I begin.

"My point is that maybe your grandfather isn't the only one still living. The checks are made out to him, but maybe you have a grandmother, too!" Maggie sounds hopeful, and it rubs off on me.

"A grandmother?" I whisper excitedly. "Maybe she bakes, and knits, and smells like roses!"

"Easy, there, cowgirl," Maggie says. "I can tell you've put some thought into what makes a grandmother, but there's no guarantee she's still around, and even if she is, you're a long way from apple pies and learning to crochet. Remember that family tree we were talking about? One branch?"

"I do," I say dreamily, now picturing myself with a sweet old lady sitting by my side on a porch swing drinking lemonade and looking at old family photos.

"I think that rather than just jumping into your gene pool without a bathing suit, you should consider dipping your big toe in to start." God, Maggie is so pragmatic. I know she's right and trying very hard to prevent me from getting hurt, so I lock away the mental image of me and the grandmother figure—who I realize strongly resembles Betty White—and decide to be cautiously optimistic.

Maybe there's more than one person out there, just waiting to welcome their long-lost sheep back into the fold.

That strange and unfamiliar motivation returns, and, thanks to the Internet, I have soon learned a few things about Mississippi.

Mississippi has 2.9 million people in the entire state, which is, like, *half* the number of people living in a sixty-mile radius of Washington, D.C.

61% of the people living in Mississippi are white, 37% are black, leaving about 2% that are anything else—*not* what I am used to in a melting pot like D.C.

A little over 1% of people in Mississippi are foreign born—in Washington it's 13%.

Per capita income in Mississippi is around $16,000, whereas in D.C. it's almost $30,000, and there's *plenty* of poverty here—I can't even imagine what it's like there.

There are about 60 people per square mile in Mississippi versus a whopping 9,378 per square mile in Washington. I try to imagine what having that kind of space would be like.

Elvis was born in Tupelo, Mississippi—I always assumed Tennessee, since Graceland is there.

Jackson native Harry A. Cole, Sr. invented Pine Sol, which I think I might actually own a bottle of for those rare occasions when I clean.

Root beer was invented in Biloxi.

Belzoni is the Catfish Capital of the World. Wow, the *whole world?*

A Mississippian named David Harrison owns the patent on the soft toilet seat. Who has one of those anymore?

The largest Bible binding plant in the U.S. is in Greenwood. *Whoa.*

I have even found Pritchard on a map. It appears to be about thirty miles from any of four major roads, two running north to south and two east to west, and not really near *anything*.

I have also discovered that my grandfather does not have a listed phone number. I begin to wonder if he might have a phone at all, based on what I've learned. This means that I cannot call him to warn him of my impending trip, ask him if he'd like a visitor, ask for directions to Pritchard, or even verify his existence beyond the P.O. Box where Nina has been sending checks for all these years.

I know myself well enough to admit that if I do not take action *now*, while I have this piqued curiosity about my family, I will never get around to it. It will end up like everything else in my life. I will lose momentum, then lose interest, and resign myself to being an orphan at age thirty-three. I have allowed this pattern to repeat too many times—not changing my major in college, settling for a crappy job, assuming that Josh was my only chance at love—and every time I end up deferring to a life that is not what I ever intended for myself. I am not happy, am not complete, and am not going to screw this up. At least I hope not.

The worst thing that can happen is that I never locate him. Or that I find him and he wants nothing to do with me, or that I find him and he unloads a bunch of family baggage on me, when maybe I'd be better off not knowing any of it. Jesus, I am talking myself out of it already. Why do I do this?

I pace my tiny kitchen—not Nina's large kitchen in all its stainless-steel glory—waiting for the guy from the moving company to finish taking the last wardrobe box from my apartment. Since all I am taking with me are clothes, books and keepsakes, I probably could have moved it all myself, but in an attempt not to lose momentum I hired it out.

When I told my landlord I was moving and asked if he knew of a place where I could donate my furniture, his eyes lit up and he said he'd keep it here and advertise my place as "furnished." I thought about the dog-smelling couch and my old, mismatched furniture and decided to let someone else fight that battle. I went to the nearest convenience store anyway and picked up a bottle of Febreeze. I'm not exactly sure what "antimicrobial" means, but it sounded like it might help matters, so I used up the entire container on the couch, the carpet and my mattress, and my conscience began to feel lighter.

I have decided that while living at Nina's I will reside in one of the two guest bedrooms. To my knowledge, neither have ever been slept in, but one is painted a cozy, buttery yellow and has a magnificent cherry sleigh bed that seems to in itself define the term *good night's sleep*. Plus, there's no way in hell I am sleeping in my dead mother's bed. It would be too weird.

Rosa came yesterday and we had the nicest talk. She said she'd like to continue working here if I need her. I doubt she'd have any trouble getting more work, but she said she spent more time at Nina's house than anyone including Nina, and that it's kind of a second home to her. I do want her to keep coming, which is selfish in several ways, but beyond the fact that my cleanliness-challenged self won't have to keep up with this enormous house, I am happy to know that I will have company some of the time. Rosa not only cleaned for Nina, but also did her laundry, her grocery shopping, and left dinner in the refrigerator Monday through Friday. I know I have not earned it, but I look forward to having Rosa in my life, at least for a little while.

I have learned that Rosa's husband, Jorge, is a janitor at a government building Downtown, and that they are putting three children through college at the same time. Their middle daughter is a junior at the University of Maryland . . . majoring in, of all things, education. Lucky girl.

Rosa is living the quintessential American dream, and I am awash in something that feels like embarrassment knowing the high price Nina paid to send me to a private school with some of the wealthiest kids in Washington, and that now I am unemployed and squatting at her house. I have accomplished nothing compared to Rosa's family, but it's reason enough to continue paying her to work here if that's what she wants to do. What the heck else am I going to do with all of Nina's money?

With all of my loose ends tied up—I am out of my apartment and somewhat reorganized in Nina's house—I can start planning my quest to find my family. I decide to call a travel agent, since I have no idea where an airport is in relation to Pritchard, Mississippi. There aren't actually many travels agents listed in the yellow pages; I guess these days people book most of their travel over the internet and don't need a real human being to help anymore.

I on the other hand need human assistance and advice, so I dial a company called Travel Time and connect with a lady named Paula who has a very thick Long Island accent. I explain to Paula that I need air travel to the airport closest to Pritchard, and a rental car with a good map once I am there. She inquires about whether or not I need a hotel room in Pritchard, and since I have no clue how I will be received when and if I locate my grandfather, I say yes.

As luck would have it, her search for accommodations in Pritchard comes up empty, so by the time we are done, I have a one-way plane ticket from Reagan National Airport to Jackson, Mississippi, assurance that I can book a return flight with very little notice, a reservation for a compact car, and a hotel room booked in Jackson. I also have a serious case of anxiety and nausea.

I spend the rest of the day going through every drawer, closet, and file in Nina's house—I don't think I'll ever be able to think of it as *my* house—looking for things to take with me to Mississippi that might back up the claim of a random crazy woman that I belong there. I am hoping to find photographs, letters, legal papers . . . anything at all would be nice.

What I do find is an original copy of my birth certificate. It is in mint condition, as though it has not been moved from the file folder since the day it was received, but it occurs to me that it probably won't help. I was born in Washington, D.C. and my father's name is not listed, so it probably won't mean anything to anyone in Mississippi, anyway.

I finger the thick, cream-colored paper and wonder when my mother decided to change her last name from Jenner to Jennings. It was obviously before I was born, because my birth certificate has Jennings on it. I wonder why she changed it at all. It's not as though changing the last couple of letters makes much of a difference, but maybe it made enough of a difference to make Nina harder to find. Maybe when Nina left home it was with the intention of disappearing. But why, then, would she work so hard to end up in the public eye? Just when I think I am starting to figure things out, it all stops making sense.

There are no photos anywhere that might be helpful. As a matter of fact, the only photos I find in the entire house are of me— school pictures dating as far back as kindergarten, pictures taken at an occasional birthday party, and one of me accepting my college diploma in which I look anything but thrilled to be graduating. None of these are organized into albums or set in frames, but rather are together in a manila envelope in the bottom drawer of Nina's desk. It makes me sad to find no baby pictures—how can a mother, even an emotionally detached one like Nina, not have scores of pictures of her baby? There is not a single photo of Nina, either, and none that could possibly be of her parents or any other family member.

There are no legal papers that might give me credence, either. Nothing at all that gives me more information or insight into my situation. I'm not sure what I was expecting to find, but I have apparently struck out.

I stand in front of the mahogany bookshelves in my mother's office, taking in the way her volumes of books are so neatly arranged. They seem to be organized by subject area and all the spines are perfectly aligned, but I note with some relief that they are not in alphabetical order. I definitely did not inherit Nina's neat gene. Most of the books are about government and politics, many are about American and European history, and on the bottom shelf there are just a few novels. I regard them, not having any clue as to what my mother would have chosen for pleasure reading, and am

43

somewhat surprised at what I see.

Truman Capote, William Faulkner, Margaret Mitchell, Willie Morris, Flannery O'Connor, Alice Walker, Robert Penn Warren, Eudora Welty—It doesn't take an English major to know that my mother had acquired an interesting collection of Southern literature. And these *are* in alphabetical order.

I am again left wondering who exactly my mother was. There clearly was more to her than the woman who abandoned her family and left Mississippi never to return. Seeing these books so carefully placed on her shelf makes me realize that there was another side to Nina. One that for some reason remained attached to, or at least interested in, her southern roots. I am suddenly intrigued about who Nina Jennings really was. For thirty-three years I could have cared less, but now I want to know more about her. Now that she can no longer push me away with her criticism and disapproval, I want to acquaint myself with my mother. It's a shame she had to die first.

I feel a throbbing lump growing in my throat, but I won't cry, so I swallow hard, close the door to Nina's office, and head upstairs. It's getting late and I have to pack. I have a plane to catch in the morning.

CHAPTER EIGHT

It's been a long time since I've traveled by airplane—my trips out of D.C. in recent years have been via the Amtrak train or Josh's Toyota Corolla—and now I remember why. My flight, which should have taken only two and a half hours, was originally delayed due to thunderstorms, and now my current problem is that the airplane has been parked near the gate in Jackson for fifteen minutes but the door still hasn't opened. I am growing extremely impatient and somewhat claustrophobic, watching out my tiny window as the airline employees attempt to roll a metal staircase toward the side of our plane.

The sun is blazing through the window, so I reach into my tote bag and find my sunglasses. By this time, most of my fellow passengers are standing in the aisles looking impatient. A man two rows in front of me is reaching into the overhead bin to pull out his carry-on bags, and I notice that his shirt has large circles of sweat under the arms. They turned the air off a few minutes ago, and I shift in my seat, feeling increasingly uncomfortable. I pull down the window shade, but now not only do I feel claustrophobic, but like I may pass out from the hot, stagnant air inside this plane. I am also keenly aware of the body odor rapidly filling the air around me.

Thankfully the intercom comes on and informs us, with apologies from the crew, that the door is now being opened and we may deplane. Ordinarily I would sit still and wait while everyone else on the plane stampedes for the door, but today I vow to not let one single human being get past my row without letting me up. I casually stick my leg out in the aisle to mark my place while the six rows ahead of me scramble to get off of this Crock Pot with wings. When it's my turn I stand up quickly, trying not to hit my head on the overhead bins, and sprint for the door and the fresh air beyond.

As I step off the plane, however, I am not welcomed by fresh air, but rather by heat like nothing I have ever felt before. It literally sucks the air out of me, and I feel like I can no longer breathe. My sunglasses have also fogged up completely, leaving me visually impaired as I descend the temporary staircase to the tarmac. I wonder if it is heat from the jet engines radiating outward and searing my face, but as I get farther from the plane and closer to the terminal, there is no relief.

I locate a restroom and have to maneuver around a couple of suitcases sitting outside the stalls. Having lived in D.C. for so long, I fear that if I leave my suitcase outside, someone will steal it while I pee, so I drag it into the stall with me and clumsily shove the door closed. The stall is tiny, and I am so crowded by my suitcase that I have trouble trying to hover over the toilet seat, so I unroll some toilet paper and wipe the seat off. Then I sit down. Much better. I begin to think about my plan of action in finding my grandfather, and suddenly get very nervous again. Every possible bad scenario runs through my head and I am almost tempted to get on the next plane back to Washington.

I gather my courage, finish up, and finagle my way back out of the stall with my suitcase. I stand at the sink, wash my hands, and assess my appearance, which is utterly appalling.

As I wash my hands I listen to two older women having a chirpy conversation about their impending flights. It is evident that they have never met before, but within thirty seconds have established that they live just a few miles from one another, and that one's bridge partner is the other's neighbor.

People just do not have conversations like this in D.C., much less in public restrooms. I smile and pull my suitcase out of the bathroom, headed for the rental car facility.

It occurs to me as I maneuver through the terminal that I am ambushing my grandparents. If they knew I was coming, would they want to prepare for it? Surely my grandmother would want to bake. I would have called and given them some warning, but I don't have a phone number. I would have written a letter to the P.O. Box, and waited for a response, but that would prolong the entire process, and I am already here. Besides, I was totally caught off-guard that day in Thomas Anderson's office when I found out I have a grandfather. I guess it's his turn to be surprised.

I am finally in my rental car, with a map in my hands and the air conditioning on full blast, but I have not driven an inch. When I made the car reservation through Paula, I asked for a compact car but when I reached the rental counter they were out of compacts and subcompacts, so the lady offered me a "tan car," or so I thought. I had no color preference, so I said that would be fine. It turns out it was not a *tan* car, but a *Town Car*—in other words, a Lincoln. A black one. It is unfathomably large, and I am terrified to even pull out of the parking spot. It doesn't help that the last car I drove was my mother's Mercedes on the day she was killed. I push that thought to the back of my mind.

The rental car lady told me that Pritchard is about two hours from the airport, and that I will surely pass more than enough motels along the way to choose from. I decide that "motel" is a cute southern term for hotel, and envision myself checking into a quaint little bed and breakfast . . . or at least a Hampton Inn.

I double-check the mirrors, gather up every last bit of courage, and put the car in reverse. I quickly find out that I barely have to tap the gas pedal to make the car move and almost hit the car across the aisle from me, which, for the record, is a Ford Taurus. I should totally go ask for another car, but it's so hot out there I can't stand it. I can do this. Tap, brake. Tap, brake. Tap, brake. Finally I put the car in drive and crank up the air conditioner, which thankfully works like a charm. The pimpmobile and I are on the road at last.

I make my way out of the airport premises, stick my face in the map the lady gave me, and before long find myself in the middle of nowhere. I panic, thinking I have gotten on the wrong road, but eventually see a sign telling me that I am indeed on track to Pritchard.

Rather than worrying about something I cannot control such as where I am going, I fiddle around on the dashboard trying to find a decent radio station. Every other station seems to be playing country music, so I end up listening to talk radio. It reminds me of Nina, but I listen anyway.

A little over an hour later I have a good grasp on current events and opinions, but am drained, no longer running on adrenaline and fear. There is a gas station ahead on the right, and it's the first non-residential building I've seen in a while. I pull into the lot thinking that at the very least I can check my directions again and pick up a snack. Caffeine and sugar are exactly what I need right now.

I park in the gravel lot alongside the station, get out of the enormous Lincoln, and stretch my long legs. There is a child's blow-up swimming pool and two plastic lawn chairs off to one side, and a dusty old pick-up truck parked next to it. It has gotten cloudy, and the heat isn't quite so cruel anymore, but my shirt clings to my back nonetheless.

As I push open the door to walk inside, I am blasted with cold air. I notice that the glass on the inside of the door is covered in condensation, and that someone has recently drawn a happy face in it. I can't help but smile back at it.

The station seems empty as I enter, so I loudly clear my throat and say, "Hello?"

A moment later I hear a toilet flush, and a woman emerges from the restroom, still buttoning her jeans.

"Oh, hey!" she greets me in a low, scratchy voice. Her smile is a mile wide, and she looks both surprised and happy to see me.

"Hi," I respond, trying to return her beautiful smile with something genuine. "I'm from out of town, trying to get to Pritchard. Can you tell me if I'm still going the right way?"

"Why in the world do you want to go there?" she asks with a pained look on her face.

I must have a shocked expression on my own face, because she quickly laughs—a gruff, smoker's laugh, but a contagious one—and says, "Oh, I'm just kiddin'! It's not so bad. Come all the way inside and outta that heat, girl! Want a drink or something?"

"Actually, I'd love a Coke and a candy bar, if you've got any."

She points to the refrigerated case, which has the door propped open wide. "Cokes are in there, and candy is behind the register. Got problems with folks stealing," she says matter-of-factly.

"Stealing the candy?" I ask, reaching into the case to grab a bottle of soda.

"Yep, the candy and the cigarettes. Guess there's not much else here worth stealing. Now, if we sold beer it'd be a different story for sure, but you have entered the Bible belt my dear, in case you hadn't noticed. " She laughs again, and I can't help it, I do too.

"Do you want me to shut the door to the refrigerator?" I ask before heading to the register.

She shakes her head and holds up a hand. "Dear Lord, no," she says. "I am up to my neck in menopause, so I keep the thermostat as low as it'll go and keep the fridge doors propped open. Only way I can get through the day, not that you'd know, young thing."

Again I smile without thinking, and walk over to the counter where the woman stands. "Do you have a Snickers bar, by any chance?"

"Sure do, " she drawls, reaching into a low cabinet under the cash register. "What's your name, darlin'?"

"Missi," I reply. "What's yours?"

"Dolly. Dolly Parsons," she says proudly, handing me the Snickers. "Not to be confused with that big-breasted gal up there in Tennessee!" She cackles at her own joke until she has to wipe her eyes.

Dolly is much smaller than I am—at least eight inches and fifty pounds—but I can tell she is larger than life. When she smiles, which seems to be constantly, her bright blue eyes sparkle like the ocean at sunset, and her short, gray hair shimmers with silvery streaks. She is beautiful in an unconventional way, and I am drawn to her like a moth to light.

I feel like I could spend the entire day talking to this stranger. I have never been so immediately drawn to someone that I wonder if her spirit is contagious or something. Suddenly remembering why I am here, I ask how far it is to Pritchard.

Dolly tells me it's only another fifteen miles or so, and asks again why I am headed there. I am just about to spill my story when a man walks in the door to pay for gas. I hadn't even noticed the big, dirty pickup truck pull into the lot. The man chats with Dolly for a minute—he must be a local—and I begin to feel like I have overstayed my welcome, so I smile, wave to Dolly, and head out the door.

"Wait, Missi!" Dolly hollers, and I realize I have forgotten to pay for my snack. Mortified, I stumble through an apology and pull my wallet out of my purse. The man gives Dolly a pat on the shoulder and leaves as I hand her some bills, but she laughs and waves them away. "Girl, I don't want your money! I just wondered if you might stay a bit. Have a chat with ol' Dolly. I'll understand if you're in a hurry to get on down the road, but I get the sense you might have something to get off your chest."

Happy to put off a theoretical confrontation with my unsuspecting grandparents and fascinated by this woman, I follow her out the door and to the little wading pool. She rolls up her jeans, kicks off her shoes, and sits in one of the chairs with her feet in the water. "Ah," she says. "Now that's better. Sure hope nobody sees fit to get somethin' that needs paying for anytime soon. I plan to sit right here a while and soak these tired toes. Sit on down, girl!"

I kick my sneakers off, peel off my socks, roll up my khakis, and join Dolly. The water does feel good, and I crack open my Coke and take a big sip. "Ah," I say, echoing her sentiment.

"Ain't this the life?" she asks. I consider this for a minute—working at a gas station in the middle-of-nowhere Mississippi, suffering hot flashes bad enough you have to practically refrigerate yourself, and taking solace in a blow-up pool with a complete stranger? Then I look at Dolly and the expression on her face. I am not sure I have ever seen a look of such contentment on another person in my entire life.

"Yes, it is," I tell her. And I mean it.

"Well, then," she says, bringing me back to reality. "What brings a girl like you to a place like this?"

What starts off as small talk between accidental acquaintances quickly takes on a soap opera quality as I spill my whole sordid story to Dolly. I'm not even sure how it happens—she just has a way of making me feel completely at ease, and she is an amazing listener. She does not take her eyes off me, even when I look away out of embarrassment. She furrows her brow, frowns, and laughs in all the right places, allows me to backtrack and tell my story out of chronological order, and at one point even hands me a tissue from her pocket, which I politely decline. It's not like I'm going to cry or anything.

Now it's out on the table—my poor, pitiful life. This woman, who just a little while ago was a total stranger, now knows more about me than anyone in the world, with the exception of Maggie.

I am momentarily afraid that Dolly will stand up in the pool, point to the Lincoln, and tell me to take my freak show on the road, but she doesn't. Instead, she sighs deeply and picks up a pack of cigarettes from the ground beside her lawn chair. She lights one, inhales, and blows a steady stream of smoke out of her nose.

"Nobody in this world deserves to watch their Mama die, no matter what kind of Mama they are. My heart hurts for you, is all I can say. Now, people 'round these parts will tell you that it's all a part of God's plan—you know, he closes a door but opens a window and all that nonsense—but I'll admit I sometimes have a hard time understanding how God would intentionally cause someone so much pain."

There is a long silence, which makes me uncomfortable, so I try to break it up. "Mind if I have one?" I ask, eyeing the pack of cigarettes resting now on the arm of her chair.

"Damn right, I do," she quickly retorts. "You're young and you're healthy, and you need to stay that way. You leave this nasty habit to us old, weathered, rotted-out types." She looks at me appraisingly, then down at my candy bar, which I have yet to open but that is losing its shape, clearly melting in the heat. "I bet you a new Snickers you've never smoked in your life."

I puff up my chest like a stubborn four-year-old. "I have too," I say proudly. "In college."

Dolly laughs deeply for a long time, which eventually becomes a raspy cough. If it were anyone else, I would feel patronized, but Dolly never loses her smile or her eye contact, which helps me understand she's just doing me a favor. I remember vividly the last time I smoked a cigarette—I was drunk at a fraternity party and trying to impress a cute guy from my Political Science class. He ended up taking my roommate home with him that night, and I woke up the following morning feeling like I'd swallowed a dirty sock.

In the past few minutes, the sky has gotten increasingly cloudy, and suddenly the wind starts gusting. Dust billows toward us from the gravel lot, and Dolly's cigarettes blow into the pool.

"My friend, I think that's our cue. You'd better get on the road before it storms, or you'll never find Pritchard. Too many raindrops might make that one traffic light awfully hard to see!" She bursts out in gravelly laughter again, and then stands, reaching her strong, bony hands out toward mine. I take them and stand, towering over my new friend, sorry that our time together is ending but grateful for our strange and surreal meeting.

We stand looking at each other for a moment, which would ordinarily make me incredibly uncomfortable, but right now I feel as though I am drawing strength from her. It's as if her hands are conduits through which courage and resolve find their way into me.

"You certainly have an adventure ahead of you, Missi, and I suspect that no matter the outcome, your life will change in ways you might not be expecting."

A lump rises in my throat. "I'm scared, Dolly. The only family I thought I had is gone, and I just don't know what I'll find when I get to Pritchard."

"Well, *I* know," she says unwaveringly. "No matter what happens there in Pritchard, whether your Granny and Grandpappy welcome you with open arms, or whether you get there and find they've passed on like your Mama, you will walk away knowing more than you know now, and there's something to be said about that."

"Dolly, I know we just met, but I feel like I've known you for a long time, and I can't thank you enough for listening to me." The wind is howling now, and my hair blows across my face, but I can't seem to break contact with Dolly.

She squeezes my hands so hard I think my fingers might break. "You said you wished you had a sister, right? Well, I think in a way you've found one in me. I liked you the minute you walked into the store, and I like you even more now. Besides, I know for sure that we'll see each other again."

"How do you know that?" Big, fat drops of rain begin to fall, and the trees behind the gas station are almost bent in half against the wind.

She smiles, and even in the darkening conditions her blue eyes glimmer. "You just may need some gas or a Snickers while you're in town! Now get going, girl. Go learn something about yourself, and maybe about your Mama, too. Bet there's a good story there."

The rain is falling hard now, so I hug Dolly tight and run to the car. I turn the engine over and switch on the wipers. Dolly stands in front of the station in the downpour, as if seeing me safely off on my journey.

As I propel the massive Lincoln down the road through the driving rain, I feel fullness in my heart that I haven't felt in ages. I shelved all expectations before coming to Mississippi in an attempt to prevent myself from being disappointed, and already I feel as though my trip has been worth something. I feel warmth and affection for Dolly and I know she's right. We will see each other again, and when we do, I hope to have something big to report.

CHAPTER NINE

The drive is grueling. The rain is falling so hard on the roof of the car that it drowns out the sound of the radio, and my hands grip the steering wheel so tightly they begin to ache. I eventually reach a flashing red light at a four-way stop and happen to notice a sign on a building that says *United States Post Office, Pritchard, Mississippi.* This is it?

There are small buildings running about a half a block in each direction at the stoplight, and I can see a hardware store, a consignment shop, a beauty parlor which actually says *Beauty Parlor* in the window, a small market, a used bookstore, and a tiny restaurant called Grits-n-Greens. I think I may have traveled back in time about fifty years.

This post office must be where Nina's checks to my grandfather come. Even though I highly doubt that anyone will hand out a home address just because I ask, I'm not exactly prepared to set up surveillance, so I dock the Lincoln in front of the post office and run through the raindrops to the door. I grab the handle and yank, but it's locked. A post office locked on a weekday afternoon?

I peer in through the plate glass at the small lobby, but see no one. The lights, however, seem to be on, and as I back away from the door I notice an index card taped just above the handle that reads *Having coffee at Melba's. Back at 4.* I grunt involuntarily, and wonder if the U.S. Government knows that postal workers in Pritchard, Mississippi take coffee breaks. Then I wonder how much mail actually goes in and out of this place. I imagine it's a pretty slow job.

My stomach growls and I realize I am starving. My Snickers bar was reduced to liquid in the wrapper earlier in the heat and although I did briefly consider drinking it, the rain sidelined a bad decision. I look across the intersection at Grits 'n Greens, which seems to be the only place other than the market to get food. I find this a little disconcerting since I'd be hard-pressed to eat a grit or a green unless I was a contestant on *Survivor* or something. Surely there are other things on the menu. If I sit down and eat, maybe I can come up with some plan to coax my grandparents' whereabouts out of the postal workers once they've returned from coffee at Melba's. Wherever that is.

I jump over puddles and run towards the restaurant, arriving in the doorway like a drowned rat. The few heads in the place turn, but rather than looking at me as though I am the idiot I feel like, they all smile and nod, and a tall, rotund woman comes toward me with outstretched arms.

"Looks like you could use a towel!" she says loudly, as I stand in a puddle of my own making, pulling my clinging shirt away from my skin. It actually would not surprise me if she pulled a towel out of thin air and started drying me off, but instead she ushers me over to a small table by the window overlooking the street. "You got a chill from the wet?" she asks. "Need some coffee?"

"No, thank you. It actually feels nice after the raging heat earlier."

"You aren't kidding," she says, wiping my table off with a small cloth, "but that's why the Good Lord sends the storms. Gives every animal and vegetable a little breathing room, and makes us complain a lot less about the heat." She smiles warmly at me and pats the table. "What can I get for you, darlin'?"

I order an iced tea and look around the room, astonished by how incredibly friendly people are around here. As two men finish their meal, they stop by three other tables on their way to the register. They seem to know the other patrons intimately, inquiring after family members and even asking about a fish another man had recently caught. Every single person receives either a handshake or friendly clap on the back, which to this human contact-phobe seems strange and wonderful at the same time.

The large woman returns with my tea, which I take a huge sip of, then gag and sputter. "Wow," I say. "This is so sweet!"

"Well, I could tell by your accent you're not from around here, but now I know for sure you're a Yankee!" she laughs. "Down here we say 'the sweeter, the better.' Now, whatcha hungry for?"

"Are you still serving lunch?"

"Honey, we serve whatever it is you want to eat."

"Okay, then," I say. It smells so good in here that I can't help but feel hungry. "Can I take a look at the menu?"

Laughter erupts from deep inside the enormous woman, and she has a hard time catching her breath, so she points over her shoulder to a chalkboard on the far wall. As I strain to read it, she regains her faculties and speaks again.

"This here's what you call a meat 'n three. We haven't got menus, but we've got meat, and we've got trimmings. Choose yourself one meat and three trimmings, plus you get cornbread."

I must look completely overwhelmed by the endless list on the chalkboard, because the woman says, "Take your time deciding, hon. I'm going to check on some pies I've got in the oven. When you're ready, just holler at me. I'm Melba."

"Oh!" I almost shout, as I make the connection. "I was just at the post office, but the sign on the door said they were at Melba's. That's here?"

"Oh, Lord!" Melba smiles. "Those two that just left a while ago? That's Roy and Willis. They come every day at three o'clock for coffee and pie. Have every day for twenty-something years, except of course on weekends and Federal holidays."

Melba heads back to the kitchen while a young blond girl clears off the now mostly vacant tables. I turn my attention back to the chalkboard to ponder my selection. I have no earthly idea what pole beans or butter beans are, am not a coleslaw fan, of which there are three types to choose from, cannot fathom what comprises sweet potato casserole—other than, of course, the obvious—and as previously mentioned would rather lick the road than eat a grit or a green. And come on, mustard, turnip, *and* collard greens? Seems like overkill to me.

As I ponder the remaining identifiable foods, I am startled by the young blond girl, who has suddenly crept up by my side with another glass of tea.

"Here you go," she says quietly, setting it on the table. "There was some in the back that didn't have sugar stirred in yet, so I made you a half-and-half."

The girl is so pretty, with long, silky hair, delicate hands, willowy arms and legs, and striking blue eyes that remind me of Dolly's. I feel like a moose next to her, suddenly very conscious of my size and mousy brown features.

"Thanks," I say, wanting to reach out and touch her shiny hair, to see if it is as soft as it looks. Even though people down here seem to know no boundaries when it comes to personal contact, it is nonetheless completely out of my nature, and besides, I am certain this girl would still think I was crazy. Instead, I occupy my hands by picking up my new tea glass and taking a drink.

"This is much better," I smile. She clears the other glass just in time for Melba to emerge from the kitchen.

"Okay, missy, what's it going to be?" Melba inquires jovially, approaching the table.

"How did you know my name is Missi?"

"Well, I didn't, but I s'pose now I do. I'll just stick a capital M on the front next time!" She places her hands on her wide hips and beams at me. "You know, I've got so much food cooked up back there in the kitchen. Why don't I just bring you a little bit of everything?"

I've smiled more today than I have in ages, so much that my cheeks are actually beginning to ache, but I can't help smiling back at Melba. "Sounds great," I say, but she has already turned back toward the kitchen before I can ask her to hold the grits.

Moments later, there is a veritable buffet of southern food laid out in front of me on my little table. Melba has brought fried chicken, for which I am grateful—it is familiar and looks and smells delicious—and several little dishes of side items, or trimmings, as she calls them.

I attempt to joke that she no longer runs a meat-n-three, but rather a meat-n-ten, but my humor is lost on her as she stands expectantly, waiting for me to start eating. I pick up a chicken thigh and bite hungrily into it. It is the most mouthwatering thing I have ever tasted. The chicken skin is lightly battered and crisp, not greasy in the least, and the meat is tender and moist.

Melba is standing over me, watching delightedly, and I realize I am making borderline orgasmic sounds without meaning to.

"Oh, Melba," I say, trying to maintain my composure. "This is *unbelievable*. Martha Stewart's got nothing on you."

"Except for a prison record, I reckon," Melba says, and bursts out laughing at her own joke. Her laugh is deep and smooth, and I can understand why Roy and Willis from the post office have come here so often for so many years. I imagine they aren't her only regulars, and make a mental note to ask before I leave if Melba knows my grandparents. Right now, however, I wipe my mouth with a paper napkin and reach for a fork. The macaroni and cheese is calling my name. I take a bite and moan again. It is creamy and smooth, with a buttery breadcrumb crust.

"This is truly the best food I've ever eaten," I tell her, and though I want to make her happy, I also mean it. Her broad smile widens even more, and she claps her hands joyfully as I plow through my lunch.

Melba stands and watches, wallowing in the compliments that fly from my mouth every time I take a bite. I think of Maggie and her legendary appetite and wish she were sitting in the empty chair across from me. She would love this place.

As the heaps of food before me dwindle, I notice Melba eyeing the only two bowls that remain untouched—the grits and the greens. I don't know whether they are of the mustard, turnip, or collard variety, but they are not going in my mouth. I am terrified of hurting this kind woman's feelings, but I just cannot bring myself to ingest either.

I take a long sip of iced tea and lean back in my chair. "Melba, that was amazing, but I can't take another bite or I'm afraid I will explode." This is actually true. I have never eaten so much in one sitting, and I'm generally not afraid to put it away when the mood strikes.

Melba hesitates for a second before she starts stacking and clearing plates and bowls. "Well, you'll just have to come back soon, then. I make greens every day, so you can save room next time! How long you in town for? Or are you just passing through?"

"Good question," I say thoughtfully. "I'm actually here to see family."

"That right?" she asks raising her eyebrows. "Now, I know everyone in this town, and don't you know this is the place to bring guests for a dinner out. Not many folks come this way for a visit, so I usually hear about visitors long before they arrive." She has every serving piece from my table stacked and balanced on her left forearm, and reaches across with her right to wipe the table clean with a rag.

"So, then. Who is it you're here to see?"

"My grandfather, Charles Jenner."

CRASH.

The dishes in Melba's arms fall to the floor in a cacophonous mess, and Melba begins to wipe her brow with the dishrag she just used to clean my table. She begins to sweat profusely, and I jump to my feet. I have seen this sort of thing on television.

"Help!" I yell out to the blond girl. "She's having a heart attack! Call 9-1-1!"

I grab onto a thick forearm and push Melba into a chair. I take the rag from her hands and dip it into a pitcher of ice water sitting nearby. I squeeze out the excess water and lay it across her forehead.

"Oh, dear Lord, help me," she moans.

I am completely in control and calm. "Melba, you are going to be just fine," I say confidently. "An ambulance is on the way." But even as I say this, I see the blond standing in the exact same place, just watching us and shaking her head.

"Why are you just *standing* there?"

The girl lets a smile creep across her unblemished face and says, "She'll be fine. Just give her a minute to collect herself."

I look down at Melba who is pale but clearly breathing. "Jesus, are you okay?"

"I'm fine," she drawls. "Not havin' a heart attack, hon. And don't take the Lord's name in vain."

"Well, what's the matter, then?"

"I'm just a bit shocked, is all," Melba says, staring at me as if I am a ghost.

"Shocked about what?" I ask, thinking I must have missed something huge. Then it dawns on me. I mentioned Charles Jenner's name and Melba almost passed out. This can't be good. Meekly, I gather the shred of courage necessary to ask, "You know my grandfather?"

CHAPTER TEN

I have never been more flabbergasted in my life than on that day in Thomas Anderson's law office . . . until now.

The haze of confusion that surrounds me now feels familiar, since I have felt it more times than I can count in the past few months. Melba is standing again, and now it is me who sits in the chair with the dishrag on my forehead. I cannot take all of this in.

"I'm sorry, Melba," I croak. "Can you say all that again? I don't understand any of it."

"Charles Jenner, crusty old bird that he is, is my father," Melba goes on. "Your mother is my sister. That makes you my niece. And Dory over there," she says nodding proudly to the beautiful blond, "is my daughter and your cousin." My head swims.

Dory has yet to come any closer, and appears to be as fazed by this revelation as I am. My stomach begins to churn, but it is not indigestion from the enormous lunch I just ate. It is more of a sinking feeling as I realize what I have to do right now.

"My mother is your sister," I mutter, without meaning to say it out loud.

"Mm hm," Melba says.

I hate that I have to be the one to tell her. She obviously has no idea that my mother is dead . . . that she no longer *has* a sister, even one she evidently never spoke to. The enormous lump in my throat leaves me unable to speak, but Melba is clearly waiting for me to respond in some way.

I clear my throat. "My mother *was* your sister," I begin, but am quickly interrupted.

"No, darlin', your sweet mama *is* my sister."

Sweet? Did she just say *sweet*? Not to think ill of the deceased or anything, but that is hardly a word I'd ever use to describe Nina. Smart? Absolutely. Well-groomed? Yes. *Sweet*? Not even close.

"Okay," I begin. "As much as I would love to have just stumbled upon my mother's family, I am beginning to wonder if we have had a complete misunderstanding of some sort. I am here looking for Charles Jenner, father of Nina Jennings, who may at one time have been Nina Jenner. Nina Jennings was my mother."

"Nina? Nina *Jennings?*" Melba booms at me, and begins pacing in front of my table. "Oh, Lord, I never would have figured this." She starts to pace and talk under her breath, but I am no longer paying attention. I am becoming more and more freaked out, and begin concocting a way to get out of here.

This all started out odd, but is quickly becoming something of a totally different nature. This has got to be a huge, bizarre misunderstanding, and I need to remove myself from it immediately. I push my chair back and stand up, grabbing my purse off the floor in one fluid movement. I pull some bills from my wallet, toss them on the table, and head for the door.

"This has been really lovely," I say, edging away from Melba. "Best food I've ever had, actually. But I have to go now. I'm terribly sorry to have bothered you." I turn my back to her and make it to the door, but as I press my hands to the glass, something makes me stop. There is complete silence behind me, and I squeeze my eyes shut, thinking that if I turn around there will be no one there. All of this will have been a dream, and I will open my eyes to see my old apartment, or my office, or maybe I will find myself sitting across from my mother at that table at the Palm. Right now I'd give anything for just that.

I turn around slowly and open my eyes. Melba has sunk into a chair and is crying. She pulls a Kleenex from her sleeve and dabs at her eyes. Dory is no longer rooted to her spot, and has approached her mother with a look of care and concern. Melba senses her presence and turns to her, wrapping her massive arms around Dory's tiny waist. It is a wordless exchange, but carries more meaning than volumes could ever convey. A mother and daughter supporting one another during a moment of emotion and confusion; Dory's touch acting as a salve to ease Melba's pain. And here I stand, watching and knowing that I feel the same pain, but that nobody is coming to put a bandage on my heart.

If there were ever an appropriate moment to cry, it would be now. I have clearly hurt Melba in a way that I do not quite understand, but just the same, I know she would not be so upset right

60

now if I hadn't walked into her restaurant today. My own emotions are so raw and close to the surface, but all I can truly feel is that nagging lump in my throat.

Maybe crying is like so many other skills in life—if you do not practice it regularly, you will eventually forget how to do it altogether. Maybe that lump in my throat is full of unused tears, and each time I suppress the need to cry the lump gets bigger, and more full, and I am beginning to wonder if at some point I will no longer be able to swallow it. The lump will grow and grow until I can't breathe around it anymore. This is self-defense, I tell myself. Nina always told me that crying never changes anything and only allows people to see where your weaknesses lie. Now is not the time to be weak.

I clear my throat loudly, pushing that lump out of the way, and Melba and Dory turn towards me.

"Oh, I thought you'd gone," Melba says, her voice sounding nasal and scratchy.

I am not sure what to say, so I shake my head.

Melba lets go of Dory and pats the table in front of her gently. I know it is a silent request for me to return to her, so I do. I sit back down at the table where not long ago I was happily eating lunch, unaware that my life would momentarily be sent into a tailspin. Again.

Melba shifts her large body uncomfortably in her chair so that her knees are almost touching mine. She reaches out, as if to pat my leg, but changes her mind and folds her hands in her lap, for which I am grateful. She takes a deep breath.

"Sit tight, sweet pea. I'm going to turn this place over to Artie in the kitchen. We've got bigger fish to fry, and there's someone I think you need to meet."

It is still raining when I leave the restaurant with Melba and Dory. I have yet to go to the Post Office, but as fate would have it, it's no longer necessary. Melba has all the information I could possibly need, and mobilizes the troops to go to "the farm" to see Charles Jenner.

I ask if it might be better to wait until morning, when everyone is fresh and less emotional, but Melba sees right through me. She suggests that Dory ride with me in my car, in case I get lost. We walk unhurriedly through the raindrops, which are thankfully falling with far less conviction than they were earlier.

Dory puts a hand on my arm and says, "Missi, you're nice."

It is a kind and well-intended compliment, but my head starts to spin, because in Dory's twangy southern accent it comes out sounding like "Missi, you're an ass," which were the last words Nina spoke to me before stepping into the path of an oncoming bus. I haven't thought of it since the instant the words came out of her mouth, but suddenly I feel the full onus of having spent my last moments with Nina despising her. Perhaps I am not cut out for the whole family thing. Maybe I should cut my losses before disappointing anyone else.

As we near the rental car, however, Dory gasps, bringing me back to the present. "Is this your car?" she asks in astonishment. She drags the word *car* out so that it has three syllables.

"Well, no . . . I mean, I rented it at the airport in Jackson, but it doesn't *belong* to me." I look at Dory, who is climbing into the passenger side with wide eyes. She is so small and cute I can totally picture her behind the wheel of a little red sports car. She must think this car is ridiculous.

"This is *amazing,*" she whispers once I have slid into the car beside her. "I've never been in a limousine before! Sometimes at night I watch reruns of *Sex and the City*—please don't tell my Mama, she'd have a fit—and Mr. Big gets carted all around town in a car like this!"

I am shocked at how naïve Dory is, but can't bear to ruin the fun for her. "Well, climb into the back seat, then, and I'll be your driver. Just don't let me get lost."

Dory squeals and crawls between the seats into the back. I hear her seatbelt click as I back out into the road. "Turn left here, Hoke Colburn," Dory says, and giggles. She's obviously seen *Driving Miss Daisy*, too.

Ten minutes later I am commanded to turn onto an unmarked dirt road, and find myself increasingly annoyed by Dory. She is taking this chauffer thing a little too seriously, and while I judge her to be around fifteen years old, she is acting more like six. She may be pretty, but she's a bit of a pest.

Melba has pulled in just ahead of us driving an old gray minivan with the words 'Grits 'n Greens—We cater' emblazoned on the side. I follow her up the long drive until we reach an old, white house with a sprawling porch. There is an old pickup truck parked out in the rain, even though there is a carport attached to the house. Under the carport protected from the elements, however, sits an ancient tractor.

It occurs to me that Dory is finally quiet, so I turn around in my seat and say, "I guess this is it."

Dory is no longer having fun. She sighs and says "I hate it here."

This does nothing for my confidence, so I turn off the ignition but make no move to get out. "Is it that bad?" I inquire, not really wanting to know the answer.

"*He* is," she says softly.

I don't realize that I am holding my breath until Melba raps on my window, startling me. "You coming? Or are you just going to marinate out here in the rain?"

I swallow hard and resume breathing so that I can heave myself out of the Lincoln. My legs feel heavy, and the day's events have left me completely drained—could it possibly have been just this very morning that I left Nina's house in Virginia an orphan? And stand now in front of a strange house in Mississippi with my Aunt Melba and cousin Dory? About to walk in yet another door that I know will change my life? It is all too much, but Melba has already taken shelter under the carport with the tractor, and is beginning to look impatient. It appears that Dory plans to stay in the car.

I follow Melba to the back door leading from the carport to the main house. She tries the knob, but the door is locked, so she rattles her key ring until she finds what she is looking for and slides a key into the slot.

"You have a key?" I ask, incredulous.

"Of course," Melba says. "This is the house where I grew up. Why wouldn't I have a key?" She turns the key and twists the knob, but the door still won't open.

"I've just never had a key to anyone's house before . . . except my own," I explain.

"You didn't have a key to Nina's house?" Melba inquires curiously, standing on her tiptoes and peering through the glass.

"Not since I lived with her as a child. When I moved out and went to college, I gave her the key back. Nina and I weren't that close, and usually only saw each other for lunch or dinner. At a restaurant." Even as I say it I realize how sad it sounds, so without thinking I add, "I have a key now." *That* sounds even sadder, so I stupidly say, "But that's nice that you have a key to . . . your . . . Dad's house."

"A fat lot of good the key's doin' me," Melba remarks sourly. "He's dead bolted the door again."

"Again?"

"Again," she echoes with a sigh. "Wait here." She walks through the rain out to my rental car and smacks the back window with the palm of her hand. Dory quickly opens the door and scrambles out.

"Ma'am?"

"Baby, go around the side of the house and tap on Sandra's window," Melba says gently, taking off her huge raincoat and draping it over Dory's tiny body to keep her dry.

"He lock you out again?" Dory asks, smiling at her mother.

Melba is visibly amused as she watches Dory disappear around the corner of the house. I am still thinking about the way that Melba gave Dory her raincoat to protect her from the rain. She literally gave her the shirt off her back. That's a mother's way, I suppose. Well, most mothers. Just not mine.

Melba seems to sense my discomfort, because she sets her large hand on my shoulder—she is nearly as tall as I am—and says, "Don't you worry yourself none. We're going to straighten all this out just as soon as the old crow lets us in the house."

I try to smile, but can only muster a grimace, so I look away from her and out into the darkening yard. There is an enormous oak tree several yards away, and I see the silhouette of a swing dangling crookedly from a low branch. I envision an old couple sitting together on the swing, swaying slowly in the warm breeze on a sunny day. Is it my grandparents I am thinking of? I'd give anything to know them. *Them.*

"What about my grandmother?" I ask Melba abruptly. "Your mother. Is that who Sandra is?"

"Oh, Baby Girl. My mother's been gone a long time. That's half his problem." She is about to say more, but a light inside the house comes on and there is some rattling on the other side of the door. A moment later, Dory lets us into a large kitchen. There is a massive stone fireplace at one end of the room, a long table with four chairs along each side, three rocking chairs along the wall by the door, and an unsightly old pink couch on the wall opposite, where two mangy dogs sleep, completely undisturbed by our presence.

"How did you get in here?" I ask.

"Sandra," she says.

"You see him?" Melba asks Dory in a hushed voice.

"No, ma'am, but I didn't look, neither. This is weird." Dory shivers.

I can't help but agree, although I am not sure why Dory thinks so. I mean, this is *her* grandfather's home and she is with *her* mother. What's so weird, then, other than the fact that her cousin, whom she's never met until today, is standing here feeling like a complete interloper?

As steamy as it was earlier in the day, we are all damp and chilly now, so Melba sets about making a pot of coffee at the other end of the kitchen. I am still standing near the door, half wondering what exactly is going on, and half ready to sprint out the door if necessary. And where is my grandfather, anyway?

Ever the mind reader, Melba turns to me. "Sit down, Baby Girl. He'll come."

I choose one of the rocking chairs close to the door, not ready to commit to being fully in the room, and definitely not wanting to get any closer to the dogs. Whoever said '*Let sleeping dogs lie*' was right on. I can smell them from here. And I thought my old couch was bad.

The aroma of coffee fills the room, and I feel myself relax a little. "That's much better," I say to myself.

"Hm?" Melba asks over her shoulder.

"Oh, nothing. Fresh-brewed coffee is my all-time favorite smell," I explain, inhaling deeply.

Melba turns and smiles broadly at me. "Well, then. You most certainly have the Jenner nose."

"How's that?" I ask, reaching up to touch my nose self-consciously, but before Melba can elaborate, a horrible noise comes from the hallway beyond the kitchen. It is clearly not a human sound, so I lurch out of the rocking chair toward the door, knowing I was smart to stay close.

The noise is quickly followed by a flash of black fur that comes into the kitchen and straight under the pink couch. The dogs, completely unfazed by our arrival a few minutes ago, are now not only awake, but barking up a storm and trying like crazy to get after whatever has just disrupted their slumber and dared to take refuge under their chosen resting spot.

I am at the door with one hand on the knob, so thrown by the commotion at the couch that it takes me a minute to realize there is a man standing in the doorway leading from the hall into the kitchen. Looking right at me.

Although logically I know who this must be—clearly this is not the Sandra I have been hearing about—I have absolutely no idea how to act or what to say. So as usual, I do nothing. I stand with my hand on the doorknob and I stare back.

He takes his eyes off me long enough to slap each dog on the rump and yell, "*Git*," which sends them running from the room. "Stepped on Missi's damn tail coming down the hall."

I am confused. "Missi?"

"The cat," he says, as if that clears up anything other than what the thing under the couch is.

I grip the doorknob even tighter. "You have a cat named Missi?"

"We've had a cat named Missi for thirty-something years," he says gruffly, no longer looking at me, but at the floor in front of him.

I am blown away. "That cat is thirty years old? I didn't know cats could live that long."

He looks back at me like I am an idiot. "Not one cat. Lots of 'em. One dies or runs off and we get another. She names every one Missi."

Now I *feel* like an idiot. "Who does?"

"Sandra."

Melba ambles heavily across the kitchen and gently pries my hand away from the knob. "I think it's finally time you came all the way in and sat down. We've got some family business to tend to."

She leads me over to the table where I reluctantly sit down. The man—my grandfather—is still standing in the doorway. He is tall and strong looking, with broad shoulders and enormous hands, which he clasps and unclasps as though unsure of what to do with them. He eventually shoves them deep into the pockets of the coveralls he is wearing.

A cup of steaming, fragrant coffee is set on the table in front of me, and I wrap my hands around the mug in a feeble attempt to get them to stop shaking. Melba slides a sugar bowl and carton of half and half toward me, and turns to her father. "You just going to stand there?"

He shrugs and looks over his shoulder back down the hallway. I can hear music in the distance that sounds like the theme song from *Happy Days*. "I expect you want me to go get her," he says to Melba, but doesn't move from the spot.

"Dory can get her," Melba tells him quickly. "You come over here and meet your granddaughter."

Dory, who has been perched quietly on a countertop in the far corner of the kitchen, climbs down and slips past my grandfather, happy for a reason to leave the room.

Not wanting to seem too interested, I busy myself by spooning sugar into my coffee. I try not to look up, but I sense that he has moved closer. I pour cream into my cup and stir some more. Why on earth I find the need to put off this moment is beyond me, but I do. I continue to intently stir and stare at my coffee until the vortex made by my spoon becomes a blur.

"You're gonna turn that cream into butter, you keep stirrin' it like that." His voice is deep and loud, and extremely intimidating.

I set the spoon down on the table and look up to meet his eyes. I feel like I am looking into my own. His eyes are the same mottled brown as mine, set deeply and framed by long, thick eyelashes. He has the most beautiful white hair I have ever seen, and his skin is tanned and leathery, I imagine from hours spent on that tractor sitting under the carport.

I don't have a clue what to say to this man, a stranger, so I do the only thing I can think of. I introduce myself. I stand and extend my arm. "Hi. I'm Missi Jennings," I declare.

He stares for a moment at my hand and I am about to pull it away, feeling stupid, but thankfully he reaches out and surprises me by taking my hand in both of his. He doesn't shake it, though, just sort of stares at it. It makes me uncomfortable.

He looks me directly in the eyes. I am flooded by emotions ranging from fear to relief, and somewhere in there is also the pure joy of meeting my long-lost grandfather. The lump in my throat is huge, and prevents me from saying anything else. I think that this may be it—I am going to cry, unabashedly, for the first time in my life. I can actually feel the tears making their way up the ducts and heading for open air. My grandfather opens his mouth to speak, and I wait for the words I've waited my entire life to hear.

"They grow 'em big up North, don't they, Melba?" He drops my hand and turns to his daughter to accept the mug of coffee she is holding out to him.

I am not going to cry after all. As abruptly as the tears had formed, they have now evaporated. *They grow 'em big up north'?* Welcome to the family, Missi Jennings.

Melba is refusing to give him the coffee, and they have engaged in a sort of tug-of-war over the cup. My grandfather pulls one way, and Melba pulls back the other, steaming brown liquid sloshing over the side and onto the floor. She is talking under her breath, demanding that he behave himself and act a little more hospitably. He appears to not give a shit.

"Give me the coffee, woman," he says sharply.

"Use you manners, Daddy, or I'll pour it in your lap," Melba snaps back. She lets go of the cup, bends down to wipe the coffee off the floor, and walks around to my side of the table.

I have returned to my seat, hiding my excessively large, northern body under the giant table. I am increasingly self-conscious and cannot look him in the eye again, so I trace the grain of the wood table with my finger and wait for something else to happen.

Melba sits down in the chair next to mine and nudges me with her elbow. "He's so old and decrepit he's got no idea what he's talkin' about. I'm twice your size, and I've never been further north than Nashville."

I can't help but laugh a little, and am grateful that Melba is there. I don't know what I was thinking when I came all by myself to Mississippi to find my grandfather. I know for certain that if I were alone with him right now, I'd run for the door, navigate the pimpmobile back to Jackson, get on a plane headed for D.C., and forget I'd ever been here. Melba radiates strength and courage, though, and I can tell she's not going to be pushed around by a grumpy old man.

I take a long sip of coffee, which is almost as good as Melba's fried chicken, and steal a glance at my grandfather. He looks incredibly uncomfortable, rather than thrilled, to have me at his table. His brow is furrowed deeply, and I wonder what he would look like if he smiled. I bet that doesn't happen very often.

I hear Dory's voice coming from the hall and suddenly remember that she had gone to get Sandra. The thought enters my mind that this Sandra could be my grandfather's wife—I mean, if my grandmother is dead, then perhaps he remarried. Maybe I have a step-grandmother. I am intrigued to meet this woman who has agreed to spend the rest of her life with *him*. She must have the patience of a saint.

Dory enters the kitchen smiling, something she hasn't done since we arrived at this house. Following closely behind is a short, stocky woman with mousy brown hair and thick glasses. She, too, is smiling, and I immediately recognize the countenance of someone with Down syndrome. This has got to be Sandra.

She seems surprised and happy to have company in the house, and goes straight to Melba to administer a long, tight hug. Melba rubs the back of Sandra's hair and gives her a kiss on the cheek. Sandra then makes her way to the other side of the table and stands behind my grandfather, setting one pale, pudgy hand on his shoulder. He reaches up, pats her hand, then turns and smiles up at her. This is the first I've seen him smile.

Melba speaks first. "Sandra, this is Missi," she says loudly, motioning to me. "She's come for coffee."

Sandra's smile widens. "I have a cat named Missi."

"I know," I tell her. "She's under the couch."

Sandra walks to the couch and clumsily lowers herself to the floor. She lifts the pink skirt of the couch off the floor and peers underneath it. The next thing I know, the cat is in her arms and she is bringing it to me. She leans forward, as if she wants me to pet it, so I do. Sandra is so close to me that I take in her oddly lemony scent, and child-like face, full of love for this cat. Her smile is so broad and sincere that I can't help but smile too.

I glance over Sandra's shoulder at my grandfather, and as soon as we make eye contact, his smile disappears. I remind myself that we are still strangers, and that perhaps in time he will find me worth smiling at. Then again, I could be completely wrong. Without saying anything else, Sandra, still smiling, carries the cat out of the kitchen and back down the hallway.

"She's sweet," I say, more to my grandfather than anyone else.

"I told you," comes Melba's voice, scratchy and raw. I turn to look at her and her eyes are full of tears.

"Told me what?"

"That your mother's sweet," Melba answers.

"Goddammit, Melba," my grandfather booms, "don't you go causing any problems!" He pushes back from the table causing cups to rattle and spill over, and angrily leaves the room.

I am speechless and very confused. What, exactly, just happened? I turn back toward Melba, who is wiping her eyes that now sparkle with anticipation. Dory stands behind her, eyebrows raised and biting on her thumbnail.

"Missi, whatever Nina may have told you," Melba says cautiously, "she was not your mother . . . not God-given, anyway. Sandra carried you. She gave birth to you. *She* is your mother."

And so it begins, the unraveling of my life, in unabridged form.

CHAPTER ELEVEN

I am on the brink of an identity crisis of massive proportions. My head feels as though it is going to spin completely off my neck as I attempt to process what I am being told. Apparently, Nina Jennings started out as Nina Jenner and was not my real mother. This, actually, explains a lot. A fact far more difficult to grasp is how I came to be.

My grandmother died while giving birth to Sandra, and it wasn't until a few days later that they realized Sandra was affected with Down syndrome. Many people urged my grandfather to have her institutionalized, but he refused, saying that Sandra was all he had left of my grandmother. He kept her, took care of her, and when she reached school age, my grandfather sent her each day to a special school with other mentally disabled kids.

"She loved it there," Melba remembers, "until one day when she just flat out refused to get up and go. It wasn't like her, and it scared me a little. I was only seventeen at the time, but I was as much a mother to Sandra as I was a sister, and I knew something wasn't right."

"At any rate, we didn't force the issue, and she never went back." My aunt continues, "Daddy didn't question it, and was just happy to have Sandra around more. She helped out on the farm some, sold eggs from the front porch and could pick up more pecans in an afternoon than anyone I knew. Not long after, though, we noticed . . . things. Decided to take her to see a doctor, and found out she was expecting."

She was expecting *me*. I sit here and listen, engrossed in Melba's story, but somehow cannot wrap my brain around the fact that she is talking about me. The way *my* life began. I clear my throat and nod my head, for lack of anything to say. This is definitely the closest I have ever come to actually crying, but the tears seem to be stuck. Maybe my tear ducts are blocked, or maybe I am afraid that if I start crying now, I'll never stop. The ever-present lump in my throat is now the size of a boulder, and I am taking short, shallow breaths, which is making me slightly light-headed.

"Daddy was fit to be tied, as you might imagine," Melba plows on, and I can tell how painful it is for her to relive these events, because she is involuntarily shredding her paper napkin as she speaks. "He took that school by storm trying to find out who was responsible for victimizing a child, and one like Sandra, no less. There was a new recreation director at the school who had been giving Sandra and a few other kids special treatment—letting them eat lunch in his office, help set up for school programs—and we just thought it was because Sandra was such a good kid. She was so helpful, friendly and responsible . . ." Melba breaks off and starts to cry. She attempts to wipe her eyes with her napkin, but it falls like confetti to the table. I hand her my napkin, which she takes with an appreciative smile, unfazed by the fact that I have used it to wipe my own eyes and nose.

"She just loved to make people happy," Melba weeps.

"How old was she?" I ask, my mind struggling to keep up with the information I have been given in the past several minutes. If my grandmother died while giving birth to Sandra, then that makes her younger than Melba. And Melba said she was seventeen when Sandra started acting strange about school. I decide quickly that I do not want the answer to my own question, but it's too late.

Melba looks right at me. "Thirteen," she says, her voice almost a whisper.

I gasp and hold my breath. "I can't believe anyone could have taken advantage of her like that," I finally say, disgusted by the concept that I share genes with someone capable of such an abominable act.

"He sure enough did," Melba says sadly. "If something like that happened today, he'd be in prison. But rural Mississippi in the 1970's was not prepared to face something like that."

I sit up in my chair a little straighter, countless hours in a law library getting the better of me. "You mean he got away with it?" I almost shout, livid.

"Not entirely," she replies, with the trace of a smile on her lips. "Daddy blew up his truck and ran him out of town."

"Probably would've cut his wiener off if he'd had the chance," comes Dory's voice. I had completely forgotten she was even in the room.

"Dory!" Melba gasps. "That's no way for a lady to talk . . . though you're not altogether wrong, I suppose."

Dory is drawn out of her corner and comes to sit at the table. She takes the next question right out of my mouth. "So how did Missi end up with Nina?"

"Well, the doctor who examined Sandra recommended that Sandra get rid of the baby."

"You mean put her up for adoption?" Dory asks.

"No, angel," Melba patiently answers. "The doctor was suggesting that Sandra's pregnancy be terminated. That she have an abortion."

Dory gasps, clutching her hands to her chest. "Mama, no!" she says disbelievingly. "Reverend Dobbins would freak out!"

"Now, Dory," her mother reassures, "the doctor was more concerned about Sandra's health and the possibility that the baby would have Down syndrome like Sandra."

I am dumbfounded. Not that I have ever spent any time reflecting on the subject, but it has never occurred to me that people with Down Syndrome could *have* kids, let alone "normal" ones, if that word even applies to me.

Dory seems appeased for the moment, and Melba turns her attention back to me.

"Your granddaddy and I wouldn't hear of putting Sandra through an abortion, but Nina, my older sister by three years, thought we were certifiable. She was away at college when all of this happened, and as far as she was concerned, smarter than all of us small-town hicks put together. Brilliant Nina had her scholarship to that fancy school up there, and said she was going to go live down the street from the President. Hah," Melba laughs. "Fat lot of good that did anyone down here. Nina got sucked in by all that Washington nonsense and never did see fit to come home and help out any. Until you came along, that is."

I have to ask. "What happened then?"

"You were born, perfect as a peach if not a little small . . ."

"Me? Small? Not possible," I interrupt.

Melba closes her eyes and smiles, reliving my first moments. "Oh, yes, Missi. You were the tee-tiniest thing I'd ever laid an eye on. Four and a half pounds, but just perfect otherwise. Had to stay at the hospital a couple of weeks for observation, but we planned to bring you home and all pitch in to take care of you." She tightly wraps a chubby hand around her empty coffee cup and continues. "Daddy even told me I could quit high school and stay home to take care of you and Sandra, which tickled me to death. Even at seventeen I was dying to be a mother, to you and to Sandra. But Nina came back and saw it quite another way."

"What way was that?" Dory questions.

Melba sighs and rubs her eyes with her thick fingers. "She didn't think we had any business raising a baby that way. Said we were creating 'yet another uneducated country bumpkin' that would send us further into financial ruin. See, we'd been in a terrible drought for a couple of years at that time, and the farm had all but collapsed. The fields dried up, we couldn't keep the cows fed, and absolutely nothing was growing. Only things going were the pecans and the chickens, and Daddy was having trouble scraping by. He got desperate and even built a still out in the barn. Started selling hooch to some of the old boys, but all that did was give high and mighty Nina more to go on.

She insisted that you would be better off with her, not in a situation where the most responsible party was only seventeen, the others being 'a drunk and a retard'."

"She said that?" I ask, horrified.

Dory is clearly agitated. "So you just let her take the baby? Sandra's baby?"

"She wasn't completely wrong." Melba puts a hand on the table close to mine. "Missi, you have to know that we loved you from the minute you came into this world. But Daddy and I were afraid of doing wrong by you. Nina said she could give you a life full of knowledge and experiences that you would never get here in Pritchard, and she clearly did that. We had no idea that all this time she never told you the truth about your mother, and to be honest, I'm surprised. Nina was always kind of a martyr. She needed people to know everything she was doing to *help* them."

"But when Nina died I went through some things and found my birth certificate," I tell them, remembering the perfect, untouched piece of paper I'd found. "It says I was born there, in Washington. And it certainly doesn't say I weighed four pounds."

"Who knows?" Melba says, shaking her head. "Maybe she had a new birth certificate forged by some big shot friend up there. All I can attest to is that you were born here in Mississippi, in the very same hospital that every single one of your cousins was born in."

I can totally envision Nina swooping in like a hawk and taking me back to Washington in her talons. What I cannot imagine is her keeping this tremendous secret from me for my entire life. For crying out loud, I am an adult, and at some point I deserved to know. I try to think if there was ever a time that she even *attempted* to tell me, but all of our "family" occasions were so forced and formal, and certainly the dining room at the Four Seasons isn't the place to drop a bomb like that. I wonder—if she hadn't been killed, would she ever have found it in her heart to tell me the truth?

I flash back to our last argument, moments before she died. She was so angry with me, and said something suggesting that I had no idea what she had been through for me. Was that it? Had I finally pushed her far enough that she was willing to let it slip? I will never know the answer to that, because I cut her off and drove her into the path of a bus.

I feel faint, and realize that I am almost hyperventilating. Melba waddles to the sink and returns with a glass of water. I take a sip and will myself to calm down. My head feels like it weighs a thousand pounds as the information settles on me like a thick fog.

"I still don't get it, though. Why didn't you keep track of me? You could have come visit, or sent cards on my birthday. Something." My voice breaks and I realize how tired and unconvincing I sound. Melba understandingly tries to put out the fires of frustration that are building in me.

"Nina did send us pictures for a while. They came every few months, and we could see that you were healthy, always dressed like a princess, and that made us happy. Before long, though, the pictures stopped coming and I got married and pregnant myself. We were poor and life got in the way, but we always assumed that your life with Nina was far better than it would have been here. She more or less told us we were too stupid to raise a child, and I guess we were stupid enough to believe her. We had no idea what she did or didn't tell you about Sandra, but we certainly didn't know you'd grow up without an inkling of the truth. Sandra had no recollection of having a baby, and her instinct to nurture was exhausted on all the cats she took in. It is no coincidence that she names all her cats Missi, you know. We let her name you."

She pauses for a while, and I can hear for the first time the ticking of a clock on the mantle of the fireplace. The television down the hall must have been turned off, and the old house is still.

Melba takes a deep breath and breaks the silence. "We had no idea about Nina's passing until well after the fact. Though I can't say what we'd have done if we had known. I know that's hardly an excuse, but it's all I can offer. I'm sorry we weren't there to support you."

I stand and walk to the fireplace, needing some distance. I know in my heart that I should not be angry with Melba—she was practically a child herself when I was born—but I can't help feeling that my family gave up on me a long time ago. They let themselves forget that I was far away with Nina, assuming I was happy and thriving. Boy, were they wrong.

I look back at my aunt and my cousin sitting at the table. Melba looks back at me pleadingly, while Dory stares at the floor and chews on her fingernails. My anger begins to dissipate, but there is a burning feeling in my chest that I know isn't going away anytime soon.

"It's getting late," I say quietly, "and I should get to a hotel. But if you think it's okay, I'd like to say goodbye to Sandra."

"I think Sandra would like that," Melba smiles. "As for the hotel, however, you may have some trouble. You'd have to go almost all the way back to Jackson to find one. Now, if you want a *motel*, all you'd have to do is drive ten or fifteen miles back toward the highway. Personally, I would recommend the Little Inn, which is just a couple of miles from here in the next town over. I just so happen to know there is a vacancy." Dory snickers and nods.

"A little inn sounds nice," I respond gratefully. "Can you help me find it?"

"Sure can, Baby Girl," Melba answers.

I am led down the hallway toward the back of the house. My senses are heightened, and my nerves and emotions are being pushed to their limits. There are two doors on either side of the hall, one on each side open to dark rooms, and one on each side closed with light seeping underneath the door onto the hardwood floor. It smells like cleaning supplies, not that I've had much experience around those. I point a finger each direction and whisper, "Which one?"

"The one on the left," Melba says loudly. I guess there's no need to whisper—it's not like we're sneaking up on anyone, except that it feels like we are.

We decided there's no point in telling Sandra that I am her daughter. It wouldn't correlate in her mind, and might end up upsetting her. I feel as though I've rocked the boat enough already.

Melba taps on the door, waits a few seconds, and turns the knob. We enter the room and I immediately notice how neat it is. A few books line up perfectly on low shelves, and framed photos stand like soldiers in formation on the tops of the bookshelves. A small bed in the corner is simply but flawlessly made up, and a rocking chair occupies the opposite corner. In the chair sits Sandra, still holding the cat.

Sandra looks up at us, smiling broadly. "Come see," she invites.

Melba goes over to stroke the cat, and I stand in the center of the modest but cozy room. I turn slowly, taking it all in—everything in neat rows, pillows centered on the bed, and a bottle of glass cleaner on the bedside table. It is immaculate . . . that is, until Dory flops down on the bed disturbing the previously un-rumpled quilt. I look to Sandra to see if she seems bothered by this, but she is completely engaged with Melba and the cat.

Generally not a fan of cats, I join them anyway, reaching out to scratch the animal behind its ears. Sandra looks at me through her thick lenses and grins.

"She likes that," she tells me. The cat begins to purr contentedly, and Sandra hands it up to me. "You can hold Missi. She likes you."

I take the cat from Sandra and cradle her awkwardly in my arms. It immediately begins to squirm, so I try scratching her ears again. It works, and Missi settles in nicely to the crook of my elbow.

"I like her name," I say, making eye contact with my mother. I would have said earlier that I look nothing like her, but now I can see some similarities; our hair and eye color are the same, and her wide forehead mirrors mine. There is something about her, though, that I know does not exist in me. This woman . . . this victim of rape whose child was ripped away from her, this mentally challenged individual, has a contentment within her that radiates outward. Her smile is real. It is sincere. And I know it comes from having lived a life full of love and support from those around her. What I would give for that.

"I like your name, too," Sandra says thickly. "Do you live here?"

No, I live in Washington . . . uh, D.C.? Where the President lives?"

"That's far away."

"Pretty far. I flew here on a plane. It took about two hours."

"Wow. Air Force One." she says, impressed.

It takes a second for me to understand what she means, but I do and laugh. "Actually, I flew on Delta Airlines. But you obviously know a lot about the President."

"I know a lot about a lot," Sandra informs me proudly as she slowly ascends from the rocking chair. "You sit," she offers.

I do, and look up to see Melba, beaming. She wraps a gigantic arm around Sandra, and Sandra folds herself into the warm embrace. I watch this beautiful, wordless exchange of love between sisters, and think of the myriad things Nina chose to miss out on by running away from her family with me.

Sandra breaks away suddenly when she sees Dory sprawled on her bed. "You're making wrinkles," she tells Dory, but seems more amused than bothered.

Dory climbs off the bed, and Sandra immediately runs her hands over the top of the quilt to smooth it and center the pillows. She then picks up the glass cleaner, heads for the bookshelf, and begins spritzing the photo frames and wiping them dry. Melba and I watch quietly as she looks for a moment at each one before setting them back in exactly the same place.

The pictures are clearly special to Sandra, and I see among them photos of Sandra, of Melba and Dory and what must be the rest of their family, of some smiling little boys, and then others that look older. Perhaps one is of my grandmother, who Sandra never knew. There is no photograph of anyone even closely resembling Nina, and I sadly note that there is no picture of an infant that might have been me. I know that Sandra most likely does not remember having given birth to a child, and that my relationship to her is not something that has ever been discussed in her presence. I still can't help feeling a pang of disappointment anyway. There isn't a home on this planet that has a framed photo of me sitting out on a shelf or table. The thought makes me deeply sad.

Dory sees me assessing the photos and picks up a frame to show me. "This is the rest of my family," she says, handing me the frame. "Your cousins," she adds in a whisper.

I look at the photograph, where Melba and a man, presumably her husband, sit on a wooden porch swing, flanked by Dory who looks to be about six or seven, and six boys ranging in age from maybe twelve to twenty-something.

"You have *six* brothers?" I ask loudly, unable to suppress my surprise. Sandra comes back over to see what we are talking about, and gently takes the frame from my hand. She mutters something softly that I cannot understand, wipes the glass again, and sets it back in its place.

"I'm sorry, Sandra," I say, making a mental note not to disturb her things again. Dory, it seems, does not exercise boundaries where her aunt is concerned.

Melba lays one hand heavily on my shoulder and with the other picks the frame up again. "No need to apologize, Missi. She was just telling you their names—Little Dewayne, Lamar, Clayton, Jerome, Stanley, and Neil Ray. The handsome fella in the middle is your

Uncle, Big Dewayne." She carefully places the frame exactly where Sandra had put it.

"You've got a whole mess of people to acquaint with," Melba says cheerfully, "and boy, will they be surprised to meet you!"

I think about my best friend when I was in elementary school, Melanie, who literally had dozens of cousins. Her family got together every year for a big reunion in the Poconos, and practically had to rent an entire hotel to accommodate them all. She always came home with rolls and rolls of Instamatic film to develop, and waited with bated breath the week or so it would take for them to come back. Then she would pore over the photos, reliving the week in the Poconos and all the familial hilarity. Every year I listened intently, drawn in by the antics of such a large family, simultaneously green with envy considering my own total lack of relatives.

Melba nudges Dory and excuses them both to go clean up the kitchen. I am left alone with Sandra—my mother who will never understand that fact. I, however, understand perfectly. Sandra is perched on the edge of her bed, and I cautiously sit beside her. I notice that the bed's headboard is intricately carved and looks quite old.

"Is this an antique?" I inquire, running my hand across the beautifully crafted wood.

"No, it's a bed," Sandra answers. "It was my mother's when she was a girl."

I smile because of the way in which she answered my question, but also at the thought of sitting on a piece of furniture that both my mother and grandmother had slept on. I feel, for the very first time in my life, a connection to my roots

"You're lucky," I say absently

"No I'm not. My mother died," Sandra says without emotion.

I turn to face her, unsure of what to say. "So did mine," is what I come up with, and not entirely untrue.

Sandra sighs knowingly and wraps her soft, pudgy hands around one of mine. "That's okay, Missi. We have each other."

I sigh too, not having any idea that this release of air would unleash a flood of emotions that have been bottled up for a lifetime. Suddenly my vision blurs and Sandra becomes an indistinct flesh-colored blob. My cheeks sting, and I wipe at my eyes, not expecting to find moisture there. But I do. My God, I am *crying*.

I try to compose myself, thinking that I should be embarrassed by this public display of tears to which no single person has ever been privy, but it feels so good, I decide to let it ride. I cry silently, the tears rolling generously down my face, but I smile also. Sandra hugs me so tightly it takes my breath away, but instead of feeling suffocating, it feels like home.

I feel like a lost sheep that has been brought back into the fold, and while I have been deprived of so much for thirty-three years, I have it all within my grasp now. This wonderful, compassionate person next to me is my mother, and the strong, caring woman washing coffee cups in the kitchen is my aunt. I have seven cousins. Seven! And I have a grandfather who loves his Sandra more than life itself, so he can't possibly be all that bad.

Over Sandra's shoulder I see a figure appear in the doorway, and I wipe my eyes expecting to see Melba. Instead, it is my grandfather, and he is glowering at me. Maybe I am giving him too much credit. Maybe this little sheep still has a long way to go.

My eyes stop leaking as I break the embrace with Sandra. My grandfather has left the doorway, so I assume it is safe to leave the room. I tell Sandra good night and that I will see her very soon. She smiles that warm, wide smile, adjusts her glasses, and returns to the rocking chair where Missi the cat sits patiently waiting for her.

I head back toward the kitchen, skirting quietly past my grandfather's room in an attempt not to make any noise that might alert him to my presence. Light spills from the kitchen into the dim hallway, and I can hear Melba talking. I am excited to tell Melba and Dory about how I've bonded with Sandra, but before I round the corner into the room, Melba's voice grows louder and angrier. I stop short and hold my breath.

"You can't control everyone's life forever," she reasons. "Sandra and Missi both deserve this! They have been robbed of each other until today, and you have no right . . ."

"The *hell* I don't have the right!" my grandfather responds bitterly. Shit. He's in there. There goes my stealth attempt at leaving.

"She is all I have left," he continues. "Your mother left, Nina left, and then you left. Sandra needs protectin', and I'm the only one who can do it!"

Melba has regained her composure a little, I think, because this time she addresses her father in a calm, sympathetic tone. "Daddy, Mama didn't leave. She *died*. It wasn't a choice she made. For that matter, I didn't leave, either. I just grew up. And I know how you feel about protecting Sandra—we couldn't protect her all those years ago, but I think we've done a fine job of it since then. That's why I stayed here . . . I'd have loved to run off and see the world like Nina did, but I just couldn't leave."

"You *did* leave," my grandfather contradicts. "You went over yonder to Neville."

I hear a snap then, which sounds like a dishtowel directed at my grandfather. "Well, Daddy, you may think they grow 'em big up north, but they grow 'em even bigger down here, and there just ain't room enough in a one horse town like Pritchard for a biggun' like me and a big head like yours. I had to find me a town with two traffic lights!" Melba laughs heartily, and I take this as a sign that it's safe—or at least *safer*—to enter the kitchen.

I gingerly step into the room, and Melba smiles welcomingly, although I have a feeling she knows I've been listening. She wipes her hands on the dishtowel, hangs it on a hook over the sink, and turns back to me. "Well, Baby Girl, we best get goin'. It's been a long, exciting day, and we can all use some rest."

My grandfather is at the table with his back to me, so I extract my rental car key from my pocket and follow Melba to the door. I remember how close I came to bolting out that same door earlier tonight, but feel grateful now that I didn't. As I am about to step out into the dark, humid carport, I turn back.

I walk over to where my grandfather sits and clear my throat nervously. "It was nice to meet you," I say. I wait for some kind of a response, or at least for him to turn his head and look at me, but he is like a statue, frozen in position.

I quickly exit the house, my cheeks burning with something akin to embarrassment or shame. He wouldn't even look me in the eye.

Melba is waiting at the edge of the carport, and the look on my face must be telling. "You need a hug from Aunt Melba?

I nod involuntarily, and she envelops me with her soft, ample arms, and gives me a squeeze. "I don't think he likes me," I say wearily.

Melba laughs scratchily and holds me at arms length. "Girl, that old fart doesn't like *anyone*. Now, let's get you put up."

I am back in my Town Car, thankfully alone this time. I assured Melba I could follow her to the inn without getting lost, and I needed a moment to collect my thoughts. Dory was already sitting in Melba's van when we left the house, and honestly I don't think I could have handled a play-by-play of events with her.

I pull out of the gravel drive behind Melba and follow her van down the dark, wet road. Thankfully the rain has stopped, but the roads glisten with reflected moisture from the light of my headlights.

My brain has reached full capacity from all the information of the past few hours—information which is highly pertinent to me, but which is also so shocking and unexpected that I can't make heads or tails of it. I honestly can't even tell which fleeting emotion is closest to what I really feel.

One minute I am angrier than I have ever been, at my aunt, at my grandfather, at my mother—that is, at *Nina*. My real mother, Sandra, seems to be the only person I am not the least bit angry with. She is as clueless as I've been, but lucky for her she gets to stay that way.

My anger fades quickly to confusion. Is Sandra really lucky to never know what she lost all those years ago? Or is she deprived of something even she deserves to know? And why didn't Nina ever feel that I deserved to know the truth? Maybe I would have understood her better, and liked her more.

Sadness sets in now, and guilt that I spent a large part of my life disliking Nina without knowing the whole story. I begin to think that in her strange, self-absorbed way, she really did believe she was doing something good for me . . . for the poor little baby whose mother was not capable of raising a child, and whose father was a sexual predator.

I take a deep breath and loosen my grip on the steering wheel. Now I am wistful, wondering if Nina did me a favor after all. I am not a confident person, and perhaps I couldn't have handled knowing what I know now at an earlier time in my life. Maybe Nina was trying in some strange way to protect me from stereotypes and self-image issues by hiding the fact that my mother was mentally impaired. I was not *her* unwanted, accidental child, but someone else's. I guess that kills Maggie's theory that my father was scared away by Nina and her high standards. The truth is that he was a disgusting criminal who got his vehicle blown up by my grandfather.

Thinking of my grandfather depresses me. He was not happy to see me today. Not the least bit happy to have his long-lost granddaughter back in his life. As far as he is concerned, I am a secret best kept swept under the rug, so that my presence doesn't disrupt the little safe house he has created for himself and Sandra.

Sandra. The smile creeps slowly back across my face as I think about how sweet and nurturing she is. How quick she is to cradle her cat or give someone a hug or a smile. I remember how it felt to hug her, and how she told me so knowingly that we had each other. Warmth creeps outward from my heart, and I feel something I haven't felt in a very long time. I feel hopeful. As Melba's turn signal begins to blink, I decide to embrace this feeling for now. It is strange and comforting, and I'd like to think I have earned it.

I park my car next to Melba's van, and in my headlights see a small, two-story, yellow house. Lights glow in every window, and I watch Dory get out of Melba's car and bound into the house like a golden retriever. I cut the engine, turn off my lights, and climb out into the warm, humid air.

"Is this the inn?" I ask, thinking that the proprietor must be a close friend of hers for Dory to just run inside like that.

Melba laughs her deep, sincere laugh. "Sure is, angel. Welcome to the Little Inn. Didn't I mention I married Dewayne Little?"

I can't contain my smile. "This is your house?" Then suddenly I feel a little hesitant. "You want me to stay here?"

Melba takes my hand and leads me toward the door. "I wouldn't have it any other way," she says. "I think you're a little overdue for a visit."

We enter through the kitchen just as we had at my grandfather's, and Melba sets her purse down on a small table around which several chairs are crammed. The kitchen smells much like Melba's restaurant did, like fried chicken and cooked vegetables. Dirty dishes are piled up in the sink, which Melba notices and quickly waves off.

She turns to me and sighs. "Can't expect a couple of men to clean up after themselves, now can we?" She says it with a mix of exasperation and affection that tells me that this is not an uncommon situation for her to come home to, and motions for me to follow her out of the room. I pick up my small suitcase and comply.

The house is small but tidy, and it feels familiar somehow. The furniture is old looking, as though it has been carefully passed down for generations, and I wonder if some of it belonged to my grandmother like Sandra's bed had. We pass through a hallway lined on one side by huge windows, which Melba tells me used to be an open porch, and into a living area where lamps sit on every table, emitting soft light throughout the room. The only non-antiques in the room appear to be two comfortable-looking couches and a hunter green recliner, in which sits a large, sleeping man. His legs dangle off the end of the footrest, and he is barefoot, a pair of socks and dirty work boots on the floor beside the chair. There is a television turned on in front of him that has been muted, and he is completely unaware of our presence. Dory is nowhere in sight.

Melba switches the television off, which wakes the man. "I was watching that, darlin'," the man mumbles, reaching out to her with one hand.

She reaches back and gives his hand a squeeze. "You were watching the inside of your eyelids, Dewayne," she says, teasing. "Anyway, I brought someone home to meet you. Dewayne Little, this is your niece, Missi Jennings."

Dewayne furrows his brow, confused for a second, but then quickly sits up, causing the footrest of the recliner to snap back under the chair. He pushes himself up to standing and attempts to compose himself. He clears his throat and stammers for a moment before finding the right words.

"Do what?"

I was expecting something else when he finally spoke, and am not sure how to answer, but as usual Melba steps in, saving me from having to answer a question I don't really understand.

"Your *niece*, Dewayne," Melba says tightly, as if willing him to comprehend the magnitude of the situation. Still Dewayne looks perplexed, so Melba continues through clenched teeth, "Sandra's daughter."

"Well, I'll be a monkey's uncle," Dewayne says, a wide, toothy grin spreading across his face. Before I know it, I am swathed in an excessive, sweaty, man-smelling bear hug that leaves me breathless.

"I guess that makes me the monkey, then," I gasp, which has the fortunate effect of making Dewayne laugh and loosen his grip on me.

He holds me at arms' length and looks me over like the long-lost relative I suppose I am. "Land sakes alive, child. I never thought I'd have the pleasure."

"She's come home," Melba declares, and proceeds to swat Dewayne on the backside. "Now you go on and make yourself more presentable—or at least smell better," she says, shaking her head and picking up his discarded clothing off the floor. "Come on, Baby Girl," she says, heading for the stairs herself. "Let's get you a room made up."

We reach the top of the stairs and head down a dark, narrow hall, and Melba flicks on a switch to illuminate our way. There are three doors on the right, one on the left, and one at the very end of the hall. She points out her and Dewayne's room on the left, and Dory's door, which is the first on the right. I can hear Dory talking excitedly on the other side of the closed door, and Melba informs me that she has given Dory permission to call her best friend, Bobbie Jean, and tell her the news of the day.

"No need to act like this is some big secret," Melba says. "We're just so happy you're here."

83

She ushers me past a bathroom and another bedroom before opening the door at the end of the hall.

"This isn't very pretty, but it's about time it had an occupant. It's been empty a while." There are two twin-size beds in the room covered with denim spreads, and a large chest of drawers sits between the beds, the top of which is covered completely by baseball trophies, photographs of baseball teams, and baseballs in clear plastic boxes.

"Wow, which one of your sons plays baseball?" I inquire.

"This room belonged to Clayton and Jerome," Melba says, coming to stand beside me and regard the paraphernalia. "They were ten months apart in age and thick as thieves. Getting one to do anything without the other was nearly impossible, and those boys could play baseball like it was what they'd been born to do."

I notice that she is speaking of them in past tense, and suddenly have a sick feeling in my stomach. "And now?" I ask tentatively, turning to look at my aunt. Our eyes lock for a few seconds before she sits down on one of the beds.

"When they were in high school—Clayton a senior and Jerome a junior—they took their baseball team to the state championships. Rode on a bus up to Ackerman to play in the big game, and the bus got hit head-on by an eighteen-wheeler. The driver and six boys were killed, including Clayton and Jerome."

"Oh, God, Melba, I don't know what to say." My eyes well up, and my heart feels like it is breaking.

"You know, it's always been easier knowing that they are still together. I'm not sure either one could have gone through life without the other." Melba wipes her own eyes and takes a deep breath.

"What is it with buses and this family?" I ask. "I'm never going near one again."

Melba chuckles and reaches out to take my hands in hers. "You can't quit living just because someone else has. God has his reasons for taking people away from us, and I figure that Clayton and Jerome brought us more than our share of joy and pride, and maybe they were needed elsewhere. There aren't two better angels in heaven, of that I am certain."

Melba stands and leaves me to unpack my things, and as I unzip my suitcase and begin arranging clothes in the drawers that once belonged to Clayton and Jerome I contemplate our last exchange. It amazes me how warm and accepting Melba is, and how she can view all the horrible events that have plagued her family over the years as justifiable because it is God's plan. Her strength, her constitution, and my God, her *faith*, are astonishing.

I reach into my suitcase to grab a handful of underwear. I open the top drawer to deposit it, but find that it is already full. I am about to push it shut again when my eye catches something that prompts me to look closer. The drawer is stacked full of yearbooks, papers, newspaper clippings chronicling the athletic achievements of my cousins, and a stack of envelopes bound by a thick rubber band. It is the envelope on top that has drawn my attention, however. It is familiar, expensive-looking, sage green linen paper, and in the upper left-hand corner is a circular, swirly, embossed return address stamp that I recognize unmistakably as Nina's.

Without stopping to consider how disingenuous it is, I pull the envelope from the stack and hold it in my shaking hands. It may be my imagination, but think I can smell Nina's Chanel perfume rising from the paper. I turn the envelope over and slide a letter out.

Through rapidly developing tears, I read:

May 20, 2003

Dear Melba and Dewayne,

I am utterly deprived of words to hear of the loss of your sons. I am sorry to never have known them personally, but it seems they were good, honest, talented boys that certainly made you proud to be their parents.

My dear sister, please know that while I have not remained close, I have never forgotten you, and at this time I hope you know in your heart how deeply penitent I am. You do not deserve this pain and your family does not deserve to suffer in such a way. I hope you will find peace in God the way you always have.

Always,
Nina

I am both touched and amazed as I read the words that Nina wrote years ago. I would have been about to turn twenty five, and would have had lunch or dinner with Nina shortly after the letter was written to celebrate my birthday, but she certainly never let on that something so tragic had happened to anyone she knew. She worked awfully hard at hiding the rest of the family from me.

It relieves me to know that she had at least taken the time to send her condolences, and adds something else to my newfound

Pandora's box of emotions toward Nina. Respect, maybe? Not that I didn't respect her before. I did. But before it was respect for the career she built for herself, her steadfast independence, and her ability to stand up for what she believed in even when I didn't agree with it. The respect I feel now comes from knowing that while she did her best to leave Mississippi behind, she at least had the courtesy to reach out to her sister at a painful time. I just wish she'd reached out to me as well.

I have the sudden feeling that I am not alone, and turn to find Dory standing in the doorway. "You okay?" she asks, her eyes wandering around the room.

I quickly shove the letter back in the envelope and return it to the stack. I gently close the drawer and turn back to Dory. "Melba just told me about your brothers."

She nods and comes in to sit on the floor next to my suitcase. "They were like two beans in a pod," she reflects, still looking around the room. "They did *everything* together. But it wasn't annoying, you know like there are these girls at my school who are practically stuck together and can't make a decision without checkin' with each other first? But Clayton and Jerome weren't that way. They just loved all the same things and loved each other even more. It makes sense that they died together, too."

I tread carefully. "Your mom says that God needed them and that's why they died. Do you feel that way, too?" I ask more out of curiosity than anything—I just can't fathom what God could possibly have to do with the fact that one family lost two members on one horrible day.

"You know," Dory begins, "she used to tell me that, and I was so young I thought she meant that God had one doozy of a baseball tournament going on up there in heaven. Like He needed some delegated hitters or something." She stands and goes over to the chest of drawers. She picks up a framed picture of a baseball team and traces two of the faces with her finger. "I wish I could turn it over to God as easily as Mama, but the older I get, the harder it is. I miss them more now than I did when I was eight."

She turns to me and looks me right in the eye. "What about your mama? Not Sandra, but the other one. Do you think he needed her, too?"

I am at a loss for an answer, and don't want to admit that while I have never exactly felt *mad* about her death, I am also not sure what use God would have for Nina unless He wanted to be bossed around and criticized. So I channel Melba's faith and optimism and tell Dory, "I don't know if God needed Nina, but I think He knew I needed all of you." As I say it, I realize that I believe it . . . and then I start to cry. Again. Damn it.

A few minutes later I have unpacked what little I brought and head back downstairs. Dory told me there was blueberry pie in the kitchen, and I am starving again. I find my way back to the kitchen and am pleasantly surprised to find Melba, Dewayne, Dory, and a guy who looks to be about twenty sitting at the table together. The new guy smiles and stands as I enter the room.

"Hey, cuz," he says, grinning from ear to ear. "I'm Neil Ray. Sure is nice to meet you."

I extend my hand and shake his, which, I realize a second too late, is filthy. My hand is now smudged with some kind of dirt and grease, but I frankly don't care. He seems genuinely glad to meet me, which is definitely my preferred reaction of the day.

I sit down at the table, aware that Neil Ray is watching me and still smiling like the cat that ate the canary. Melba sets a huge piece of pie in front of me, and Dewayne pours a glass of milk from a ceramic pitcher on the table and slides it over to me. I thank them and tear into the pie, which is even better than anything I'd eaten earlier today. We all sit quietly, eating pie, and I am overcome with a feeling of comfort and belonging that I have never felt before. This is a real family, and I'm part of it. Better yet, they actually seem to be okay about it.

I don't even realize that I am smiling until Uncle Dewayne says, "You look almost as happy as Neil Ray, Missi. He's just glad there's somethin' else to talk about around here besides the truck he wrecked today, but tell us what's making you so happy."

I look down at what is left of my pie and think about all of the things that have happened to me in the past several weeks. "I'm just happy to be here," I tell them with a content sigh. They all smile at me, and Dewayne nods understandingly. I am exhausted and no longer wish to be the center of attention, so I look at Neil Ray and grin. "So, Cuz. How did you wreck the truck?"

Dewayne laughs so hard he nearly chokes on his pie, and Neil Ray shakes his head, feigning shame. Dory reaches across the table to high five me, and tells me I fit right in.

Within minutes I have figured out that Neil Ray is the family troublemaker, albeit a lovable one. The truck he damaged was one of a fleet of trucks used by the family land-clearing business. Uncle Dewayne and his remaining sons, Dewayne, Lamar, Stanley, and Neil Ray, work with Uncle Dewayne's brothers and some of *their* sons. I was proudly informed that the company owns excavators, backhoe loaders, skid steer loaders, dump trucks and even a recently acquired rock crusher. The truck that Neil Ray wrecked today was just a pick-up truck, but it happens to be his third wreck this year. Evidently Neil Ray may have been more cut out for stunt-car driving, but strangely enough, nobody seems to be angry with him—just a bit irritated and somewhat amused.

I remember when I got my driver's license. I was nearly seventeen before Nina determined me to be mature enough to get behind the wheel of a car, and was informed in no uncertain terms that if I ever so much as scratched her car, I would never drive again.

Yet here is Neil Ray, having crashed his third truck this year, being unconditionally loved and supported despite the financial loss he has caused his family's business. I get the feeling that this type of behavior is something Dewayne and Melba have come to expect from him, but still . . . this is something. It must be an awesome thing to be yourself and not worry about being excommunicated by your parents.

Melba begins to clear the table and tackle the heap of dishes that had already been left in the sink. I offer to help dry, and she gratefully agrees. As Dory and Neil Ray disperse to go watch TV and shower, respectively, Neil Ray gives me a friendly punch on the shoulder on his way past, and Dory reaches out to give me a sweet but fragile hug.

"God, she's tiny," I say after Dory has left the kitchen. "I feel like I could break her."

Dewayne pushes his chair out and stands. "She's petite like her Daddy," he says, patting his ample belly and chuckling. "Well, I do believe I can hear my pillow calling my name. You girls don't stay up too late getting to know each other, you hear? You got a lot of years ahead of you to do that." He puts a massive arm around each of us and plants a kiss on my forehead, which is the single most paternal thing that anyone has ever done to me.

"He's a good egg, that Dewayne Little," Melba says, after he's left the room. I can't respond because I have begun to cry again. It's funny, because right now I am not sad in the least. Just overwhelmed and relieved to be where I am.

"Oh, Baby Girl," my aunt whispers, and wraps me in a warm, soft hug. "I think you're a bit overwhelmed for one day. Why don't you go on and get some rest? We've got a tough nut to crack tomorrow."

"What do you mean?" I ask, wiping my nose with the back of my hand.

She picks up a sponge and immerses it in a pot of soapy water. "My Daddy. We need to make him understand that you are a part of this family, a fact which is not going to change."

I look down at my feet and the tennis shoes I put on almost eighteen hours ago. A lifetime ago, it seems. "I have a feeling he's going to be hard to convince."

"You just leave it to your Aunt Melba. Everything is going to be just fine." She gives me a knowing look. "Now get on to bed, my angel, and have you some sweet dreams."

CHAPTER TWELVE

I wake the next morning in the same clothes I left Washington in. I'd had the strength to take off my shoes and socks, and I might have brushed my teeth, but for the most part all I can remember is falling into the bed, too tired to even reflect much on the whirlwind of a day I'd had, which was probably a good thing.

I think I might have awoken wondering if it had all been a dream, but the first thing I see as I open my eyes is the array of baseball paraphernalia on the dresser. It is a grim, yet comforting, testimony that yesterday actually occurred as I remember it.

I sit up, stretch, and run my hands through my hair. It is tangled and feels greasy. I open the bedroom door and peer out into the hallway. The bathroom door is open and everything is quiet, so I grab some clean clothes and my quart-sized Ziplock bag of toiletries and head for the shower.

The bathroom is tiny and is tiled entirely in pink. Even the sink and toilet are pink. I laugh to myself, imagining Melba's six sons spending their formative years bathing in a sea of bubble gum pink. Not that it seems to have mattered; they sound like quite the masculine array of athletes and dirt pushers.

My train of thought somehow leads me to Josh. He shared a bathroom growing up with two sisters, and told me once—I dismissed it at the time as just being juvenile behavior—that his sisters would wash their bras in the bathroom sink and hang them to dry in the shower, and he would try them on and parade around the house to terrorize his sisters and freak out his father. If only I'd known then what that story really meant.

I step into the steaming spray of water and scrub extra hard from head to toe, trying to cleanse myself of these thoughts. I take extra care to shave my legs, knowing I will be forced to wear shorts in order to survive the insufferable heat of Mississippi. I even condition my hair, something I usually don't take the time to do. I hadn't planned on making quite so many first impressions yesterday, and am going to try to make up for some of them today.

I consider blow-drying my hair, but I didn't pack a dryer and don't feel comfortable rummaging through the bathroom cabinets looking for Dory's, so I pull it back wet into a neat, low ponytail. I brush my teeth and put on some tinted moisturizer and lip-gloss, which is as close as I ever come to actually wearing makeup. I put on a light blue t-shirt and khaki shorts, and eschew my tennis shoes for flip-flops. I am ready to take on my grandfather, for better or worse.

The living room is empty as I descend the stairs, but I find Dory in the kitchen with a bowl of Frosted Flakes and a box of Pop Tarts. "Breakfast of champions," she says with her mouth full. "Want some?"

It's tempting, it really is, but I have something else in mind. "Is there any pie left?"

Dory looks at me as a worried expression takes over her face. "My Mama would never let me have pie for breakfast."

"But Pop Tarts and sugar-coated cereal are fine?" I spot an aluminum foil-covered round dish on the counter and make a beeline for it. "At least the blueberries in the pie are real fruit, and it's not like I'm going to eat it a la mode." I cut myself a generous slice, locate a fork, and sit down next to Dory.

"Well," she starts, "I mean, you can eat it outside if you want."

"Not *al fresco*," I correct, amused. "*A la mode* is with ice cream."

Dory's cheeks color and her brow furrows. "Oh," she says awkwardly. "But if you eat pie for breakfast because it's healthier than Pop Tarts, then why not eat the ice cream, too? Like, instead of drinking a glass of milk?"

"Dory, you're a genius," I tell her, and head for the freezer.

"I'm definitely not a genius. Clayton and Jerome were the smart ones. They were going to finish high school and go to college on scholarships," Dory says proudly. I calculate that Dory would only have been in about second grade when her brothers were killed, and must have looked up to them incredibly. I locate the ice cream and sit back down.

"Do you remember a lot about them?" I inquire, wanting to know more about them, but not wanting to upset Dory.

She grins, and I immediately know that Dory has retained all the best memories of Clayton and Jerome. "They were funny," she begins. "Used to hide under my bed or behind my door and when I'd walk in the room they'd jump out and scare me to death. Tried to do the same to Mama, but one time she nearly had a heart attack and they quit it. Clayton had a girlfriend named Sara Jane, and was forever playing jokes on her, like once he put a bullfrog in her shoe and when she went to put her foot in she screamed like you would not believe. We always wondered why she kept on going out with him."

I laugh and can almost imagine the two inseparable boys ganging up on the people they loved.

Dory does not seem to be finished reminiscing, and I am happy to indulge her. "They used to set up a pitching machine in the field behind the house and practice hitting home runs. I'd run around for hours, collecting all the baseballs and bringing them back so they could keep hitting 'em. Mama says that's why they were so good at baseball."

"Because they had such a good ball girl?" I ask. Dory nods. My heart physically hurts for her, but at the same time I am touched that Clayton and Jerome continue to be loved so deeply and remembered so clearly by their mother and sister. I think of my relationship with Nina and feel something much more than a pang of regret about what was missing between us. I wonder if knowing about my real mother and the sacrifices Nina made on my behalf would have changed the way I felt about her. I would like to think so, but know that there is no point in speculating. It was what it was.

Dory is staring at me curiously. "What?" I ask, a bit more defensively than I mean to.

"What are you thinking?" I know it is an innocent and sincere inquiry, but I am not ready to go there yet, so I put her off.

"Nothing important." I quickly get up and set my plate and fork in the sink, which is what I'd have done if I were at my own place. Then I remember the mountain of dishes that Melba had to wash last night, so I rinse them and put them in the dishwasher. I turn back to face Dory. "So, what are your plans for the day?"

Her pleasant expression abruptly turns sour. "Mama told me to wait for you to get up and take you back over to the farm."

"Your grandfather's farm?" I ask.

"No," she answers. "*Your* grandfather's farm."

I am determined to get to the bottom of why Dory seems to loathe her, or rather, *our* grandfather so much. I mean, he's no warm-and-fuzzy-sit-on-my-lap-and-I'll-tell-you-a-story-about-when-I-was-your-age type of guy, but surely there must be some redeeming quality hiding underneath that grouchy façade. Surely.

Dory doesn't seem to think so. The only words she can come up with to describe him as we cruise the Lincoln back over to Pritchard are "mean as a snake." I drive slower.

As we pull up to the farmhouse, I can see in the daylight that it, to be polite, needs some work. The white paint is peeling off in large sheets, the front porch is sagging, and the roof is missing more than a few shingles. There is a dilapidated old barn just beyond the house, which I did not notice through the dark and rain last night.

"Thank the *Lord*!" Dory exclaims as I put the car in park and turn off the engine.

"What?"

"Fergie's gone," she says, climbing out and almost running to the door of the house.

I have no idea who she is talking about. "Who's Fergie?"

"His dumb old tractor," she informs me with a sweep of her arm indicating the empty carport. Then she disappears inside.

I take in the space where the tractor had been sheltered from the rain last night, and then look out at where the old pickup truck is still sitting. It looks as though at some point it must have been green, but is so rusted out now that there are actual holes in the metal.

As I head for the house I am stopped by a distant sound. I turn and look out into the field behind the barn. I can barely make out the shape of the tractor, but there it is, rumbling along out there. And there *he* is. A shiver runs up my spine and I hurry to the house to take refuge.

I barely have a foot in the door, however, when I get mauled by a couple of rabid dogs. Well, almost. They are across the room on that disgusting pink couch, but they are barking at me as though I am a burglar or something, teeth bared and saliva flying from their hideous jowls. It occurs to me that to them I *am* a stranger and thus will be treated as an intruder by the animals, so I run back out the door, slamming it behind me.

I stand under the carport, clutching my chest in terror, but thankfully the barking stops and my fear dissipates. Unless those crazy dogs come crashing through the door, I think I am safe. I do not need to go inside, even though I'd love to go in and see Sandra. At some point, surely, Dory will realize I am not there and come find me.

My grandfather is still a long way out in the field on Fergie, so I stroll over to the old barn and step inside. It is dark and damp, and feels nice compared to the heat outside. Once my eyes adjust to the murky light, I see that the barn is full of junk. Old farm equipment, stacks of rotting lumber, and tools of every shape and size litter the place, none of which looks like it's been used in quite some time.

As I turn to leave the barn—God forbid I get caught snooping around by my cantankerous old grandfather—I notice one single object that does not seem to be in the same state of decay as everything else. It is, upon closer investigation, a beer keg, but with an angled steel pipe coming out of the top. I cannot imagine that my grandfather has a habit of throwing wild parties, so I assume he has come up with some new use for the keg. If he's been known to blow up someone's truck, then perhaps he makes his own explosives out in the old barn. I decide to get the hell out of there.

I wander over to the barbed wire fence that separates the yard from the field. A slight breeze has kicked up, and I close my eyes and let the sun warm my face. There is a smell here that I have never smelled before. It is earthy but clean, with a trace of sweetness. I inhale deeply, taking in the sounds and scents of the farm. I can hear the far-off rumbling of the tractor, the birds singing nearby, and the stirring of the trees in the breeze. I can smell that smell—that wonderful, organic smell that must be a combination of a million things out here. I can feel the wind on my face, the sun on my shoulders, and an unbelievable burning sensation on my feet.

I open my eyes to see hundreds of ants climbing all over my feet and ankles—and they are biting the ever-living shit out of me. I start to scream, and run back toward the house, kicking off my flip-flops as I go. The pain is searing, and I smack at my feet trying to get the hangers-on to let go.

Dory must have heard my outburst, because she and Sandra come running out of the house to my aid. "What happened?" Dory shrieks.

"Ants!" is all I can answer. My feet are on fire, and are quickly beginning to swell. I cannot stand still for the agony, so I run back and forth, stomping my feet and screaming.

Dory runs back into the house, and Sandra comes over and takes me by the arm. She pulls me to the brick steps leading to the door and gently helps me inside. Not that I care at this point, but I do notice that the two heinous dogs do not so much as lift their heads from the couch when I enter this time. Sandra shoos them away and sits me down in the warm place they have left behind.

Dory is talking excitedly on the phone and filling a plastic bag with ice. "It's *bad*, Mama. She must have a hundred bites on her feet and legs." She comes over, stretching the telephone cord as far as it will go, and places the ice across my ankles. I squeeze my eyes shut and rub them with my fists, and when I open them again, Dory is staring at me in shock.

"Mama, her whole *face* is swellin' up now. I'm not kiddin'. Her eyes are puffy, her legs are puffy, and she's got welps everywhere." She turns away from me and begins to whisper into the phone.

"Dory, *what*?" I holler, panic setting in. My *face* is swelling? How? Those things were on my feet, not my head! My mouth feels tingly, and my tongue feels thick. I try to fuss at Dory to stop whispering and tell me what's happening, but the sound comes out slurred and slow. Beside me, Sandra takes my hand and squeezes it, and then everything goes dark.

I remember the wonderful, fresh smell of the farm, and how good the sun felt beating down on me. But now the smell is fading and becoming something else—a musty, furry, fetid stench. The dogs. Now it's all coming back to me.

I attempt to sit up, but am pushed back to a reclining position by large but gentle hands. My eyes are still swollen shut, so I can't see very well, but I hear Dory's voice, so between that and the smell I know I am still at my grandfather's.

The hands on my shoulders have a voice, too, one I am unfamiliar with. It is decidedly male, but definitely not my grandfather, and is explaining to Dory that I have had an anaphylactic reaction to the ants. Fire ants, he calls them, and with good reason.

As I regain my senses, I am aware that while my legs no longer feel like they are on fire, they itch like crazy. I reach down to scratch them, but my hands are gently redirected by the large, warm hands of this stranger. "Don't scratch. They'll ooze."

"Ooze?" I am horrified. "Gross."

Big Hands laughs and folds my hands across my middle. "Just rest. Everything is going to be fine." He says it like everyone else around here—*fahn*—and I feel strangely comforted despite the fact that my heart is racing. I reach up with one hand and place it on my heart.

"Wow," I say, feeling it beat as though it is going to jump out of my body.

"I gave you a shot of epinephrine," Big Hands tells me. "That's what is making your heart race, but it's also reducing the swelling in your throat, opening your airway so that you can breathe more easily, and maintaining your blood pressure. You had what is called an anaphylactic reaction to the ant bites."

"You could have *died*!" Dory cries from somewhere behind Big Hands. I turn to look at her and can make out her blurry form. I also get a hazy glimpse of the man who allegedly saved my life, but can't make out his features.

"Well, it was definitely a serious reaction, and Dory, you were smart to call your mama. I'm glad I was close by when she called me," he adds.

I am about to ask just who, in fact, he is, when the door bursts open and Melba literally fills the room. "Dear Lord, Missi! Are you all right? Oh, my stars. Look at you! They absolutely ate you alive!" She all but shoves my knight in shining armor out of the way and kneels down beside the couch.

She runs her hands over my legs and feet, barely touching them, and then cups my face. She leans in so that our noses are almost touching and takes a deep breath. "Don't you ever stand on a fire ant hill again, do you hear?"

I nod, finally beginning to feel calm and collected again. "Where is Sandra?" I ask, suddenly aware that she is no longer in the room.

"*He* is with her out on the porch," Dory informs me. "She was pretty upset when you passed out, and when he saw Darryl pull up like his hair was on fire he came in to see what all was going on."

I try again to sit up, and this time I am allowed. I shift uncomfortably, cognizant of yet another burning feeling—this time on another body part. "Why does my butt hurt?" I ask warily.

Big Hands, who Dory just called Darryl, clears his throat. "That's where I gave you the shot."

As the full meaning of that small statement dawns on me, my heart starts racing again and my cheeks burn. "You saw my butt?"

"I saw it, too," Dory says with a giggle, and I want to kill her.

Darryl closes up something akin to a toolbox and stands. "Well, I've been an EMT for a few years now, and you'd be surprised how many butts I see doing this job. Missi, it's been a pleasure to meet you. Mrs. Little and Dory, as always, it's great to see you, and please tell Little Dewayne hello for me. I haven't seen him in months."

Melba walks him to the door. "You know, Darryl, he just mentioned your name last Sunday and said the same thing. Why don't you and Lucy come have supper with us after church this

Sunday? All the boys will be here, and y'all can catch up."

"Mrs. Little, I'd like that very much. Are you sure it's no trouble?"

"I'd be upset if you didn't come," Melba says, and hugs Darryl. "Plus, you can check up on the patient. Thanks again for coming to help Missi. She's my niece and we've only just been reacquainted after many years, so we'd like her to stick around for at least a little while."

Darryl turns back toward me. With my somewhat improving vision I can tell that he is tall and broad shouldered with dark, wavy hair. "I'm happy to help any cousin of Little Dewayne's," he says, and walks out the door to his truck.

"See you and Lucy on Sunday," Melba calls out after him.

She comes over to the couch and lowers herself down next to me. "Baby Girl, is every day with you going to be this exciting? Because if that's the case, I need to prepare myself."

"Aunt Melba," I say, awkwardly initiating contact by placing my hand on top of hers, " until very recently I would have said that I am one of the world's most boring people. All this . . . this *excitement* . . . is new to me, too."

"Well, maybe let's tone it down. At least a little," she says, turning her hand over so that our palms are touching and we are holding hands.

Melba has set about preparing food in the kitchen. In her wonderful, motherly way, she has decided not to return to the restaurant and has left Artie in charge yet again. I feel guilty, but at the same time I am relieved to have her here.

I take a deep breath and head down the hallway. Dory is at the back of the house watching television, but it is not Dory I am looking for. On the right side of the hall, before reaching the threshold where the bedrooms are, a door stands slightly ajar, and daylight filters in through the space around it.

I push the old door open, expecting it to creak loudly and thereby alert someone to my presence, but it does not make a sound and for a moment I am able to stand and watch Sandra and my grandfather sitting side by side in rocking chairs, rocking in unison, hands clasped between them and not saying a word.

Risking upsetting Sandra all over again, I gingerly make my way to a vacant chair next to her and sit down. I rock along with them in silence for a long time, inhaling the fresh farm air and listening to the sounds of the birds, just as I'd been when I disturbed the ant hill earlier. Thinking of it makes my bites itch, so I stop rocking and lean forward to scratch.

"Leave 'em be," comes a voice from the other side of Sandra.

"Excuse me?" I ask, leaning further and turning to look at my grandfather.

"Scratchin's the worst thing you can do," he says, without really looking back at me. "Makes 'em ooze."

Again, gross. "They itch like crazy. I guess it's a visceral response to want to scratch," I say, cautiously optimistic that we are at least communicating in some way.

He grumbles and looks straight ahead, out at the barn. "Well, I don't know what the hell visceral is, but I've got something that will make those bites quit itchin'. When Melba ain't lookin' I'll fetch you some."

Rather than ask questions, I decide to play it carefully, so I thank him and return to rocking alongside Sandra. The itching is excruciating, so it is all I can do not to scratch. I try to focus on the cadence of the rocking and the fact that at this moment I do not feel loathed by my grandfather, but the itching is winning out. Sandra is scratching her chest with her free hand and watching her makes it even worse. Just as I am about to lose control and tear at my legs with my fingernails, Sandra stops her own scratching and reaches out toward the arm of my chair to take my hand. Hers is warm and clammy, but it soothes me, and for now I forget about the itching. We rock—the three of us—in silence again, my grandfather and I finally making a connection, albeit one held together in the middle by Sandra.

Then, as abruptly as it happened, it *un*happens. He lets go of Sandra's hand, gets up, and walks from the porch toward the barn without saying a word.

I need distraction, so I ask Sandra where Missi the cat is. She grins and heads for the house, and I follow. Not surprisingly, the cat is in Sandra's room and seems genuinely pleased to see us. Sandra picks her up and gently passes her to me, so I sit in the rocking chair in the corner. I notice that there is also a straight-backed chair in the room that was not here last night.

"Is that new?" I ask her, pointing to the chair.

"No, it's from the kitchen," Sandra says thickly. "I needed another one."

"Why?" I ask, rubbing Missi the cat behind her ears.

"So we both have a place to sit when you come," she answers, and then takes up residence in the extra chair.

We sit together in her room for a long time, talking a bit, but mostly just sitting. Normally this would be incredibly awkward and uncomfortable for me, but for some reason the silence is reassuring. It's nice to be with someone who expects nothing but your presence. I hear the television from the other room—Dory is watching Oprah—and closer, the ticking of an old wind-up alarm clock next to Sandra's bed. I again take in the order that exists in Sandra's room, and imagine that the meticulousness of it gives Sandra a sense of control and comfort.

I think back to my apartment in D.C., and how disorganized and untidy it was. After Josh, I had nobody to impress, so I let my life get even more out of hand than before, and completely lost all the sense of comfort that home can bring. This place, though, or at least this room, seems to be a haven of comfort and belonging. I felt the same way last night in Melba's kitchen eating pie. There was a sense of belonging that just automatically came with the place. This is not simply a house, but a home. Melba and Dewayne's house is a home. I feel at home.

Melba's voice comes from down the hall. "Anybody hungry?"

The pie I ate for breakfast is long gone, and I realize I am starving. I stand up still holding the cat, and ask Sandra if she is hungry. She nods and stands, too.

She takes the cat from me and carries her down the hallway, saying that Missi must be hungry, too. She holds the cat close to her face and hums quietly to it. It is a tune I recognize, but can't quite place.

She continues humming as she sets Missi down by a food dish in a corner of the kitchen. I am pleased to note that in the time since I vacated the pink couch, the dogs have not returned, so I sit complacently at the table where Melba has laid an impressive spread. There is sliced ham, pasta salad, coleslaw, some type of beans, and corn muffins. It is enough food for ten.

Dory joins us and begins piling a plate with food. I look at her tiny body and wonder where it all goes as I scoop far less onto my own plate, knowing precisely where it will go. For now I decide that my aching butt deserves some comfort food after what it's been through today. I generously butter a muffin and take a bite.

Sandra sits across the table from me, having seen to it that her cat has been properly fed. Melba places a plate in front of her, and she picks up a fork. "Missi is her nickname, you know," she says randomly.

"The cat has a nickname?" I ask with my mouth full.

"Her real name is Mississippi Moon." Sandra scoops some beans up with a fork and shovels them into her mouth.

Melba smiles knowingly at me, as though we share a secret, and I take another bite of muffin at the exact moment that understanding hits. '*It is no coincidence that she names all her cats Missi, you know. We let her name you.*'

I nearly choke as I try to swallow, but my mouth is dry and my throat is constricted again. I reach for a glass of tea and take a gulp, then sputter and spit as I realize it is even sweeter than the tea at the restaurant.

Somehow I manage to regain control and raise my eyebrows at my aunt. "*Mississippi Moon?*" I ask through clenched teeth, lowering my voice so that Sandra doesn't hear.

She narrows her eyes at me. "I suppose Nina didn't tell you that, either?"

I feel like I am about to lose my mind. My name . . . my given name at birth . . . is *Mississippi Moon*? I sound like the offspring of some pothead, not of a sweet, naïve, thirteen-year-old! I put my napkin on the table and am about to leave the table when I hear Sandra start to hum again as she chews her food. This time I recognize the song, and as she hums the words materialize in my mind. *Old black water, keep on rollin', Mississippi Moon, won't you keep on shinin' on me.*

Dear God, can this possibly get more bizarre? My instinct is to be mortified by this revelation, but then something hits me, and my perspective changes completely. I am named after a Doobie Brothers song, a song that Sandra is humming on this day, over thirty-three years after I was born, as if she knows somehow that we have been reconnected. Mississippi Moon might be a name better suited for a pole dancer than for me, but I am so deeply moved that I can't bring myself to be offended by or ashamed of it. It is a name that was given to me by the one person in this world that had a right to give it, and it means something to her. So I put my napkin in my lap again, sit alongside my family, and eat.

When Sandra finishes eating, she takes Missi the cat back to her room without a word. As Melba, Dory, and I begin clearing the table of plates and serving dishes, my grandfather walks in the back door with a stomp and a slam. We all turn to look at him, and he looks back at us with a rather annoyed expression on his face.

"Daddy, can I fix you a plate?" Melba asks.

"I'm not hungry," he snaps, and crosses the room in the direction of the hallway. Then he stops short and faces Melba. "But thank you," he says softly, as if offering an apology for more than just his tone. He leaves the room and I hear Dory exhale.

I feel empowered for some reason and can't help myself, so I carry a plate to the sink and address Dory. "Why are you so afraid of him?"

"Him?" she asks, pointing an elbow at the door through which he just left.

"Yes, him. You seem to almost hold your breath when he's in the room, and I haven't heard you speak three words to him. He terrifies you, I think, and I just wonder why."

Dory's cheeks turn scarlet, and she looks sheepishly at her mother. She shrugs and contemplates her answer for a moment. "He's mean," she says with reservation, but Melba does not react, so she continues. "He never says anything nice to anyone, never says please or thank you—except for a minute ago, which I am telling you is the only time I've ever heard it in my life—never seems happy to be around anyone other than Sandra, like the rest of us being here is some big pain." She gains momentum with every word, and I think I see the trace of a smile at the corners of Melba's mouth.

Dory goes on. "He acts like he's the only one who's ever lost someone he loved, and that he can just huff around all the time for the next hundred years. But he's wrong. We lost people, too, and Mama says that's no reason to be mad at the rest of the world and feel sorry for yourself. You've got to be grateful for what you have." She takes a deep breath, looking surprised and pleased, as though she'd been waiting an eternity to say all of that.

"Then why be afraid of him?" I inquire. "Why not just pity the fact that he is such a miserable old man?" I think I am trying to convince myself of the same thing.

Dory gets quiet again and says hesitatingly, "I'm afraid to get in his way and make him mad, I guess. People all over town talk about his temper, you know. Bobbie Jean's grandfather used to be friends with him, and they got into a fight about something or another, like a million years ago, and he swears that my granddad came after him with a BB gun and took out the seat of his pants with it."

I laugh out loud at the thought, and Dory smiles a little, too. "Then there was the truck . . . now *that* story is famous, only I didn't know the story behind it or whose truck it was." Dory says, stopping abruptly and looking to her mother.

"My father," I say, under my breath, goose bumps rising on my arms.

Melba turns away from the sink and wipes her hands. "The truck that belonged to the man that raped Sandra. He was no father

101

to you Missi, so don't you ever think that you are in any way a part of him. But that story is indeed a popular one. Daddy's temper is legendary, and the day he blew up that truck in the parking lot of the Winn Dixie, I think people figured he'd lost it completely. Nobody in town knows the real reason why. Just that someone had crossed Daddy for the last time and got a shotgun to the gasoline tank."

"I still don't understand why that makes you scared of him, Dory," I press. "I can't imagine there is anything you could possibly do to make him mad. You are a reminder of what he still has, not what he's lost."

Dory throws her hands up. "I guess I'm just not Sandra. Even Mama's not Sandra," she says, as though resigned to it all.

Melba wraps a fleshy arm around her daughter and presses her lips to Dory's hair. "There is only one Sandra," she sighs. "But there is also only one Dory, one Melba, and now one Missi . . . well, maybe two." She grins at me, her eyes twinkling, and I let out an approving snort at the thought of the cat. "And I think that he knows that the rest of us can take care of ourselves. Sandra is what God gave him to protect when Mama died, so she gets a little special attention, and that's okay."

She turns to look Dory in her beautiful blue eyes. "Missi is right, though, and I've been waiting years for you to come to this on your own, but I guess we had to give you a little push. You should not be afraid of your grandfather. He is rough around the edges for certain, but inside he's just as scared as you."

Dory looks appeased, if not wholly convinced, and hugs her mother around her enormous middle. I leave them together and seek out my grandfather.

It takes some looking, but I follow my instincts and return to the barn. The shadows are long, the breeze has completely disappeared, and the birds seem to have taken a break from the late afternoon heat.

I clear my throat as I approach the barn door, not wanting to sneak up on anyone. I hear rustling coming from inside, and the sound of glass clinking. "Hello?" I call into the darkness.

He appears into the shaft of light that the door lets in, looking agitated. "Well, come in or get out. Just shut the door," he says, and disappears from sight again.

I decide to go in, since he actually gave me the option. I find him standing by the beer keg, filling a small jar with clear liquid. "What's that?" I ask.

He raises his eyes to meet mine without moving his head. "Hooch."

"Hooch?" I ask.

"Hooch," he answers.

I recall Melba mentioning that there was a still in the barn, but somehow this wasn't what I'd expected a still to look like. "Well, I guess it's about that time," I say jokingly.

"What time is that?" he snaps.

"Looks like happy hour," I answer, trying to lighten the mood.

He screws a lid onto the jar and stands in front of me. "This ain't for me. It's for you." He holds it out to me. Even with the lid on, I can smell the strong scent of alcohol.

"What do you want me to do with it?" I inquire.

"It'll make those bites quit itchin'," he says matter-of-factly.

"I bet it will," I say, wrinkling up my nose at the thought of drinking it, but he sighs exasperatedly, and thrusts the jar at me again.

"You put it *on* the bites," he says impatiently. "With a cotton swab or something."

"Oh," I say, finally understanding. "Thanks." He just stands there, looking at me, so I take this as my cue to leave the barn.

As I reach the door, and step out into the sunlight, I hear him call out after me. "Don't let your aunt see you with that."

I stop at my car to hide the jar before returning to the house, definitely not wanting to cause a problem between my grandfather and my aunt. After the events of the day, I am exhausted. I step back inside the house and find the kitchen immaculate and Melba on the phone.

I sit in the rocking chair closest to the door and see that the dogs have returned to the pink couch. Thankfully, they did not bark when I came in. Maybe everyone around here is starting to get used to me.

Dory wanders in from the hallway and sits in the rocker next to mine. "What are their names?" I ask, motioning toward the animals. They are looking at me with wary eyes, but I am beginning to think they wouldn't hurt a fly.

"Big Dog and Little Dog," she says with a drawl. "Real creative, ain't it?"

The dogs appear to be almost the exact same size, but I don't ask which is which. It probably doesn't matter, anyway. As Dory and I rock, Melba begins talking, as if she'd been on hold for a while.

"I need to schedule an appointment for Sandra Jenner," she says, "with Dr. Boudreaux." She listens for a moment and then lowers her voice as her eyes meet mine. "It's just a checkup on her pacemaker."

It takes a moment to register, and I am pretty sure Melba was hoping I didn't hear her, but I did. Sandra has a pacemaker. I'm no cardiothoracic surgeon, but I'm fairly certain that having a pacemaker means Sandra has a bad heart. My own heart sinks.

I wait as patiently and respectfully as possible until Melba finishes her phone call, then join her at the kitchen table. She looks at me expectantly, knowing that I have questions. I collect my thoughts before I speak, wanting to ask appropriate questions without getting emotional. As I prepare to speak, Melba reaches across and wraps her hands around mine. It is a gesture that I am quickly getting used to, and that brings an incredible amount of comfort to me. We sit like that for a minute, but I finally find my voice.

"She has a pacemaker? What does that mean? Is she going to die?" I ask, feeling like a child but wanting that answer straight out.

"Baby Girl, we're all going to die," Melba says. "It's just a matter of when the good Lord decides it's our turn. Sandra has lived a long life for someone like her, and I expect she's going to live a whole lot longer. But she has a condition that makes it necessary for her to have a pacemaker, and it's just something extra we have to fret over."

"What kind of condition?" I inquire, desperately needing to hear that it's just an irregular heartbeat or something.

Dory joins us at the table, and is quick to share her take on things. "Sandra's heartbeat was irregular, so they did an AV node invasion." You'd think from the proud expression on Dory's face that she'd just aced the MCAT's, but Melba patiently ignores her and keeps her eyes focused on mine.

"It's called an AV node *ablation*," she says. "Do you know what that is?"

I shake my head, knowing that my freshman Biology class didn't come close to addressing it. Melba goes on. "Well, heart conditions are not uncommon for someone with Down syndrome, and for Sandra this meant that eventually her heart wasn't able to keep ticking at a proper rate by itself." Melba speaks calmly and with a complete understanding of the situation. "She's had the pacemaker a long time and it seems to be doin' a fine job. We just get it checked out often to make sure the battery and connections are strong." She smiles then, genuine and reassuring, and I know she believes what she says, and is not simply trying to make me feel better.

I inhale and do feel somewhat better, knowing that this condition of Sandra's is something that has been addressed for a long time. Still, I hate knowing that there is so much more to this family's pain and suffering than I had imagined. I sigh deeply and cover my eyes with my hands. As much as I've cried the past twenty-four hours, Melba must think I do it all the time, because she slides a tissue across the table to me.

Melba looks tired. More tired than she did when I met her just yesterday. I know that I am partially to blame for this. I came barging into her life without any warning, have forced her to confront and discuss some of the most painful moments of her life, and am camped out in her dead sons' bedroom.

"Is having a family always this hard?" I ask.

"*Having* a family is the easiest thing in the world," she answers wisely, "and almost any knucklehead can do it. But now, loving a family? Taking care of a family? Not so easy, baby doll, but worth the effort, I promise." Dory leans against her mother's shoulder and closes her eyes.

Inside my head, I consider the ease and lack of thought with which I moved through my former life in Washington. I got up every day, went to work, came home, and started all over again the next day, with very few exceptions. Every day was exactly the same. But that routine, that daily rhythm of events, also included a hefty measure of boredom, sadness, and regret. Even on the occasional obligatory mother-daughter outing with Nina, I never had to work hard at acting like I'd rather be anywhere else. Those events, as painful and unpleasant as they often turned out, were easy in a bizarre way, because they were always exactly the same: greet each other icily, make small talk, eat in silence, bicker about some inane topic, leave angry. Lather, rinse, repeat. Easy.

This, though, this sudden onset of family in an entirely different context, is not easy. I feel an intense attachment to these people whom I have known for such a short time, but have felt just as much pain in their presence as I have joy. Not pain that they have caused me, but rather *their* pain, *their* loss, *their* struggles. I am typically not a terribly empathetic person, usually focusing on my own problems, of which at any point in time there seem to have been plenty to choose from. But I think that empathy is precisely what I am feeling right now, and that this empathy is what is causing my pain.

I think what hurts the most is that I know with absolute certainty that none of these people deserve what has happened to them. These are good, kind, loving people. With the exception of that cantankerous old man who portrays the family patriarch, these are perhaps the most marvelous people I have encountered in my life.

Prior to knowing them, the family that in my book outranked all others, was without question, Josh's. It always felt like an honor to be in their presence, and they exemplified everything that I thought a family should be—holidays at home, sibling banter, cut-throat games of Scrabble and Monopoly, and two or three weekly phone calls home just to "check in" with mom, dad, and the basement-dwelling grandma.

This family, however, sets itself apart somehow. Maybe it's that where Josh's family was jovial and fun, they were also cynical and raw, which made them more authentic to me. I was comfortable because cynicism was something I was intimately familiar with. But Melba, Dory, Sandra, Dewayne . . . even Neil Ray, seem to possess a familial bond that exceeds simply being related to and liking one another. There is a cohesiveness that exists perhaps because of what they have lost, but that completely surpasses anything I have ever witnessed. Their love for each other is genuine and effortless.

It has only been a day that I have actually known them, though, which means I know almost nothing. That grandfather of mine is certainly no peach, and there are still several of Melba and Dewayne's offspring that I have yet to meet. Maybe I am a fool and just want this to be the case simply because this is *my* family and I want so badly for it to apply to me as well. Maybe they are cynical after all. I guess time will tell.

CHAPTER THIRTEEN

I play a few games of dominos with Sandra before I can bring myself to leave. She does not chat while we play, instead focusing intently on the game and winning every time. My focus, however, is on Sandra, not on the dominos—although I am confident I would lose anyway. I spend a long time memorizing her face, which is round like the moon and equally as luminous. Even as she furrows her brow in concentration, her eyes smile. Deep and brown, framed by thick, arching eyebrows, Sandra's eyes are truly the corner stone of her face, around which every other feature plays a supporting role.

She has a small nose, which is flattened at the bridge, and when she is deep in thought she wrinkles it up, causing her glasses to slip. When this happens, Sandra reaches up with one stubby finger and pushes them back. It seems to be almost a reflexive action, and I begin to count the number of times per turn Sandra pushes her glasses back up on her nose. Her mouth is small, and most of the time her tongue sticks out just a little bit. Even when she catches me looking at her and flashes me a smile, her tongue does not retract, and I return the smile until she goes back to ruminating about which domino to play next.

I look at her ears, which are the tiniest I have ever seen. They look as if they belong on an infant, and I wonder if they have grown at all since the day she was born. The top of her left ear is slightly folded over, and I want to touch it, to unfold it, but I don't. She is fine exactly as she is.

On Sandra's next turn she reaches out with one hand and slides a domino toward the length of right angles we have made on the table. Her other hand absently scratches her chest, and I wonder if she has an itch or if it's something she does when she's thinking hard. I notice that her pinky finger curves in toward her other short, chubby fingers. Her fingernails are short and uneven, and I decide that she must bite them. I smile again at the thought, because that would be something we have in common.

I am drawn back to Sandra's eyes, though, which sparkle with pride and accomplishment as I realize that she is out of dominos and I have lost yet again. I feign disappointment and shock, but inside I am happy, for her and for me.

Melba sticks her head in the door and tells me she and Dory are going home. I have the option of staying a while longer, but I am tired from the day's medical crisis and family acclimation. I am also afraid I'd end up in Alabama somewhere if I tried to find my way back to the Little's on my own, so I hug Sandra and tell her I will see her soon.

She smiles and nods, and then holds up one finger as though she's forgotten something.

"What it is?" I ask.

"The ants," she says, wagging the finger at me. "Stay away from them."

I laugh and assure her I will, and follow Melba out the door. As she passes my grandfather's room, Melba taps on the door and calls out, "Bye, Daddy."

In response, there is an audible grunt from inside the room. Melba just shakes her head and continues down the hall to collect Dory.

I am actually glad to have Dory's company on the way back to the Little's. It is beginning to get dark as I pull out of the drive behind Melba's van, and Dory is chatty. Apparently the pep talk Melba and I gave her about not being afraid of Charles Jenner has gotten her off on a tangent about those girls at school again. I remind her that it is still summer for a little while longer, and that she doesn't have to face them just yet, but she is on fire. I wonder if we unknowingly unleashed a monster.

I let her yammer on about the popular girls at her school while my mind drifts to the events of the day. I work my way backwards, thinking of the time I spent with Sandra, the conversation—loosely defined—I had with my grandfather, the closeness I felt to Melba and Dory today, and the hands I felt on mine while coming out of the ant bite-induced fog. Cute, tall, Darryl hands.

Oh, for God's sake, the man gave me a shot in the ass that very well may have saved my life. Of course I am putting him on some huge pedestal and thinking that he's beautiful, when in fact, I never really saw him. He was blurry the entire time he was there. Plus, he

108

drives a pick-up truck. Oh, and there's also the issue of Lucy, who is his wife or at the very least, his girlfriend. Not to mention the man lives in Mississippi. I, on the other hand, live in Washington . . . or actually Virginia, now that I have Nina's house. At any rate, it's far, far away from here.

My bites begin to itch again, and I reach down to scratch, which causes me to inadvertently swerve the car. I overcorrect to avoid crossing over into the other lane, but my front right tire catches on the shoulder and I have to overcorrect again to avoid running off the road completely. Dory is screaming, and by the time I get myself together and tell her to shut up, there are lights flashing behind me. Red and blue lights. Shit.

I pull off onto the shoulder as the police car stops and a swaggering officer disembarks from his vehicle. In the rearview mirror, I read the words *Sherrif's Department* on the grill of the car. The words must be written backwards in order to appear correct when viewed by offending vehicles. How considerate.

Dory is crying and saying something about her life flashing before her eyes, and for just a second I feel bad to have scared her. After all, her brothers were killed in a vehicular accident, and I bet just getting into a car after that was hard for them all. I reach over and pat her arm, and tell her I'm sorry and that everything is going to be okay.

By this time the officer is at my window, so I roll it down and begin to barrage him with apologies. He asks for my license and registration, but since I am driving a rental car I don't have one of those, so I hand him my license and rental agreement, and try to look innocent.

"You from Washington?" he asks upon reading my license. He pronounces it *Warshington*, which is a pet peeve of mine, but I decide to let it go this time, in the best interest of avoiding a ticket.

"Yes!" I proclaim a little too cheerfully. "I'm in town visiting family," I add proudly.

The officer leans down to look in the window at my passenger, who is still sniffling and muttering to herself. "That Dory Little?" the officer asks. "Dang, girl, you're all growed up!"

"Dory is my cousin!" I exclaim cheerfully, hoping that like everyone else in this town, they are great friends in which case he will surely not issue me a ticket. I am totally off the hook.

Just then, I hear shouting from up ahead, and look up to see my aunt's car parked a little way up the road on the shoulder and Melba charging towards my car like an angry bull. What have I done? I have put her daughter in harm's way and she'll probably never forgive me. After all this family has been through, here I am scaring the crap out of everyone by practically running off the road with one of their own in my car.

As she gets closer, however, her angst appears not to be directed at me, but at the policeman. I am so *on* the hook.

"You get away from that car, you hear me, Lowell Brown?" She is shouting and waving her arms frantically, like they say you should do if you're ever attacked by a bear—make yourself look bigger and more imposing, although I think Melba's got that covered without the dramatic arm movements.

The officer cowers and starts backing up toward his patrol car. He is holding both hands out in front of him, and from what I can tell is trying desperately to calm Melba down and ward off an offensive.

"Miz Little, ma'am, I realize this lady is kin to you, but I've been following her for at least a couple of miles. She ain't got her headlights turned on, and she ain't got her seatbelt buckled. Then she crossed over the center line and nearly ran into the ditch back yonder—"

Melba cuts him off. "Lowell, you have no earthly idea what all this girl has been through in the past twenty-four hours. You can't possibly write her a citation."

"Yeah," adds Dory, leaning across me, now evidently over her near-death experience. "She almost *died* today. Got eaten up by about a million fire ants and had to get shot up with Excedrin. You look at her legs, Lowell. She's got welps all over the place!"

"That sweet, wonderful boy Darryl Fortson came rushing out to my Daddy's to give my niece here a shot of *epinephrine*," Melba says, eyeballing Dory. "The girl could hardly breathe and he saved her life, which is more than I can say for you, *Deputy*." She speaks with such ire that I know there's a good story here, but I am wise enough not to ask. Not now, anyway. I decide to let my aunt do the talking.

"Miz Little, I'm just tryin' to do my job, and this here lady was not obeying the safe driving laws of the Great State of Miss'ippi. Niece or not, I feel that it is my obligation . . ."

"Oh, hush, Lowell. Your obligation my . . ."

"What's this?" comes Dory's voice from the passenger seat.

"Don't interrupt, baby," Melba says coolly. "We are just going to clear this little matter up and get on home. Daddy's going to wonder where in the Sam Hill we are."

"But it smells *awful*!" Dory persists, and I turn to see what she is talking about.

110

Oh. My. God. I had completely forgotten about the jar my grandfather had given me, but Dory has found it in the cup holder and removed the lid. The strong, pungent smell is wafting towards me and I know it won't be long before it reaches Deputy Brown's nose and then my aunt's. I grab the jar and replace the lid quickly, flashing Dory a look warning her to keep quiet. I am screwed. I will probably end up in some hellish women's prison facility in the middle-of-nowhere Mississippi, where my poor aunt and uncle will be too ashamed to even visit me on weekends. I can picture my mug shot already.

By some small miracle, however, neither Deputy Brown nor my aunt have paid much attention to what is going on inside the car. Melba is still giving Lowell a good talking-to, and it is becoming quite clear that there is no way I am going to end up with a ticket. This man is crumbling right in front of my eyes, and I can tell he will not dare cross Melba Little.

Finally it is Deputy Brown's turn to speak. "Well, Miz Jennings," he says very officially, looking again at my license. "I s'pose I can let you off with a written warning this time . . ."

Melba clears her throat loudly, prompting Lowell to amend his statement. "Or rather a verbal warning." His cheeks are turning red and he looks extremely uncomfortable as he turns back to me. "But if I see you disobeying the rules of the road again while you are in town, I will have no choice but to give you a citation." He tips his Ranger Rick-looking hat at my aunt and practically runs back to his car.

Melba gives me a triumphant look. "Buckle your seatbelt, Baby Girl, and cut on those lights. I'll see you at home." She starts to walk back to her van, but turns again and reappears at my window, holding out her hand. She doesn't appeal to me as the "slap me five" type, so I lay my hand in hers in a sort of sideways handshake. To my surprise, she shakes free of my hand and snaps her fingers. "The jar," she says, sounding more irritated than angry.

I take it from the cup holder again and pass it to her. "I didn't think you'd seen it," I say, ashamed. "It was supposed to help the ant bites. Please don't tell him you found it. I think he was actually trying to be nice."

"That *man*," Melba mutters under her breath. She then uncaps the jar and pours the contents onto the road, then ambles off toward her van.

We return to Melba and Dewayne's to find total pandemonium breaking out. There are five pick-up trucks parked haphazardly in the yard, and all kinds of noise coming from the house. I must have a look of sheer horror on my face as I get out of the car, because Melba takes one look at me and starts to howl.

"Nothin' to be scared of, Baby Girl," she laughs as she takes my hand and leads me to the door. "Just the rest of my boys come to meet their hooch-smuggling, drag-racing, ant-bitten cousin from up North." I have to laugh at the description—if I didn't know me I might even think I sound interesting—and feel somewhat delirious as I follow Melba and Dory into the house.

"Cuz!" shouts Neil Ray as we enter the kitchen. The room seems insanely crowded, even though I count only five people other than Dory, Melba, and myself. Neil Ray puts a strong hand on my shoulder and ushers me toward the throng of men. First up is Uncle Dewayne, who envelops me in a hug and shouts his relief that "those little bugger ants" didn't eat me up today.

Next, I am introduced to Lamar, who nods shyly and holds out a hand for me to shake. Stanley is right behind Lamar, and he is ready with a handshake and a big grin. I notice that Stanley looks almost like a clone of my grandfather. His size, broad build, brown eyes flecked with gold, and thick hair are all Charles Jenner. The only difference is that the smile seems totally at home on Stanley's face, whereas it is completely absent from my grandfather's.

Finally, Neil Ray introduces me to "Little Dewayne," whose nickname is completely contrary to the man towering over me. I have never before felt small, but in this room I do. Little Dewayne reaches his massive arms out to me and I worry for a moment that I am about to be squashed like a bug, but his embrace is gentle. When I pull away from Little Dewayne there are tears in his eyes, but Neil Ray quickly explains that while he may look like a grizzly bear, Little Dewayne has a heart like a marshmallow. I love him immediately.

Melba rushes around, sending grown men to the sink to wash up, putting on the coffee pot, and pulling various boxes and cartons out of the refrigerator and freezer. In no time, there are eight of us crowded around the kitchen table eating cookies and bowls of homemade peach and blueberry ice cream, and drinking incredibly strong coffee. I am assaulted by questions from my cousins—what I do for a living, what living in a big city is like, what having a famous mother was like. I do not split hairs by telling them that Nina was not really my mother. I owe her that much; after all, she did raise me.

112

I find myself laughing and answering even the questions I would ordinarily find invasive, because they all seem genuinely interested in getting to know me. When Neil Ray asks me if I have a boyfriend, however, I take an absurdly long time to swallow the bite of ice cream I'd just put in my mouth, then take a drawn out sip of coffee. I am procrastinating, but nobody at the table is fazed. They are all waiting patiently for my answer.

"No," I say definitively. I am all set to let that be it, but some unknown force inside my head decides to elaborate on that answer, and suddenly I have told them everything about Josh. *Everything.* When I finish my sordid tale of love lost, the room is silent. I have said way too much. Dory looks horrified.

Lamar, who has yet to say two words, is the first to speak, and I am initially taken back by his smooth baritone voice. The smallest of all the Little's sons has the biggest voice I have ever heard. "You went with a gay?" he asks. Evidently smooth only describes his voice.

My cheeks feel hot, and I suddenly wish I had not been so forthcoming.

"Well, yes, but in my defense I was completely unaware of his—preference while we were dating." I am stumbling over my words in an attempt to reclaim the dignity of the conversation. "I mean, as soon as he told me, that was it." I look to Dory and Melba, hoping that one of the women at the table will bail me out.

My savior turns out to be Little Dewayne. "Well, too bad for him. Anyone that chooses to let you get away ain't no kind of genius." I smile my thanks and try to change the subject, but Dory isn't ready to let it go.

"You must've been so heartbroken," she says dramatically, "and *mad.*"

I am mortified, and really do not want to continue this line of discussion. "Yes and no," I say quickly. "I just wanted him to be happy. He deserved to be happy." I shovel more ice cream into my mouth, which ironically is exactly what I did after Josh and I broke up.

Everyone at the table is staring at me, as if they are expecting me to pull another skeleton—or boyfriend—out of the closet. I decide to change the subject. "So, who's Lowell Brown, and why does your mother despise him so much?"

I look around for some sort of response, but everyone's eyes are on Stanley. Smiling Stanley, who is currently not smiling at all, but instead looking down at his empty bowl. Without looking up, he asks, "How do you know about Lowell Brown?"

113

"He pulled me over on the way back here, and would have given me a ticket if it hadn't been for your mother." I wait for the rest of the family to stop holding their breath, but no one does. They are waiting for Stanley to breathe first.

Stanley cuts his eyes over to his mother and the trace of a smile forms on his lips. "Mama?"

Melba is indignant. "I simply told Lowell that it was not acceptable to give my niece a ticket."

"You told him a lot more than that," Dory mutters under her breath. Neil Ray stifles a laugh.

"Mama, it's been a long time," Stanley admonishes. "Don't you think it's time to let that sleeping dog lie?"

Little Dewayne snorts. "That sleeping dog slept with Stanley's girlfriend."

I gasp. "Are you serious? How awful!" I feel so bad for this man who at first glance seems to percolate happiness. He obviously harbors some serious pain underneath that cheery exterior.

"It's not the girlfriend I miss so much," Stanley says, with a smile that belies his heartache. "It's my best friend."

"Lowell Brown was your best friend?" I ask, deciding that having a boyfriend who turned out to be gay maybe isn't quite as terrible as having your best friend steal your girlfriend.

Lamar, evidently, disagrees. "Least she wasn't a gay."

"Well," Little Dewayne says, again saving me from another tragic turn in the conversation, "it sounds like Mama took care of Lowell Brown, and I've got a family to go see after. I can't wait to tell my kids all about their cosmopolitan cousin come to town. Welcome to the family, Missi. We sure are glad to have you."

He kisses his mother on his way out, and Lamar and Stanley get up to leave as well. Stanley gives me a friendly pat and tells me he'll see me at supper on Sunday.

"Oh, that reminds me," my aunt says, snapping her fingers. "I forgot to tell Little Dewayne that Darryl is coming to supper, too."

"I'll tell him, Mama," Stanley assures her as the door closes behind him.

"He bringing Lucy?" Neil Ray asks, stopping at the door leading to the back of the house.

"I told him to," Melba answers.

Neil Ray turns to me. "That Lucy is really something. You'll love her."

"I'm sure I will," I respond with false optimism. I am suddenly drained of energy, and want nothing more than to climb into bed. I notice that all of the men have fled the room. The driveway has three fewer pick-up trucks than before, and Uncle Dewayne and Neil Ray have disappeared to other parts of the house. Dory, Melba, and I load the dishwasher and wipe off the table, and then Melba shoos us out with orders to get some rest.

I head straight for my room, or rather, Clayton and Jerome's room. I flop down on the bed and wish my ant bites would stop their infernal itching. Too bad Melba dumped the moonshine. I have a feeling my grandfather knows a thing or two about killing pain.

A sound comes from the doorway and I look over to see Dory standing there. "Hey," I say. "Come on in."

Dory walks over to the dresser, fingers a couple of the trophies, and joins me on the bed.

"Is it weird for you, having me stay in this room?" I sit up and turn to face her. "Because if it is, I completely understand, and would be happy to stay somewhere else."

Dory shakes her head and looks past me to the menagerie of baseball keepsakes. "It's actually nice to have someone in here. For the first time in forever it doesn't make me think of what we lost. It makes me think of what we found."

I feel choked up, not having expected Dory to say something quite so eloquent. It occurs to me that the way I feel about Dory—annoyance alternating with affection—is probably something comparable to sisterly love.

She folds her hands in her lap and looks down at them. "You know, I don't have very many girlfriends. I think most people don't know what to say to me, so they don't say anything at all. Nobody wants to get too close to the girl with two dead brothers and a grandfather who's crazier than a June bug in May." She takes a deep breath, and I let her continue.

"I mean, I got Bobbie Jean, and she's great. We've been best friends since kindergarten, and I know she'd do anything for me. She doesn't treat me any different from the next person, and it's easy to forget everything else when I'm with her. I just don't know what I'd do without her." I think about Maggie and know exactly what she means.

"And I know you've only been my cousin for two days, but I already don't know what I'd do without you." All I can do is smile at this adorable person through the tears that perch precariously in the corners of my eyes. I am at a total loss for how quickly and openly I have been accepted into this family, when I never felt completely accepted by Nina in the thirty-three years we were a family.

There are no words to accurately express how I feel, so I squeeze her little hands and just say, "Thanks."

CHAPTER FOURTEEN

I wake the following morning feeling like I've slept for a year. I have been so tired for so long, that I think I'd honestly forgotten what it feels like to *not* be tired. The sun is streaming through the curtains, but when I look at my watch I discover that it's only eight o'clock.

I lay in bed letting various fragments of information wash over me. The story I came to Mississippi looking for is not in any way the story I found, but in so many ways it has helped me piece together the person I am. I have always felt as though my life has been lived on one of those rope bridges suspended high above a dark, rocky gorge. With each disappointment, failure, and criticism that I encounter—and God knows there have been plenty—the bridge sways and seems to sink lower into the chasm, reaching closer and closer to the danger below, making me lose sight completely of who I once was or wanted to be.

On that day, on my last birthday, I think I was at my lowest point ever. I was completely dissatisfied with my life, my job, and my relationships with other people, but what was I doing to change it? Absolutely nothing. Since then, I have been dangling precariously, not making any move to save myself . . . that is, until the day before yesterday, when I got on a plane and came to Mississippi.

I feel now that with every step I take here, with every new person I meet, I am slowly rising a little bit higher. On one end of this bridge is the life I left behind, and on the other end is the life I want to have, and it is up to me which direction I choose to climb out.

Right now I have only one direction to choose when getting out of this bed, since on one side of it is an actual wall. I push back the covers, throw my legs over the side, scratch the ant bites on my ankles, and stand. I have some very important things to do today.

After a refreshing shower and a thick coat of Benadryl cream on my bites, I head downstairs. Melba and Dory are at the table eating breakfast, and I join them, grabbing a big, fluffy, flaky, biscuit from a platter as I sit down.

"Good morning, sunshine," Melba smiles, sliding a jar of honey towards me.

"What's the honey for?" I ask, pulling the biscuit apart.

Dory looks at me sideways. "For your biscuit. You never had a biscuit before?"

I laugh. "I have, but never with honey on it. I usually have jelly." Just to be gracious, I spoon some honey over the top of the biscuit and take a generous bite. It is like heaven, warm and buttery, and proceeds to literally melt in my mouth. I will never put jelly on another biscuit as long as I live.

I ask Melba and Dory what their plans for the day are, and they inform me that they both have to be at the restaurant for the lunch and dinner shifts. "Artie's great at gettin' the food to the table, hot and tasty, but he's not much for cleaning up or bookkeeping, so I've got to see to things today. You think you can stay out of harm's way?" I nod. She grins, eyes shining, and starts clearing the table.

"I'll do kitchen duty here this morning," I tell her, reaching for another amazing biscuit.

Melba stops short and looks at me, for a moment speechless. "Do what?" she finally asks.

"The breakfast dishes," I tell her. "Leave them on the table and I will wash and put them away. You have more important things to do."

Dory snorts, but Melba is clearly touched. "I'm not sure I've ever walked out of this kitchen without cleaning it up first."

"Well, try it," I say. Melba sets the plate she is holding back on he table and heads out of the kitchen to get ready for work. On her way past, she leans down and kisses the top of my head, just like I'd seen her do to Dory before. I look to Dory, who is grinning at me.

"What are you going to do today?" Dory asks. "I wish I didn't have to work. I'd rather hang around with you, since school starts up next week and this is my last weekday of freedom 'til next May."

I feel a little bit sorry for her, but could actually use some time alone today. "I've got a few things to do. Can you give me directions to get back to the road I came into Pritchard on when I came from the airport?"

Dory looks shocked. "Tell me you're not leaving already! You just got here!"

"No, no, no," I tell her, not having meant to upset her. "I've just got somewhere I need to go." I really don't want to explain, so I offer, "Maybe I can come get you after the dinner shift so you don't have to stay too late with your mom. Then we can hang out."

Dory brightens. "Really? And do what?"

I hadn't thought that far. "Uh, watch *Sex and the City* reruns?" I quickly conjure. "And maybe tomorrow I could take you back-to-school shopping."

She gets this happy, excited look on her face that reminds me of a puppy about to get a treat. "*Shopping*? I'd love to! I bet Mama'd even let me skip work to do that! Saturday usually isn't too busy. And there's a Walmart not too far away . . ."

Walmart is not what I had in mind. "Not school supplies, Dory. Clothes. How far is the closest mall?"

Dory shakes her head. "Have to go all the way to Jackson for that," she says glumly.

"I'll talk to your mom. Maybe she'd let us anyway."

Dory can hardly contain herself, and runs out the kitchen door squealing, off to call Bobbie Jean before she goes to work. I start cleaning up the kitchen, actually enjoying the chore knowing how much it means to my aunt. When I am done, my fingers ache from scouring the biscuit pan and a skillet that had scrambled eggs encrusted in it, but the kitchen shines and even smells clean. Maybe this is a hidden talent of mine that I've just never tapped into. I feel truly proud of myself, and head upstairs to get my cell phone.

It feels so good to talk to Maggie that my entire body is buzzing with energy. I miss her so much, even though it's only been a few days since I last saw her. I usually talk to her so frequently that she knows almost moment-to-moment what is happening in my life—which, more often than not, is *nothing*—and now suddenly more has happened in the past couple of days than in the entire six years that I've known Maggie, I have to dump it all on her in one telephone conversation. Several times during the call she has to put me on hold to answer an incoming call at the law firm, so it takes a while, but finally we are caught up.

"Wow! It's like a Lifetime movie," she whispers into the phone. "After all that with Nina, you still have a mom! Missi, this is positively the craziest turn of events I could have imagined. How do you feel about it all?"

I tell her about the incessant string of raw emotion that seems to work its way through my heart and my mind throughout the day. Maggie listens intently, cutting in occasionally and calling me Ms. Blackwater, both to throw off whoever is within earshot and to poke fun at my given name, which I just finished telling her about.

When I finish my story, Maggie sighs. "Wow. Sandra sounds really special, and your aunt sounds like an amazing woman. That paramedic sounds nice, too."

"You mean the *married* paramedic with a gorgeous wife named Lucy?"

"Bummer," Maggie retorts. "Anyway, it's almost too much to digest. I can't imagine how you must feel . . . uh, Ms. Blackwater." Her voice gets significantly louder. "I'll have one of our clerks contact you to gather more information."

I laugh. "You'll have to do that, Maggie. The next time I come down here to visit, maybe you can come with me!" I can just see her fraternizing with my redneck cousins and eating Melba's food until she makes herself sick.

"You mean you're coming home?" Maggie sounds surprised.

"Of course I'm coming home. I need to look for a job, need to see after Nina's house, need to hang out with my best friend . . ."

"You're loaded," she quips. "Remember? You don't need a job."

"Seriously? I am thirty-three years old. What do you think I'm going to do, retire?"

"You just sound so happy, and you finally have a family like you always wanted. I just wonder if you'll meet some hot farmhand named Bubba, buy some land with your millions, and pop out a few kids."

"Really," I say impatiently, "you know me better than that. I'll spend a few more days here and then head back north. I'll use the money to come visit whenever I want."

"Okay then, good. Because God, I miss you! This place is about as much fun as a pelvic exam without you . . . uh, Ms. Blackwater," she says again loudly. "Shit," she whispers. "I think I'm busted. Call me later!" The line goes dead and I can envision the scene of Maggie sparring with Richard over having a personal telephone conversation during work hours.

I pull a pair of socks out of the dresser, having decided to wear tennis shoes today to ward off ant attacks. As I sit on the edge of the bed to tie my shoes, there is a knock on the door. "You decent?" comes Melba's voice.

"Nope, but I'm dressed," I say, and she pokes her head in. She nods at my choice of footwear. "Good thinkin'," she commends. "Well, Little Bit and I are off to feed the masses. She said you wanted to pick her up later?"

"Only if it's okay with you" I say, suddenly thinking that I would be taking away one of her few valuable employees, and that perhaps I should have asked Melba about it first.

"She's like a kid in a candy store, she's so excited. She also said something about you taking her into town to go shopping?" She steps all the way inside the door, making the room feel about half its size.

"I'm sorry, Aunt Melba, I really should have discussed it with you first. I didn't mean to cause a problem."

Melba takes a step toward me, turns, and sinks down on the bed. "Come, sit," she says, and I am afraid I am in serious trouble. I sit beside her, and she begins to cry. Nina was right. I *am* an ass, an inconsiderate, unthinking ass.

"Melba, please don't be upset with me. I just . . . she said she wanted to hang out with me, and I thought it would be fun. I didn't realize she has to start school on Monday, and she seems a little bummed out about it, so I figured I could take her shopping and maybe she'll be a little bit more excited to go back to school. New clothes always give me a fresh perspective." I finally work up the courage to look my aunt in the eyes, and realize that she is smiling through her tears.

"I'm not angry in the least," Melba says, pulling a Kleenex from the sleeve of her shirt and dabbing at her eyes. "Sometimes I think Dory's the forgotten child. She's the baby, the only girl, and where at this age her brothers were playing *Field of Dreams* out in the yard, Dory's stuck at the restaurant with me during almost all of her free time. After Clayton and Jerome died, she had to grow up real fast, and I know she's had a harder time than any of the rest of us. Her whole world got tossed upside down, and she was too young to understand any of it. I used to worry about Neil Ray in the same way, but his spirit is still intact. With Dory I'm not so sure sometimes, but since you got here, she's had a sparkle in her eyes that I don't see very often." She sniffles and shifts her weight on the bed.

"I know she's always wanted a sister, and God seems to have sent you at just the right time. She's got two years of high school left, and I'd love for her to go to junior college, at the very least.

121

She's said before that she wants to be a teacher, and I think she'd be good at that. Dory is so good with children, especially little ones, but I think these days you need to go to a four-year college to teach, and I'm afraid she'll worry that Dewayne and I can't function without her. Maybe that's true, but I'd like to try, for her sake." Her sniffles become sobs again, and I can't help myself. I instinctively put my arm around her expansive shoulders.

She pats my leg, whips out another Kleenex from her magic sleeve, and blows her nose so loudly that I am startled and my arm recoils. Her voice is nasal now, but she continues.

"To make a short story long, I think spending time with you will be wonderful for Dory, and of course you may take her shopping tomorrow. It's exactly the sort of thing a mother ought to do with her daughter, but I'm too busy to do it. Besides, you can probably pick out clothes for a sixteen-year-old a whole lot better than a big ol' hillbilly like me. I'll have some cash at the end of today, so I'll give that to you in the morning."

"Not necessary," I tell her sincerely. "This was my idea, and I've always daydreamed about having a sister, too. This is what I want, and that's all there is to it."

Melba hugs me so tightly that I think my ribs are going to shatter, and I am aware of a squeaking sound, which at first I think may be the air getting squeezed out of my body. When Melba lets go, however, the squeaking continues, and we both realize it is coming from the hallway. I get up and peek out the door to find Dory, who has been eavesdropping, squealing with delight and doing some sort of dance. I clear my throat, and she immediately stops, her cheeks turning scarlet.

"So, I guess we're on for tomorrow," I say calmly.

Dory rushes forward, kisses me on the cheek, and then goes straight into her mother's arms. "Mama, I love you, I love you, I love you!"

Melba's eyes glisten as she returns the sentiment. "Let's get going, Baby Girl. We're gonna be late, and I'm not sure Artie can handle another day on his own." She heads out of the room, stopping to cup my cheek in her large hand. "Have a good day, angel," she tells me, and ambles down the hallway toward the stairs.

Dory squeals once more, tells me to pick her up at six, and follows her mother down the hall. "Mama?" she says, catching up to Melba.

Melba turns around at the top of the stairs. "What is it, baby?"

"You don't have to worry about me. I don't feel like the forgotten child. I feel like I'm pretty lucky to have you, Daddy,

122

Little Dewayne, Stanley, Lamar, Neil Ray, Sandra, and now Missi. That's more than a lot of people have."

Melba embraces her daughter, and I know the magic sleeve is about to produce another Kleenex. I close my door gently and give them their moment, thinking about what I'm going to do with my day.

Forty-five minutes later I reach my destination. It's not really that far, but the directions Dory wrote down for me leave something to be desired—go back through town, turn left at the old slaughterhouse, which is now ironically a recycling drop-off, then right at Roscoe Waller's junkyard—plus, I get delayed by some cows just casually crossing the road without any supervision whatsoever.

At any rate, it takes a bit longer than I expected, but I am here. I park the Lincoln and brace myself for the Arctic blast as I step inside the door.

"Well, hey, girl! I was hopin' to see my friend again. What's the good word?" Dolly cheerfully inquires, coming out from behind the counter to greet me. "You find what you were lookin' for?"

"You won't believe it, Dolly . . ." I begin, but she slaps her leg and holds up a hand.

"Hold that thought, darlin'. When someone tells me I'm not going to believe something, I know my full attention is required. Let's do this properly." She grabs two Cokes before shutting all the refrigerator doors, locks the cash register, takes a couple of Snickers bars from their safe place behind the counter, and leads me out the door.

We take our seats by the wading pool and remove our socks and shoes. It is hot again today, but not as oppressive as it was the day I met Dolly. As I set my feet in the water, Dolly gasps.

"Sweet Jesus, what happened to your legs?" She leans over to inspect them closely. "Oh, honey, you got into the ants, didn't you?"

I quickly fill her in on my recent medical emergency, but just thinking about it makes the bites itch all over again. I begin to scratch frantically, and Dolly jumps up from her chair. "I've got just the thing you need. Be right back!"

I want to yell after her that I've already been told about the hooch remedy and narrowly escaped arrest for possessing it, but she disappears into the store before I can get the words out. A moment later, she returns with a small tube of ointment and hands it to me.

123

"No freaking way," I tell her firmly when I read the label. "That is not meant for insect bites . . . on my *legs*!"

"Don't be silly, Missi," Dolly says dismissively. "Preparation H has a million uses besides the obvious. Taking the itch out of insect bites is just the tip of the iceberg." She opens the tube, squeezes some onto her index finger, and dabs it all over my feet and ankles. "You know, beauty queens used to use this stuff to tighten sagging under-eye skin."

"Is that why you have it?" I ask, thinking that Dolly's skin is gorgeous for a woman her age, especially one who smokes.

"No, darlin', I've got it for the usual reason. Dolly's got the 'rhoids." She finishes doctoring my wounds as I try very hard not to laugh out loud. Dolly isn't one to mince words.

"Alrighty, then," she says, finally twisting the top off her Coke and settling back in her chair. "Time's a wasting. Scoop the poop."

I open my own Coke and lean forward in my chair to describe the events of the past three days. Just as she had the other day, Dolly listens with her entire body. She grabs my arm to convey surprise when I tell her about Sandra, never breaks eye contact except to squeeze them shut as her tears roll down her cheeks as I recount the horrible crime committed against Sandra, and laughs so hard her whole body shakes when I tell her about my curmudgeonly grandfather, the jar of illicit liquid he bestowed upon me, and my run-in with the local Sherriff's Deputy.

At one point, a rusty old Ford truck pulls into the station and a sweaty, dirty man gets out and heads for the door to the shop. "Sorry, Floyd," Dolly hollers to him. "Shop's closed."

"What for?" he asks, one hand on the handle and ready to go in. "I need somethin' cold to drink."

"Copperhead's loose inside. We're just waiting for animal control to come fish it out. Unless you want to give it a go." Dolly looks at me with a wink, and Floyd hightails it back to his truck.

"Men," she says amusedly, clicking her tongue. "Now, where were we?"

When I finally conclude my account of the previous seventy-two hours, Dolly looks down at her reflection in the pool and shakes her head. "I just cannot imagine how you must feel about all of this. This is a barrelful of information that I bet you weren't expecting. I have to say, though, you seem . . . good. When you came into the store today, I knew something good had happened."

"You did? How?"

She smiles and leans back again. "You seem taller, lighter. Like the weight of the world has been lifted from your shoulders."

I consider this. "You might be right. I mean, I have a family—a big one—after thinking I'd lost the little dysfunctional one I grew up with." I choose my words carefully, not wanting to sound thankless. "But the weight isn't totally gone, it's just shifted a little. Now I feel so guilty that I was never able to appreciate Nina for what she *did* do for me, even if it was dishonest and unorthodox."

Dolly nods, as if she understands completely. "You're in an emotional pickle," she says, "and you can do one of two things. Leave the pickle on your plate where it will get limp and brown, or eat the damn thing and be done with it."

"Well, in that case," I say, unwrapping my Snickers bar, "I suppose I'll eat the pickle."

Dolly grins at me. "That's my girl."

Dolly and I sit with our feet in the pool until the bottoms of our toes are pale and wrinkled. She has chased away three more customers with her snake story, but nobody seems all that upset or even surprised.

I have monopolized the entire conversation, just as I had the last time I was here, and realize that although I feel I've known Dolly my whole life, I know almost nothing about her, other than that she suffers from both hot flashes and hemorrhoids.

"Tell me about you, Dolly," I implore. "What's your story?"

Dolly waves off the request, saying that there's nothing to tell, but I am stubborn. "I told you every last detail of my life—even that my last boyfriend was gay! You owe me a good story, too."

Her expression softens, and I can tell she's going to cave. She shakes her pack of cigarettes and puts one in her mouth, but does not light it. She looks at me out of the corner of her eye. "Just remember sweet girl. You asked."

I am breathless after listening to Dolly's life story. She was born and raised in a tiny town in west Texas. She was daughter of a schizophrenic mother and a highly abusive father, and managed to marry someone who was both. Her husband was an alcoholic who hid every fork, knife, pair of scissors, and any other sharp object in the house, at the bottom of the kitty litter pan in order to keep the "people that wanted to kill him" from finding and using them. He would stay up all night, wandering the house and peering out of windows, and to keep himself alert would drink a pot of coffee spiked with whiskey—or as Dolly put it, a bottle of whiskey spiked with coffee.

Whenever Dolly would try to intervene and put him to bed, close the curtains, or hide his liquor, he would accuse her of being "one of them," and beat her senseless. One night after being thrown to the floor in close proximity to the cat's litter box, Dolly reached in among the lumps and granules and found a carving knife just in time to prevent her husband from hitting her over the head with a rum bottle. He was declared dead at the scene when the police arrived, and everyone in town knew him well enough to know that Dolly had acted in self-defense. Even so, she left Texas and used every penny she had to buy the filling station in Mississippi and create a new life for herself here. This was a little less than ten years ago, so Dolly endured her nightmare of a marriage for a long time before it was over.

I ask if she and her husband had ever had children together—I still have no idea what his name was, because she never called him by it, just a string of *he's, his',* and *him's*—and she cries as she tells me that she was once pregnant with what she knew in her heart was a baby girl, but that she miscarried after a particularly bad thrashing compliments of her husband. She took every measure after that *not* to get pregnant again, because she was terrified of bringing a child into an abusive household, not to mention the fact that the poor child would have mental illness on both sides of the family to worry about inheriting.

"I would never have guessed you'd gone through all of that, Dolly," I tell her, finally loosening my grip on the arms of my lawn chair. "From the moment I met you, you've exuded a zest for life and an inner peace like I have never seen in another human being. I would never have guessed what you've been through. I'd think anyone would need therapy after all that to help sort it out."

Her crying subsides, and she finally lights her cigarette. She closes her eyes as she takes a long drag, and actually smiles as she blows out a long line of smoke.

"This place has been all the therapy I need, darlin'. It's all mine, gives me a place to go most days, and folks around here are usually so nice that I feel like I have a thousand friends." She looks up into the cloudless sky. "People generally find me a little bit strange because I'm here on Sundays instead of sittin' front and center at the Baptist church, but I have a strong relationship with God, and I always have—we just chat off and on all day every day instead of just on Sunday morning when half the world is yankin' on His ear. I believe that He has a path He wants each of us to walk, and mine has just had a few more potholes than most. Ultimately though, my path led me here, and lucky for me so did yours."

126

"Dolly?"

"What, sweet girl?"

"I want to be you when I grow up."

Dolly smiles and kicks at the water with both of her feet. "No you don't, baby. It's so worth being you that it ain't even funny. You just wait. But that is most definitely the highest compliment I have ever been paid, and I love you for that, Missi."

My heart expands in my chest, and a warm feeling washes over me. It's good to be loved.

Eventually I leave Dolly to her work and head back to Pritchard. I don't want to let a day go by without seeing Sandra, but I am nervous about showing up at my grandfather's without the moral support of Melba or Dory.

On my way, I drive through the center of town and pass Grits n' Greens, which is packed. This makes me happy for Melba, and I wonder where all of the patrons have come from.

When I pull up next to Charles Jenner's house, Fergie is sitting under the carport. It occurs to me that either my grandfather has some bizarre crush on the Dutchess of York, or that he's into popular music, but as I get out of my car I see the raised words on the side of the thing and realize that the tractor is a Massey Ferguson. There you go.

I approach the door nervously, but the rusted out pick-up truck is absent so it's possible that no one is home. I knock on the back door and wait a couple of minutes, but I get no answer. Maybe my grandfather and Sandra went somewhere together.

The breeze kicks up and I decide to wait a while. Avoiding anthills, I make my way to a massive old oak tree, under which hangs a rickety-looking swing. I take my chances that it will actually hold me and sit down. I have not sat in a swing of any sort since I was probably ten years old, and it is nothing short of heaven—the shade of the spreading branches, the breeze in my hair, the fresh farm smells, and the rhythm of the swing moving back and forth. I close my eyes and almost rock myself to sleep, when I hear a sound over my shoulder.

I turn and open my eyes to see Sandra coming out of the house. When she sees me she stops and beams. She has the best smile, and it thrills me that she is happy to see me.

"Hi, Missi," she calls out, and waves. She stops a couple of times on her way over to the tree and inspects the ground. She squats like a child, scratching her chest with one hand while waving the other over the blades of grass beneath her. She picks something up and continues toward me.

"What are you looking for?" I ask, curious and wanting to know her every thought.

"Four-leaf clovers," she says, holding out her hand. In it is a perfect four-leaf clover, and her thick fingers cradle it as if it were a baby bird. "I'm good at finding them."

"Those are supposed to bring good luck. Something wonderful will happen to you."

Sandra looks at me kind of sideways. "Want me to help you find one?"

"I'd love that," I say, and climb out of the swing. Sandra leads me to a large, grassy area, and sits down. I sit beside her and start scanning the ground for four-leaf clovers. I see a million with three leaves, but after ten minutes have found none with four. I suppose that's why they are supposed to be good luck—you have to have luck just to find one.

I look over at Sandra who now has four of them nestled in the palm of one hand while she meticulously surveys the patch of clover. I study her patience and then emulate it. My fingers graze the tops of the tiny green plants, pushing them apart gently to uncover the ones hiding beneath. I breathe slowly and deeply, listening to the quiet and perusing the clover, until my hand freezes. I lean closer and can hardly believe my eyes.

"I found one!" I squeal, startling Sandra and completely disrupting the peace.

I pluck it out of the ground and hold it out to show her. She grins.

"Good job," she says proudly. "Now you have to press it."

"Like this?" I ask, pressing it between my palms.

Sandra looks at me, amused, and shakes her head. "Come on."

She pushes herself up off the ground and I follow her into the house. We go back to her room and she pulls a dictionary from one of her bookshelves. A tasseled bookmark hangs from the book, and Sandra opens to the marked page to reveal two waxed-paper sheets between which rests a half-dozen four-leaf clovers. She places the new ones in the book and flips to several other pages hiding more waxed paper and dozens more clovers.

"Holy crap, Sandra," I say without thinking. She looks at me sternly—just like a mother would—but doesn't say anything.

She closes the book. "I'll take good care of it," she tells me, and I know she will.

I spend the next long while in the chair meant just for me, playing dominoes with Sandra on a TV tray. The shadows are getting long and my stomach is rumbling, which reminds me that except for the Snickers bar and Coke at Dolly's, I have not eaten a thing since breakfast. I heard my grandfather's truck pull in a while ago, but he has not come in to address either Sandra or me. A strange smell—hot cooking oil or something—wafts down the hall and into Sandra's room.

"I think your dinner is about ready," I say to her. "We'd better call it a day. Thanks for letting me win a few games this time."

She smiles. "You're welcome, Missi." I seriously think she *did* let me win.

We walk together to the kitchen, where the smell is really strong and, frankly, nauseating. My grandfather stands at the stove with a spatula in one hand and a saltshaker in the other. He is cooking what might be fish.

"Hi," I offer, not going any farther into the room than the doorway. He does not look at me or respond other than to give an almost imperceptible nod.

Sandra has pulled napkins and silverware from a drawer and is setting the table for three. I am *so* not staying for dinner. It would be horribly uncomfortable sitting across the dinner table from a surly old man who seriously lacks conversational skills, not to mention that there is not a chance in hell I am eating whatever is in that skillet.

"Well, I'd better go. I told Dory I'd pick her up at work after the dinner shift." I hope I don't come off rude—I don't want to hurt Sandra's feelings, but I thankfully have not been issued an official invitation, either, so I pick up my keys and go to hug her goodbye.

"You'll stay," my grandfather barks. He turns from the stove to face me and waves the spatula in the air. "She don't have company for supper very often." He points the spatula now in Sandra's direction. "Stay for her."

He returns to the stove and aggressively shakes salt onto the fish. Sandra has finished setting the table and now pours tea into glasses. I set my keys down and sit at the table, noticing that Big Dog and Little Dog are in their usual spot on the pink couch, but have not moved or made a sound since I entered the room. Not only are they getting used to me, but I might be getting used to *them*, too.

My grandfather comes to the table with his pan and the spatula and sets a large hunk of fish on my plate. He then serves Sandra and himself before setting the hot skillet in the sink. He turns the faucet on, and as the water hits the pan it makes a hissing sound and causes steam to billow out of the sink. He tosses the spatula on the counter and joins Sandra and me at the table.

I feel like I might throw up, but pick up my fork in an attempt to be polite.

Charles Jenner snaps at me. "We ain't said the blessin', yet." He takes one of Sandra's hands and closes his eyes. I quickly drop my fork and put my hands in my lap.

The blessing consists of some mumbled, incoherent, angry-sounding words from my grandfather and then a resounding "Amen" from Sandra. I wait for them both to pick up their forks before I dare to pick mine up again.

They start eating quietly, but ever the procrastinator I put off the first bite to sip some tea. I take a drink, which causes me to gag and cough, and my grandfather shoots me an annoyed look. "It went down the wrong way," I apologize, but in actuality it is the worst tea I have ever tasted. It is twice as sugary as Melba's and has an absurd amount of lemon juice in it—not the fresh-squeezed kind, either. The fish may actually be the safer choice.

I cut into the dark, oily fish with my fork and lift it to my mouth. It smells pungent, and when I finally get up the nerve to put it inside my mouth, I have to swallow it whole. I lived on canned tuna and ramen noodles for much of my adult life, but this is absurd. I have no idea how I am going to make it through the rest of the meal without vomiting.

Sandra and my grandfather seem to have no trouble eating it, though, which makes me feel bad, so I take another bite. Heinous.

"What kind of fish is this?" I ask, putting off bite number three for as long as possible.

"Catfish," answers my grandfather without lifting his head.

"Oh," I say casually, but in my head I envision a bottom-feeder with long whiskers, which does not help my situation at all. I remember as a child not liking certain things that Nina or the housekeeper made for dinner, but my solution was always to mix the offending food item with something more palatable. Meatloaf, for example, is a whole lot better when hidden inside a big dollop of mashed potatoes. Peas? Try them with a bite of buttered rice, and you almost don't know they're there. The trouble now is that the catfish stands alone on my plate. There are no potatoes. There is no rice. I would even consider eating grits right now. This calls for drastic measures.

"Excuse me," I say, trying to sound as polite as I can. "Do you have any ketchup?"

Sandra kindly gets up from the table to retrieve it from the refrigerator, but my grandfather narrows his eyes. "What for?"

"Um, up north? We eat our fish with ketchup." I am so unconvincing, but I stammer on, trying to salvage my only hope of ingesting the catfish. "Well, actually, we eat it with cocktail sauce, which is ketchup mixed with a little bit of horseradish . . . but plain ketchup will be fine. Thank you, Sandra." I take the ketchup from her and pour a generous amount on my plate.

"You ask me, it ruins perfectly good fish," grumbles the naysayer across the table.

I shrug in mild disagreement, but manage to force every bite of catfish—and a few errant bones—down, thanks to the Heinz. When I finish, I smile proudly.

"You musta liked it," my grandfather says, assessing my empty plate. "I can send some back to Melba's place with you. I caught six of 'em over at Skinny O'Dell's pond yesterday."

Uh oh. I am in trouble. "Oh, that's really nice of you. I'm definitely full, though. Thanks." I make a big show of leaning back in the chair and rubbing my belly as though I'd just finished Thanksgiving dinner. I lean a little too far, however, and the next thing I know I am on the floor on my back, looking up at the fluorescent lights on the ceiling.

Sandra jumps from her chair and helps me up off the floor. I am mortified, and more than a little bit irritated that my grandfather looks amused. My cheeks are blazing, and my heart is racing.

"On that note," I say abruptly, "I should help clear the table and get going. Dory is expecting me."

I carry my plate and still-full tea glass to the sink. Sandra brings the rest of the dishes to me while her father remains at the table watching us clean up. I rinse, Sandra stacks the plates in the dishwasher, and he just sits there.

When we are done, Sandra says she has to go feed Missi the cat, so I give her a hug, issue a blunt thanks and good night to my grandfather, and gratefully head out the door. Outside, I take a deep breath and look out at the fields in the waning sunlight. Everything has a golden glow—even the old pickup truck. It's not what I am used to, but it's pretty. Just grass, trees, and sky as far as I can see. I slap at my neck. Evidently, there are mosquitoes, too. I run for the Lincoln and jump inside.

I walk through the front door of Grits 'n Greens and immediately discover that I am still hungry. The aroma of fried food and something sweet that I can't put my finger on, along with the warmth of the place and friendly chatter of the customers, bombard my senses.

Dory rushes from a table with a tray full of dirty dishes, deposits them in the kitchen, and proceeds to refill at least ten glasses of tea. Someone asks her for coffee, but before she can respond she sees me and comes running over.

"Oh, Missi! Don't leave without me." She is breathless. "We have been so busy tonight! I think the whole county decided to go out for supper, but it's starting to clear out. Sit down and I'll get you somethin' to eat."

"Can I help?" I ask, wanting more than anything to eat some of Melba's cooking, but knowing I couldn't just sit and watch my aunt and cousin work their tails off the way my grandfather had earlier.

Dory's eyes light up, and she drags me by the arm to the kitchen. She instructs me to wash my hands and put on an apron, hands me a coffee pot, and charges me with refilling every mug in the place.

"What if someone wants decaf?" I ask.

"Missi," Dory answers patiently, "this is Mississippi. Nobody drinks decaf!"

And with that, I get to work. Incidentally, nobody asks for decaf.

At one point I almost crash head-on into Melba as I head back into the kitchen for a fresh pot of coffee. She is startled, but when she sees me her face lights up. "Well, now," she says cheerfully, "this I like." She shouts introductions to Artie, who is up to his armpit stirring a huge pot of something, and Nelson, the dishwasher. I say hello, grab a full pot off of the burner, and return to my task.

It is more than an hour later that things finally settle down. Word got out that Melba's dessert special today was old-fashioned banana pudding—the kind with actual meringue on top—and people have come out of the woodwork to eat here. What I can't get over is how charged the atmosphere is the entire time. Just as it was on my first visit here, there is a constant buzz of friendly conversation punctuated by laughter and smiles, and that indescribable feeling of being a part of something . . . like a family, only not related. Maybe this is what community is at the heart of the definition.

The people that are eating together here somehow seem to mesh with the ones around them, and there is cross-fraternization between tables, which would never happen at a restaurant in D.C., where people are so intent on their own thing, on their own group. I have to say, though, that I like it. I really like it. Before people even know that I am Melba's niece, they include me, talk to me, and want to know me.

I finally set the coffee pot down on a table and fall into an adjacent chair. I am physically exhausted, but my brain is on hyper drive. I am trying to commit at least twenty new names to memory, while savoring the wonderful feeling that overwhelms me.

I close my eyes and smile, and the smell of bananas, vanilla, and cooked sugar seem to have permanently taken up residence inside my nose. I open my eyes, however, to find a bowl of steaming banana pudding resting on the table in front of me. Dory is sitting across from me, and she is smiling, too.

"Dory, where did you get that?" I ask in a sharp whisper, as though she robbed a bank or something. "I thought that was long gone. Mr. Bennett had to settle on peach pie, and he'd driven twenty miles for banana pudding!"

"Mama put it aside for you a while ago, and just heated it up a smidge." She leans across and sweeps a fluff of meringue off the top with her finger. "Hurry up and eat it. It's not nearly as good cold."

I feel as though I've just been given an unexpected gift. Melba deprived a paying customer his banana pudding in order to save *me* a huge, warm bowl of it. I happily accept my gift and tear into it, thinking that I would eat catfish with ketchup every day if it meant having Melba's banana pudding afterwards.

Every new thing that I eat here tastes even better than the last—with the exception being, of course, the catfish—and I practically lick the bowl clean. Dory watches me with a mixture of delight and amazement. If I stay here much longer, I am going to be enormous.

"Mama, Missi didn't like it one bit," Dory calls back to her mother.

A loud "Ha!" echoes from the kitchen, and Melba emerges. She is sweaty and the hair around her temples curls in damp ringlets. She wipes her forehead with the back of her hand and tucks a dishtowel in the front of her apron.

She comes to the table and lifts my empty bowl, turning it around and upside-down as though she is inspecting it. "Is that a fact?"

I yawn, stretching my fatigued arms. "That was the most delicious thing I have ever eaten, and this was the most fun I have ever had," I tell them.

"The most fun you've ever had? That's prophetic," Dory says disgustedly.

"And *pathetic*," adds Melba, pulling on Dory's golden hair.

"Whatever," Dory dismisses, but then grins at me. "If this was the most fun you've ever had, you need to get a life."

I laugh in agreement, but deep inside I am breathing a little easier and I feel like I finally *have* a life.

Melba spreads her arms wide, so that she can wrap a plump arm around both Dory and me. "My girls," she says.

Instead of going back to Melba and Dewayne's to watch *Sex and the City* reruns, Dory and I end up staying at the restaurant to help Melba close up for the night. As tired as we all are, I think we just aren't ready to let go of the feeling of togetherness and camaraderie. I wipe down every table with kitchen spray and a dishrag and take all of the condiment containers to the kitchen to refill them and put them away.

Dory stacks chairs on the tables and vacuums, and Melba, Artie, and Nelson tidy the kitchen until it gleams. You'd never know there were so many pots of meats and vegetables bubbling away in here just a little while ago.

Wearily, we turn off the lights and lock up, say goodnight to Nelson and Artie, and head for our cars. Still, I can't wipe the smile off my face as I drive home, Dory in my passenger seat babbling away about our big outing to the mall tomorrow. Bobbie Jean is coming with us, and while I know I am in for something I haven't quite bargained for, I am looking forward to getting to know Dory better and meeting her best friend.

When we reach Melba's, I am too exhausted to be social, so I hug my aunt and cousin goodnight in the kitchen, give my sleeping Uncle Dewayne an affectionate pat as I pass his lazy boy, and climb the stairs to collapse in bed.

I sleep deeply and dream of Nina and Josh. In my dream I walk into Grits 'n Greens, surprised to find them sitting together at a table. They are engaged in deep conversation until I approach the table. "What are you doing here?" I ask them.

"Checking on you, *dahling*," Nina drawls, squeezing a lemon into a glass of water.

I look to Josh, who says nothing but reaches out to squeeze my hand. His hand is freezing cold, so I offer to get him a cup of hot coffee. I leave them for just a moment, but when I return from the kitchen to fill his cup, they are gone. I sit at their table, fill the cup, and drink it myself.

I wake with a start and realize that I have only been asleep for an hour. I am groggy, but I remember the dream vividly. Why did they leave without saying goodbye? I lay in the darkness listening to the chorus of frogs and crickets outside, and just as I am about to fall back to sleep, I remember that in the dream Nina said she and Josh were checking on me. Maybe they decided I was fine, that I am doing fine without either of them, so it was okay to just go.

I drift off feeling content, and I know without a doubt that I am not just doing fine, but better than fine. I dream more during the night, but instead of Nina and Josh, this time I dream of Sandra, Dory, Melba, and my cousins. The dreams are noisy, colorful, and happy, and wrap me in a blanket of security until I wake in the morning greeted by the sun and the anticipation of what today will bring.

What the day brings is a whirlwind of activity and an epic trip to the mall in Jackson that will remain always in my memory as a collection of giggles, gasps, small-town teenage gossip, and mostly the satisfaction of watching Dory's pre-school-year jitters dissipate and her confidence grow. We return to Melba's at the end of the day loaded down with bags and a fresh outlook on the impending start of her sophomore year.

The entire day is a blur, but Bobbie Jean is delightful and a perfect friend to Dory. As for me, I miss Maggie even more than before and am physically and mentally drained from the adventure. I know I was not as energetic and excitable as those girls when I was a teenager, and I feel as though I have experienced yet another event that I missed out on growing up.

I excuse myself to my room early and collapse onto the bed. Tomorrow is an even bigger day, but even my nervousness about Melba's Sunday supper can't keep me from falling hard into a deep, dreamless sleep.

CHAPTER FIFTEEN

Sunday morning arrives and I am a wreck. I really have no idea why, except that today my entire family will be in one place. My cousins will all be present, along with Little Dewayne's wife and kids, and Lamar's wife, whom I have yet to meet.

I am also nervous because I am sure I will be dragged off to church with the rest of the family, where I will no doubt be called out as the freak that I am when it is discovered that I have no idea how to act there. Nina's funeral was easy, because nobody expected anything of me other than to sit in a pew and look distraught. Other than that, I have been in a church maybe ten times in my life, all for weddings of high school or college friends . . . also very easy, because at those particular functions I would make a point to sit with my Jewish friends so I could blend in with the people who didn't kneel or flip through hymnals when everyone else did.

Today, however, is a totally different ball of wax. The Littles are hard-core Baptists, and from what I've heard around the dinner table, they spend up to three days a week at the church for various reasons. Melba even feeds the entire congregation every-other Wednesday night before Bible Study. This is not a place where I can blend in or pretend I am Jewish. I have brought absolutely nothing to wear to a church, and it never occurred to me at the mall yesterday to think ahead and buy something. That will have to be my excuse to miss the service . . . I have no appropriate attire, and would hate to embarrass my family in front of their congregation.

With that in my back pocket, I head to the kitchen in my pajamas. As I get close, I can hear someone banging pots and pans around, and something already smells amazing. I round the corner

136

into the room to find four pies cooling on the counter, and three large pots on the stove.

"You get busy awfully early," I say to my aunt as I inhale deeply. "Pie for breakfast is my personal favorite!"

Melba turns, flashes me an enormous smile, and waves a wooden spoon at me. "Baby Girl, you better not be cuttin' into these pies until after supper, you hear? Neil Ray Little will have your head on a plate!" She laughs and stirs something bubbling in a pot. "Got some collard greens goin' just for you!"

I suppress a groan and lift the lids on the other pots, feeling relief when I find green beans and a mushy yellow substance that smells like corn. I *like* corn. It all smells delicious, though, and I am salivating like Pavlov's dog.

The back door opens and Uncle Dewayne enters, carrying a huge fork and wearing an apron that says *Kiss the Cook* in red lettering. "Good mornin', sunshine!" he says cheerfully, setting the fork in the sink. "I hope you're hungry today."

"If I wasn't before, I am now," I tell him. The smells are enough to wake anyone's appetite. "Isn't it a little early to get dinner ready, though?"

"Missi, you ever fed seventeen people? Got to get up with the chickens to get a head start," Melba says, stirring the other pots and turning down the heat. "Plenty of things that can get done before church. Warming it all up again is easy."

"We eat our big Sunday meal in the middle of the day—when we get back from church. The rest of the day we spend digesting it all," Dewayne laughs, rubbing his belly.

"Speaking of church . . ." I begin, knowing I am going to sound like a jerk.

"Oh, yes!" Melba interrupts. "I was going to ask you if you didn't mind staying at the house while we go and keeping an eye on the smoker."

"The smoker?" I ask, wondering which family member was the culprit.

"I got the meat put on the smoker at five this morning," Uncle Dewayne says, "and it's goin' real good, but it won't be done until noon and then has to set a while. You mind holdin' down the fort and making sure the meat comes off?" he asks, as though his request is a huge inconvenience for me. "I'd do it myself, but I've got collection duties at the church today."

I am so relieved to have escaped church-going responsibilities that I almost hug my uncle. "I'd be happy to," I say a little bit too cheerfully. "What kind of meat is it?" I ask, wondering what in the

137

world kind of meat would require eight whole hours to cook, other than an entire cow . . . or possibly a bear.

"It's a turducken," Uncle Dewayne says. "Your Aunt Melba makes the best turducken you will ever eat in your life!" Dewayne washes his hands in the sink and excuses himself to shower for church before I have the chance to ask, but the image has already taken over my thoughts. *Turducken?* What in God's name is that? That is no animal I have ever heard of, and I find it more than a little disturbing that the first syllable is *turd*.

I shake my head to rid myself of the horrible thought pervading my mind, and run out of the kitchen just as my stomach begins to churn. Safe in my room, I inhale deeply and sit in the bed. Surely I am overreacting. Nothing that Melba has cooked up to this point has been anything short of heavenly, and this can't be any different, can it? I mean, people in the South do eat some weird stuff, like grits, mustard greens, and peas that swim in bacon fat, and frankly I do not care for any of those things—not that I've actually *tried* any of them yet, but they are definitely offensive by sight, which prevents me from even getting them near my mouth. Maybe I can chalk this up to being another southern delicacy that I will avoid.

My curiosity is piqued, however, and I can't help myself. I am an educated woman, and should at least know if there is an animal running around North America that I have never heard of—I know what a *narwhal* is, for crying out loud, and it doesn't get more obscure than that. I return downstairs and find Melba still in the kitchen making "supper" preparations.

"Hey, sunshine," she says cheerfully as I sit down at the table, not knowing exactly how I should broach the subject. I do not want to sound disrespectful, nor do I want to sound like an idiot. I trace the ridges on a placemat with my fingers, and before I know it a steaming cup of coffee appears in front of me.

I thank Melba and take my time stirring sugar into the cup, while she goes from the stove to the oven, to the refrigerator, and back again. Finally, she turns the dial on an egg timer and sits across from me with her own mug.

"I hope you know, Dory had the time of her life yesterday," she tells me. "That was really special."

I am flattered, and under any other circumstance would feel all warm and fuzzy inside remembering our field trip to the mall yesterday, but I am distracted by my quest for answers about little-known animals, and simply smile at my aunt, all the while working up the courage to ask.

"Speaking of Dory," Melba says, "I hope that sweet thing is up. She's got a solo with the choir today, so she can't be late." Melba gets up and starts out of the kitchen just as a pot on the stove bubbles over. She hurries to turn down the heat and turns to me. "Missi, do you mind going to see if Dory's awake? I need to wipe up this mess before it sticks for eternity."

"Sure," I say, postponing my inquiry, and head for the stairs to wake Sleeping Beauty.

As I get to the top of the stairs, I am stopped short by a noise. The sound is coming from Dory's room, so I take a few steps toward her door and listen more closely. It's music that I hear, and just as I think that it is perhaps the most beautiful music I have ever heard, it registers that it is actually *Dory*. Singing.

I can't help myself, so I continue to stand outside of her room eavesdropping on what must be practice for her solo. I cannot make out the words, but it doesn't matter. Her voice is sweet and pure, and I suddenly wish I was going to church today, too.

Down the hall a door opens, and Neil Ray emerges from his room, freshly shaven and buttoning the front of a crisp, ironed, white shirt. I have yet to see him when he is not just back from work and extremely dirty, and apparently the shock is evident on my face.

"I clean up pretty good, don't I, cuz?" he says with a wide grin.

I nod my approval as he passes me, and knock on Dory's door, sorry that my private serenade is over. Dory answers, dressed in a bathrobe. A towel is wrapped around her wet hair.

She greets me with a smile and opens the door wide, inviting me in. "Are you coming to church with us this morning?" she asks excitedly.

"No," I answer disappointedly. "Your dad asked me to keep an eye on the turducken." I wait for some emotion or another to register on Dory's face at the mention of the mystery meat, but she gives me nothing to go on. "I hear you're singing, though, and I'm sorry I won't be there to hear it."

She smiles and removes the towel, so that her damp hair cascades around her shoulders. "That's okay," she assures me. "If I do a good job today, maybe the choir director will let me solo again."

I want to tell her how incredible her voice is, but I hate to admit that I was listening outside her door without her knowing. I just nod and tell her she'll do great. I leave her to get ready, deciding not to bother Dory about such matters as the provenance of turducken while she prepares for her big debut.

139

I skulk back to my room to put on my best turducken babysitting clothes, brush my hair and teeth, and return to the kitchen to get another
cup of coffee.

Neil Ray is at the table eating cereal and toast. I help myself to more coffee and join him. "I was really hoping for pie," I whisper, pouring myself a bowl of Cheerios.

"Gotta save room for turducken," Neil Ray winks. "Then pie."

Before I can ask the obvious question, Melba comes in the back door carrying an aluminum pan full of yellow liquid. She sets it on the counter and addresses Neil Ray.

"You bringing anyone for supper I need to know about?"

"Yes, ma'am," he answers politely. "You remember the girl I met clearing the lot for the house over by Uncle Alton's?"

Melba nods and says "Mm hm," but I can tell she is not thrilled, because she starts banging pots and lids and slams the oven door for no reason.

"What's her name?" I ask, trying to deflect Melba's obvious irritation at Neil Ray's choice of guest.

"Sorbet," he says, dragging out the name to make it sound alluring.

"Like the dessert?" I ask, eyebrows raised.

"Oh, yeah," Neil Ray answers with a wink, and promptly receives a snap on the back of his head from his dish towel-wielding mother.

Between Neil Ray's obscene interest in the woman, Melba's evident distaste, and the girl's name itself, I envision Neil Ray arriving at the family meal with a pole dancer in tow and I know that things are going to get interesting. Neil Ray gets up from the table, Melba clears his dishes, and before I know it, the entire family has headed for church. I, however, am left behind. With a turducken . . . whatever in God's name that is.

The smoker is outside in the yard, set a little ways from the house. My sole responsibility is to make sure the coals underneath the smoker continue to smolder so that whatever the hell is inside cooks properly. I have been advised that under no circumstances should I remove the top of the smoker and expose the turducken to the fresh air. This will change the temperature inside and throw the whole cooking process off, and it seems may also send planet Earth off its axis. At precisely high noon, I am supposed to take off the lid and carefully transfer the meat to the kitchen counter, where it will sit and wait for Uncle Dewayne to return and deal with it.

What I know for certain is that this turducken got everyone at the house pretty excited, so I set about my task very seriously. I stand staring at the thing for a while, as though it's a live grenade that I am expecting to go off, but it is already getting incredibly hot outside, so I decide I need something to sit down on.

There is an old shed in the yard, and as I pry open the door I am accosted by the smell of mothballs. Fortunately, I also find a dirty white plastic lawn chair, which I drag out into the yard near the smoker.

I sit in the sun, baking, and begin to sympathize with the meat. Watching the smoker, it occurs to me that it looks like some strange space capsule, and my mind drifts, and I imagine that I am an astronaut inside the capsule, ready to land on an uncharted planet. I see stars outside a small window and watch asteroids fly past, thankful that they do not make contact with my spacecraft. It is incredibly warm inside the capsule, even though the temperature out in space must be very cold.

Just as I can see an oncoming planet growing larger in the distance, my stomach growls, and I root around in the capsule for some astronaut food. I find a foil pouch filled with a brown, dehydrated substance, which looks hideous, but smells heavenly. My mouth waters as I lift the food to my lips . . . and suddenly my head rolls to one side, waking me from what I realize was a dream. I am sweating, I have drool rolling out of one corner of my mouth, and I am starving. The smell from my dream is still there. The turducken. Shit! I am supposed to be keeping an eye on the turducken!

I look at my watch and panic when I see that it is ten minutes after twelve. I have been asleep for over two hours, and the Littles will be home any minute! Melba is expecting the turducken to be *on the counter covered in foil.*

I jump up from the chair and rush toward the smoker. The coals are not radiating the same haze that they had been. Shit, shit, *shit.* I grab the lid of the smoker and pull, but it weighs a million pounds, and is . . . extremely hot. I think I have left a layer of skin on the handle, but I don't care.

I run into the house and find potholders hanging from a hook in the kitchen, then hurry back out the door, tripping on the three steps leading to the ground and skinning my knee in the process. I brush myself off, return to the smoker, and grab onto the handle with both hands. The lid comes off, and I drop it onto the grass, finally face to face with the turducken.

For a moment all I can do is stare at it. I am not sure what I conjured up in my mind that it would look like, but this is not it. It looks—pretty normal, actually, and smells absolutely incredible.

Gingerly, I lift the pan the turducken rests in, and not wanting to mess up any more than I already may have, carry it slowly into the house. It is heavy, and I have to set it on the steps while I prop the door open, but I eventually get it inside without sloshing too much of the juice run-off on my shoes. I cover it with foil and mentally review my checklist: make sure coals don't go out, take meat off smoker at noon, and let it sit on the counter under aluminum foil. Well, I suppose one out of three is better than zero.

I know that my family will be returning any minute and I am a total wreck, so I run upstairs to freshen up, wanting to make a good impression on my cousins' families. I am especially looking forward to meeting the kids, and Little Dewayne has three of them.

I head into the bathroom to brush my hair and apply a much-needed second coat of deodorant following my two-hour nap in the blazing sun. I turn on the faucet at the sink and stop short at my reflection in the mirror.

I am purple. More accurately, I am *magenta.* My face is completely fried, and my hair is matted to my head in greasy, sweaty wisps. I am certain I have never looked more disgusting in my whole life, and I am about to have Sunday supper with my entire living extended family and some chick named after dessert.

I have to do something. I gently splash cold water on my face and blot it with a towel, which hurts. I attempt to smooth on some tinted moisturizer, but not only does it sting, it succeeds only in making me look like an idiot trying to cover up a sunburn. I rinse it off and move on to my hair. I pull it back into a ponytail, which looks okay, but it seems to draw more attention to my face, so I take it down again and try brushing and fluffing it. This is unbelievable.

Finally, I do the only thing left I can think of. I brush my teeth. I may look like a total freak, but I will not have bad breath on top of everything else. I go to my room and put on clean clothes and flip-flops since my sneakers have turducken juice on them, and make a mental note to steer clear of anthills.

I hear sounds coming from outside and run to the window to see the first cars pulling up. I have no choice. I look ridiculous, but they are my family, and hopefully they will like me anyway.

Downstairs, things are getting crowded quickly. I enter the kitchen to find Melba and two other women pulling things out of the refrigerator. The oven is preheating and Uncle Dewayne is peeking under the foil to inspect his beloved turducken.

"Mm," he says, inhaling deeply.

"So how'd I do?" I ask innocently. All heads turn toward me, and there is a collective gasp.

"Sweet Jesus, what happened to you?" Melba shouts, rushing over and cupping my face in her hands.

I can feel my cheeks blazing, which at this moment is as much from embarrassment as it is from the sunburn, so I try to sound nonchalant about it. "I just forgot to put on sunscreen while I was keeping tabs on the meat."

Dewayne clicks his tongue. "You mean you were out there the entire time?"

I feel so stupid. "I wasn't about to let those coals go out," I say cheerfully. I put my own hand on my cheek, wishing the heat would go away, or that I might shrink and disappear.

Melba brushes some hair from my forehead and turns to introduce me to the two other women, Little Dewayne's wife, Regina, and Lamar's wife, Angie. Regina gives me an enormous hug, and I immediately know why she and Little Dwayne are married. They are equally friendly and convivial, and she seems genuinely happy to meet me.

Angie, on the other hand, is timid and quiet, and instead of hugging me, she offers her hand, which is so thin and pale that I am afraid I will squash it in my own.

"Where are the kids?" I ask Regina, who laughs and explains that they are coming from church in the back of Uncle Neil Ray's pick-up truck, which is strictly a Sunday privilege.

"Devon's only three, though, so we make him ride in the front, car seat laws be danged. Plus, his big brothers might conspire to toss him out of the truck for wrecking their Lego contraption before we left the house this morning." Regina laughs again, and I find myself smiling at the idea, but Angie looks horrified, as though she thinks Regina may actually be serious.

A new wave of noise comes from outside, and Regina takes my hand and pulls me toward the door. "I bet that's them," she says cheerfully.

We exit the house to see four more pick-up trucks pull into the yard in a cloud of dust and dirt. The first contains just Stanley, but the second brings Neil Ray, three of the most adorable children I have ever seen, and Neil Ray's date, Sorbet, who is not that far from what I expected. She is very pretty with platinum blonde hair, but wears a denim dress that shows off quite a bit of both her substantial breasts and skinny legs. She is carrying Regina's youngest, Devon, in her arms, and is quickly relieved of the child by Melba, who has followed us outside.

The third truck I recognize for all of the rust and metal rot, so I know that it must be my grandfather and Sandra. The last pick-up to arrive looks familiar, but I'm not sure why, until the driver's side door opens and out climbs Darryl, the EMT. Crap, I'd completely forgotten he was coming . . . with *Lucy*. Her name alone is cute.

I decide to busy myself with Little Dewanye's kids, who I expect to be shy around a stranger, but surprise me by wrapping their skinny arms around my waist and legs and telling me how happy they are to meet me. I am pretty sure they've been coached, but I don't care. I love the attention, and it's been forever since I've been around kids their age. They are energetic and funny, and ask so many questions at once that I have to wait for the noise to stop before I can even answer.

Daniel, who is five, holds my hand and swings it back and forth while asking how close I live to the Air and Space Museum. "He's a little bit obsessed with planes and rockets," Little Dewayne says, coming up behind us. "Give Missi some peace," he tells his children gently.

"No," I counter, "I love it. They're great, and I never get to spend time with kids. They can ask me anything they want."

"Really?" asks Marcus, the seven-year old, jumping up and down.

"Really."

"Why is your face so red?" he asks.

"Marcus!" his mother scolds, setting a stern hand on his shoulder. "Mind your manners."

Marcus looks embarrassed. "I did say they could ask anything," I say, meeting Marcus' eyes. "I just wasn't very smart and sat out in the sun for a long time today without putting on any sunscreen first. I don't always look this way."

"Nope, sometimes she has great big welts all over her legs and her eyelids swell shut," comes a voice from behind where we stand gathered. Darryl steps forward, carrying a little girl who is two or three years old. I am so mortified that for a second the situation does not register.

"Uncle D!" Marcus shouts, running to Darryl, who sets the girl down on the ground.

"Boys, do you remember Lucy?" he asks, squatting beside the girl and holding her around her waist. "She was still a little baby the last time you saw her."

144

Daniel shakes his head, but Marcus nods. "I remember her," he tells Darryl quietly. "Her mama died."

Darryl forces a smile and rumples Marcus' hair. "You have a very good memory, buddy." He stands again, lifting Lucy off the ground, and greets the rest of my family. It has obviously been a while since anyone has seen Darryl, and even my grandfather gives him a handshake and a pat on the shoulder.

I seek out Sandra and spend a few minutes finding out about her day yesterday. She tells me that my grandfather took her to get Missi the cat a new flea collar, because Big Dog and Little Dog brought fleas into the house. No surprise there.

A little while later, Darryl finally approaches me with a shy grin. "Hope I didn't embarrass you too much back there."

I attempt to be casual. "Oh, I usually do a decent job of embarrassing myself," I say, covering my cheeks with my hands. "As you can see, I've already moved on to my next careless incident."

"I do see," Darryl says, nodding. "I've got some stuff for that, too."

The child in his arms starts to fuss, so he shifts her weight and turns her to face me. "Can you say hello to Missi?" he asks her quietly.

Lucy buries her face in Darryl's shirt.

"She's awfully shy," he apologizes. "I thought it'd do her some good to be around other kids. It just may take a while for her to warm up."

"She's your daughter?" I ask, knowing that she must be. She has the same dark, wavy hair, and as I look at them side by side, I see that they have identical blue eyes. Lucy's skin is perfect and pink, and she has a dimple in only one cheek, which I notice when Darryl nuzzles her neck with his nose and she giggles.

"She's my everything," he says proudly, but a flicker of sadness runs through his eyes. "My wife passed away when Lucy was not quite a year old."

I look at his little girl and can't help myself. "What happened?" I ask.

Regina, who apparently has been listening from nearby, comes over and takes Lucy from Darryl. "Faith was my very best friend, and ever since we were kids she would have these terrible headaches from time to time. She was so tough, though, she'd just push through them and move on. When she got pregnant with this little angel she didn't have any for a while. We all thought the headaches were a thing of the past." She kisses Lucy on the cheek, and Darryl finishes the story.

"Until she *did* have one again, and didn't tell anyone how bad it was, just tried to push through it on her own like usual. This time it was an aneurysm, and she died while she was at home alone with the baby."

My heart physically hurts, and the tears I have grown so familiar with are brimming at the corners of my eyes. I sniffle, and both Regina and Darryl sigh. Between them, Lucy squirms.

"Well, that's our little red wagon," Darryl says, suddenly breaking the silence. "I hear there's some turducken that needs eating!"

I nod my head and dab at my eyes with my fingertips. I *still* have no idea what a turducken is.

After several games of hide-and-seek, I wash the hands of Regina and Dewayne's kids and usher them back into the kitchen where supper awaits. I take a seat at the folding table that has been set up for all of the children. Neil Ray and Sorbet join me, leaving two seats available. Darryl comes to sit down with Lucy, but Regina cuts him off, insisting that he sit beside Little Dewayne so that they can catch up. She puts Lucy in an empty chair beside me, and begins bringing plates of food for each of the children.

On each plate is a piece of meat that is three different colors spiraled together—brown, light brown, and sort of pink. I am asked to help cut the meat into small pieces for the kids, and as I stand next to Daniel with a fork and knife, I seize the opportunity to get some information from an unsuspecting source.

"Do you know what turducken is?" I ask Daniel quietly.

"Yes, ma'am. It's good's what it is," he answers a little too loudly.

I lean in to cut his meat, and lower my voice to a whisper. "That's great, but do you know what a turducken actually *is*? Like, what kind of animal?"

Daniel straightens up in his chair and turns his head toward me. "It's actually *three* animals," he says excitedly. "I think a duck eats a chicken, and then a turkey eats the duck. Right, Mama?" He turns to Regina, who has overheard everything.

She smiles at her son and clarifies the story for me. "A turducken is a multi-bird roast," she says as if this clears everything right up, and I look at her blankly. "See, you de-bone a turkey, lay it out, and spread some cornbread and sausage dressing on top. Then

146

de-bone a duck, add it to the pile, and add more dressing. Repeat with the chicken, roll it all up, and sew it shut with kitchen twine."

I must have a look of sheer relief on my face, because she winks at me and says, "Why, you don't think we'd feed you opossum or anything, do you?"

"Of course not," I say lightly, trying to hide the fact that at this point anything was possible.

"Aunt Missi, you don't have to cut my meat that small," Daniel tells me politely, tapping my arm. "I *am* five and a half." I look at his plate and realize that I have cut his meat so small that he could almost swallow it without chewing.

"Sorry, buddy," I say, but am frankly too floored by the fact that he just called me *Aunt* to care.

Regina reaches over and picks up Daniel's plate. "This is the perfect size for Devon over here." She scrapes the meat onto Devon's plate, puts more onto Daniel's, and sets it back in front of him. "Here you go, Aunt Missi. Why don't you cut this up for the big man?" She smiles at me, and I feel warm inside. This time, I cut it just right.

The turducken is fabulous. It is moist, savory and smoky, and the cornbread stuffing inside is absolutely scrumptious.

"How in the world did Melba come up with this?" I ask Neil Ray, who sits across from me, one arm wrapped around Sorbet's shoulders.

"Wasn't her original idea to begin with," he tells me, "I think the crazy Cajuns came up with it, but Mama does it better than anyone." Melba looks over from the other table and smiles at the compliment.

"I'm Cajun on my daddy's side," Sorbet volunteers. "My grandmother from Lafayette makes *the best* turducken, you know, *authentic*." She wipes the corner of her mouth with a long, red-nailed finger, and Melba's smile turns into a scowl.

"Aren't Cajuns descendants of the French?" I ask her, steering the conversation in another direction. "Is that where your name comes from?"

"Well, I suppose they are," she says with a drawl that puts the rest of the room to shame, "but I'm actually named after my parents. My daddy's name is Sorrell, and my mama's name is Betty." She smiles proudly, takes a sip of tea, and chews loudly on a piece of ice.

While my brain mulls this over, I am pretty sure my mouth is hanging open. I have never heard of a person taking a syllable from their name and a syllable from someone else's name to create a new, socially acceptable name, but there you go. Sorbet. Classy.

147

"Isn't that precious," Regina says loudly, rescuing me from having to come up with a response. She shoots me a look that makes me shut my mouth and force a compliant smile. Meanwhile, Neil Ray stares at the girl as though she has truly hung the moon.

A giggle is bubbling up inside of me and I know I have to get out of the house before I upset Neil Ray by laughing at his girlfriend. I say out loud to nobody in particular that I am in the mood for some freeze tag, and immediately turn into the Pied Piper, leading three kids to the door. I turn and see Lucy, still sitting in her booster chair watching us leave the room, and ask if she wants to come play. I can tell she's considering it, and she climbs down carefully from her booster, but instead of coming to me, she runs to where her father sits at the other table and climbs into the safety of his lap.

Freeze tag on a full stomach is a recipe for heartburn, and within fifteen minutes I fall into my trusty plastic lawn chair and revisit the taste of turducken, which is not nearly as appetizing the second time around. My lack of stamina has let the children down horribly, and they stand in front of me whining that they want to play some more. Lamar is busy dismantling the smoker and dumping ash into a bucket, plus I am not sure he likes me very much, so I do not seek help from him. As I swallow the bile that continues to creep up my throat, the back door opens behind me and I turn to see Little Dewayne coming out of the house with Lucy in his arms, followed closely by Darryl and Stanley.

As Lucy is carried out into the yard, she does not take her eyes off her father, and there is a look of fear, almost, on her face—as though she can't bear for one second to be away from him. I glance at Darryl, who trails just a step behind, and see the exact same look on his face. I imagine they both must feel that the other is all they have in this world. On one day, they lost the single most important person in the world to them, and now seem to cling to each other for dear life. No wonder that little girl is so painfully shy.

I push several strings of hair out of my face and wipe the sweat from my forehead, relief filling me as the kids see their father and scream in unison, "You're it!" Little Dewayne passes Lucy to Darryl, growls, and in one motion scoops up all three of his own children and tucks them under his arms.

They squeal and shout as he carries them to his pick-up truck and dumps them gently into the bed. He wipes his hands dramatically on his slacks and says, "Well, it's time to head to the dump! Anyone want to ride along?"

Marcus, Daniel, and Devon squeal again and scramble to get out of the back of the truck. The boys run out to the field where

Darryl and Stanley are now playing with Lucy, but Devon is too little to get out by himself, so Little Dewayne goes back to the truck to rescue his smallest son. He lifts Devon high into the air and plants kisses all over his tiny face.

I watch with a mixture of amusement, fondness, and self-pity, knowing that there was never a moment—not one in my entire life—when my own father expressed any affection toward me. Honestly there were precious few moments when Nina did, either. The thought enters my mind that I never really *belonged* to anyone. Not to Nina, except for the obligation she had to clothe me, feed me, and send me to a good school, not to Sandra, whom I was taken from almost at birth, and certainly not to my father, crap-bastard that he was. I shudder at the thought just as Uncle Dewayne sets another plastic chair down beside mine and takes a seat.

"Whatcha thinkin', girl?" he asks, although I have a feeling the direction of my gaze and the tears in my eyes have already given me away.

"Nothing," I say, shaking my head and trying to push the sadness away.

"I knew Nina growing up, you know," Dewayne says, which surprises me for some reason. "She was in my grade. I knew her since the first day of kindergarten."

"Were you friends?" I ask cautiously, afraid that I already know the answer, that Nina was incapable of having real friendships even at a very early age.

"When we were real young we were, actually. I remember how smart she was. Always miles ahead of everybody else, but didn't lose her first tooth until the second grade." He grins at the memory, and I close my eyes and try to picture Nina as a child. This is difficult for me to imagine, and I realize that I have never done it before. She was always the epitome of an *adult*, never playful or joking, and never sharing stories of her childhood with me.

I turn to my uncle questioningly. "You said you were friends when you were young. What happened later on?"

"Nina always had something that none of the rest of us did, and it set her apart. She had ambition, and a lot of it. That girl knew she was going to leave this place and never come back, and she spent an awful lot of time making sure that it happened. Stepped on a few toes along the way, but I give her credit for getting there." Dewayne looks me in the eye and I can't help but look right back.

"Did *you* ever think of leaving?" I ask.

"Naw, I got my whole family here. Mama and Daddy are gone now, but I've got two brothers I always knew I'd go into business

149

with—see, we've loved playin' with trucks our whole lives—and probably the biggest thing is that I've loved Melba Jenner since I was sixteen years old." He winks at me. "I just had to wait until she was old enough to get my hands on. But no, I never thought about leaving. Everything I needed was right here." He looks out at the field, where three of his sons are now standing and watching his grandchildren run around.

"Nina may have left, but I don't think she ever really found what she was looking for," I say sadly.

"That's no surprise," Dewayne says, turning again to face me. "What she was hunting was bigger than all of us, and my guess is it never really existed. You were probably the best thing that she had." He kicks at the gravel in the drive. "You may not have been Nina's to take, but at least having you in her life gave her something besides herself to think about. I mean look what she did for you, despite what she may have done *to* some others at one time."

I sigh and look down at my own feet, thinking to myself that I always felt like more of a nuisance to Nina than anything else, but at the same time I desperately want to believe my uncle's theory that I may possibly have meant something to her.

"You remind me of all of them, actually," Dewayne says after a minute, and I can feel his eyes on me.

"All of who?" I inquire, honestly not knowing who on earth I could remind him of.

"The three of them," Dewayne answers, pointing over his shoulder toward the house. "Nina, Melba, and Sandra."

Something in my chest catches as he tells me this. I sit there beside my uncle, who I have known for five days, and hold my breath, trying to come to terms with who I am and where I come from—I mean *really* come from. I am frozen as I wait to hear what he has to say, since I have never been told that I remind anyone of another person. I have always been Missi Jennings, unique in my plainness, and impossible to link to the traits of any other human being.

Dewayne clearly senses my nervousness, and reaches over to take my hands, which are involuntarily balled up into fists, my fingernails digging into the palms of my hands.

He looks into my eyes, and where normally I would look away out of self-consciousness, I cannot take my own eyes off his.

"You remind me of Nina because you are smart, independent, and ready to take on the world."

I swallow and exhale, grateful that the words *condescending* and *bossy* were not among the others, and wait expectantly for further analysis. Right now, it is not how I remind him of Nina that matters to me.

"You remind me of Melba because you are strong, funny, and care so much about other people. Take Dory, for example. Do you know what you did for my baby yesterday with that shopping trip? You have given a shy, uncertain girl the chance to shine, where in the past she's always felt like an old penny."

I want to tell my uncle that Dory couldn't be an old penny if she *tried*, that her beauty and sweetness alone set her apart from any girl that could possibly exist at her school, but I don't want to change the subject yet.

Dewayne's face breaks out into a grin so huge that I can see every tooth in his mouth, and he lets go of my hands and moves his to my cheeks, which he cups gently, in that fatherly way that I am so unfamiliar with.

"And Sandra? I think you've got her very best qualities of all. There is no bigger heart in this world, and no smile that brings more joy to the people around her than Sandra's. You're a lot like that, too."

My eyes brim with tears, but I feel the corners of my mouth stretching out in opposite directions. Dewayne raises his eyebrows at me. "See?" he says. "That smile can light up the world." He lets go of my face, but does not move away.

"She's brave, too. She takes the world by storm every day, never seeming to realize how challenging it is to be different, or how much more she has to put up with compared to everyone else."

"She is amazing, isn't she?" I ask, finding my voice. I am sincerely humbled by the comparisons my uncle has made, and I love that my connection to Sandra runs deeper than my brown hair and eyes.

"Honey, so are you," Dewayne says, hugging me tightly, "and we're just so glad you're here."

As I hug my uncle back, I see a figure move out of the corner of my eye. It is Sandra, and she is holding a camera, grinning widely having caught us in a candid moment. "Good one!" she says. "Now smile." Dewayne and I stand together and smile for Sandra as she clicks a few more pictures.

"Give me your camera, Sandy," Dewayne offers. "I'll take one of you and Missi."

Sandra hands him her camera and comes to my side. I tower over her, so I squat down a little, making our heads even, and put my arm around her shoulder. Just before Uncle Dewayne snaps the photo, she tilts her head towards mine so that our temples are

151

touching. It is not lost on me that this may be the only photo ever taken of us together.

"Good one!" Sandra approves. She takes her camera from Dewayne and heads for the field to take pictures of the children. I give Uncle Dewayne one last squeeze and turn to the house, one strong, smart, caring woman going to help another wash dishes.

I enter the kitchen to find chaos as Melba attempts to clean up with far too much help. Regina is at the sink scrubbing pots and pans, and Sorbet is drying. Neil Ray and my grandfather sit at the table talking, as Angie tries to wipe it clean with a cloth. As the cloth nears my grandfather, whose arms are folded on the table, he swats at Angie in irritation, and she flinches and looks as though she is about to cry. Melba shuffles around, piling leftovers into the refrigerator and looking over everyone's shoulder to inspect their work.

As I watch, Sorbet picks up a glass bowl from the drain board. She uses her long fingernail to pick at something still stuck to it, then spits on the dishtowel and cleans it to a shine. Melba sees it, too, and her eyes bulge as though they are about to come out of their sockets.

"Pictures!" I suddenly call out. "Everyone out to the yard! Sandra is taking family pictures, and she wants everyone to come outside."

Regina dries her hands, Sorbet sets the spit towel on the counter, Angie practically runs out the door to escape my grandfather, and before long the kitchen is empty except for Melba and me. She looks absolutely relieved.

I pick up the bowl that Sorbet "cleaned" and set it back in the sink. An arm reaches around me and gives a gentle squeeze, and as I turn to Melba she sighs wearily.

"This is just what I needed," she says, turning on the hot water and rewashing the bowl. She sets it in the drain board, opens a cabinet, and pulls several dishes out. She puts these in the sink as well, and begins to wash.

"Did Sorbet dry those, too?" I ask, knowing I should not encourage my aunt.

"Baby Girl, I have absolutely nothing kind to say about that woman, so I will follow my mama's good advice and keep my mouth shut."

"Well, you're a better person than I am then, because she's a real piece of work." I face Melba, who is scrubbing dishes with water so hot the sink fills with steam. "I know you think he can do better."

"My goodness, Missi, that girl has *talons*!" She clamps a plump hand over her mouth and shakes her head. "I promised myself I would not do this."

I start to dry the newly washed dishes and put them away. "It's okay, Melba. You're Neil Ray's mother, and she's hideous!"

Melba looks downcast. "It's just that Neil Ray's such a sweet young man, Missi. He went through so much at a young age when his brothers were killed, and never really set any goals for himself. He saw how that can all be taken away in a split second, and decided there wasn't any point in working so hard. He's spent every minute since "enjoying" life, living it without much in the way of rules, and spending his time with tacky women who simply don't deserve him."

She turns off the sink and sits down at the table. "I couldn't have chosen a better wife for Little Dewayne if I'd picked her out of the JC Penney catalog myself. Regina is a good woman, a wonderful mother, and has a great sensibility about her. And I know Angie's like a scared church mouse sometimes, but she has a big heart and loves Lamar so much, which is not necessarily an easy task. Poor Stanley lost his girl to that no good Lowell Brown, but I know he'll make a good choice when it presents itself, and thank the Lord I have some time before I've got to worry about Dory. No boy's getting anywhere near her anytime soon if her daddy and brothers have their way." She wipes at a spot on the table that Angie must have missed.

"But I do worry a whole lot about Neil Ray," she says, turning to me. "And now I have you to worry about, too."

"Oh, Melba, *please* do not worry about me." I am suddenly uncomfortable, but at the same time touched that she cares. "My life has been completely thrown into the air in the past few months, and the pieces are just now falling back to the ground. Give me time to see where they land, and then I promise I'll work on my love life. Okay?" I plop down in a chair beside her.

She covers my hand with hers and gives it a good squeeze. "Alrighty, then. I might can give you a break for now."

"Thank you," I smile. "Besides, you've got your hands full getting rid of Sherbet out there."

Melba cackles, then quickly chokes it back. "Mississippi Moon Jennings, you're going to get me in such trouble!"

I wince. "I suppose I am the last person who should be making fun of someone else's name."

"Your name is just perfect," she says, getting up from the table. She gently places her hand on the top of my head before turning toward the counter. "Think you could help me serve up some of this pie?"

I spend the remainder of the afternoon playing with Marcus, Daniel, and Devon, which not only helps burn off at least one of the slices of pie I consumed, but also makes it easy to prevent any further contact or conversation with Darryl. I honestly don't know why I find it necessary to avoid him. He seems like a great guy and is incredibly good-looking—normally the kind of guy who I would stare at from a distance, sure that he'd never notice me back. For some reason, though, I feel compelled not to even glance in his direction or listen to his conversations, and I stay far enough away that there can be no accidental interactions.

Lucy, however, is another story. I cannot keep my eyes off her. She has warmed up to Little Dewayne's boys beautifully, and has been trying so hard to keep up with them that her yellow dress is filthy, both knees are grass-stained, and her brown hair has started curling in sweaty ringlets above her forehead. She seems so happy, in total contrast to the shy, clingy child I met just a few hours ago, but it pains me to think about what this little girl has been through in just the couple of short years she has been alive.

As I play among the kids—every other adult there is standing on the perimeter, graciously letting me be the superstar—I keep imagining myself when I was Lucy's age. I remember almost nothing from when I was that young, but I wonder what my life was like. Nina would have been working non-stop getting her foot in the door at the RNC, so where was I? Who took care of me? Although I cannot remember a time when Nina and I were close, I also don't think that my childhood was altogether unhappy. I was obviously cared for by *someone*, and at least I had a mother figure at home, however imperfect she was. Lucy, on the other hand, will never have real memories of her mother because she was so young when Faith died. Thankfully, she will also never remember being in the room when it happened. I had a front row seat to Nina's death, and it is an image I cannot seem to rid myself of.

Maybe it isn't Darryl that I am avoiding. Maybe it's that I am aware that Lucy and I have the loss of our mothers in common, but where I was lucky enough to get a second chance by discovering Sandra, there is no second chance for Lucy. Faith was her real, biological, loving mother, and she is gone. Sure, there is the chance that Darryl will find someone else to love and marry, but Lucy will never get her mother back. It seems so unfair.

I watch her run through the high grass in the field, for now wonderfully oblivious to anything but the joy she feels, when

154

suddenly she disappears from view. One second she's running, and the next I can no longer see her. Without hesitating, I run full-speed toward where I had just seen her, and nearly trip over her. She is lying on the ground, obscured by the tall grass growing around her, and is beginning to cry. I pick her up and cradle her in my arms.

"You're okay, you just fell down. Let me see your knees and elbows," I say gently. There is a tiny bit of blood on her left elbow. I turn to carry her back toward the house, but Darryl has already reached us and takes her from me.

"It's okay, baby. Daddy's got lots of Band Aids in the truck," he says, turning his back to me. He walks away to take care of his daughter, and it is all I can do to not start crying myself, and I don't even know why.

I tell the boys that I will be right back, and go inside to pour myself a glass of tea and get a hold of myself. I no longer wince at the sweetness of the tea, and the cool liquid calms me. Being part of a family is an emotional roller coaster, but I'd be stupid not to realize how lucky I am, and this thought compels me to return to the madness outside.

Back in the yard, I find an empty chair next to Regina and sit down. We talk easily for a while and watch Stanley and Neil Ray, who have found a wiffle ball and bat in the shed, and are now tossing the ball to Marcus and Daniel. Dory jumps in, taking Devon by the hand and resuming her old job of ball girl. Everyone seems content and happy, and Regina smiles and cheers her boys on.

I look over at Darryl's truck, curious to see how Lucy is doing. Little Dewayne is squatting down beside her, holding one of her small hands in his enormous one. Darryl places a Band Aid on her elbow, and both men plant a kiss on it. All better.

Sandra approaches and pats Regina's shoulder. "He's practicing," she says, pointing now to Little Dewayne, who has hoisted Lucy up on his shoulders and tickles the bare feet that dangle in front of his chest.

Regina nods and squeezes Sandra's hand. "He's praying, for sure," she answers.

I am not following. "For what?" I ask.

"For a little girl of his own to protect," Regina tells me. "I'm expecting another baby."

"Really? That's wonderful!" I practically shout, and am suddenly filled with excitement at the prospect of this family—*my family*—getting even larger. Besides, I like Regina and Dewayne tremendously, and I know there couldn't be two better parents.

Regina tries to suppress a smile, but can't. "Dewayne wants a daughter so badly he can taste it, and I suppose if this one's a boy we'll just keep on trying until God sees fit to give us one. At least if it's another boy we've got a whole mess of clothes and toys to use again."

"I think it's a girl baby," Sandra offers. She sits down in the grass and starts looking through a patch of clovers. It's still hard to imagine that this is the woman who gave birth to me. She is so child-like and innocent to have been through all of that—being raped, delivering a child, and then having me taken from her life completely. I guess my grandfather has done a pretty good job of making sure that nothing else bad ever happened to her again.

I glance around, wondering where my grandfather is, and locate him standing with Big Dewayne in the shade of a large tree. They are talking, but my grandfather's gaze is on Sandra, picking clovers. Even now, he is vigilant about the well-being of his youngest child. As I watch him, his eyes meet mine, and for a second we just look at each other. I smile at him. He frowns and then looks back at Sandra.

CHAPTER SIXTEEN

Monday morning is hectic. I awake early to the sound of showers running, doors opening, and pots and pans clanging. Downstairs, Big Dewayne and Neil Ray are getting ready to head off to work, Dory flutters around in a blur of nervous excitement on her first day back to school, and of course Melba is busy filling stomachs and packing lunches for everyone.

I pour myself a cup of coffee and join them at the table, happy for the moment to be a part of this productive chaos. Dory is dressed in one of her new outfits, and looks adorable. I wonder how many phone calls were placed to Bobbie Jean before a decision on what to wear could be made.

She spoons honey onto a biscuit and chats rapidly about how thankful she is to have gotten Mrs. Aldridge for math this year instead of mean old Ms. Weems, and her disappointment at having third period lunch. "I mean, who wants to eat lunch at ten o'clock in the morning?"

Big Dewayne asks if Bobbie Jean has the same lunch period, and Dory grins. "Yes sir, thank heavens, and so does Travis," she tells him. Travis, I learned on the trip to the mall Saturday, is Dory's cousin who Bobbie Jean has an enormous crush on. This is a small fact I am proud to be privy to.

"Then what do you have to gripe about, darlin'?" Uncle Dewayne asks.

"Nothing, Daddy," Dory answers. She gasps and jumps up from the table. "I better finish getting ready or I'll be late for the bus!" As she scurries from the room, she calls out to Melba. "Mama, put extra mayonnaise on my sandwich, please!" I have no earthly idea how that girl can be so thin.

157

After Dewayne, Neil Ray, and Dory have left, I help Melba clean up the kitchen. It seems like all we have done since I have gotten to Mississippi is eat and clean. I make this observation to Melba, who laughs out loud and says, "And now I get to go to work and do it all over again! Twice!"

The phone rings and Melba chuckles as she ambles over to answer it. I start to leave the kitchen to go get dressed, but as she responds to the person on the other end, her voice sounds panicked. I stand at the kitchen door, knowing it isn't polite to eavesdrop, but I can't bring myself to walk away.

"What's happening?" she asks. "Is there any blood? How much? Where are the children? I'll be there just as soon as I can get there." She hangs up, clenches her fists to her chest, and takes a deep breath. "Missi, go get dressed. I need your help."

I run through the house, up the stairs, throw on some clothes and, for the sake of time, flip-flops. I toss my hair into a ponytail, contemplate brushing my teeth but remember I have gum in my purse, and am back in the kitchen in less than three minutes. Melba stands by the door with her purse. "Let's go," I say, having no clue where we are going.

In the car, Melba fills me in. Regina woke up this morning with horrible cramping and bleeding, and needs to go see her obstetrician. I know this can't be good, but Melba reads my mind, and ever unflappable, puts me at ease.

"She's going to be fine," Melba assures me, but there is a crease in her brow that I have not seen before, and I know she's worried, too. We ride the rest of the way in silence, and though it is early in the day, the pavement in front of us glistens in the summer heat.

Little Dewayne and Regina live in a pretty yellow house on a large, woodsy lot. Little Dewayne's truck and a minivan are parked in the gravel drive, but when we enter the house it is strangely quiet. Melba heads toward the back of the house, and I am relieved when I hear little voices yelling "Granny, Granny!"

She returns to the foyer where I still stand, Marcus and Devon trailing behind. "Missi, can you please get these rascals to the kitchen and help them get their shoes tied? The school bus will be here in just a few minutes, and these babies can't be late on the first day of school!" She sounds far more chipper than I know she feels.

"I'm not a baby!" Daniel quips at his grandmother. "I'm in kindygarten! I get to go to big school with Marcus!"

Melba kisses his head. "You'll always be *my* baby, even when you're as big as your daddy! Now give Granny hugs, and make sure you remember everything about your day today, so you can tell me all about it later." She squeezes both boys and leaves the room to find Devon, who apparently has decided to play hide and seek.

I tie Daniel's shoes while Marcus does his own. He has not said a word yet, so I try to get him to talk by asking him what grade he's starting today.

"Second," he answers quietly.

"Do you know your teacher's name?"

He nods. "Miss Parker. She was my first grade teacher, too, and got promoted with us kids." I had a teacher in elementary school that did the same thing. She taught my fourth grade class and then looped with us to fifth. I tell Marcus this and he smiles, just a little.

"Is Mama gonna be okay?" he asks, and I can tell he is fighting back tears.

"Yes," I promise him. "And I know it will mean so much to her to know that her big boys are having a great first day at school. Can you do that for her?" Marcus nods. "Is this your first day riding the school bus?" I ask Daniel.

"Yes, ma'am!" he tells me excitedly, putting his giant backpack on his shoulders.

"Then your job just got even more important," I whisper to Marcus. "You've got to make sure your brother gets on and off the bus, and to the right classroom. Think you can show him how it's done?"

Marcus stands a little taller and nods seriously. "I sure can."

I hand Marcus his backpack and walk them out the front door, just as the big yellow bus pulls up to the end of their drive. It is not until the bus pulls away and I am waving at the boys that I realize I am holding my breath. I look to the sky, and for the first time in my life say a prayer to God to watch over this family today. The stagnant air stirs a little, rattling the leaves in the tree above my head. I wonder if this is a sign that maybe He is listening.

I return to the house to find Regina and Little Dewayne coming down the hall leading to the front door. Regina is pale and moves slowly, while Dewayne gently guides her. She smiles weakly at me. I can tell they are attempting to leave without being seen by Devon, so I hold the door for them and wish them good luck while trying very hard not to cry. I close the door quietly behind them and go find Melba.

She is in a room at the back of the house, lying on her side on the floor next to a bed.

"Are you okay?" I ask, rushing to her side.

She rolls onto her back and sighs. "I'm fine," she says, "but I seem to have lost something under this bed, and for the life of me I can't get at it."

I walk around to the other side of the bed, lift the edge of the quilt, and kneel down. Looking out at me from the shadows is Devon, grinning like this is the most fun game he's ever played.

"Melba, I think I've found your lost object," I say, but Devon seems in no hurry to get out from under the bed. I think fast. Bribery. "Devon, I'll bet Mister Rogers is on," I say in my best conspiring voice. Instead of scampering out of his hiding spot, however, he just looks puzzled.

"Try Diego," Melba whispers from the other side of the room.

"Okay." I try again. "How about Diego?"

To my relief, Devon squirms out and runs past me to the door, disappearing into the hallway. I help Melba up off of the floor and we follow Devon to the family room. I have no clue what this Diego is all about, but Devon is clearly a big fan. Before long, we are all engrossed in the action, and I even learn what a kinkajou is. I am disappointed, however, when at the end of the show Diego does not sit down and trade his Keds for loafers and his cardigan for a coat.

After a few minutes I sense that Melba is getting edgy, so I clear my throat. "I can stay here with Devon if you need to get to the restaurant. If Regina and Dewayne call, I'll let them know where to find you."

She looks grateful but hesitates for just a second. "Are you sure? Artie can always handle things, but after Sundays off, Mondays can be crazy."

"Please go, then. We'll be fine, and I know where his hiding place is now." I wink at my aunt.

"Alrighty, then. Devon?" she says sternly to her grandson. "You need to be a good boy for Missi, you hear?" He looks at her through thick, dark eyelashes and nods very slowly.

"Good," Melba says, gathering him in her massive arms and kissing his rosy cheek. "Granny'll bring you something special for dessert tonight." She sets him down on the ground and leans in to kiss my cheek as well. "Thank you, Baby Girl. I'll call in a while and check in."

She picks up her purse and heads out the front door, and I am alone with my cousin's child while his wife potentially miscarries their baby. I wonder if I have just gotten in over my head.

I am amazed at how television has changed since I was a child. It has graduated from simply teaching kids how to count, and instead teaches them to count in Spanish and even Chinese, depending on

160

the program. Instead of puppets there are talking animals and aliens of all types in every episode. I think I have even learned a few new dance moves after spending the morning watching TV with Devon.

He tells me that he's hungry, so we relocate to the kitchen and search for a snack that I think his mother would let him have. As he sits happily nibbling graham crackers, the phone rings. It's Melba. She forgot to tell me that Daniel's kindergarten is only a half-day, and that the bus will drop him off at noon. I promise to meet the bus and retrieve Daniel. Neither of us has heard from Dewayne and Regina yet.

Afraid that I will lose track of the time, I set the oven timer to ring a few minutes before Daniel's bus should arrive. I want to be right there, waiting, when he gets home. Surely he'll want to share his exciting day with someone, and just because he hardly knows me, it shouldn't mean that he get any less of a hero's welcome.

Devon demands that I get out his Play-Doh, but cannot tell me where to find it, so I give him a couple more crackers and start opening cabinets. I finally locate a bin in the laundry room full of paints, crayons, paper, and thankfully a large bag of Play-Doh. This keeps both Devon and I occupied for quite a while. I make flowers and little animals, while Devon makes blobs and mixes colors, and we are both happy.

When Devon tires of Play-Doh, however, I discover what a pain it is to clean up, especially when it is sticking to the seat of a three year-old's pants. I try to scrape it off, but decide to just put clean shorts on him instead and leave the others on top of the washing machine. Then there is the matter of the rug underneath the kitchen table, which now has teeny tiny wads of bright blue Play-Doh stuck between its fibers. I attempt to scrape it out bit by bit with the tines of a fork, but am only marginally successful. Maybe once it dries I will be able to chip it out. Great.

Next, Devon wants to play Candy Land, which might have been fun if he knew the rules even a little bit. He does understand that the goal is to get to the candy castle at the end, so he takes card after card from the top of the pile until he gets one of the "fun" ones that let him jump ahead to each character's location. This allows him to win every game while I remain stuck somewhere near the shady-looking guy with licorice for hair.

I am relieved when I hear the timer in the kitchen going off, so we clean up the game and go out into the yard to wait for Daniel. Devon is visibly excited about his brother coming home. He's probably a lot more fun to play with than I am.

161

We hear the engine of the bus rumbling before we see it, and we both start waving as soon as it comes into view. It comes to a noisy, hydraulic stop, and just as the diesel smell brings bad memories to mind, the door slides open and out jumps Daniel. He is wearing a hat made of paper apples and a nametag that says *Daniel L.*, and is positively beaming. Kindergarten was awesome, evidently, and he seems perfectly happy sharing the events of the day with me as we walk toward the house. His teacher is good, his friends are good, so it was a good day. He even got to go to music class and bang rhythm sticks together. I guess some things stay the same after all.

We enter the house to the sound of the phone ringing. I run into the kitchen and grab the receiver, afraid I have missed the call. Thankfully, there is a voice on the other end. It is Little Dewayne calling to check on the "big kindergarten man." I put Daniel on the phone and listen as he divulges to his father the same details I'd gotten a few minutes ago. When he's done, he hands me the phone and informs me that he's starving.

I tell him that I'm going to say goodbye to his daddy and then make him lunch, and he scampers from the room saying something about peanut butter.

On the phone, Dewayne tells me that they still don't know anything for sure. They are still getting a heartbeat, but it isn't as strong as they'd like, and Regina is a wreck. She is only ten weeks along, he says, but they have already gotten attached to the idea of having another child. I say some things that I hope sound encouraging and assure him that everything is fine here. He hangs up to call his mother, and I set about making two peanut butter and jelly sandwiches. I cut them in halves and call to the boys, who come running to the kitchen table like starving cats.

"How did you know I like pbj's?" Daniel asks, taking a massive bite.

"You told me," I remind him, pouring milk into a couple of plastic cups.

"Dev neeths a thippy cup," Daniel warns me through a mouth full of sandwich. "An' cut off hith crusths."

I locate a sippy cup in a cabinet, pour Devon's milk into it, tighten the lid, and cut the crust off his sandwich. He picks up the cup, takes a sip, and milk runs all down the front of him. Shit. I jump up and wipe his shirt off with half a roll of paper towels.

"You forgot the thingy, Aunt Missi," Daniel says, getting down from the table. He opens a drawer and hands me a small, strange-looking, white plastic object.

162

"What do I do with this?" I ask.

"Take off the lid," he instructs.

I do, and he points to the hole into which I need to shove the white plastic thing. Apparently this will somehow keep the milk from coming out when you don't want it to. Who knew?

The boys are eating and nobody is making a mess, so I make myself a sandwich and join them.

"When did I tell you I liked pbj's?" Daniel asks, and then adds, "Can I have some grapes?"

"When you got off the phone with your dad," I remind him, locating a container of washed grapes in the refrigerator. I put some on his plate, then put a few on Devon's.

"You need to cut his," Daniel says. "And no I didn't."

"I need to cut his *grapes*?" I ask. I've never heard of cutting grapes. "And no you didn't what?"

"So he doesn't choke, and no, I didn't tell you I like pbj's." Daniel pops a grape in his mouth and crunches loudly.

I cut up Devon's grapes and sit down for the third time. "Yes, you did," I say, trying not to sound bossy. "You handed the phone back to me, told me you were starving, and ran down the hall saying you wanted peanut butter."

Daniel grins at me and his blue-green eyes twinkle. "I said I was going to *feed* Peanut and Butter, silly."

"Who are Peanut and Butter?"

"Our gerbils," he explains. "Want to see 'em?"

We head back to the room Daniel and Marcus share, armed with some sunflower seeds. I suggested carrot sticks, but was looked at with pity by a five year-old. "They aren't *rabbits*, Aunt Missi." So sunflower seeds it is.

I have to admit I have never been a fan of small, furry, rodent-like animals—of any sort. Particularly after living in DC in my seedy apartment, where I have had more than a couple of run-ins with those of the rat persuasion.

I stand a decent distance from the plastic cage while Daniel opens a small hatch and sprinkles the seeds into a little bowl inside. The cage is really more of a gerbil dream house, with elaborate tunnels, several rooms, and a running wheel. I suppose that even gerbils need personal space, and they've definitely got it here.

In one of the rooms is a half-chewed toilet paper roll, and as soon as the seeds have hit the bowl, out of the tube comes a furry white creature with a tiny pink nose and a long tail. The creature scampers through a tunnel into the dining area and gets to work on the sunflower seeds. It is actually somewhat charming, the way the gerbil holds one seed at a time between its front paws and cracks it open with its teeth to get to the good part.

"Which one is that?" I ask, moving slightly closer.

"Buttah," Devon volunteers, "'cause he's yella."

"Well," Daniel corrects, "he's not *really* yellow, but Peanut is brown, so we named the whitish one Butter, so they go together. They're brothers, just like me, Marcus and Dev."

I keep watching as Butter intently works on another seed. "Where is Peanut?" I inquire.

Daniel points to a pile of wood chips in the corner of another compartment. "Under there. He must be sleeping. When I put in the pellets right after school, he didn't come out then, either. Guess he's tired."

"Well, maybe we should let him sleep, then," I suggest.

"Okay. Can we get them out later and play with them? Mama lets us do it in the bathtub with the plug in so they don't go down the drain. Without water," he adds.

The thought of loose gerbils in the house sends shivers up my spine. "Maybe," I lie.

I lure the boys back to the kitchen with the promise of making chocolate pudding from a box I'd seen in the cabinet earlier. I even find one of those old hand-held crank beaters in a drawer, so that both Daniel and Devon can take turns mixing the pudding. When it is sufficiently thickened, I put the bowl in the refrigerator to chill, wipe up the pudding that has been flung around the kitchen, and tell them that when their big brother gets home, we'll all have some for snack.

"By the way," I say, realizing that I have already forgotten, "do you happen to know what time Marcus's bus drops him off?" I suppose I can always call Melba at the restaurant.

"Three ten," both boys say on cue. No need to call Melba after all. This family is a well-oiled machine.

After a lengthy Matchbox car race on the living room floor, Devon starts to whine—about nothing. I am at a loss about what to do until Daniel advises me that it is well past Dev's naptime. I hadn't thought about a nap, but I guess he *is* only three.

I scoop Devon up off of the floor and give him a squeeze. "You ready to go get in your bed for a rest?"

"*No!*" he shouts, kicking his legs so forcefully that I am afraid I will drop him. I look to Daniel in a panic.

He shakes his head. "Think you might be a little too late," he says wisely. "Sometimes he gets *too* tired, and then there's no way you're gonna get him to sleep."

Fabulous. I guess I'll just have a tired, whiny child on my hands for the rest of the day. It occurs to me that I don't know when Dewayne and Regina might be home, and what shape they'll be in when they do. I start to feel a little frustrated, but I think about them and the possibility that they are losing a baby, and I know that this is a cakewalk in comparison.

We don't have long before Marcus will return from school, so although it is insanely hot and humid out, I suggest we go outside and wait for him. Devon perks up.

"Can we turn on the hose?" Daniel asks.

Why not?

When the bus arrives at *exactly* three ten, Marcus hops off and surveys the motley bunch awaiting him. We are all soaking wet, and Devon and Daniel are shirtless.

"You put sunscreen on them?" Marcus asks suspiciously. Uh oh. I've been busted by a seven year-old.

"Um, no," I stammer, "but we haven't been out here long."

"Why isn't Dev taking a nap?" Marcus queries. Busted again.

"Well, I didn't realize he needed one until it was kind of too late." I look into Marcus's eyes to gauge whether this is an acceptable answer. Maybe now that he's home, *he* can be in charge. He just shrugs.

"How was the first day of second grade?" I ask, hoping to change the subject.

His bright smile returns, and the rest of the way to the house he chatters happily about his day. There is a new boy in his class who moved "all the way" from Texas over the summer, and he is pretty sure they are going to be great friends, because the other boy's name is Mark, so in his mind they are practically twins.

Just outside the front door, Devon and Daniel peel off their wet clothes and go running to their rooms to find dry ones. Marcus drops his backpack on the kitchen floor and unpacks it, setting his lunch box next to the sink and putting a folder on the counter by the phone. I am amazed at this display of responsibility from such a young kid. Regina's got her kids well trained.

"Mom needs to sign my behavior chart tonight," he says, facing me. "Will she be home to do that? I got a smiley face."

My heart breaks. "I'm pretty sure she will, but if for some reason she isn't, maybe I could sign it for you." It is a question more than a statement.

"Okay," he agrees. "One time in first grade, Sam Pruitt's aunt signed his, 'cause his daddy and mama went to Florida for a week, and that was okay."

I really hope that his mother will be home to sign his paper, but it's good to know that my signature will be sufficient in a pinch.

"Want to go get Daniel and Devon and see if they're ready for some pudding?" I ask cheerfully.

"We get *pudding*? After *school*?" Marcus yelps, as though I'd just offered chocolate cake for breakfast. "Yahoo!" he yells, running off down the hall to fetch his brothers. I totally rock.

Twenty seconds later, Marcus and Daniel are at the table awaiting their treat. "Where's Dev?" I ask.

The other boys shrug. "He was in his room getting dressed," Daniel responds.

I put a bowl of pudding and a spoon in front of each of them, and another at an empty seat. "You get started," I instruct. "I'll go get Dev. Maybe he needs help."

The back of the house is quiet, and I enter Devon's room to find nobody. "Dev?" I call.

His dresser drawers are open, and a few articles of clothing hang out, so at least I know he *was* here. I decide that perhaps he's in the big boys' room checking out the gerbils, but when I go in there, there's no sign of him. I passed the TV room on my way back here, and I didn't see him there, either. I am about to return to the kitchen to enlist the help of the older boys when I recall the scene this morning, with Melba lying on the floor in Devon's room.

I go back in and lift the quilt, and can just make out a small body in the shadows. "Come on out," I entice. "Your pudding is on the table waiting for you." But the body doesn't move. I reach out to tickle him, but am rewarded with only a grunt and a snort. Devon has fallen asleep in his hiding spot under the bed.

I am afraid to leave him there, so I slowly pull him out and place him on top of the bed. He is wearing a green and yellow striped t-shirt and red plaid shorts, and the combination makes me stifle a laugh. I pull a thin blanket over him, and close the door on my way out.

Back in the kitchen, Daniel and Marcus have both finished their pudding, and look at me expectantly as I enter the room.

"He fell asleep," I report.

"Whew," Marcus says, dramatically wiping his brow, "'cause you don't even want to know how unpleasant he can get when he hasn't gotten enough rest."

166

I laugh and wonder if he's overheard his mother deliver the same sentiment.

"Can we play with Peanut and Butter now?" Daniel asks, wiping pudding from his mouth with the back of his hand.

I consider this, and decide that since the little one is out of the picture, surely the two older boys can handle their pets in a bathtub. Before we go, we rinse out the pudding bowls, and I make the boys promise to be quiet so we don't wake Devon.

I learn that Peanut is actually Marcus' gerbil, and Butter is Daniel's. The Easter Bunny brought them last spring after Santa Claus failed to deliver the puppy they'd requested for Christmas.

"Mama's allergic to dogs," Marcus explains, "so Santa took her side. It's better than having a mama that's sick all the time sneezing, I guess."

"Maybe we can get a dog when Mama dies," Daniel speculates. I am about to bite his head off for making such a horrible remark, but he salvages the situation by adding, "But then we'll be so old and wrinkly, we might not even *want* a pet anymore."

"I think you're pretty lucky to have these guys," I offer, watching Daniel pull Butter out by his tail. "I never had a pet growing up."

They look at me sympathetically, and I am amazed by what sweet, kind boys they are. Melba was right. Regina has done a spectacular job of raising them, and God would be crazy not to give them another one. I start tearing up at the thought of what she might be facing at this exact moment, but know I can't get upset in front of the kids, so I dab at my eyes and hold the hatch open for Marcus, who is attempting to coax Peanut out from under the pile of chips where he's been all day.

Daniel has already gone into the bathroom, and I can see him leaning over the side of the tub, which means that Butter has safely made it there without escaping. "Did you put the plug in?" I call out to Daniel.

"Yes, ma'am," he calls back over his shoulder, "but he already pooped in the bathtub."

"That's okay," I tell him. "We can handle that." I turn back to Marcus, who is having no luck getting his gerbil out. "You know," I say, "Peanut has been sleeping all afternoon. Maybe he's not feeling well." Marcus looks concerned, and I start to worry, too. I have not actually *seen* Peanut move today; he's been hunkered down in the chips the entire time. I begin to wonder if he's even breathing.

I stick my arm into the cage and poke around at the bulge in the corner. Nothing. Using just the tips of my fingers, I scrape some chips off the top of the pile. Eventually, I uncover light brown fur, which seems to be moving up and down intermittently. He's breathing! Thank goodness nobody's pet has died on my watch.

I sigh out of sheer relief, and Marcus does, too. "Uncover him more," he advises.

I continue scraping until there is an entire gerbil exposed. Peanut is considerably larger than Butter and seems in no hurry to get up. He peers up at me with what might actually be a look of disdain, and I apologize to the little rat for the disturbance.

"We just wanted to make sure you were okay," I tell it. Turning to Marcus, I smile. "Maybe if you pick him up, he'll perk up a little."

Marcus reaches in and quickly withdraws his hand. "He peed on me!" Marcus exclaims. He holds his hand away from himself. "Ew, what is *that*?"

On Marcus' fingers is not pee, but rather a slimy, pink substance. I panic, and start scraping at the chips around Peanut frantically. The poor thing tries to squeeze itself further into a corner, but he is so plump that it does little good. I try to find the source of the slime, but as I throw caution to the wind and am about to pick Peanut up, a tiny, hairless *thing* emerges from underneath him.

"What is that?" Marcus hollers. Suddenly, Daniel is next to him, peering into the cage.

Another icky, fleshy alien appears, and it dawns on me, "Peanut's having babies!" I say out loud without meaning to.

"He *is*?" the boys ask together.

"*She* is," I correct. "Whoever told you Peanut was a boy was wrong."

Marcus and Daniel stand, mouths gaping, and watch with a mixture of horror and amazement as four additional babies squeeze out from under Peanut. I notice that Daniel's hands are empty.

"Daniel, where is Butter?"

Without looking, he points to the bathroom, and I run, fully expecting to find an empty bathtub. My fears are mollified, however, when I see Butter scurrying around the bottom of the tub. A few little poops dot the white porcelain, but that is easily remedied. I saw Clorox wipes in the kitchen.

I pick the animal up carefully, cupping him in my hands so that he can't escape, and return to the cage. I push Butter back through the hatch, thankful that a large-scale crisis has been avoided. He seems to want no part of the excitement, however, and scoots through the tunnel to his own apartment where the toilet paper roll awaits. That's a man for you, I think to myself. Let her do all the work while you go chew on cardboard.

Thankful that the drama is over, I give Marcus a congratulatory pat on the shoulder. "Good for Peanut. She's a mother!" This is my attempt to give closure to the moment, but apparently it's not the right thing to say, because Marcus starts crying.

"Are you upset that Peanut is a girl, when you thought all this time she was a boy?" He shakes his head as a snot bubble comes out of his nose and bursts. I try to ignore this, but between gerbil afterbirth and snot bubbles, I am about to vomit.

"Then what's the matter?" I implore. "Aren't you happy? You have a whole bunch more gerbils now than you did a few minutes ago!"

Marcus wipes his nose with the back of his hand and points at the cage with a look of sheer revulsion on his face. "Is that what's going to happen when Mama has the baby?"

Faced with the options of either telling a seven-year-old that in reality having a human baby is actually even more gruesome, or telling him that there is a good chance his mother won't be having a baby at all, I am overwhelmingly relieved to hear the telephone ringing down the hall.

I command the boys to stay put and run for the phone, not thinking of who it might be on the other end until I answer it and hear Regina's voice.

"Hey, Aunt Missi. Have my little angels driven you out of your ever-living mind yet?" Her voice is scratchy, but sounds cheerful. In the event that this is just for my benefit, I tread lightly.

"Regina, how are you? How is the . . . how are you feeling?" I stammer, my heart racing.

"Oh, I'm just fine," she says. "How are you holding up? I can't thank you enough for helping with the boys today."

"Oh, Regina, it was the least I could . . . wait, okay. You say you're fine, but *how* fine? I mean, how is the . . . um, baby?" I wait through a painful pause, thinking I've upset her. Then thankfully I hear Little Dewayne come on the line.

"Missi? Sorry, about that. Gina's got to chat with the doctor for a second."

"Dewayne!" I gasp. "How is she?" I am coming out of my skin, and have unconsciously begun to walk in circles around the kitchen table.

"Oh, she's holding up," he answers, keeping his voice down. I can hear another man's voice in the background and assume it is Regina's doctor. "I think they're going to cut us loose in a few

169

minutes, so we wanted to let you know we'd be home soon. How are the big boys doing?"

"They're great," I say, but rather than elaborating for a concerned father, I press for information for my own sanity. "Please tell me the baby is okay."

"Oh, yes! The baby's fine," he says. "I guess this happens from time to time, and Gina spends all her time on her feet running after the kids, so it's no wonder. She needs bed rest for a couple of weeks and she'll be good as new."

Tears are now streaming down my face, and I feel my very own snot bubble forming in my right nostril.

"Missi? You there?"

Now I am full-on sobbing, because I am so happy for Dewayne, Regina, and their children, present and future, because I know how happy it will make Melba, because Sandra will have one more person to take pictures of, and because in some small part of my mind I recognize that the prayer I said this morning has been answered.

I sniffle and clear my throat. "Dewayne, I am so happy for you. I've been so worried all day, and the gerbil had babies and it just seemed unfair that it could have *six* when you were potentially losing one . . ."

"Do what?"

"I'm sorry," I say. "What?" What in God's name does that mean?

"What did you just say? That durn thing had babies?" Dewayne is incredulous.

"Yes, six of them," I tell him.

"No, five," says a small voice from behind me.

I turn to see Daniel standing in the doorway of the kitchen. "What's that, buddy?"

"Well, there *were* six, but now one's gone," Daniel tells me.

"Where did it go?" I inquire. Daniel shrugs, turns, and starts to walk back down the hall. I follow, forgetting that I have a phone to my ear until I hear a deep voice say my name. "Oh, Dewayne! Sorry. Daniel just told me . . ."

"Missi, go on and see to those rodents, and Regina and I will be home as quickly as we can." Dewayne laughs and says goodbye, and I vow to have this situation taken care of before a mother who needs to rest gets home.

When I get back to the boys' room, Marcus is on the floor looking under furniture, Daniel is rummaging through a toy box, and Devon, who evidently has woken up during my brief departure, has his little arm elbow-deep in the gerbil cage.

"Get down!" I try not to shout, extracting his arm and lifting him off the chair on which he is standing. "Let's leave the mommy alone with her babies, okay? We don't want to scare them."

"Marcus, are you sure there are only five babies in there?" I poke around the woodchips a little, not wanting to disturb the new family or touch something potentially slimy, like a hairless newborn gerbil. Peanut is nestled in deep, the babies in a pile at her belly. I only see five, too, but one could be underneath the others or obscured by the chips.

"I'm sure," he says confidently. "There were six at first, and then Butter came to visit Peanut and carried one off. Daniel tried to get Butter back out again, and then the baby was gone. Disappeared."

"Like them planes in the Bermuda Triangle," Daniel chimes in, sounding older than five. "Gone."

I feel panic rising in my chest. "Did Butter drop the baby when you took him out?"

"Must've," Marcus shrugs, " 'cause we haven't seen it since."

I'm no expert on animals, but I seriously doubt that a ten minute-old gerbil can get around very easily, which would mean that if it had been dropped right by the cage, it would still be there.

"Did Butter take the baby back to his room with the toilet paper roll?" I ask.

"Yes, ma'am, but as soon as he got there, I pulled him out," Daniel says proudly. "I thought it was too little for him to play with."

I open a hatch on the top of Peanut's room and lift up one end of the cardboard roll. Peanut slides out, but there is no sign of a baby. Shit.

"Okay, I need you to leave the cage closed and not bother the gerbils for a while," I calmly instruct. "I will be right back." I decide for safety's sake to take Devon with me as I return to the kitchen to locate a phone book. I may not be a veterinarian, but I can sure as hell call one.

To keep him occupied, I get Devon's uneaten pudding out of the refrigerator and situate him at the table. As I start looking through cabinets for the yellow pages, there is a knock on the front door. Surely Dewayne and Regina have not gotten home that quickly, but just in case I rush to open it and help them get inside. It is not my cousin and his still-pregnant wife, however. It's Darryl.

"Hi," I say. "Are you looking for Dewayne?"

Darryl shakes his head. "I stopped by the G 'n G for lunch and heard about what happened." He has a look of serious concern on his face.

"Well, they aren't home yet, but the news is really good. Where did you say you were?"

"The G 'n G? Grits 'n Greens. Melba was a wreck, so I told her I'd stop by and check on everyone." Darryl looks past me, and suddenly I feel bristly. Check on everyone? As if I am incapable of handling things here? I am, after all, an adult, for God's sake.

I attempt to smile, but am fairly certain that I have just bared my teeth at Darryl instead. "Things here are great! Um, *super*! Devon is just up from his nap . . ."

"And in need of a bath," Darryl interrupts, which serves to irritate me further.

"At four-thirty in the afternoon?" I ask. This guy may have helped me through a medical crisis *and* have his own offspring, but I have never heard of a child having to take a bath in the middle of the afternoon. My level of annoyance increases. Darryl now leans to one side and looks behind me into the house. I suppose this is his way of asking for an invitation, so I'll just invite him in and show him what a competent babysitter I am.

As I step aside to let Darryl through the doorway, I realize what he'd just been looking at. And why he suggested that Devon needs a bath. Apparently I used poor judgment when I left a three year-old and a bowl of pudding alone in the kitchen, because behind me stands a green-striped t-shirt and a pair of red plaid shorts attached to a head entirely covered in chocolate pudding.

"Devon!" I gasp. "Did you forget to eat it? Or did you just decide it would be better to wear it?"

Underneath the slimy brown mask, two huge eyes look back at me. Then Dev smiles, revealing the most perfect set of tiny white teeth.

I turn back to Darryl. "Well, it was your idea. *You* give him a bath."

Darryl scoops him up as Devon giggles, and carries him down the hall. I follow to check on the other two and the litter of newborn gerbils.

"There still five?" I ask, entering the room to Daniel standing sentry over the gerbils and Marcus lying on his stomach on his bed.

"Yep, still five," Daniel reports. Marcus does not say anything, but his shoulders are shaking, and I realize with alarm that he is crying again. I am completely unprepared for a crying seven-year-old boy twice in one day.

172

"Marcus, what's the matter?" I ask, sitting down beside him, but at a distance to give him a little space. I have not known a seven-year-old since I *was* seven, and I am fairly certain that they are fragile.

"Butter is a cannonball!" he wails, kicking his feet on his mattress and beginning to sob.

I have no idea what he means or what to do about it, so as much as I hate to, I go for backup. I enter the bathroom that connects the big boys' room to Devon's, where I find Darryl and a half-naked three year-old. Darryl looks perplexed.

"Can you help me?" I ask, trying not to sound desperate or in any way pathetic. "Marcus is crying, and I'm afraid his gerbil might have, um, eaten one of the babies. I think he might feel more comfortable talking to a guy . . . what's the matter?"

Darryl points to the bathtub and scratches his head. "I have no idea what that is," he says, pointing to the tiny pellets that still speckle the bottom of the tub.

"Oh, that." In the excitement of the past hour, I had completely forgotten to clean up the gerbil poop. "Uh, I'll handle that if you'll handle Marcus." Darryl almost runs out of the bathroom, and I hit the jackpot when I find a container of antibacterial wipes in a cabinet under the sink. I clean the tub, pull Devon's second set of clothes off, and get the adorable little mess clean.

A few minutes later I have dried Devon off, redressed him in clothes that match, and resorted to another episode of *Diego*, which seems for the moment to make him happy and, more importantly, keep him out of trouble. Daniel comes in to report that the remaining animals are all still accounted for and to make the unsolicited remark that *Diego* is a "baby show," but nonetheless settles in next to his little brother. I sit in a chair and take a deep breath.

Darryl comes in then and sits on the floor. Without looking at me he says, "I think Marcus is all set."

"All set?" Is that guy talk for *not crying anymore*?

"He was just confused about the whole eating-of-the-baby thing." Darryl starts to laugh. "You've had quite an exciting day, haven't you?"

I start to laugh too. "It definitely wasn't what I'd had planned when I got up today, but I'm glad I could help. I can't imagine how much harder this day was on Regina and Dewayne."

Darryl nods, and we sit in uncomfortable silence for a minute until Marcus joins us.

"Hey, buddy," I say. He smiles bashfully and leans against the arm of my chair. "You feeling a little better about things?"

"Yes, ma'am," he answers. "We changed his name."

"Oh, really? What did you change it to?" I think he's on to something, though, because now that there is proof that Peanut is female the name seems a little androgynous. Maybe Fluffy, or Peaches, or something more maternal like that would suit her better.

"Rex," Marcus states, derailing my train of thought.

"But . . ." I start, about to remind him that *Rex* just gave birth, until a large hand rests unexpectedly on my shoulder. My head jerks to meet Darryl's eyes, which are silently advising me not to pursue this line of questioning.

"Then Rex it is," I acknowledge. "How are Rex's little ones doing?"

"I'll go check!" Marcus energetically volunteers, and as quickly as he entered the room, he has left it again.

I turn again to Darryl, raising my eyebrows in search of an answer.

"He was having some issues regarding the sudden gender change of his pet," Darryl explains, "and was not happy that it was *his* gerbil that was squirting out babies all over the place."

" *'Squirting out babies'*?" I ask.

"His words, not mine," Darryl defends. "So, anyway, I suggested changing Peanut's name as a way to sort of start fresh, or give his pet a new identity since he knows a little more about it now. I wasn't thinking along the lines he was, though, and he picked Rex because a T-Rex was a meat-eater and so, as it turns out, are gerbils on occasion."

"Oh, *that's* what he meant by cannonball," I say, putting the pieces together. "Cannibal. But she wasn't the one that ate the baby, was she?"

Darryl holds his hands up, as if imploring me to just go with it. "He also convinced Daniel to change Butter's name to Barry."

"Barry?" I ask, clearly not doing a very good job of following the mind of a seven year-old.

"Um, evidently there was a meat-eating dinosaur called a Baryonyx." It comes out more like a question than an answer. "And since Daniel's gerbil is the one who seems to have actually eaten the baby, Marcus thought the name Butter no longer suited it, either."

I look over at Daniel, who is next to Dev, their arms touching, engrossed in the resolution of Diego's latest adventure. "He doesn't seem too fazed by it," I tell Darryl.

Just then there is rumbling coming from outside the house, and I look out the window to see Little Dewayne's truck in the drive. "They're home!" I shout, and everyone, without exception, runs for the front door.

Darryl reaches the truck first, and opens the passenger-side door to help Regina out. Dewayne joins him and takes her arm to gently guide her toward the house. The boys are jumping around in front of her, and although she is still pale, the smile on her face is the only reassurance her children need.

"Mama, you're home!" Daniel yelps.

"Mama, where's the baby?" Daniel inquires. Regina pats her belly, which, I might be imagining, seems to have grown a little since this morning. She stops for a moment to touch each of her darling boys.

"Mama, you won't *believe* what happened here," Marcus begins, but Darryl clears his throat loudly and shakes his head. Dewayne's eyes get wide, and I can tell he forgot to mention this to Regina.

"That can wait, at least until your mama gets inside the house. She needs to find a place to put her feet up for a while," Darryl says kindly to Marcus. Then he adds in a whisper, "Besides, you need to think about what you're going to name those five babies, so you can tell your parents the whole story all at once."

Darryl offers me a ride back to Melba's, but I decline knowing that I can still help here and that Melba will be back after the dinner shift at the G 'n G is over. Not to mention the fact that he still makes me incredibly uncomfortable, making the idea of a silent, awkward drive completely unappealing.

The evening goes by quickly, and the boys are perfect. It is as if they know, without ever having to be told, that Regina needs quiet and cooperation in order to rest. We play with Matchbox cars, build with Lincoln Logs, and play several games of Chutes and Ladders—which is only marginally more fun than Candy Land, but thankfully has fewer rules for Devon to ignore—all without one complaint or unkind word from any of the kids.

I can tell the entire time that Marcus is almost biting his tongue not to say anything about the gerbils to Regina, who has spent the past two hours on the couch with her feet up, not wanting to be away from her boys any more than she already has today.

"Tell me about school today, boys," she requests at one point, resulting in a barrage of answers from both the new kindergartener and the seasoned veteran.

"I drew an apple with a worm coming out of it," Daniel tells her, "and Mrs. Bailey let me pass out rhythm sticks in music."

"I made a new friend today, Mama! His name is Mark and he's from Texas," Marcus divulges.

"Aunt Missi made us chocolate pudding after school!" Daniel adds.

"She did?" Regina asks enthusiastically, smiling broadly as her two oldest children report about their days.

Marcus is completely animated at this point. "Yeah, and then Dev fell asleep and didn't get to have his pudding, and then—" he catches himself from telling too much of the story.

"Then what?" Regina encourages.

"Um, um, then Uncle Darryl came over to help Aunt Missi," Marcus covers, though I am not pleased with the fact that he thinks Darryl came to *help* me. I didn't need any help. Well, not much, anyway.

"Yeah," Daniel chimes in, just as Little Dewayne enters the room, "and while Aunt Missi was talking on the phone, Peanut had babies!"

"Peanut did *what*?" Regina asks, shocked, but I am still thinking about how that last remark sounded. While Aunt Missi was on the phone? Unless I have lost my mind, I was in the room when the gerbil had babies. I watched it with my own eyes and swallowed my own bile. It was afterwards that the phone rang.

Little Dewayne lifts Regina's feet, sits down on the couch, and rests her feet in his lap, gently rubbing them. It is a small but incredibly sweet and intimate action, and I look away for a moment, feeling like an intruder.

"I forgot to tell you about that earlier," Dewayne tells his wife. "I was the one Missi was on the phone with when all this was happening." He looks at me. "You ever find that other one?"

"Other *what*?" Regina asks, her face getting pale again. "Please tell me there isn't a gerbil loose in my house!"

"No, no," I assure her. "It's just that . . . well, um, Peanut? Had babies?" I sound like a total idiot, but I go on. "And, um, Butter? We think he ate one."

Dewayne starts shaking, and tears begin to roll down his cheeks. I panic, because if a crying male child freaks me out, then a crying male adult is going to send me over the edge. I have just gotten comfortable with my own tears, for heaven's sake! I am at a

176

total loss until I realize that Little Dewayne is not crying. He is laughing . . . *hysterically* . . . at my expense.

"Well, hell, we should have stayed home today, Gina! Sounds like there was quite a show going on." Dewayne is almost breathless at this point, and as Regina swats him and tells him to watch his mouth in front of the children I begin to shake, too, and howl until my side hurts.

Finally we get ourselves under control, only to find three small boys staring at us as though we've lost our minds. I suppose a gerbil eating a baby isn't very funny to them. I swallow the last of my guffaws and compose myself again.

"The boys were very brave and helpful," I commend. "But yes, we are ninety-nine percent sure that Butter ate one. It was pretty chaotic for a few minutes—you called, and when I got back Devon was awake and one of the babies was missing."

"Devon, baby?" Regina says tenderly. "Did you try to take one of the gerbils out of the cage again?" Devon just looks at his mother, wide-eyed, admitting to nothing.

"Those poor things are terrified of Devon," she informs me quietly. "He's not the gentlest at three. I wonder if he tried to take one out and sent the others into a panic. You know, I've heard that some animals do that if they think they are in danger."

"Eat their babies?" I am shocked.

"Yes, if they think they are in danger, they will take the babies' lives themselves. It's some sort of primal instinct or something." Regina is cool and calm, not the least bit thrown by the actions of her children's pets.

I wonder how long you have to be a mother before you learn to handle these things, and if all mothers know that gerbils will behave this way when frightened. That would be a total red flag for me in the pet selection process. Goldfish sound like a far more genteel choice. Then again, I am not a mother, and I do not have the incredible sense of serenity and composure that Regina does, even after what she's been through today.

I watch her sit there, surrounded by her family, her hands resting on her stomach and her eyes on her boys. She's got to be at least three years younger than I am, but she is so much wiser and surer of herself. Maybe that's what being a mother does to you. Melba certainly possesses the same qualities, and come to think of it, Nina even did, too. She never seemed unsure about anything, especially when it came to me. She was always sure she knew what was best, even when I disagreed, and I'd never have admitted it before now, but she was usually right, if not tactful.

A small, warm hand touches mine, and I look down to see Marcus beside me.

"Aunt Missi," he begins, "don't you think it would be good to get a new cage for Rex?"

"Why, buddy?" I ask, looking into his dark brown eyes.

"Well, that way Butter . . . I mean *Barry* . . . can't eat any more of the babies. I think it would make Rex sad if he did." Marcus no longer looks sad, just serious.

I look over to Regina and Little Dewayne. "Where's that Walmart I've heard about?"

Five minutes later I am behind the wheel of Regina's minivan, directions to Walmart are on a sticky note on the dashboard, and a kindhearted seven-year-old sits in a booster seat behind me, on a mission to protect a litter of gerbils.

"Aunt Missi?" he says softly. I really like being an aunt, even though I'm not technically one.

"Yeah, buddy?"

"I'm so glad you came here. I've missed you my whole life."

Tears begin rolling down my cheeks without warning, and although it will be hard to tell him that soon I'm going to have to go home, for now I let us both believe what we want.

"I've missed you my whole life too, Marcus."

I do not know how mothers do it every day. Back at Melba's much later, I fall into bed, so exhausted that my entire body aches, but too tired to sleep. I replay the day in my mind, and vacillate between laughter and tears remembering it all.

I am not sure how a person learns to be a parent, although I suspect it's more of an on-the-job-training sort of thing. Days like today will serve to both thicken one's skin and make you love your family more, if that's even possible. Just being a part of Regina and Little Dewayne's family today made me realize how fiercely a mother can love her children, how a man as large and strong as Little Dewayne can become so vulnerable when his wife is in distress, how completely resilient children can be, and how it is possible for someone as emotionally detached as me to so deeply love people that I barely know.

It seems unfathomable to me that Nina wanted no part of this incredible family, and I wonder how and why a person would ever *choose* to be alone. Maybe that's why she swooped down here in an effort to "rescue" me from a life of what was, in her opinion, ignorance and destitution. Maybe what she really wanted was

178

company—maybe she found out quickly that being alone is overrated and was too proud to just apologize and come home.

So I deserve this, now. I deserve to love my family and to feel loved in return. This is what I have always wanted, and regardless of how unconventional my being brought back here may have been, I have them now, and I feel so lucky and so sad. Sad because Nina clearly had no idea what she was missing out on, and consciously left behind the people on this earth that loved her in exchange for loneliness. I'm afraid that I ended up being no company to her either, and instead became just one more chore for Nina to complete.

All the love and gratefulness that currently courses through my heart now, however, cannot obscure something else that my brain is trying to communicate, which is that I am playing house. Yes, I am related to these lovely people, and yes, I love them immensely, but they are not *mine*. They are each other's, and I am an outsider. They did not ask for me to come barging into their lives unannounced, and while I feel nothing but acceptance and affection from them, I was not a part of their lives until just last week, and when I am no longer a novelty will I be merely a distraction?

I need to call Maggie and talk to her. I need to bounce these feelings off someone who will tell me the truth, even if it's not what I want to hear. I reach over to the dresser for my cell phone and flip it open, but it's dead. I haven't charged the battery since I got here, and don't have the strength to rummage through my things and locate my charger, so I close it and fall asleep fully clothed and clutching my phone, and dream about gerbils.

CHAPTER SEVENTEEN

I wake in the morning to an empty house and a note from Melba wishing me a happy "day off." I look at the oven clock and am shocked to see that it is past eleven. Dory left for school long ago, and Melba, Dewyane, and Neil Ray all headed off to work, and I never heard a peep. I suppose that yesterday took more out of me than I realized.

Not sure what I should do with my time, I pick up the phone and dial Maggie's cell number. It's noon in Washington, and I miraculously catch her at lunch, so she can talk without fear of losing her job or having Richard wrap the telephone cord around her neck.

"Missi!" she shouts into the phone. "I've left a thousand messages on your cell! I was afraid you'd been carried off by a herd of rabid armadillos!"

God, I miss her. "My battery died and I haven't done anything about it yet. I spent Sunday at a family supper that lasted the entire day, yesterday with my cousin's three little boys, and am just now rolling out of bed." As I say this, I realize what a vacation this sounds like.

"I think retirement suits you," Maggie quips. In the background I hear plates clanking and a man's voice.

"Where are you?" I ask, wondering which cheap D.C. deli she is in, and whether or not her foot-long has extra mayonnaise or oil and vinegar on it.

"Bangkok Bistro, baby," she says, and the man's voice echoes her words on the other end.

I am jealous, but only for a second. Maggie may be at our favorite restaurant, but I have been consuming vast quantities of heavenly southern food that is far more delectable than anything I have ever eaten during the lunch rush in the District.

We chat for a couple of minutes, but the man in the background is chatting incessantly. The Maggie *I* know would typically ask him to "please shut the fuck up while I talk to my best friend in the whole world whom I have not seen in person in an entire week," but today she addresses the loquacious individual with a calm and accommodating tone that I've only heard her use at work.

"Give me a moment, won't you? It's Missi, and we're catching up for just a sec." The vociferous man responds, and although I can't make out what he's saying, he is charming and agreeable in tone.

"Are you with someone?" I ask. This is an idiotic question, because she is *clearly* with someone. Either that or she has an incredibly attentive waiter who has spent the past five minutes at her table addressing her personal needs, which is unlikely in D.C.

"*Yes*," she practically sings. "You went and left me here all alone, so I had to find someone to keep me company!" She lowers her voice to a whisper. "I met him at the National Gallery on Saturday. He's a security guard there, and pulled me aside as I came out of the ladies' room to point out that I'd accidentally tucked my skirt into the back of my underwear."

I laugh out loud, because I can envision this as though I were right there. "So you've taken him to lunch to what, thank him?" I choke.

"Oh, no," Maggie corrects. "I took him to dinner Saturday to thank him, and then took him home with me. Then he took me to breakfast Sunday to thank *me* for . . ."

"I get it!" I interrupt. "What's his name?"

"*Se llamo Carlos*," Maggie purrs into the phone. I had no idea she knew any Spanish, and suddenly I am bizarrely possessive. I should be happy for Maggie. In all the time I've known her, she's never had a boyfriend, and she supported me through the entire Josh thing—beginning to horrific end—and then pulled me from the depths of depression afterwards never wavering in her loyalty or the sincerity of her friendship. So why then, upon hearing Maggie's very obviously happy declaration that she has been seeing someone for the past *four days*, do I feel compelled to get on the next plane to Washington and reclaim my best friend?

I regain my composure and casually ask, "Did you go see the Calder exhibit?" It's one that Maggie and I both love, and we once spent several hours at her apartment trying to recreate his wire sculptures with coat hangers.

181

"Of course," Maggie says. "It made me feel like I was with you. That's why I went there to begin with. I just got to have my cake and eat it too, as it turned out."

I can't help but smile. "Then go and enjoy your lunch with Carlos. Maybe I'll get to meet him when I get back."

"Okay, but seriously. Watch out for rabid armadillos." Maggie is too much.

"I haven't seen one yet," I assure her, "but maybe I'll start carrying a sharp stick just in case."

I hang up and sigh. I really miss her. There just aren't many people in this world that I would say are my *friends*, and I'd take one Maggie for a thousand acquaintances any day. I wish she'd had more time to talk, but on a cell phone in a public venue just isn't going to cut it. I want to tell her about the myriad emotions I have been experiencing that until very recently had not been known to me. I have always been good at being sad, apathetic, disappointed, and even pissed, but extreme euphoria that is speckled with bits of—at any given time—exasperation, sympathy, shame, reluctance, respect, affection, and awe, is totally not something that has ever resided within me. Maggie would understand that and help me sort it out, but she's on a lunch date. With Carlos the security guard.

I decide to go to the person who, by the laws of nature should always be there to bestow ones' deepest thoughts to. I run up the stairs, dress, brush my hair and teeth, and sniff my tennis shoes. They still smell like turkey but are at least dry today, so I slip them on, grab my keys, and hit the road.

I pull up to my grandfather's and am relieved to see that the rusty old truck is not in the driveway. I wonder if this also means that Sandra is not home. I park the Lincoln and pass Fergie on my way through the carport to the back door. The tractor's paint is faded red and almost as decayed as the truck, and my guess is that relatively little, if anything, has changed around here in a long time.

I tap on the door and am rewarded with a cacophony of barking from the other side. Big Dog and Little Dog frantically scratch at the door until I see Sandra through the small window as she enters the kitchen and gently swats them away. She squints through the window and grins when she recognizes me, turning the locks and welcoming me in with a hug. It makes me happy to be here with my mother, even though she will never know the truth. All I have to do is look at Sandra, and I know without a doubt that I am a better person for knowing her, and knowing that *she* is where I came from. I no longer care who my father is, not only because he is clearly someone not worth knowing, but because Sandra is enough for me.

182

We spend a heavenly half-hour playing chase-the-ball-of-yarn with Missi the cat, and then instead of our usual domino match, we settle in for a friendly game of Uno. I love spending time with Sandra, but for some reason I am having trouble focusing on a game today, and begin to feel restless. Looking around for an excuse to get up, I notice something on Sandra's bookshelf that was not there the last time I was here.

I push back the chair that was added especially for me, walk the couple of steps to where the object sits, and pick it up to look at it. It is the photo that Uncle Dewayne took of Sandra and me at Melba's on Sunday afternoon, in a shiny silver frame that has *Best Friends* etched at the bottom. I look at the two of us—mother and daughter—heads touching and smiling widely, our eye and hair color identical to one another. In the photo, we look as though we've known each other forever, without the thirty-three year break. Our smiles are easy and genuine, as though we are any average mother and daughter posing for a picture.

I turn to Sandra, so touched that I am speechless, and hold the frame out to her. She takes it from me and holds it to her chest.

"It's my favorite," she says. "All the people I love are on my shelf, but you weren't. Now you are." She polishes the shiny frame with the hem of her shirt before setting it carefully back on the shelf.

"When did you have it developed?" I ask. "That picture was just taken a couple of days ago."

"Yesterday," she says, sheepishly for some reason. "My daddy took me."

I am rendered speechless again at the thought of Charles Jenner driving Sandra to get her pictures developed and purchase the frame. Is this a sign of some sort that he is beginning to accept my relationship with Sandra? At the very least, perhaps he loathes me somewhat less than he did last week when I showed up here.

Not sure whether it is that my grandfather might possibly be coming around to the idea of me, or that I now have a place of honor on Sandra's shelf, I am suddenly feeling something beyond content—jubilant, I think. I want everyone to know Sandra. I want her to meet Maggie, and even Josh, because I know he would find this whole turn of events wonderful and be truly happy for me. Unfortunately, they are a long way away, and Sandra is not supposed to know that she is my mother. Still, I am coming out of my skin with the desire to share her with the world.

"Where is your father?" I ask excitedly.

"In town, I think," Sandra says, scratching her chest with two pudgy fingers. "He needed jars."

I suppress a smile and take her hands. "Want to go for a ride with me?"

She nods enthusiastically and follows me to the kitchen, where I scribble a note for my grandfather and leave it on the table where he'll see it as soon as he returns home. We leave the house for our first outing together.

Dolly couldn't be more thrilled to see us pull up and soon she has abandoned her post inside the gas station and we have settled comfortably around the wading pool. Sandra kicks at the water with her feet while drinking a root beer, looking as happy as a kid in a candy store. Dolly watches her, grinning from ear to ear, every now and then looking back at me with a wink or a comment about how sweet Sandra is or how much we resemble one another. I can tell by watching her face how happy Dolly is for me. *I* am happy for me, unabashedly so at the moment, just being able to share Sandra with Dolly.

We enjoy the sunshine, which feels far less oppressive when you have your feet in water and your hand wrapped around a cold drink. I tell Dolly about Sunday dinner at Melba's and about my day with Little Dewayne's kids yesterday, and she listens intently, which is one of the many things I like so much about her. She seems as relieved as I am that Regina's baby is going to be okay, and doubles over laughing as I narrate the birth of the baby gerbils.

Sandra tells Dolly about Missi the cat, and Dolly is clearly affected by the fact that thirty-three years after naming me, Sandra would have a cat with the same name. She asks Sandra simple, kind questions to keep her talking, and I can tell that they are enjoying each other.

After a while, Dolly laughs her hearty laugh and leans forward to address Sandra conspiratorially. "You and me need to come up with a plan to keep our friend Missi in Mississippi, Sandra. We don't need her runnin' off back to Washington, because we'd just miss her too bad, wouldn't we?"

Sandra looks concerned, and I realize that it's never occurred to her that at some point I will leave here. I think Dolly recognizes this, too, because she keeps talking and attempts to lighten the subject.

"Maybe we can find her a boyfriend here," Dolly suggests excitedly.

Sandra smiles and looks at me mischievously. "Missi already has a boyfriend," she informs Dolly. I think she must be confused, or perhaps overheard a conversation or remark about Josh somewhere along the way, but she surprises me again. "She loves Darryl."

Dolly eyes me suspiciously. "You been holding out on me, girl?"

"No!" I defend, a bit too harshly. "I barely know him! Sandra, what makes you think Darryl is my boyfriend?"

"He never came by much until you got here," Sandra explains. "You look at him a lot."

I am so embarrassed that I can feel my cheeks reddening, and suddenly the pool is no match for the heat. I remind Dolly that Darryl is the EMT that helped me during my ant incident, and assure her there is absolutely nothing going on.

"He actually makes me a little uncomfortable," I tell Dolly quietly, trying not to let Sandra hear, not knowing what she may repeat later.

"He cute?" Dolly inquires, raising her eyebrows.

"Yes," I answer too quickly. "I mean, I guess so, but I haven't really thought about it much." I immediately think of his thick, wavy hair and blue eyes, and wonder if I am the least bit convincing. "Why?"

Dolly looks at me and shrugs her shoulders. "Well, I'm not sure what you'd be starin' at, then, if he weren't good lookin'."

"I don't stare!" I snap, now completely belligerent. I am afraid that Dolly can read my feelings better than I can. Her face goes from questioning to serene again, and she reaches out to squeeze my hand.

"Wishful thinking on my part," she says. "I just hate to think that as quickly as you came into my life, you could leave again. I didn't realize how badly I missed having a friend to chat the afternoon away with until that day you showed up tryin' to find Pritchard. I swear I've been happier ever since."

The knowledge that I have somehow made Dolly happier makes my chest ache, and I squeeze her hand back tightly. I look over at Sandra and smile at her, thinking how much happier I am for knowing *her*. She grins back.

"I had a boyfriend one time," Sandra says coyly, tilting her head to one side and kicking at the water with her bare feet.

"Is that right?" Dolly asks. "I bet he was a looker, too."

"He was my teacher," Sandra answers, and it dawns on both Dolly and me at the same time who it is she must be talking about. I am rendered speechless and look to Dolly in sheer panic. She clears her throat and smiles kindly at my mother.

"Was he sweet to you?" she inquires gently.

"Mm hm," Sandra responds. "He sat by me at lunch and gave me extra dessert." She is still smiling, as though she is remembering

185

something pleasant, and I am relieved to know that these are her memories. I decide we should leave it at this, so I stand and turn to Dolly.

"We'd better get going." I look at my watch then and realize that I've had Sandra away for almost two hours. I feel as though I am monopolizing her, and I bet my grandfather is home by now. We say goodbye to Dolly, promise to visit again soon, and Dolly hugs Sandra affectionately before returning to her post inside the gas station.

"I like your friend," Sandra says as we pull out onto the road.

"She likes you, too," I tell her, smiling from the inside out.

As we cruise back into my grandfather's drive, I see Melba's van parked in front of the house. I haven't seen her yet today, so it makes me happy that she is here. Sandra and I get out of the car but have barely taken a step toward the house when my grandfather comes barging out the door, yelling at me.

"God damn it, girl! Where have you been?" His face is scarlet, and he glares at me with pure rage. I am dumbfounded.

"*I said, where have you been?*" Saliva flies from his mouth, and his hands are curled tightly into fists. Sandra has stopped a few feet away and is watching her father curiously.

I finally manage to speak. "I took her for a ride to meet a friend of mine," I stutter.

"You have no right to take her anywhere!" he shouts, pointing a crooked finger at me.

I start shaking all over. "I didn't mean to worry anyone. I left a note for you on the kitchen table."

He narrows his eyes and growls. "You did no such thing."

I feel like a four-year-old being scolded, but am also so angry I can't see straight. Sandra is *my* mother, and if I want to spend time with her, why can't I? I consider running inside to redeem myself by finding the note. Maybe it fell on the floor underneath the table.

Melba appears in the doorway with a piece of paper in her hand. "Daddy, you need to settle down." She approaches us and holds up the paper so that he can see it. "This was on the kitchen table." I recognize the note immediately.

"Well, so what?" he demands.

"It explains where Sandra was and that she was with Missi." Melba looks at me and shakes her head slightly, as if to tell me something. I just stand there, afraid to say anything else.

My grandfather scowls at me one more time, turns, and stomps off to the barn. Sandra still has not moved. She looks confused.

"Why is he mad?" she asks Melba.

Melba ambles over to her sister and takes Sandra's chin in her hand. "He was just worried about you," she says warmly. "Did you have fun with Missi?"

Sandra nods enthusiastically, smiling again. "I made a new friend and drank a root beer." She looks toward the house. "I better go check on Missi," she says, and disappears into the house to see her cat. Melba rubs her temples as though she has a headache. I feel responsible.

"Melba, I am so sorry," I begin, but she holds up one hand and shushes me.

"Baby Girl, this is not your fault. That man is truly exasperating." She leads me into the house and pours us each a glass of tea. I sit in a rocking chair, still not understanding exactly what I did that was so terrible.

"I should have waited until he was home to ask his permission. Or taped the note to the door where he'd have seen it," I think out loud.

Melba shakes her head. "Honey, taping it to his forehead wouldn't have done any good. Your note was still on the table, right where you said you left it."

The only way I've ever seen people enter this house is through the back door, which takes you directly into the kitchen and past the table. It seemed like the most obvious place.

"He can't read," she says quietly after a while. "Words on paper mean nothing to him."

I am both shocked and saddened. My grandfather is illiterate? "Oh, Melba, the thought never entered my mind.

"Well, why should it?" she booms. "I'll bet you've never encountered a single adult human being in your life who couldn't read. Those fancy schools up north wouldn't hear of such a thing."

I stop rocking and look at my aunt, unsure if that last remark was a jab at me, at Nina, or just the truth. She squeezes her eyes shut and shakes her head again.

"I'm sorry," she whispers. "He is like a child in so many ways, and he's just so stubborn!" She paces the kitchen with her glass of tea and finally sits heavily in a chair. "He's not a stupid man, Missi, he just never had the opportunity to go to school. He's been working on this very farm since he was old enough to walk, and with precious few exceptions has never left it. After Mama died and the rest of us realized he couldn't read and could only write to scrawl out some

187

version of his name, we tried to help him. Nina and I tried so hard, but he refused to let us treat him like he was less of a man."

I can see in her eyes how painful this is for Melba. I get up from the rocking chair and join her at the table.

"You know, I think that may be part of the reason Nina left. Daddy flat out refused an education, so she went to the other extreme and ran away to become the exact opposite. I guess she showed him." Melba drains the tea in her glass and rattles the ice absentmindedly.

"Melba, I am so sorry for causing all of this to be dredged up." I feel horrible, but honestly only for making Melba feel the sting of her past and for creating a situation that so clearly confused Sandra when we arrived back here. I do not, however, feel bad for my grandfather. He seems to have a knack for intimidating the people in his life, which is totally unfair.

"It's not your fault, Baby Girl," she assures me, "and you know, sometimes these things happen for a good reason. I mean, the cat's out of the bag, isn't it? There's one more person in this world who knows his big, ugly secret."

"I just thought maybe he was beginning to like me, or at least get used to the idea of me," I say quietly.

Melba reaches across to lift my chin with her soft, warm hand. "Don't worry about him. We've been trying to live with Charles Jenner without losing our minds for a long time, and let me tell you, it isn't easy." She lets go and smiles at me. "Where did you take her, anyway?"

I relax a little and tell Melba about our time with Dolly and how much Sandra enjoyed sitting around with her feet in the pool. I tell her about Sandra's recalling having a boyfriend once, and how it seems that Sandra only remembers the special attention she got from my—I can't help but wince at the thought—father, and not the abuse. Melba smiles through tears and seems truly relieved, although I'm sure the wounds have still not healed for her or my grandfather, even thirty-three years later.

188

CHAPTER EIGHTEEN

We say goodbye to Sandra a little while later, but my grandfather has not reappeared. Melba mutters under her breath that he's probably in the barn "playing with his science project," but he certainly has not made any attempt to speak to us or to check on Sandra's well being after our unauthorized adventure.

Melba has to get back to the restaurant for the dinner shift and closing, so I sail back to her place alone, realizing that I know my way around now without having to think much about it. Not having to think about where I am going to turn next allows me to take in more details than before, such as the goats occupying the many old cars in a yard along one road—I had thought perhaps it was just a junkyard at first, but evidently those old cars serve a greater purpose—and the many signs imploring passersby to "Bring Jesus Christ back to the U.S.A." I wasn't aware that he'd left.

As I pull into Melba's driveway, I park under the shade of a large oak tree. The shadows are getting long, and I am sure that Dory is somewhere inside the house. Uncle Dewayne and Neil Ray will be home as soon as it's dark.

I heave the Lincoln's huge door open and climb out, wondering why I am so exhausted. As I muster up the strength to shove the door closed, I hear a rustling sound coming from some bushes on the other side of the tree. I freeze, listening for the sound again. There is absolutely no breeze blowing, so as I mentally rule out the wind, I hear it again. It's sort of a rustling *and* a scratching, and I can see the bushes shaking as whatever it is moves around inside them.

I decide it's probably a cat, although I have yet to see a cat at Melba's at any point over the past week, and take a couple of ginger steps toward the house, not wanting to call attention to myself. It is

189

at this moment that the thing decides to call attention to *itself*.

I have never seen anything like it, and am once again rooted to the ground, unable to move. It has pointy ears and a sharp nose, and otherwise looks like a giant football. It stops and scratches at the ground with long claws, and then makes a beeline for me.

I start screaming, thinking that those claws could easily rip my eyes out, and God knows what kind of teeth that thing has to also tear me apart with. I run as fast as I possibly can to the back door, and thankfully it is unlocked. I slam it behind me and peek out the window at the creature. It is nowhere to be seen.

"Missi, are you okay?" shouts Dory as she runs, panting, into the kitchen. "I could hear you screaming from upstairs!"

"It was charging me," I tell her breathlessly, clutching my chest and keeping one eye on the bushes by the tree.

"What was?" she asks, turning the locks on the door to keep our unwanted guest at bay. "Is there a perpetuator out there?" She runs for the phone and picks it up. "I'll call 9-1-1."

"No. It's okay," I say, catching my breath and feeling my heartbeat return to a somewhat normal rhythm. "It's gone. I think it went back into the bush." I turn to her quizzically. "What did you call it?"

"A perpetuator," Dory repeats. "Like on *Law and Order*. The bad people the police are always trying to catch. You know, robbers and drug dealers and people like that."

"A *perpetrator*?" I question. She nods, still holding the phone and peeking through the window blinds. "Dory, you can put the phone down. There's not a criminal out there. I was just . . . um, charged. By a creature."

"Oh," she says, setting the phone down, clearly disappointed by the apparent lack of drama now. "A creature?"

I point to the bushes. "I was getting out of my car and it came running out of the bushes over there. It was crazy looking, and covered in a shell or something. It ran right at me, and scared me to death."

Dory wrinkles her nose. "A snail?"

"No, it wasn't a snail! I know what those are, and they aren't scary." Sometimes talking to Dory is painful. "They can't run, either," I add, matter-of-factly.

Dory unlocks the door and starts out into the yard, curious. I panic. "Dory, please stop! It has sharp claws and big teeth!" I follow her closely, since she seems completely unafraid. She must really think it was a snail.

190

She tiptoes to my car, and then beyond it to the oak tree. I am on her heels. We stop when the large trunk of the tree is between us and the bushes, and sort of peek around the tree. The rustling starts again, and so does the racing of my heart. I grab Dory by the arms and push her in front of me like a shield, not that her tiny frame would protect me from much . . . other than maybe the snail she mentioned.

Scratch, scratch, rustle, scratch. I feel like I am living out a horror film, waiting for the psychopath or werewolf or something to jump out at us, and in the meantime I am having difficulty remembering to breathe.

Dory stands completely still, but the noise stops and I feel her relax, as though the danger has passed. "What is it?" I whisper, but as if the thing knew we were standing here waiting for it to reappear, it rustles around and emerges again from the bush, in all its freakish glory.

"There it is!" I holler, running for cover back toward the house. I turn to hold the door for Dory, but she has not followed me. In fact, she is still standing right by the tree. And she is *laughing*.

"Dory, come *on!*" I yell.

"Aw, he's not gonna hurt you," Dory calls over her shoulder. "He probably can't even see you—they have terrible eyesight." The thing is wandering around the base of the tree, poking around in the dirt and grass with his cuspidate snout.

I inch back toward Dory, ready to sprint again if the thing decides to launch an offensive.

"What is it?" I ask again quietly, stopping a few yards from the creature.

"An armadillo," she whispers back, annoyed, as though I should know these things. "Haven't you ever seen one before?"

"No," I snap. "I don't think we have those in Washington."

"Well, at the zoo, then? Don't y'all have a big old zoo up there?"

"The National Zoo has *real* animals," I say, sounding like a total urban snob and wondering if there might in fact be an armadillo there. I take a few steps closer to the armadillo, suddenly recalling Maggie's advice to avoid rabid ones. I proceed with caution.

When I reach the tree, I can hear it sniffing and scratching, but I begin to think that Dory may actually be right. It is smaller than I remember it being, and there is no clear evidence of teeth or foaming at the mouth, for that matter. The claws seem to serve the sole purpose of scratching in the dirt, rather than eye-gouging. I am pretty sure we are safe, and, embarrassingly, that I was probably never in any sort of real danger. I feel completely idiotic, but in all honesty, it *was* scary. The thing looks utterly alien.

There is a rumbling sound coming from behind us and getting gradually louder. Dory turns toward the sound and a mischievous smile spreads across her beautiful face. I turn, too, to see Uncle Dewayne coming up the drive in his truck, kicking up gravel and dust in its wake.

"Dory, please don't say anything," I plead.

She reaches up and cups my face with her diminutive hands. "Missi, having you here is just like having a sister, and I've always wanted a sister." She winks at me and I exhale in relief.

"So the armadillo incident . . . is our sisterly secret?" I ask.

Her smile grows even wider. "Not a chance, sister."

For the most part I have received nothing but sympathy and support following my run-in with the armadillo. This is only because Neil Ray is at Sorbet's this evening, and has not had the opportunity to hear the story and spread it to his brothers . . . yet. Melba and Dewayne got a good chuckle, but otherwise have been kind about it.

I sit at the kitchen table, too full to move. Melba brought chicken and dumplings and blueberry pie home with her tonight, and I have eaten until I am nearly ill. I keep thinking that if I don't leave Mississippi soon, I will weigh three hundred pounds. I have been here a week as it is, and don't know how much longer I can loiter here without overstaying my welcome.

I want to see Little Dewayne, Regina, and the boys before I go home, and of course, I'd like to spend more time with Sandra, although I don't know if my grandfather will even allow me on his property again after today. I shiver involuntarily as I recall the seething anger in his eyes when I brought Sandra home this afternoon. He acted like I'd *kidnapped* her, for crying out loud. My own mother! I know he was just scared—It's been his job for Sandra's entire life to protect her, and the one time he didn't, look what happened. *I* was born, and his family was torn apart. God, he must hate me, and I can't really say I blame him.

My thoughts are interrupted by the silence in the room. I snap back to the present to find Melba, Big Dewayne, and Dory staring at me with concern on their faces.

"Do what?" Uncle Dewayne asks.

"Huh?" I *still* don't know what that means.

"Who must hate you, Baby Girl?" Melba inquires gently.

"Probably the armadillo," Dory answers for me. "She scared the pants off that poor thing."

"What are you talking about?" I ask, irritated. I must have missed something big while I was deep in thought.

"Just now," Dewayne says. "You said, 'God, he must hate me.' Who were you talking about?"

Great. I was thinking out loud. "Was that all I said?"

"Why, is there more?" Dory leans toward me as though she is about to get dished some serious gossip.

"No, I was just thinking about how much it upset him . . . um, my . . . your father, Melba . . . when I took Sandra with me today." I rub my hands, which suddenly feel cold. "I suppose he'll be glad when I leave. One less thing to protect her from."

"Missi," Uncle Dewayne starts. "I usually try not to give my two cents worth when it comes to Charles Jenner, because it rarely does any good other than to get Melba all stirred up. But I can tell you this: Charles Jenner is a man whose life didn't turn out at all like he'd expected. He had three daughters when all he ever hoped for were sons to help on the farm, and he lost his wife on top of it, leaving him to care for two girls and an infant with Down syndrome."

When Dewayne pauses and looks to Melba, I do, too. Her eyes are watery, but she nods at him, as if to encourage him to continue. He wraps his rough, enormous hands around hers, and turns back to me.

"All he knew to do was work as hard as a man could to put food on the table, and I do believe that he made it his life's purpose to watch over those little girls like a hawk. Melba's Aunt Lucille took care of the girls during the day while he was out in the fields, but Charles worried himself sick every time they left the farm to go to school, knowing he couldn't keep watch then." My uncle takes a breath and shakes his head.

"So imagine the guilt he felt when Sandra ended up pregnant, barely a teenager. Guilt *and* hatred, and I'm not just talking about hatred toward the fella who got Sandra pregnant. He's hated himself ever since for allowing it to happen in the first place, and I reckon it's hard to get through each day when you hate yourself."

Dewayne lets go of my aunt's hand and reaches across to pat mine.

"What I'm trying to say is that he doesn't hate you, Missi. You are simply a reminder of what is, in his mind, his own greatest failure." Dewayne looks again at Melba, who sighs deeply.

193

I clear my throat and can barely manage to squeak, "So Nina may have actually done him a favor by taking me away. He could forget, in a way, about what happened to Sandra?"

Melba eyes me sadly. "I think he allowed himself to pretend it hadn't happened. He pulled Sandra out of that school and the two of them haven't spent much time apart since. Unless she's with me she's with him, and that's how it's been for a long time."

I feel sick, and this time it has nothing to do with the amount of food I have consumed. "So I show up and it all comes rushing back front and center, and today he comes home and she's gone. How could I be so inconsiderate?"

"Missi," Melba pleads, "don't you blame yourself for any of this. You are as innocent as Sandra in all of this. The woman you believe your whole life to be your mother is killed in front of your very eyes, then you come here to try and connect with what family you're told you have left, only to find out that Nina wasn't your mother after all—" As she rambles on, her words keep getting louder and more agitated, but she finally stops to take a breath and when she speaks next her voice is just a whisper.

"And to top it off you find yourself in the middle of this crazy, dysfunctional group of hicks from down South. Oh, what you must think of all of this."

I ponder for a moment exactly what I think of all of this. Then I look at my aunt, my uncle, and Dory, who is oddly silent, and see that their eyes are full of love and concern for me. For the first time in what seems like ages, my head ceases to spin, and I can see everything clearly.

"I think," I begin, "that this 'crazy, dysfunctional group of hicks' is the most kind and loving group of people that I have ever had the pleasure of knowing, much less being a part of. I even think, Melba, that your father only does what his heart and conscience tell him are the right things to do. And, I think that we should all stop trying to figure out whose fault it is and whose fault it isn't, because the one thing I am certain of is that regardless of what's happened before, you have all managed to stand by and support each other through a lot of pretty sad situations." I take a deep breath and know that in some small but significant way, I have just changed my story forever.

"Why do you look so happy?" Dory asks, looking confused. I shrug, but can't help smiling.

"I'm proud of myself," I say, sounding surprised even to myself. "I have never been proactive about a thing in my life, and for some crazy reason I decided—well, with a little encouragement from my friend Maggie—to come here and try to figure out who my family is or was." I push my chair back and get up from the table, feeling a sudden rush of energy.

"I had no idea what to expect, and what I imagined was a sweet old grandfather and possibly a grandmother with lemonade and a rocking chair." I am pacing now, and my family is watching me cautiously now, possibly waiting for my head to spin around.

"Sorry 'bout the sweet old grandfather part," Dory mutters under her breath, and Melba swats at her and shushes her, as if she knows that my epiphany is not over yet. Uncle Dewayne is staring at me wide-eyed, as though my euphoria borders on psychosis.

"But look what I got instead," I ramble on. "An aunt, an uncle, cousins out the wazoo, and my real, honest-to-God mother!" My voice is shrill with emotion, but I am not losing my mind. I feel something that I just can't quite put my finger on it's so foreign to me.

"And there's no reason to be sorry, Dory," I say. "He's part of the package. The only thing I'm sorry about is the way it had to happen. That Nina had to die. It would have been great to know all of you at the same time. Maybe I would have understood her better. But I actually don't regret having spent my life with her if it eventually led me here. Right now." I feel so jubilant that I am afraid it may bubble up from inside me and spew all over the room. I feel...

"Lucky!" I practically shout as the word comes to mind, and I realize that this is what I've been trying to put words to. The room is silent except for my voice, which seems to be echoing off the kitchen walls.

"I feel lucky," I explain, "and truly happy for the very first time in my life. It may have taken a long time for me to get here, but every bit of it was worth it, because . . ." I swallow hard, afraid that words will fail me, but thankfully they don't, "I love you all. I just love you."

Nobody moves for a second that feels more like an eternity, but finally I find myself wrapped up by three sets of arms, and strangely I am the only one now who isn't crying.

CHAPTER NINETEEN

If having people to love feels good, then there are no words to describe how it feels to know that you are loved in return, and not the kind of love that will one day change its mind and decide it no longer loves you, or that it loves you, but not in "that way" anymore, because it is gay.

I will never get tired of having my family tell me that they love me, which has happened at least a dozen times already today. Even Neil Ray hugs me on his way out the door early this morning adding a quick, "Love ya, cuz."

I am halfway through my first cup of coffee and not completely coherent yet, but just the same, my head snaps up at the words. A smile spreads across my face and I am about to answer him back when he adds, "Even if you are afraid of a little old armadillo," and runs out the door.

My suspicious eyes find Dory who is concentrating way too hard on her bowl of Frosted Flakes, but I can't turn my grin into a scowl for letting him in on my secret. I am enjoying being awake during this hectic morning at the Little's, as my family prepares for work and school.

More hugs and *I love you*'s are exchanged all around before I am now alone at the table in a quiet house, but not the least bit lonely. I contemplate pouring myself another cup of coffee before I shower and head over to see how Regina is doing. Melba told me Regina's mother is there for a while to help with the boys while Little Dewayne works, but maybe I could run some errands for them or entertain Devon for a while. I could even check on the baby gerbils in their new women and children's shelter, and see how Barry is doing in his bachelor pad.

I opt for a Pop Tart from Dory's stash instead of the coffee and have wrapped it in a napkin to take upstairs with me when the phone rings. I grab a pencil and paper to write a message on, and pick up the phone.

"Missi? Is that you?" a familiar voice asks. It takes a moment to register that this call is actually for me.

"Maggie!" I shout, jumping up and down with the excitement of hearing my best friend's voice on the line. I didn't realize until just now how unfinished our conversation yesterday had felt.

"Wait, how did you get this number?" I ask, suddenly afraid that this is some sort of emergency. "Is everything okay?"

"You're asking me if *I'm* okay?" Maggie asks back jovially. "I have been calling your cell phone since two o'clock yesterday afternoon, and you haven't picked up! I finally decided to call this number, which is the one you called me from yesterday during lunch. I'm a clever one, you know."

Ugh. My cell phone has had a dead battery for several days now. I make a mental note to plug it in today.

"Maggie, I'm so sorry! My phone is dead. But . . . why have you been calling since yesterday if there's nothing wrong?" Maybe she felt the same way about our call. Or maybe something exciting has happened at work. Maybe Richard has been run over by . . . no wait, that's not funny anymore.

"I'm engaged!" Maggie screeches into the phone, and I have to momentarily pull the receiver away from my ear and shake the noise out of my head before reacting.

"You're *what*?" I almost screech back. "To who?"

Maggie clicks her tongue, and I am grateful that she is such a kind person. She could have just totally hung up on me, but she knows me well enough to know that it takes me a minute to catch up sometimes.

"Carlos, you moron. Who do you think? *El es mi amor verdadero.*" Maggie giggles, and although I have no idea what she just said, I know in an instant that this is no joke.

"The guy you had lunch with yesterday? He proposed to you?" I fight the urge to sound incredulous, sarcastic, or unsupportive, knowing it will come out sounding simply jealous and mean.

"Can you believe it? Like, five minutes after I talked to you!" She is ecstatic, and I hold my breath and will myself to be as happy for her as she deserves me to be.

"Maggie, that's amazing! Congratulations!" I think I have successfully pulled off the thrilled-best-friend tone, and start in on the barrage of questions, still trying to keep my voice light.

"How did he propose? When did he have time to find a ring? I mean, it sounds like you two have been together non-stop since you met!" Which was just days ago, I think to myself. Stop it. I need to be supportive. This is Maggie, for heaven's sake. If I told her tomorrow I was going to marry Josh, she'd drag me off to pick out a wedding gown and a strap-on penis.

"We're going to wait and pick the ring out together on our honeymoon in Mexico! You know, there are silver mines down there, and we can buy something close to the source. Carlito's family is in the jewelry business!" Maggie is elated and still yelling, which leads me to believe that she is not at work today. Richard would take her head off for a personal call of this nature and volume at the office.

"This is so exciting! And just like you, Maggie, to go to Mexico and pick out your ring *after* you get married." This I mean. It is exactly the sort of thing Maggie would do. "Okay, so you already have your honeymoon figured out, but surely the wedding will take a little more planning. Surely you've told your parents?" I think of her quiet, homely parents, who I have had the pleasure to meet a few times when they've come to visit D.C. Maggie is originally from Iowa, and while her folks couldn't be lovelier, they must have had a cow when they found out Maggie is engaged to a security guard named Carlos whom she's known for less than a week. I can't help smiling. This is totally Maggie.

"Oh, my parents know, all right," she says, and then bursts into guttural laughter. "That was quite a moment. Total silence on the other end of the phone, and then my father, who would rather kiss a pig than get personal, busts out with, 'Margaret, you know you have other options, such as adoption or single-motherhood.'" Now we are laughing together, because I can completely visualize Mr. O'Leary's kind face, flushed with embarrassment, inferring that Maggie must be planning a shotgun wedding.

"He does realize you've only known Carlos a few days, doesn't he?" I ask, trying to catch my breath.

"Well, I might have mentioned that," Maggie replies, "but Dad never was too good at math." We both start laughing again, and I wish more than anything that we were not having this conversation over the phone.

"I miss you, Maggie," I tell her, wiping the tears of laughter from my eyes.

She is silent for a second, and then says quietly, "Well, I was hoping I'd see you sooner, rather than later. We're flying to Vegas this weekend to make this thing official on our one week anniversary, and I don't think I can do it if you won't be there as my maid of honor."

My shock at this revelation quickly becomes sentimentality at the idea of being Maggie's maid of honor, which in turn becomes anxiety as I realize that I am in Mississippi on a Wednesday, and am expected in Las Vegas before Saturday . . . in a dress. I take a gulp of air and stammer out a response.

"Of course I'll be there, Maggie. I'm just—I've got to figure out logistics." I set the note pad and pencil that I am still clutching in a death grip down on the kitchen table and sink into a chair. Maggie is getting married in three days. What does this mean for me? I shake the thought from my head, because this isn't *about* me, and flex my fingers before I pick up the pencil again and start making notes. As I write, I read the words out loud so that Maggie can follow my train of thought.

"Well, I don't have time to come back to D.C. first to get clothes," I say as my hand unthinkingly writes the word *dress*. "I actually know where a mall is, though, and it's close to the airport." My pencil scrawls the word *ticket* next. "I can book a flight out on Friday afternoon and get to Jackson early enough to pick up a dress and some shoes before my flight leaves." *Hotel* is next on my list. "Where are you guys going to stay, so I can call and get a room there? Oh, and are you guys doing one of those Elvis-as-justice-of-the-peace things?"

There is total silence on the other end and I think for a moment that we may have been disconnected. "Shit," I mutter, blowing into the receiver. "Maggie, are you there?" I am about to hang up when I hear sniffles coming through the earpiece.

"Maggie?"

"I'm here," she says, and then begins sobbing.

"What's the matter?" I ask. Any other person would assume that she might be having second thoughts about getting married to someone she barely knows, but I know Maggie better than that. Maggie always knows what she wants, and never makes a decision she regrets. "Why are you crying? I was joking about Elvis!"

"I'm crying because I'm happy," she answers, blowing her nose loudly into the phone. "I am madly in love with Carlos, as strange as that may be, and I am getting *married*, which I honestly thought would never happen to a troll like me."

"Maggie, you are not a troll," I tell her, and while I know how unusual-looking she is, I mean it. There is so much more to Maggie than what you see just by looking at her, and Carlos has no idea how lucky he is to have figured it out so quickly.

"You know what I mean," she retorts, "and anyway, here I am calling you while you're getting to know your real mother and the rest of your family, asking you to leave on my account, and you're ticking off the to-do list that will get you there without so much as a thought." She starts bawling again. "That's why I'm crying!"

I am touched, but also a little surprised. "Do you honestly think I would miss your wedding for anything in this world? Mags, wild horses can't keep me away. I'll come and help you get married off properly, and then come back here for a few days before I head back to D.C. As much as I love being here, I'm beginning to feel like I am overstaying my welcome . . ."

"You could *never*," Maggie interrupts.

"Well, I know they'll never say it, but I think they might find that they like me better in small doses. I think their lives were a little bit calmer and less dramatic before I showed up, and whether or not they realize it, I know they'll be thankful when things get back to normal."

"Bah," Maggie quips. "Normal is highly overrated."

We exchange more information, and I am armed with everything I need to book a flight to Las Vegas and a hotel room once I get there. I wish again that we were having this conversation in person, because I want to show Maggie how much I've changed in the past week by wrapping her up in a giant hug. She would be shocked and thrilled. I vow to do it the minute we meet up in Vegas.

We say goodbye and giggle at the thought of seeing each other in two days.

"Charge your cell phone!" she yells, just as I am about to hang up.

"Yes, ma'am," I holler, setting the phone back in its cradle. Holy crap, Maggie is getting married.

Thirty minutes later I am booked on a ridiculously expensive flight leaving Jackson on Friday afternoon and have a room reserved at the Venetian as per Maggie's instructions. I have also had the most bizarre conversation with an airline agent who said he was having trouble understanding my "southern accent." What the hell?

I have never been to Las Vegas before and have never particularly wanted to go, but am strangely excited about it. I am suddenly craving a vacation... not that my time here has been hard work, exactly, but definitely emotionally draining, and between ant bites and sunburn, a little hard on the body, too. I still have little scabs all over my legs, and my arms are peeling so badly it looks like I have contracted leprosy.

I call Melba at the G 'n G to let her know about my plans, locate my abandoned Pop Tart, and finally make my way to the shower. Now that I know I will be gone this weekend, I definitely want to go see Regina and the kids today. Maybe I will stop by my grandfather's and *ask permission* to take Sandra over there with me. The worst that can happen is that he will scream at me some more and I'll leave without my mother. I'll take the chance.

As I get ready, my heart beats at breakneck speed, and I vacillate between thinking that I am simply excited about going to Las Vegas or if I may be having a panic attack. I drag a brush through my wet hair and look at myself in the mirror. Aside from the skin on my nose falling off in sheets, I think I actually look better than I have in a long time. Younger? Wiser? Maybe not, but my eyes look rested instead of bloodshot and tired. My hair seems to be enjoying the break it is taking from a hair dryer, too, and looks shiny and healthy. The deep furrows that usually inhabit my forehead are gone, and there is something else. I can't quite decipher it, but it's there.

I lean in closer and assess my face, which in the past I would have described—quite accurately—as plain. Today, however, I might go out on a limb and upgrade it to attractive. It's definitely not pretty in a traditional way, but it's not nondescript anymore, either. There is character there that I have never observed in my own face, and I suppose which can be attributed to the recent events in my life. The mother with whom my relationship could be called—at best—strained is gone. The job which I hated with a passion is gone, and gone along with it the boss who took great pleasure in making each day utter misery. My fleabag apartment and funky couch are gone, too. Everything that made my former life feel so tragic and pitiful are not factors anymore.

I think of all the new factors—Melba, Big Dewayne, my cousins, sweet, innocent, clueless Dory. And Sandra. My *mother*. I watch my reflection as a smile slowly snakes its way across my lips. Screw the guilt and paranoia. There is no good reason that I should be feeling either, and I choose at this moment not to. Can I really do this? Can I choose to eliminate the negative emotions? To focus on and only feel the good ones? I can certainly try. My smile gets markedly wider, and my decision is made. Happy only.

I am ridiculously, gloriously giddy as I dress for an active day of family time. Keys in hand, I leave my aunt's house and set sail in the Lincoln for my grandfather's farm. I arrive to find the crusty old truck in the drive and Fergie sputtering around out in the field. I stand by the fence for a few minutes, waiting for Charles Jenner to spot me and stop the tractor, but it dawns on me that even if he did see me, he would probably not stop driving that thing around. I make my way through the gate and, with my head held high, walk out to where my grandfather and his tractor move in slow, perfect lines across the land.

As I get close, my resolve wavers and I fear for a moment that he will ignore me, but suddenly the tractor lurches to a stop and the engine goes from a roar to a metallic hum, and then quiet. My grandfather sits on his throne looking down at me as I make the final approach, and hesitantly climbs to the ground.

"You gonna get hurt, girl, walking around out here," he says too loud, as though still trying to talk over the sound of the tractor's engine.

I try hard to maintain the cheerfulness that I have committed myself to. "You wouldn't run me over with that thing, would you?" I ask, looking at the strange contraption attached to the rear of the ancient Massey Ferguson.

"It's not the tractor you need to be careful of," he says. He glances down at my feet and moves his eyes a fraction. I follow them and realize how close I am standing to a massive anthill, thankful that I put on my tennis shoes again today.

"What's that?" I inquire, taking a large step away from the ants and pointing to the flat, wheeled mechanism that Fergie had been pulling.

My grandfather picks something out from between his teeth before answering. "Bush hog," he says matter-of-factly.

"What does it do?" I ask, making an effort to force conversation before asking if I can borrow Sandra for a couple of hours.

"Cuts," is his reply. I have clearly set my expectations too high.

I look out at the field where he has made straight, perfect lines in the grass. It occurs to me to compliment my grandfather on his precision, but I decide it will come off sounding insincere, so I don't. Instead, I cut to the chase.

"May I please take Sandra with me to Regina's for a while? I want to check on them, and I know Sandra would . . ."

"If she wants," he interrupts to my surprise. "Don't know if she will, though. She's tired." It comes out sounding like *tard*.

"Why is she tired?" I ask.

He shrugs and turns away from me to climb back onto his tractor. I stand there like an idiot, not certain whether or not our conversation is over, until he fires up the engine and Fergie lurches forward.

Blood from a stone, I think as I scurry around anthills back toward the house. The back door is unlocked, but I still knock loudly as I enter, not wanting to startle Sandra or send the dogs into a barking frenzy. The kitchen is devoid of people and animals, so I head down the hallway to Sandra's room.

She is laying on her back on top of the bed, but her eyes are open. I tap on the door and am thrilled to see the smile spread across her face when she sees me. She sits up slowly and I ease myself down beside her.

"Hi. Are you feeling okay today?" I ask.

She swings her short legs over the side of the bed and nods, "A little tired." She yawns and stretches, standing to assess her now-wrinkled bed linens. I stand, too, allowing her to pull and adjust the quilt until her bed is neat and smooth once again.

"Do you want to play dominos?" Sandra asks, pulling the familiar tin box from her shelf.

I shake my head. "Actually, I came to see if you wanted to go with me to Regina's for a little while. Devon is at home and we could play with him until the older boys get back from school." She does look tired and a little pale, so I give her an out.

"We could play dominos for a little while instead and then I can go over by myself if you'd like to rest."

She perks up. "Let's go see Devon," she says cheerfully, and heads for the door. I follow her through the house and into the kitchen, where she takes two jars of light-colored jelly out of a cabinet.

"What kind of jelly is that?" I ask, holding the back door open for Sandra.

"Scuppernong," she answers. "It's Gina's favorite."

I have never heard of a scuppernong, but the jelly is a pretty pinkish-purple color, so I imagine it can't be all that bad. "Did you make that jelly, Sandra?"

She grins and nods as I open the passenger side door to the Lincoln. "Daddy and I did."

I close her door gently and walk around to the driver's side, trying to imagine my grandfather and Sandra in the kitchen making jelly together. It doesn't seem like something he'd do, but then again, *I* seem to bring out his cranky, non-jelly-making side. It makes me happy to think about him spending that kind of time with

Sandra. I think I'd been under the impression that she goes largely ignored around here, while he spends his time riding around on that rusted out tractor.

I get in the car and look at Sandra, who is cradling the jars on her lap like they are babies. I reach across her and buckle her seatbelt, an ironically maternal thing for me to do, but I don't want her to have to set the jars down.

"Thanks, Missi," she says.

"You're welcome. I just want you to be safe."

She smiles, exposing her small, perfectly square teeth. "I love you," she tells me.

My eyes burn with tears as I grin back. "I love you, too, Sandra."

CHAPTER TWENTY

As impossible as I think it will be to have a better day than the past several, today tops them all. Sandra and I arrive at Regina's, and she couldn't be happier to see us. It seems that having her mother there to "help" is driving her a little bit crazy, so upon our arrival she promptly dispatches Vernadeen to run a series of needless errands "in town," guaranteeing at least a couple of hours of peace.

Regina and I sit on the couch in the family room and watch Sandra and Devon build with giant Lego-looking blocks. Devon takes great pride in knocking down each structure and then watches with amusement as Sandra feigns surprise or disappointment and starts over again. The repetition would annoy me to no end, but Sandra smiles bigger and laughs harder with each demolition.

We pop some frozen chicken fingers in the oven for lunch, and Devon and I sit in the shade of a huge tree and wait for the school bus to bring Daniel home from kindergarten. When the bus pulls up, Daniel steps off slowly, and he looks truly unhappy. He looks up as his feet hit the road, however, and brightens up considerably.

"Aunt Missi!" he shouts. "I didn't know you were coming today!" He gives Devon a kind pat on the head, as if he was a Golden Retriever rather than his little brother, and then hugs me around one leg.

"How was your day, buddy?" I ask, and Daniel's face turns somber again.

"It was *okay*," he says unconvincingly.

"Did something bad happen at school?" I inquire, wondering what awful thing could possibly have transpired on the third day of morning kindergarten.

He scowls and discards his backpack on the grass at my feet. "I didn't get to be the line leader *again* today."

I suppress a chuckle, knowing that this is clearly a serious matter to a five year-old, and that I need to respond in an appropriate manner. I think quickly. "Well, who have the line leaders been so far?"

He shuffles his feet and looks down at them. "Emma, Thomas, and David," he says.

"Do you know their last names?" I inquire, not sure that he will have picked up on such details in just three days. I am wrong.

"Emma Brown, Thomas Carter, and David Egan," he answers without missing a beat.

"Ah!" I say, thrilled with myself for anticipating the teacher's pattern. Thank goodness some things never change. "Your teacher is going in alphabetical order by your last names," I tell him.

"So I'm going to be *last*?" he implores.

"No, Daniel, you'll probably be near the middle, because your last name starts with an L, which is in the middle of the alphabet." I wait for this to make him feel better, but the sour expression on his face does not change. I try another approach.

"That's actually good, you know," I begin. He looks up at me and shades his eyes with one small hand. I continue while I have a captive audience. Even Devon seems interested in my theory.

"You're just learning your way around your new school, right?" Daniel nods. "So for the kids who are the line leaders this week, and even the beginning of next week, your teacher probably has to tell them when to turn right or left, and when to go straight. But, when it's *your* turn, you'll pretty much know where everything is, and your teacher won't have to give directions anymore."

Daniel raises an eyebrow questioningly, but then smiles. "We *do* have to stop at every corner in the hallway now," he informs me. "So nobody gets ahead of the group. I already know when to stop and even how to get to the gym!"

I nod back and hold up my hands in triumph, and Daniel is quick to get on board.

"Oh, man, I'm going to be the best line leader *ever*!" He grabs a strap of his backpack and drags it behind him as he runs for the house. Regina stands in the open doorway and stoops down to hug her middle child.

"Hi, sweet boy!" she welcomes him. "How was kindergarten today?"

"It was great, Mama!" He plants a wet kiss on her cheek. "I'm starving!"

"Well, I just came out to tell y'all that there's some chicken fingers sitting in there ready to be eaten. Sandra's in the kitchen setting out plates."

Daniel runs past her into the house. "Sandra!" I hear him yell cheerfully.

Regina stands up slowly, and I gently herd her and Devon back through the door and into the kitchen. She turns when we are out of earshot of the children and grins at me. "Good job out there, Dr. Phil."

"Ah, you were witness to my quick thinking and vast child psychology skills?" I ask sarcastically.

She takes one of my hands and gives it a quick squeeze. "I saw my baby go from devastated to elated in about ten seconds. Don't think that doesn't mean something to me." She turns again and eases herself into a chair at the kitchen table. "You coming, Aunt Missi?" she asks loudly, and Daniel, Devon and Sandra all look up at me, still standing in the middle of the room.

I walk to the table and sit down opposite Regina, pick up a piece of battered chicken from the plate in front of me, and take a bite. It is warm and juicy. I watch my family start eating, too, and as Devon picks up his sippy cup, I smile inwardly at the knowledge that there is a little white thing that fits into a hole under the lid, preventing the liquid inside the cup from spilling. This is knowledge gained in the field, which means that perhaps I am not just playing house after all.

Regina's mother has returned from her errand running and I can immediately see why she has gotten under Regina's skin. Vernadeen hovers incessantly, shushes the boys, fusses at Gina for not being prostrate with a pillow beneath her knees, and wads up the Play-Doh creations Daniel and Devon made for Sandra to take home and plops them into the trash bin. I try very hard to avoid being in the same room.

When the bus bringing Marcus home from school rumbles its way up the street, Vernadeen hustles out the door and makes a scene of introducing herself to the bus driver as Marcus' grandmother who has "moved in with the family to help Regina, who is now on strict bed rest, until the baby arrives."

"Over my dead body she's here until the baby comes," Regina mutters under her breath. We are peeking out the family room windows watching the show.

207

"I thought she lived here in town," I say, thinking that surely once Little Dewayne got home in the evenings, they could usher Vernadeen back to her own place for the night at least.

Regina squeezes her eyes shut as if warding off an enormous headache, and shakes her head. "She lives just over the county line, which is all of thirty minutes away, but she swooped in here the other day with two suitcases! My poor Daddy is going to starve—the poor man can barely make toast without burning the house down, and for what? So she can nag me and my kids half to death?" She sighs, and the creases around her mouth and tired eyes soften a little. "I should be grateful, I know. I'm lucky to have her, willing to drop everything and take care of me like I'm a child again. You must think I'm awful, Missi."

"I don't at all," I say, and I mean it. "If I've learned anything lately, it's that family dynamics are strange and awkward, and that you can hate someone, or think you do, your entire life and then realize one day that maybe you never took into consideration their side of things."

Regina is still looking out the window as her mother ushers Marcus and another boy up the front porch steps. Her eyes are watery but she is smiling and I know that, for the next little while at least, she is going to cut Vernadeen some slack.

"Maybe I'll wait until tomorrow to evict her," Regina says softly. "Let's go see how second grade was today."

I follow her out of the room to find Marcus and his friend shedding their backpacks and shoes just inside the front door. Marcus hugs his mother around her slight belly and is quickly scolded by Vernadeen to be gentler. Regina tussles her oldest son's hair before turning to her mother.

"Mama, would you mind going to the kitchen and washing some apples or grapes for these big boys? I bet they're hungry!"

Vernadeen hurries into the kitchen to fulfill her task, and I slip around Regina to collect discarded sneakers, socks, and school bags from the foyer floor.

"Aunt Missi!" Marcus shouts, startling me with both the volume and sheer surprise in his voice. "I didn't know you would be here!" He leaps into my arms, causing bags and articles of clothing to spill back onto the floor, but I don't care a bit. I am still not used to people being so happy to see me, and I revel in it. I squeeze this lovely child and wink at his friend, who stares at us as if we'd just climbed out of an alien spacecraft.

"Mark," Marcus says, "this is my Aunt Missi I was telling you about!"

"The one who got your hamster a new cage?" the boy asks shyly.

"No, the one who got my *gerbil* a new cage," Marcus corrects. "Want to go see Rex?"

"Yeah!" Mark answers, suddenly enthusiastic, and the two boys run down the hall in search of the rodent.

I am barely able to contain the ridiculous smile that now occupies my face after hearing that Marcus has told a new school friend about me, and feel positively giddy as I bend over and push the backpacks out of the way, once and for all.

Regina smirks and looks at me sideways. "Must be nice to be a rock star, Aunt Missi."

An involuntary giggle bubbles up, and I am feeling buoyantly charitable. "Why don't you go park yourself on the couch with Dev and Daniel, and I'll go help your mom with the snacks."

"Don't help too much," she quips, and then shuffles down the hall to the playroom.

Sandra is in the kitchen watching Vernadeen meticulously peel an apple, slice it, and spread peanut butter on each slice. She observes with as much intensity as if she's watching a magic show, but she looks tired again. I worry that I have worn her out and kept her away from home too long, so I sit down next to her, forgetting my offer to help Vernadeen.

"Sandra, are you ready for me to take you home?"

Sandra nods, but does not say anything.

"I'm going to go say goodbye to Regina and the boys, and I'll send them in here to see you before we go," I tell her, and excuse myself from the room.

Vernadeen calls out after me that the boys' snack is ready, and I mumble something back about already going to get them. When I get to the playroom, Devon is curled up sleeping at one end of the sofa, and Regina is on the carpet helping Daniel put together a large puzzle of a farm.

"I'm going to take Sandra home," I say, squatting down beside them and ruffling Daniel's hair. He makes a face and fits part of a horse into the puzzle.

"Is she okay?" Regina asks, a look of concern flashing across her face.

"Just tired, I think, but we've been gone a while, and I got royally chewed out the other day for taking her out at all."

"Mr. Charles is pretty protective of her," Regina says with a nod, and this is the first time I have heard him referred to as something other than "Daddy" or "the crusty old man." I kind of like

209

the way it makes him sound almost human.

I decide not to get into the whole story about leaving the note and all. It seems like a good thing to keep to myself, and the more I think about his protectiveness over Sandra, the less annoying and suffocating it seems. "She's lucky," I say instead, "and so will your little girl be, with three big brothers and Little Dewayne to worry about her."

Regina rubs the tiny bump that separates the rest of us from the tiny being inside and raises her eyebrows. "You'd better hope it's a girl, or Dewayne's going to want to keep on trying until we get one." She sighs. "I'm not sure I can do this another time."

She takes Daniel's chin in her hand so that he is looking her in the eyes. "You go with Missi and say goodbye to Sandra and give her an extra hug from Devon," she tells him. "I'll try to pry Marcus away from his friend and his pet and bring him up, too."

I help her up off the floor and follow Daniel back to the kitchen. He climbs into the chair next to Sandra and puts a small hand on her shoulder. "Bye, Sandra. Thanks for coming over to play today. Aunt Missi says you're tired, so I hope you get to take a nap and feel better."

Vernadeen swoops between them with some apple slices on a plate, but Daniel ignores her and turns his attention back to Sandra to finish saying his goodbyes.

"Kindygarten makes me tired, so Mama makes me go to bed at seven o'clock. Maybe you should go to bed at seven o'clock, too. Then come back and play tomorrow, 'kay?" He leans in and plants a gentle kiss on Sandra's cheek as Marcus comes running into the kitchen with Rex in hand and Mark on his heels.

"Marcus Dewayne Little, you get that varmint out of the kitchen this instant!" Vernadeen hollers as Sandra gives Rex a quick rub on the top of her head before getting a bear hug from Marcus. Marcus and his posse exit the kitchen quickly, causing Vernadeen to stomp a foot and put her fists on her hips.

"But I've made a snack!" she whines.

Regina shuffles in and plops down in a chair. "Mother, you told him to get the gerbil out of here, so he's just doing what you asked. He'll be back to eat soon enough."

Vernadeen lets out a loud "Hmph," and picks an apple slice up off the plate. She studies it for a moment before popping it into her mouth and chewing it loudly.

We say our goodbyes and Regina follows Sandra and me out to the car despite the fussing from Vernadeen to come back in and put her feet up.

"Oh!" I say, turning around suddenly and nearly knocking Regina over. "I forgot to tell you that I'm going to Las Vegas tomorrow."

Regina looks at me in shock and then narrows her eyes. "I thought people only went to Las Vegas to get married in a hurry."

"Yes, just not me," I say, amused as relief washes over Regina's face. "My best friend, Maggie," I clarify, deciding not to get into the whole story. "And if you knew her you'd know that a Vegas wedding suits her perfectly."

"Are you coming back to Pritchard afterwards?" Regina asks, frowning. "Or are you going, well, *home*?"

Sandra is looking at me with an expression similar to Regina's now, and I bend to put an arm around her shoulder. "I'm coming back here first, as long as nobody minds. I'm not ready to say goodbye yet."

I hug Regina again, and while I am not a hundred percent sure, I think I actually see a tear well up in the corner of her eye. It hadn't occurred to me that I might be missed, even though I know how much I will miss them.

I open the car door for Sandra, wave to the group of little boys that has assembled on the front porch, and drive back to my grandfather's feeling a strange mix of emotions churning inside me.

Thankfully I return Sandra to a far less angry Charles Jenner than last time. He is quick to shoo me out, however, saying that he and Sandra are required to be at Melba's in a couple of hours for dinner, and that Sandra needs to rest a little in the meantime.

"Somethin' 'bout you leaving?" he says, not looking directly at me.

"Just for a wedding," I clarify, not wanting him to get too excited about my departure. "I'm coming back on Sunday, and I guess I'll decide then when I'll go back to Washington."

He nods and finally makes eye contact. I freeze. "Now go on. We'll be along after a while."

I give Sandra a pat on the arm and tell her I'll see her at dinner. I give my grandfather a tentative little wave and scoot out the door. In my car, I turn the radio on and fill my head with the sounds of Mississippi talk. After commercials for tractor rental and transmission repair, I get sucked into a discussion about casinos and whether or not they are a morally appropriate way to generate income for the state.

It amazes me how both sides can be so convincing—one touting the ways that the state benefits from the jobs and revenue, the other strong in the belief that casinos bring undesirables and their undesirable behaviors to a place they would otherwise not come. I wonder how I'd feel if I actually lived here, if I had kids growing up in this state. I switch off the radio as I pull into Melba's driveway. I suppose I am not the audience they are aiming either side of the debate at. I *don't* live here, and I will certainly never raise children here. I think it's ironic that I am headed to Las Vegas tomorrow, though. Heaven knows what the anti-casino people think of that place.

Dory is sitting at the kitchen table doing homework. I have never understood why teachers feel the need to jump right into things the first week of school. She looks at me with a pained expression, and as I wait for the words "algebra" or "English" to come out of her mouth, she says instead, "*Please* take me with you!" Word travels fast.

"I wish I could, but not only are you too young to go many places in Las Vegas, I am also pretty sure your parents would let you go around the time hell freezes over." Dory grimaces and I worry I've offended her with my language.

"Unlikely, what with global warming and all," she answers, and I can't help but laugh. I love Dory more every day. She is funny without meaning to be, and much smarter than I gave her credit for initially.

"I'll bring something back for you if I can find anything appropriate, okay?" I tell her, and her smile quickly returns.

"Mama's coming home early tonight and making a special dinner for you before you leave," Dory says. "Now how is it, exactly, that you just now found out that your best friend is getting married? Don't these things take a while to plan?"

"One day you'll meet Maggie and you'll understand immediately," I explain. "She generally doesn't do things the traditional way, and she's only even known her fiancée since last weekend." I stop and sigh. "But honestly? Twenty years from now they'll still be happily married. I'd put money on it."

Dory smiles. "I don't know *anyone* wild like that!" She lowers her voice to almost a whisper. "Does Maggie have tattoos?"

I shake my head.

"A nose ring?" she counters.

I shake my head again, but quickly add, "She does have a belly button ring, though."

"Wow," Dory says, looking extremely impressed.

I leave Dory to her assignments and go to my room to start packing. I am touched by the fact that Melba is making a special dinner for me when I am only leaving town for a couple of days, and

212

that my grandfather is bringing Sandra over to join us. My mouth waters wondering what she's going to bring us to eat, and I secretly hope for some of her amazing fried chicken or brown sugar ham.

I rummage through my things and realize that I have not washed any clothes since I arrived. I groan. Nothing I *did* bring would be very appropriate in Las Vegas, anyway. I make a mental note to get to Jackson even earlier tomorrow to shop for an entire weekend's worth of clothes, and fill a quarter of my suitcase with underwear and pajamas. I'll add my toothbrush and makeup in the morning and be ready to go.

I finally remember to plug in my cell phone, and flop down on the bed. It occurs to me that I have no wedding gift for Maggie and Carlos, and that I have no earthly idea what I would even get them. Maggie will understand a belated gift from her maid of honor, I think, as images of china patterns and monogrammed towels run through my head. I'll have to come up with some other idea, like maybe his-and-hers Harley Davidsons. My mind wanders and I drift off.

There is a knock at my door, and I jump. Uncle Dewayne peeks in.

"You decent?" he asks with a grin.

"Depends on who you ask," I say, wiping some drool from the corner of my mouth. "I must have dozed off."

"Got a big weekend to rest up for," he winks. "Melba sent me up to fetch you. Your grandfather and Sandra are here."

Dinner is fantastic. A smaller group is assembled tonight—just Melba and Big Dewayne, Dory, my grandfather, Sandra, and Neil Ray, thankfully without Sorbet this time. The table is so covered with food that the tablecloth is completely obscured, and with the exception of my grandfather everyone seems happy and relaxed. Dory keeps steering the conversation to my trip to Las Vegas, and Neil Ray is all fired up about it for some reason.

As the table gets cleared of the pork roast, sweet potato casserole, yeast rolls, creamed corn, okra and tomatoes, and zipper peas, it is reset with bowls, spoons, and the most enormous banana pudding I have ever seen. The meringue looms over it like Mount Kilimanjaro, and we turn into gluttonous idiots as heaping servings are passed around the table. There is total silence afterwards as we all lean back in our chairs and rub our full bellies.

"You should leave more often," my grandfather says, finally breaking the silence, and I look at him in utter shock as the rest of

213

the table dissolves into laughter. I think the crusty old man actually made a joke.

I shrug and try to act coy. "Maybe I will," I respond, and push back my chair to start clearing the dessert dishes. It is all I can do not to lick the bottom of every bowl I pick up from the table, and I know I will be dreaming about banana pudding tonight.

When the dishwasher is loaded to capacity and enough aluminum foil has been used to span the state, my grandfather rounds Sandra up to leave. She looks even more tired, with dark circles forming underneath her normally cheerful eyes, and I worry that our outing today was too much.

Sandra gets hugs from everyone as my grandfather stands sentry by the door, and I would like to say goodbye to him also, but after our humorous little exchange earlier I decide not to push the envelope. He looks anxious to leave.

I am the last to hug Sandra, and it is a long embrace. She is breathing hard into my chest and the smell of her breath reminds me of those old plastic film canisters. "I love you," she says, and we all follow her out into the yard. My grandfather takes her by the elbow and walks her to his rusty old truck like a perfect gentleman. He helps her up into the cab, gives the door a good shove, and walks around to the driver's side without looking back at his audience. We stand and wave as the truck rumbles down the drive, but I know nobody inside the truck is looking back.

Dory sighs and folds her arms. "I better go in and finish my homework," she says glumly. "Mama, where'd you say the new package of pens is?"

"I'll come in and get it for you, Baby Girl," my aunt tells her daughter, and then turns to Neil Ray. "You going out to see that girl of yours tonight?"

"No, ma'am, not tonight." He looks at me. "Thought I'd go over to Miss Millie's pond and fish a while. Maybe Missi here wants to go with me." He raises his eyebrows as if he is up to something.

I am about to tell him that I'd rather have a pelvic exam than sit outside getting eaten alive by mosquitos while waiting for some fish to eat a worm off of a hook, but he elbows me gently and gives me a pleading look, so I nod.

"Okay," I say finally, "but just for a little while. I'm not done packing yet."

Neil Ray grins and claps his hands. "It'll be dark before long, anyway. I'll get the rods and tackle box!"

I run in to put my tennis shoes on and meet up with Neil Ray in the kitchen, where he has just hung up the phone. "Miss Millie's boy, Quinton, is gonna meet us at the gate," he informs me, and we head out the door to his truck, where two fishing poles are leaning against the side. He sets them down into the truck bed and we climb in, and I can feel such excitement radiating from Neil Ray that I wonder what in the world we're going to fish *for*.

"What are you so excited about?" I ask as he pulls the truck out onto the road.

"Nothing," he says quickly, but I can tell there's more to it. I decide not to press him. Yet.

In less than a minute, he turns the truck off the road onto a wide gravel path, and we come to an old gate locked up by a large chain and padlock.

"Quinton's not here yet," he says, reaching behind his seat and pulling out a small cooler. He opens it, hands me a can of beer, and opens one for himself. Now I get it.

"I thought this was a dry county," I remark, flipping the tab and taking a long sip.

Neil Ray grins mischievously at me over his beer can. "It is, but that's why God invented the interstate." His smile fades quickly, though, and he adds, "You tell my mama, there'll be hell to pay, Yankee."

I shake my head in mock disgust. "You goofy people down here don't even know where the Mason-Dixon line is, do you?"

He shrugs, smiles again, and relaxes, knowing his secret is safe with me, then jumps out of the truck when a tall, lanky black boy emerges from the woods.

"Quinton!" Neil Ray says happily, and the two give each other a kind of clap-on-the-back man-hug. "Missi," he says to me as I also climb out, "I'd like you to meet Quinton Tate. Quinton, this is my cousin, Missi, down from Washington for a visit."

I shake Quinton's hand, which is three times larger than my own. "Nice to meet you," I say, but he just smiles and nods shyly before pulling out a key and unlocking the gate for us.

"Quinton, I'll lock up when we're through," Neil Ray tells his friend, and pulls the cooler from the truck. He hands Quinton a beer. "Thanks, man, and hug your mama for me, you hear?"

Quinton holds the can up in a toast, smiles again, and disappears back into the trees. Neil Ray and I get back into the truck and drive slowly down the path until we get to a clearing next to a large pond.

"How do you know Quinton?" I ask, helping to get the fishing equipment out of the truck.

"Miss Millie and my mama have been friends since time began," he says, setting the tackle box down on the bank of the pond. "They were playmates before anyone around here thought it was okay." I find myself feeling grateful for not having grown up in a place where friendships were based on anything other than whether or not someone was fun to be around, and the realization settles in that the person I have to thank for that is Nina Jennings. More food for thought for my starving mind.

"Millie's daddy and that grouchy old grandfather of ours were friends so long ago they had to pretend otherwise," Neil Ray continues. "The Tates are salt of the earth, every one of 'em, and Quinton has the biggest heart of all but he's the quietest, too." He sits on the ground and pulls the lid off a container. He takes out some bug-looking thing with a bunch of legs and pokes the hook on the end of his fishing line through it.

"I thought people generally used worms for bait," I say, wrinkling my nose. What kind of fish wants to eat a bug?

Neil Ray looks at me sideways. "Well, then, you don't know much about fishin'. Fish around here like crickets just as well, maybe even better. They've even been known to eat a chunk of Mama's ham." He tosses his line out into the middle of the pond, and within ten seconds has a bite. He reels it in, gently rescues it from the hook, and tosses it, flapping, back into the water.

"I suppose I have a thing or two to learn about fishing, " I say, looking around at the rest of the equipment we've brought. "Which pole should I use?"

"It ain't a *pole*," Neil Ray corrects, "it's a rod."

"Excuse me," I respond sarcastically. "I did say I have a lot to learn." I pick up the *rod* closest to me, hold my breath as I get a cricket out of the container, and suppress my gag reflex while attempting to pierce the poor insect with my hook. Out of the corner of my eye I see Neil Ray watching me, and I detect a smirk on his face as the bile rises up in my throat.

"Oh, screw it," I say, throwing the rod to the ground and flinging the cricket into the water. "You fish. I'll watch." I sit down heavily in the dirt as Neil Ray throws his line out again.

"I didn't really want to fish," he admits, wedging the end of his rod into the crook of his bent knee and leaning back. "I want to talk Vegas." I look at him and his eyes are shining with interest and mischief.

"Not you, too!" I yell, remembering how Dory had implored me to take her along. "I've never been to the place, but I highly doubt I'd live through five more minutes in your parents' house if I

216

dragged their children off to Sin City."

Neil Ray grins like the Cheshire cat and raises his eyebrows at me. "Trust me, Missi. You couldn't corrupt me more than life already has if you tried. I can tell by looking at you that you've never been to Vegas . . ."

"What do you mean, you can tell by looking at me?" I interrupt. "What's missing? Tattoos?"

Neil Ray laughs. "Nope, not tattoos. Just . . . I don't know— something. Going to Vegas just changes a person in a way that stays with them long after they leave. You'll know it when you get back, I'm sure of it."

I look at him suspiciously. "And what makes you the expert?"

The shine in his eyes is now a distinct twinkle, and if it's possible, his smile is even wider. "Five days that will go down in history, Missi. That place opened my eyes and changed me forever."

I am aghast. "You've been to Las Vegas? And you're worried that your mother is going to find out you had a *beer* tonight?"

Neil Ray is laughing out loud as he reels in his line, which has started twitching with the weight of another fish. "She wouldn't believe me if I told her myself," he says, tossing the small, brown fish back into the pond.

"Well, where did she think you were? I mean, you *live* with her, and I imagine you'd be hard to miss for almost a week." I pick up a stone and fling it.

"My buddy Cam Hopkins got married last year, and five of us that grew up together were supposed to be going to his granddaddy's hunting camp over in Louisiana for a few days for the bachelor's party. Soon as we crossed the state line, though, Cam surprised us by going all the way to the airport in New Orleans and we got ourselves tickets to Vegas. The first of many spontaneous acts over the course of that week." He sets his rod down on the ground, done with fishing for now, and drains his beer.

"I guess, if you consider giving away money to a casino spontaneous," I say snidely.

He swallows loudly and shakes his head. "I didn't lose a single bill in a casino," he informs me proudly. "There's *lots* of other stuff to do besides gamble."

"Like what, hookers?" I am appalled.

"Hell no!" he says, obviously offended. "Who do you think I am?"

I shrug. "I don't know, someone whose life was very clearly changed forever in Las Vegas? I am going to go out on a limb and say that *my* life is going to be more or less the exact same when I get

217

back here on Sunday. I can't imagine that there's much out there for me, other than Maggie's wedding." I finish talking and it dawns on me that my life will have changed dramatically when I return. Maggie will have far less time for me, and without her, where does that leave me? I shake the notion out of my head and attempt to redirect the conversation.

"Okay, then *cuz*. No casinos, no hookers. What in the world did you do that was so life-altering?" I wait expectantly while he opens another beer.

"We knew we were coming home broke regardless, but figured we could piss the money away at a casino or piss it away doing things we'd enjoy and remember," he starts.

"I thought you said no hookers!" I interrupt again.

"Hush, or I ain't telling you a thing," he says quickly, but I can tell he is amused. I take his beer from him and busy my mouth so he can talk.

"We rented a boat out on Lake Mead, went skydiving, saw some girly shows, and burned through more money than I make in a month, but I kid you not, Missi, it was the most incredible experience of my life." He retrieves his beer from my grasp and finishes it.

"Wow," I say, honestly impressed. "I'm only going for a couple of days and I'm sure the wedding will take up most of that." I also know deep down that I am not one quarter as adventurous as Neil Ray and wouldn't skydive if someone paid me. "But in the end, you came home broke just like anyone else?"

Neil Ray grins. "Every one of us was so broke by the end of the third day that we ate breakfast, lunch and dinner at Krispy Kreme on the fourth." He picks up his fishing rod and starts to torture another cricket. "That's when we discovered midget wrestling.

"*What?*" I ask, hoping I'd heard wrong, but certain I hadn't.

"Single most amazing thing I've ever seen," he says, flicking his line at least twenty yards out. "We were just sittin' eating *Hot Doughnuts Now* when this midget walks in, all bad-ass looking and covered in tattoos, like he'd just hopped off a miniature Harley. My buddy Troy was thinking about getting a tat while we were out there, so he strikes up a conversation with the midget about where he got his tattoos done."

"Can you please stop saying 'midget'? It's making me cringe. I don't think they like to be called that anymore."

"Naw, we asked him. He didn't buy into all that nice stuff, and Troy's only five-five, so Notorious told him he could technically be called a "little person," too. Also said he didn't want to be confused with a Disney character, so dwarf was out. He kinda figures it is what it is, so call him a midget." Neil Ray reels in his line and recasts.

"His name was Notorious?" I ask.

"Yep. Notorious S.M.A.L.L. Get it?" Coolest little motherf—" He catches himself. "Anyway, Notorious talked to us for a while, ate an entire dozen by himself, and invited us to come to a wrestling match that night. Called it mini-wrestling, or micro-wrestling, or something like that."

"And you went."

"Missi, I tell you it was something. Must've been hundreds of people there watching all these midgets, and every one of them was a total hard body. I haven't seen muscles like that on a regular person in a long time, and they were off the hook crazy. Picking each other up and throwing them across the ring, smashing trash cans over each other's heads, and Notorious was the main attraction."

"He was good, huh?" I ask.

"Not just good. Insane. I made a thousand bucks off that little psycho." Neil Ray turns to me. "He said he was gonna staple a twenty dollar bill to his own forehead, and some asshole in the crowd yelled out, 'No way, you freak!' So Notorious said he bet the boys from Mississippi would make a wager on that, which of course we did. Rich jerk from up north somewhere bet us five grand that Notorious didn't have the balls to do it. Idiot."

"He stapled money to his *forehead*?" I am shocked. This is not at all how I envisioned Las Vegas to be.

Neil Ray has a fish on his line, which he reels in, frees, and throws back. "He did it for us," he says, wiping his hands on his thick khaki work pants.

"What do you mean?"

"I think he figured he'd help us out and show us a good time. Nobody else thought he'd bore holes into his own head, but he did it for us. We split the money and left there with a little something in our pockets." He hooks the end of his line onto the rod and looks out across the pond at the sun, now very low in the sky.

"I left Vegas thinking that if I died the next day, I would know I had lived." He picks up the tackle box, his empty cans, and the rods and walks back to his truck. "You should try it sometime," he says to me over his shoulder, not smiling anymore.

Normally I'd get defensive and say something snippy, but I decide not to, knowing that it is not midget wrestling that he is suggesting.

"Let's get you home so you can pack," Neil Ray says, opening the passenger door for me. "Don't want you to be late for the rest of your life."

CHAPTER TWENTY-ONE

I sleep fitfully and wake when it is still dark. I can't help thinking about what Neil Ray said to me last night. Part of me has the audacity to be a little bit mad about it. I mean, I feel like I've lived more since I've been in Mississippi than I ever have, but how sad is it, then, that for me "living" means loitering around my aunt and uncle's place meeting relatives I've never met, babysitting a multi-bird roast, and acting as a midwife for gerbils? Neil Ray is right. If I really want to live, then I've got some work to do.

The thing is, I'm happy, which is not a word I would have readily associated with myself in the past. Growing up with Nina was, at best, tolerable, and even being on my own in my crappy apartment was just *okay*. Except when Josh was around. I was definitely happy then. I suppose the way I've felt the past week is similar to how I felt when I was with Josh. There's something to be said for being around people that you truly care about, and that care about you in return. Maybe that's what living is, or at least where living starts.

I decide to get a head start on my long day, so I head down the hallway to the bathroom and shower quickly, knowing that Dory will be up soon to get ready for school. As I yank a brush through my mess of tangled hair, I realize how long it's been since I've had it properly cut. I twist it and secure it with a clip, hoping that I have time in Jackson to buy a few new clothes, a dress for Maggie's wedding, and get a few inches chopped off my hair. I collect my toothbrush, razor, make-up bag, and brush, and throw it into the mostly empty suitcase back in my room. My cell phone is charged, so I toss that, the charger, and a couple pairs of clean underwear in, and I'm packed.

I dress in khaki shorts, a nice—well, clean, at least—t-shirt, and flip-flops. At least I can count on the weather being equally hot in Las Vegas. It's only five thirty but I can smell coffee wafting up the stairs, so I know that I am not the only one awake in the house.

In the kitchen, I find Melba and Big Dewayne dressed and sitting side-by-side at the table with a newspaper spread out between them. When they see me they both smile, and I think that there cannot be a better way to start a day.

"Get you a cup of coffee, sweet girl, and come sit with us. You're up with the birds this morning," Melba observes.

I pour myself some coffee, add some sugar, and sit down. "Couldn't sleep," I say. "Guess I'm excited for my trip."

"I have it on good authority that Las Vegas is a pretty exciting place," Uncle Dewayne says with a grin.

I am momentarily stunned, wondering if he knows his son has been there, and hoping Neil Ray doesn't find out and think I squealed.

"Um, do you know anyone who's been there before?" I ask, hoping to sound casual.

"Nobody who'd ever admit to it, darlin'," he answers with a wink. "But this is a pretty small town, and we've got a good idea of what people are up to around here."

Not knowing how much Big Dewayne knows, I attempt to alleviate any worries about my cousin. "I'm sure that whoever it is spent more time on a boat at that big, pretty lake than in the casinos. I have it on good authority that there's a whole lot more to do there than gamble." I wink back.

My aunt looks at me through narrowed eyes for a second, but eventually smiles and gets up from the table. She straightens her shirt over her vast belly, takes an apron from a hook on the wall, and pulls it on over her head. "What can I cook you for breakfast this morning, angel?"

I imagine she must be speaking to Uncle Dewayne, but he is looking at me, waiting for an answer.

"Me?" I ask. "Well, actually, since you have to cook for the rest of the day at the restaurant, I was going to save you the trouble and have some of that banana pudding from last night." I gauge the reactions on my aunt and uncle's faces and worry that I've said the wrong thing.

"Or eggs and bacon would be great," I add, trying to salvage the situation.

Big Dewayne jumps up from the table and retrieves the enormous bowl of banana pudding from the refrigerator. "That's the

222

best idea I've heard in quite some time," he laughs, setting it on the table and peeling the plastic wrap from the top.

"Dewayne Clyde Little!" Melba says, incredulous. "What in Heaven's name kind of breakfast is banana pudding?"

"I'd have to say well-balanced," Dewayne responds, looking like a mischievous child. "You've got your fruit in the form of bananas, your dairy in the form of the puddin', and your eggs nice and fluffy right on top!"

Melba, dumbfounded by this logic, stands for a moment just staring at her husband, and I am certain we are going to end up eating oatmeal.

"Dewayne Little, you have lost your ever-living mind," she replies, turning around and opening a drawer. When she turns around again she is holding three spoons in her hand, and there is a twinkle in her eyes. "It does go real good with coffee, though."

We crowd at one end of Melba's huge kitchen table and eat straight from the bowl, something I was never allowed to do growing up. Nina always said it was Neanderthal behavior to eat or drink directly from a container, but I have come to realize that eating out of the container—especially with someone else to help you—just makes the food taste better. Nina might not have been so darn skinny if she'd figured that out.

I stop to take a breath as Neil Ray enters the kitchen. He stops and looks at us, shakes his head in mock disgust, and gets his own spoon from the drawer. In no time, the bowl has been scraped clean and the four of us sit at the table smiling at each other as if we have just gotten away with something.

Dory straggles in mid-yawn and goes right to the refrigerator for some orange juice. She pours a glass with her back to us, and finally turns around to say good morning. "Good Lord, who ate all that banana pudding?"

"It was Missi's idea," my uncle says, pointing to me with his spoon.

"Aw, why didn't somebody come wake me up?" Dory whines. "I never get to eat dessert for breakfast!"

Neil Ray collects our spoons and deposits them in the sink. "You know what they say about the early bird," he says, poking his sister in the ribs.

"I guess he gets to finish the banana pudding at the crack of dawn," Dory pokes back. "But have you ever heard about the not-so-early bird?"

Neil Ray looks at Dory sympathetically. "She gets Corn Flakes?"

"Nope," Dory says, opening the freezer. "She gets to have ice cream, and nobody better say a word about it!"

I hear Melba catch her breath, but when I look at her, her mouth is closed and she busies herself by picking up the empty bowl that once contained a massive amount of banana pudding. She sets it in the sink and fills it with hot, soapy water before kissing Dory on the top of her head. Dory looks up from her task of scooping ice cream and grins at her mother.

"Morning, Mama," she says, dumping a scoop of chocolate into a bowl.

"Morning, baby," Melba says back.

Dory puts the lid back on the ice cream carton and slides into the chair next to me.

"Sorry we didn't save you any pudding," I apologize, sipping my coffee.

Dory leans toward me and sticks a bony elbow into my bicep. "Don't be sorry, Missi. We would never get away with this normally." She looks over at Melba, who is now rinsing the bowl and spoons and setting them in the drying rack. "I think you've made her go soft or something."

Certain I've never had that affect on anyone before, I chuckle to myself and give Dory some company for a few minutes while she eats her nutritious breakfast. I am a horrible influence on these people, but for the time being everyone seems happy.

Eventually the kitchen clears out, leaving me alone with my thoughts and my coffee as my family continues to get ready for the day ahead. Uncle Dewayne and Neil Ray leave at the same time today because they are working together on a site, and they each grab a brown bag out of the refrigerator on their way out. Melba must pack their lunches, I realize, as they wish me a safe trip before climbing into Big Dewayne's truck together and rumbling off down the drive.

Dory returns lugging a backpack almost as large as she is, takes her own brown bag from the refrigerator, and shoves it into her pack before zipping it up. I watch her and think about how every single day that I attended school, from kindergarten until graduation, I never showed up with a homemade lunch in my bag. I was one of those kids whose mother either did not have time to make a lunch for their child in the morning, or simply did not think about taking the time to pack it the night before. I decide at that moment that if I ever have kids of my own, they will never have to buy their lunch in the cafeteria . . . unless they want to, like on pizza day.

Dory puts both straps of her backpack over her shoulders and stands in front of me. "Please change your mind about taking me to Las Vegas, Missi," she implores. "I never get to go anywhere!"

I stand and hold her beautiful, tiny face in my hands. "It won't be as much fun here without you," she says. "Plus, I'll have to eat real food for breakfast again."

"You won't even know I'm gone," I assure her, "and I'll be back in two days."

I hug her, and even with her gigantic backpack on, I can easily wrap my long arms around her. "What are you going to do when I leave for good?" I ask.

She jerks her head away and looks up at me. "Hush your mouth, Missi. A sister doesn't leave another sister, even when she's just a cousin."

I laugh out loud, but know that I will have to leave sometime, and probably sooner than later. I have to go home and make a life for myself, instead of borrowing someone else's life like I am here. I kiss Dory's head like Melba does and squeeze her again before she sulks out the door to catch the bus.

I am about to head up to my room to collect my things when Melba hurries into the kitchen breathing hard and jamming her hand into her purse.

"Going in early again?" I ask.

"Not today, honey," she says, finally pulling her keys from her bag. "I've got to take Sandra to the doctor this morning. Just that routine appointment to have her pacemaker checked."

I'd almost forgotten about that. "What do they check it for?"

Melba pushes her hair away from her face, sets her purse on the table, and turns to me. "I forget that you don't know all about this; it's just part of the drill for me." She smiles and adds, "I forget that you just got here, it feels like we've had you forever."

I listen as she tells me about having the battery checked and how a technician can tell how often the pacemaker has had to correct her heartbeat. I can't help but wonder how a heart as beautiful and pure as Sandra's can be so messed up that it needs a device to make it work properly, but I know there is no answer for this question.

"I'd forgotten today was the day for this. I wish I could go with you. Maybe I can come with you and catch a later flight—" I say as my mind races to come up with a plan.

"When you told me your Maggie was getting married I decided not to mention it," Melba says. "This is just routine, and just like every other time we'll be in and out in an hour or so. You go on just

225

like you planned, and when you get back Sandra can tell you all about her checkup herself."

Melba envelops me in a hug and as we stand for a minute or two just holding each other, I feel a long-empty place inside of me fill up and overflow. Melba may not be my mother, but she is someone who instills in me all that is motherly, and while I know it is useless to wish I'd had her my whole life to help nurture and love me, I can't help being envious that Dory has had this from the day she was born.

"I am so thankful for you," I tell my aunt.

"And I for you, Baby Girl," she answers. "You have filled a void that has plagued this family ever since we lost our boys, and have brought new life to us all. For years I accepted that I would never know you, but I can't tell you how happy I am that I do."

She lets go of me and wipes her eyes with the back of her hand, suppressing a sniffle. "Well, I'd better get going. Your grandfather never has Sandra ready on time, so I've got my work cut out for me." She kisses my cheek.

"Now, you call when you get to Las Vegas so I know you're there safe and sound, you hear?" She eyes me sternly.

"Yes, ma'am," I answer without thinking. "See you Sunday."

"Be careful, sweet thing. Aunt Melba loves you."

"I love you, too," I tell her. She gathers her things and heads out the door to her van. As she starts the engine of her van she looks over to where I stand in the window watching her leave. She places her hand on her heart, blows me a kiss, and waves before slowly starting down the gravel lane.

It's still early enough that if I go directly to Jackson I will still have to wait for the mall to open, so I dock the land yacht at the gas station to see Dolly on the way. A car I don't recognize is parked next to the wading pool. I head inside the mini-mart and know instantly that Dolly isn't there. I know this because the refrigerator doors are all closed and it's at least eighty degrees inside. I almost don't see the small girl behind the counter, but she is chewing gum so loudly that the sound of it calls my attention to her.

"Can I help you?" she drawls, looking over the top of a magazine at me as though I have just interrupted something very important. She doesn't look older than sixteen, and wears a stretched-out pink tank top and an absurd amount of black eyeliner.

"Is Dolly here?" I ask tentatively.

"No," she says, looking around the room as if I should have figured this out on my own, and then back down at her magazine.

"Do you know where she is?" I ask, feeling myself bristle a little. I have no clue who in the world this chick is, but I already don't like her. "I didn't realize she had help here. I'm a friend," I quickly add, trying to establish credibility with this little punk.

Without looking up from her reading material, she grabs a Coke with her free hand, takes a loud slurp, and says, "She's at chemo."

I feel as though the wind has been knocked out of me, and walk over to one of the refrigerators and stick my head in. I take a few deep breaths and collect myself before returning to interrogate Dolly's employee.

"I had no idea she was sick," I say, trying to channel the old me that never cried, but feeling the new me winning. "She never mentioned it to me." I think about the hours we spent with our feet in the water and the secrets we shared, and wonder how on earth this could not have come up.

The girl snaps her gum and sets her magazine on the counter to address me this time. I am grateful for the half-assed show of courtesy, but know that she can now see the tears welling up in my eyes.

"My daddy makes me work here when Dolly needs time off. She's been going to chemo once a month for at least a year, far as I know. Maintenance, I think she calls it," the girl says, and I am surprised and impressed to hear her utter such a big word.

"So this is something she's been dealing with for a while?"

"Mm hm," she answers, and though I feel a little better, I feel betrayed that this news has been delivered to me by a gum snapping teenybopper. I wonder if she even paid for the Coke and gum she has clearly pilfered from Dolly's food mart.

"Listen," she says, bringing me back to the subject at hand, "I like Dolly. She's a nice lady, and I s'pose she should get some kind of award for giving me a job after I got kicked out of school. I'm just mean is all. I didn't mean to upset you."

I sniffle and try to stand up a little straighter. "She's very special to me, even though I haven't known her long. I suppose *you* should get an award for being here when she can't." I should stop with that, but my mouth continues to speak without my brain's permission.

"Why did you get kicked out of school?" I am intrigued, because while I knew more than a few privileged kids who got suspended with relative frequency, I don't think I've ever known

227

someone who was actually never allowed back at school. Maybe that's what happens when your parents pay out the ass to send you to private school. You can come back as long as the checks keep coming.

"I locked the moron principal in the janitor's closet," she says with a nonchalant shrug.

Public school in Mississippi must be tough. "You got expelled for that?" I ask.

"Probably wouldn't have, 'cept nobody found him until Tuesday morning." She takes another loud sip of her Coke.

"Oh wow, you locked him in there overnight? Man, he must have been a jerk."

"He wouldn't let me out of stupid old Home Ec to take an electronics class," she explains. "And I didn't lock him in there for one night. I did it on a Friday before we had a three-day weekend from school. President's Day."

I suppress a gasp, but actually find it amusing. "Guess you never got into that electronics class, then."

"Nope," she says. "Just a heap of trouble with my daddy. He's the pastor at that big old Baptist church up the road. His little angel went and embarrassed the family, heaven forbid."

"Well, you seem to be pretty bright. Ever consider getting your GED and taking some college courses? Bet they have some cool ones they even let girls in." I stop myself. "Sorry," I say. "You don't need advice from a random stranger with no job of her own."

She closes her magazine and stands up. She is much taller standing than she looked sitting, but she is bone-thin, and her jean shorts barely hang on her hipbones.

"No, you're right. I should do that. Dolly and my old guidance counselor have both suggested it, but I've just been too pissed off to listen to anyone who's tried to help me." She looks around and motions with her arms. "Can't work here forever, and Dolly likes being here, so she doesn't need me much. Plus, I'd die of boredom."

I smile at her, the intense dislike I'd felt for her earlier gone and replaced with sympathy. "What's your name?" I ask.

"Ginny. Short for Virginia, but who wants to be named for a Yankee state?" *God*, I think, *these people and their freaking geography!* "What's yours?"

"Missi. Short for Mississippi Moon, but who wants to be named for a rebel state *or* some ridiculous song from the seventies?" I grin at Ginny and turn to go.

"When you see Dolly, will you tell her I came by?" I ask. "I'm headed out of town for the weekend, but I'll come back to see her

228

Monday. Will she be here?" I look at the lanky teenager on the other side of the counter. She is pretty when she smiles and forgets about the giant chip on her shoulder.

"She'll be here. I'll leave her a note." Ginny pulls her chair back under her again and settles into it.

"Thanks. It was nice to meet you, Ginny," I say as I push my way out of the door.

"Nice to meet you, too, Mississippi Moon," I hear as the door swings closed behind me.

My trip to the mall in Jackson is uneventful. I am grateful for having been here before, because I park by the anchor department store and am able to find a Vegas-style Maid of Honor dress. It's a simple, knee-length one that is deep blue and covers my disastrous sunburn in all the right places. I've also picked up a pair of silvery sandals with a small heel that are borderline sexy and that I can even walk in, and enough casual clothes to fill the mostly empty suitcase in my car. I even buy my first pair of designer sunglasses just because I try them on and feel glamorous. Since they are expensive I'm sure I'll either lose them in a week or sit on them, but if they last me the weekend I'll be happy.

I venture into the food court, which was crowded and a bit daunting the last time I was here. Today there are few people, most pushing strollers, and it's relatively quiet. I grab a sandwich and sweet tea and sit down surrounded by my shopping bags. I observe the other shoppers and marvel that nobody seems to be in a hurry. Everyone is walking at a fairly normal, if even a bit slow, pace, and some are looking around and up at the glass ceiling, as though they are just taking it all in. At one food counter, a woman waives someone ahead of her in line, patiently waiting while her young daughter decides what she wants to order.

Living in Washington my whole life, I am accustomed to the mad rush that seems to occur every day without fail; hurrying to catch the Metro, hurrying to beat the lunch crowd, hurrying to get my work done so I can hurry up and go home. I have hurried my way through life without stopping to soak in the details, and cannot imagine all that I have missed in the meantime.

Maybe that's why I am here—to discover and meet my wonderful family for sure, but maybe also to learn how to live differently. I chew my sandwich slowly, close my eyes, and visualize the faces of the people I care about. I see Maggie and her crooked grin, Sandra and her kind eyes, Big Dewayne, Melba, and all their kids and adorable grandkids. I see my grandfather, Dolly and even Ginny, and when Darryl's face somehow sneaks in to my montage, I open my eyes quickly. I vow that when I return to Washington for good, I will carry this with me. I will not fall back into the routine of doing everything as fast as humanly possible. You can't enjoy life when it rushes by you so fast that it's a blur.

As I dispose of my sandwich wrapper and cup, it hits me that while I was imagining the faces of the people I love, I didn't see Josh or Nina either, for that matter. I try to conjure them now out of sheer guilt and they come, but not nearly as vividly as the others. I am a bit mystified by this, but strangely I feel relief. I wonder if I am finally leaving my past behind and looking into my future. I collect my parcels and head for the parking lot, making sure not to walk too fast.

The airport shatters any feeling of Zen unhurriedness I had felt earlier. It's not a big airport, but evidently the entire state is getting on a plane today. I navigate the ticketing line and security with as much patience as I can muster, watching the passengers around me to pass the time.

As the line continues to snake around toward the metal detectors, I stop beside a family of four and imagine that they are on their way to spend a fun-filled week at Disney World. The parents look to be in their mid-thirties and are both very attractive, and the kids couldn't be cuter. The son is five, maybe six, and the little girl in the father's arms is two. I am certain that she is two because she reminds me so much of Lucy, still covered in soft baby skin, but able to communicate to her mother that she is hungry, thirsty and tired.

"Baby, we've got to stay in this line or we'll never make it on the airplane," the woman says gently, reaching over to rub her daughter's back. "I have snacks in the bag that you can have when we get there."

"I want snack *now*," the daughter whines, twirling a long strand of dark hair around her finger.

The dad shifts her to his other arm impatiently. "We can't get the snacks out now!" he snaps, causing the girl's bottom lip to quiver and her eyes to well up with tears. Upon seeing this, the man shoves the girl into his wife's arms and sighs. "I can't deal with this shit today," he mumbles to himself, but everyone hears anyway.

As the girl dissolves into tears, her mother kisses her and rocks her back and forth. "It's okay, angel. Daddy's not mad at you, he's just sad that Pop-Pop's gone to heaven. We'll be at Nana's in a couple of hours and it will make her feel so much better to see you."

"We going to put Pop-Pop in the cemetery?" the boy asks, taking a step toward his mother and dragging his backpack along with him.

"Yes, baby," the woman answers pulling the boy to her side.

"Where Pop-Pop going?" the girl inquires.

Her brother sighs and raises his eyebrows. "A cemetery, Riley. It's where dead people live."

The explanation is clearly lost on Riley, but the dad has heard it and his shoulders begin to tremble. The mom ends the conversation as the line begins to move again, and I am no longer in earshot. I was so wrong about Disney World, and hate that those kids have to endure a funeral at their age. Thinking back to Nina's funeral, I can say for sure that there were no children there. It's just too much sadness to impose on tiny little minds and hearts. I wish I could scoop them up and take them to Disney World while their parents say goodbye to Pop-Pop.

I make it to my gate just as my plane begins to board. The seat beside me is empty, and the flight is quiet. I close my eyes and try to think about how much fun Maggie's wedding will be. Everything that has to do with Maggie is fun, and this will certainly be no different. I am really anxious to meet Carlos. Surely she's told him all about me, but what would she have said? '*My best friend Missi is pretty unmotivated and lacks ambition, but she's a barrel of monkeys otherwise?*'

That's going to change, I remind myself. I am turning over a new leaf. I am going to embrace my life and the people that are in it. I am going to stop and smell the flowers. I am going to be a contributing member of society. I am going to get a job that helps people and rewards me. I am going to volunteer in a nursing home. Okay, maybe I am getting carried away, but I decide that if the opportunity presents itself, I *will* go see midgets wrestle in Las Vegas.

CHAPTER TWENTY-TWO

I have thought that Mississippi must be the hottest place on Earth, but I'm sorely mistaken. As I step out of the airport terminal in Las Vegas I am immediately seized by heat unlike anything I have ever felt. I turn and run back inside the air-conditioned building, dragging my suitcase behind me, and find a kiosk at which to buy a bottle of water. I yank the largest one I can find out of a small refrigerator, shove it at the clerk who scans it, throw money at him, and proceed to uncap the bottle and chug it.

"Thirsty?" the clerk asks, motioning at the line of people collecting behind me.

"Oh, sorry," I say, taking a step off to the side to allow the line to move. "It's so *hot* out there. It must be a hundred and ten degrees!"

The clerk scans a magazine and pack of Kleenex for the lady behind me. "A hundred and fifteen," he says matter-of-factly.

Dear God, there is no way I am going back out there. I smell cooked meat and wonder if it is possible for my skin to have charred in the few seconds I was outside. It already had a head start from Turducken Day. I sniff my arm and am relieved when I see the fast food bag held by the person in line behind me.

"It's not that bad, actually," the clerk offers. "No humidity, just dry heat. You get used to it."

I thank him and walk away slowly, thinking he is completely full of shit. When I reach the sliding doors to exit the terminal again, I stand off to one side and watch people react as they are confronted by the weather. A few grimace, but nobody chickens out and runs back inside like I did. I take a deep breath and slide into the crowd of people brave enough to venture out into the elements. The clerk has no freaking idea what he is talking about. It is unbelievably hot, and the hair on my arms feels as though it is singeing.

232

I step into line at the taxi stand and am so thankful for an air-conditioned vehicle that when it is my turn I decide to ignore the fact that the driver looks like Charles Manson. Not that I actually know what Charles Manson looked like, but I imagine it is exactly like my cab driver. *Looks can be deceiving,* I tell myself. *Embrace life. I am sure he is a lovely man. He just hasn't had a good night's sleep or a haircut... in several years.*

As I climb in he asks where I'm going. I ask if he knows where the Venetian is and then feel like an idiot when he eyeballs me in the rearview mirror and says he's been there a few thousand times, and that if it wasn't so freaking hot I could probably walk there. I decide that I ought to shut my mouth and enjoy the short ride, so I lean back and watch the city reflect light back at me until we pull up in front of my hotel.

Charles Manson reaches a hand out over the seat as I rifle through my purse to find money. I quickly lay it in his palm and jump out of the taxi, my door having been chivalrously opened by the hotel bellman. Another uniformed man pulls my suitcase out of the trunk, and I am escorted into an absolutely magnificent lobby bustling with people, every one of which looks happy to be here. This will be an easy place to embrace life, I think. The mood is contagious, and I grin from ear to ear as I wait my turn to check in.

I look around at the intricately painted lobby, and am bathed in the rich blues and yellows that cover the room. I close my eyes and breathe deeply, inhaling the scents of perfume and fresh flowers, and listen to the sounds echoing throughout the room. I hear hushed conversations close by, a phone ringing at the reception desk, the tapping of feet moving across the marble floor, and . . . a bird? A high-pitched screeching like that of a hawk or some other bird of prey fills my ears, blocking out the other, more pleasant sounds, and causing my eyes to burst open and search the room for the avian intruder. A thorough once-over above my head reveals no bird, but the screeching continues and even gets louder. I refocus my search to the lobby floor, where I see a flaming orange blur careening toward me from across the room.

The blur closes in and wraps its arms around my waist. It is Maggie. My eyes now fill with tears as the extent to which I have missed her settles upon me. I hug her back and we jump around, arms entwined, Maggie still making that awful noise. We have drawn some attention, but she quickly addresses the stares by waving her arms and announcing to every stranger in the lobby that her Maid of Honor has arrived.

Maggie looks . . . beautiful.

"Your hair!" I exclaim, holding up a handful.

"I know!" she yells, shaking her head from side to side like a runway model. "Total lack of humidity!" Her normally wiry, wild hair lies almost smoothly on both sides of her face, which is flushed and rosy. She is wearing a loud, neon floral sundress and green flip-flops, and is positively glowing.

"Mags, you look gorgeous," I tell her, looking down at my best friend and truly feeling her elation.

Maggie snorts and swats at me with a bejeweled hand. "I think someone has been reading the *How-to-be-the-World's-Best-Maid-of-Honor Handbook.*"

"I'm serious," I say. "You look amazing, and you're a sight for sore eyes."

Maggie beams. "Thank you for saying that. You're only the second person other than my parents to ever say that to me; Carlos just beat you to it by a couple of weeks." She squeezes my hands and her eyes shine. "Missi, I'm just so happy."

"I'm so happy for you," I say, hugging her tiny frame. I realize that the check-in clerk is watching us with some degree of amusement, and that I am currently holding up yet another line. "Come on, Mags. Let's get this party started. I can't wait to meet Carlos."

By the end of the day I am as smitten with Carlos as Maggie is. He is a giant Mexican teddy bear, towering over even me at well over six feet and weighing easily two twenty-five. Fantastic security guard material on the surface, but once you get past his hulking exterior you find the kindest, most affectionate, and incredibly personable man you can imagine. He cannot take his eyes off Maggie and hangs on her every word, laughing the loudest of anyone when she says something funny and agreeing with her at all the right times, but not every time. He is lovely.

During dinner at a restaurant off the strip, he has taken to calling me Luna, which is Spanish for "moon." Nobody else would ever get away with this, but coming from Carlos it is endearing and makes me feel special. In the past couple of weeks, Maggie has very obviously told him everything he could ever wish to know about me, which makes me feel even more special, because he remembers it all and asks me about how I am doing after Nina's death without referring to her as my mother, how I am enjoying spending time with my newfound family in Mississippi, and how well Sandra and I are getting to know each other.

Carlos' entourage consists of his parents, who live in a silver mining town in Mexico called Taxco, one brother, two sisters, two childhood friends also from Mexico, and Carlos' roommate from D.C., a slightly unnerving guy named Keith, who is one of the few people at the table that is fluent in English and therefore is the person I converse with the most during dinner. He is highly irritating, continually referring to himself and Carlos as "the two amigos," and is ballsy enough to suggest that he and I become roommates, since Maggie will be moving in with Carlos when they get back. The fifth or sixth time the subject comes up, I decide to nip it in the bud.

"Actually, Keith, as tempting as it sounds, I'm not even sure I'm going back to Washington." Without revealing too much personal information, I continue my little white lie, saying, "I have family down south, and I am considering making a move and looking for a job there."

"*What?*" Maggie shouts, having overheard this remark and not understanding that it is strictly a way to get Keith to leave me alone. She hurdles three chairs at the table to get to me. "I can't believe you haven't told me!"

"Um, well, *yes*. Uh Maggie? I really need to use the bathroom. Want to come?" I politely extract myself from my conversation with Keith and push Maggie toward the ladies' room. She fusses and mumbles all the way there before I can close the door and reassure her.

"I was just trying to avoid becoming Keith's newest amigo," I explain. "He needs a place to go thanks to you, no offense, and I am not about to cohabitate with him at Nina's townhouse."

Maggie settles onto a bench just inside the ladies' room and shrugs. "I guess he is a little strange," she says, "but totally harmless, and we could double date . . ."

"Maggie, please!" I admonish.

"Sorry, sorry, sorry," she apologizes, shaking her shiny, smooth, orange hair around. "I should just be thanking my lucky stars that you aren't really moving to Mississippi."

I am surprised. "Did you think I was really considering it?" I sit down beside her.

She looks sheepish. "I just figured how could you *not*? I mean, this is the family you never had, and from the sound of it, they're wonderful and think you are, too."

"Well, sure they're wonderful, but that will just make visiting them more special and more frequent. I mean, I have a house now to take care of. And it's free!" I squeeze her pale, miniscule hand.

235

As I say the words, though, I can't help thinking about how Nina's house will never really feel like my own, that I feel a little bit like a squatter, and that it's mine by default, not because I have earned the right to live there.

"Besides, what would I do without you?" I say, but again my mind fast-forwards to when Maggie returns to Washington a married woman, and I know that the boundaries of our friendship will have to change.

Maggie smiles finally. "I have to admit, I've been really worried about it. You could sell Nina's house for a bundle in the blink of an eye, and buy up half of Pritchard with the proceeds! Marry that hot paramedic, and . . ."

"Ugh! Not this again."

"Okay, okay. A girl can dream, can't she?" she says, nudging me with her bony shoulder and then jumping to her feet. "I'm just glad you're coming home," she continues. "I missed you. Now let's go find my fiancé."

We emerge from the ladies' room to find the entire wedding party waiting outside the door. Carlos steps forward and takes Maggie's hand, explaining kindly that the bride and groom are due for a romantic gondola ride back at our hotel. Maggie squeals, Carlos beams, and he whisks her away, leaving me an arm's length from Keith. I quickly invent a migraine and bum a cab ride to the hotel with Maggie's parents.

In the taxi I chat with the O'Learys, who are quiet, calm and completely unlike their daughter. They seem genuinely happy despite the decidedly un-Irish-Catholic manner in which Maggie is getting married. My mind wanders to what Maggie said about me staying in Mississippi, and as much as I have enjoyed my time there, I just can't see myself living there all the time. I don't think I'd be happy, and I'm certain there would be precious little for me to do. Still, I wonder why Maggie's dreams for me are larger than my own. I come to the conclusion that I don't know *what* I want out of life, and that even though I came here resolving to live more fully and take more chances, I don't think it's really that easy. I can't just *decide* I am going to get more out of life, can I? If it were that simple, everyone would be happy.

When the taxi drops us off, Maggie's parents invite me to accompany them to see some show at the hotel. I thank them but decline, choosing instead to follow my cousin's advice, and end up wasting the better part of the night in the lobby trying to find out where I might go to see midgets wrestle. I realize too late that this crowd is probably a bit different from the one Neil Ray and his buddies ran with down here, and manage to freak more than a few people out with my inquiries, including the concierge. Unsuccessful and tired, I return to my room, raid the minibar, and fall into a wine and M&M-induced sleep.

CHAPTER TWENTY-THREE

I wake with a start, wondering how both a midget wrestler and Darryl Fortson have ended up in my bed and why in the hell they are hammering on the wall. Upon further investigation, I realize that it was thankfully just a dream, and that the other half of the soft, well-appointed king-size bed is still meticulously undisturbed.

The hammering continues despite the fact that my dream has ended, so I conclude that someone must be banging on my door. I hoist myself out of the bed and peer through the peephole, only to find the hallway outside my door empty. Maybe housekeeping gave up on me.

I am halfway back to the bed when the banging resumes, and again I look through the peephole to find nobody there. Pissed now, I silently remove the safety lock and wait with my hand on the knob for the next knock. I don't have to wait long, and as soon as it happens I yank the door open and lunge into the hallway before the offenders have a chance to get anywhere.

"Ha!" I shout, victorious.

But it is just Maggie, who is plastered to the opposite wall in fear. "Jesus! What is it with everyone today?"

"Oops. Sorry, Mags. You're too short to see through the peep hole," I explain, holding the door open and inviting her in.

"Oh, now I get it," she says. "I thought maybe everyone went to eat breakfast without me."

"Not me, babe. You hungry?" Stupid question.

"Starving! Get dressed, but don't bother showering. You can do that later, plus you'll be sweaty in ten minutes. It's a hundred degrees already. Hurry up. I'm starving!" Maggie finally takes a breath and flops down on my bed.

"You mentioned the starving part," I say, and an idea dawns on me. "How about a Krispy Kreme or two? Neil Ray recommended the Las Vegas version highly."

"Make it a cool dozen and it's a deal," Maggie answers.

I throw on a t-shirt dress I picked up in Jackson, a new pair of beaded flip-flops, pull my hair into the requisite ponytail, and swipe some gloss on my lips.

"Ready to go?" I ask Maggie as I step out of the marbled bathroom.

She narrows her eyes at me. "You look so great," she says, and instinctively I roll my eyes and cross my arms in front of me.

"No, really," she continues, sitting up straight and cocking her head to one side. "You look relaxed and confident. Like you feel better in your own skin or something."

I drop my arms and urge myself to accept the compliment, but feel slightly self-conscious. "Did I look that bad before?"

Maggie rolls her eyes back at me. "No. You didn't. I just haven't ever seen you look so . . . I don't know . . ."

"Well fed?" I ask. "I have been eating like a pig ever since I got to my aunt's house. Chicken and dumplings, smothered pork chops, I mean, my God, those people can even make vegetables taste like meat! And turducken! Have you ever heard of that?"

"Missi!" she interjects. "Well fed was not the adjective I was searching for, but thank you for the tirade on Southern cuisine. What I was going to say is that for as long as we've known each other, we've both struggled with our lives. Take work, for starters, which was, and still is, a miserable place where nobody makes even the smallest attempt to make anyone else feel good about themselves. Then look at our time spent together outside of work. My constant insecurities that nobody would ever want to go out with me, and you getting your heart broken when Josh decided to be, well, *himself*. Throw on top of that your problems with Nina, and then . . ."

She takes a deep breath and continues. "God, poor Nina. But seriously, do you even *realize* all the crap you have put up with? You could not be a stronger person if you tried, Missi, and I have always seen it in your face and in your eyes. Today it's a head-to-toe thing, though. Like you've carried the weight of the world around on your own shoulders all this time and finally got to put it down."

Hearing my life described in such a way makes the lump I haven't felt in a while creep back up my throat. "I couldn't have made it without you, though," I tell my best friend. "I mean, I seriously don't know where I'd be if I didn't have you, Maggie. You bore the burden of my life right alongside me, and were solely responsible for me reuniting with my family. You have been the light of my life for as long as I've known you, and you always will be."

She smiles and blinks back a tear, which in turn makes my own eyes water. "I know, and I have never taken you for granted, Missi, because you have always made me feel deep down how important I am to you. I know that I am not a pretty girl, but you make me feel so special and so beautiful that I can believe it myself. And look at me now! I'm getting married in a few hours. You are the reason I am here today."

We are both crying now, and I wipe my drippy nose with the back of my hand. "I think Carlos might have a *little* to do with you being here," I laugh.

Maggie sniffles and wipes her eyes, which look even larger than usual when they are wet and bloodshot. "Man, you cry a lot now!" she jokes.

I shrug, stand up, and smooth out the front of my dress. "Years of holding back, I guess, and now there's no stopping it."

"It's refreshing to see you express your emotions," she says. "Healthy. *That* was the word I was looking for earlier. You seem healthy. In every way."

"Hm. Then let my healthy self treat my dearest friend to some healthy doughnuts on her wedding day." I grab my purse and hold the door open for Maggie.

"This is the best day ever," she squeals, prancing past me and out into the hallway.

While the doughnuts certainly live up to the hype, I can't help but think that they don't hold a candle to having Melba's banana pudding for breakfast. We linger for a while over our dozen, but even after an hour there isn't a midget in the place to give Neil Ray's story a leg to stand on, and I have given up on asking regular-sized people about it. I am beginning to wonder if he made it up to inspire or entertain me. Oh, well. I have a wedding to attend today, anyway.

Fueled by the mother of all sugar highs, we make our way back to the Venetian to do wedding day stuff. At thirty-three I have never been a bridesmaid before, much less a maid-of-honor, so I had no idea that wedding preparation could be so much fun. Suddenly concerned with wedding day superstitions, Maggie retrieves her things from her room and comes to mine so that Carlos will be unable to find her.

She throws a gigantic garment bag over a chair in the corner of my room, calls room service to order a bottle of champagne, and flops down on the bed. We spend a couple of hours laying around watching bad television and tying on quite a champagne buzz.

I am relishing this time with Maggie, simultaneously feeling a bit selfish that I have had her to myself for most of her wedding day. I think about how Melba will want every precious second with Dory when it is her turn, and decide to suggest that perhaps Maggie call her mom to come help her dress. Before I can get the words out, however, there is a knock on my door followed by a deep Mexican-accented voice calling, "*Mahggie?*"

"Holy shit, he found me," Maggie yelps, running into the bathroom and slamming the door. "How did this happen?"

I suppress a giggle as I get up to let her fiancée in. "It's a hotel, not witness protection," I call out to my sequestered friend. "The front desk may have had something to do with it."

I open the door to a bronzed, glowing Carlos, clad in bathing trunks, a t-shirt, and sandals. Keith trails closely behind, relieving me of the guilt I felt just moments ago. I am glad that Carlos spent today with his friend, too, even if he is smarmy.

I step out into the hall, not about to incite Maggie on her big day by allowing them into the room and in possible eyeshot of the bride.

"She's here, but I think she wants you to wait to see her until the wedding ceremony," I explain, as I watch the smile disappear from Carlos' face.

"Oh," he answers. "Since I have known her, we have not gone this long without seeing each other. "Does she know I'm here?"

I grin. "She heard your voice through the door and made a beeline for the bathroom. Maybe you can talk to her at the door. Tell her you'll see her in a few hours?"

Before I am completely done speaking, Carlos brightens and brushes past me into the room. I hear him tap on the bathroom door and say something to Maggie in Spanish that sounds insanely romantic. I give them their due privacy and remain out in the hallway with Keith.

"Have you guys been at the pool?" I ask, attempting to make casual conversation.

Keith nods and raises one eyebrow. "You know it," he says. "No shortage of hot babes in thongs out there, but sappy-ass Carlos had to come find his chica, like he was going through withdrawal or something."

"I think that's sweet," I defend. "She's never going to let him in there, though. Maggie is being traditional for the first time in her life and worrying about bad luck."

"Sounds to me like you're the one with bad luck," Keith asserts, taking a step closer but then leaning against the wall with his arms crossed.

"Me?" I question, not sure what he is insinuating.

"Yeah, wasn't Nina Jennings your mom? Man, that shit was all over the news for weeks."

While I found him only moderately irritating before, Keith now dangles precariously close to repugnant. I wonder why he didn't mention this last night at dinner instead of now. In the hallway outside my hotel room.

I take a breath and calmly speak. "Well, I suppose I hadn't thought of it as my bad luck, just a horrible *accident*."

He is taken off guard and backtracks. "Oh, right. Well, you know. That's what I meant."

I am not about to let him off the hook. "But that's not what you said," I growl, still keeping my voice low.

"I just feel sorry for you, is all."

"Why do you feel sorry for me? You don't even know me, and I certainly don't need your sympathy." I restrain my emotions and fold my arms defensively in front of myself.

He stands straight again and starts wringing his hands nervously. "It's not coming out right," he starts. "Let me find the right words."

I wait while he attempts to compose himself, but continue to glare at him.

He finally looks me in the eye again. "It just, well, must be hard. To be an orphan."

"Excuse me?" I bark, no longer able to control myself. "An orphan? I'm thirty-three, for God's sake, not four! And since you think you know so much about me, you should know that Nina Jennings isn't . . . wasn't even my real mother. That *shit* you mentioned being all over the news enabled me to find out who my *real* mother is, and I *love* her. She may not be all that mother-y, but she is amazing and kind, and she makes me so happy."

I step forward, and Keith takes two steps back.

"I also have a huge family I never knew about, and have never felt *less* alone in my life!"

It occurs to me as I berate this poor fool that I have stopped thinking of *myself* as an orphan. How could I be one when I have so much family to love?

I sense movement behind me, and turn to see Carlos and Maggie standing in the doorway taking in the spectacle. Carlos looks concerned, but Maggie looks pleased.

"The whole roommate thing not working out?" Maggie inquires with a twinkle in her eye.

"Oh, Maggie! You came out of the bathroom! I'm so sorry, I didn't mean to make a scene." I run to her and put my hands on her narrow shoulders. "I don't believe in bad luck, anyway," I say, looking over my shoulder to scowl at Keith, who must have fled to the elevator, because he is no longer there to endure further tongue-lashing.

"Screw bad luck," Maggie says with a wave of her hand. "I'd already come out of the bathroom to make out with my fiancé, but it sounded like things were getting a little heated out here, so we came to help."

I look at Carlos apologetically. "I know he's your friend, but he called me an orphan."

Carlos shrugs. "He means well, but Maggie says he has no feelters."

"Feelters?"

"Filters," Maggie translates. "He has no filters. Just says whatever comes to mind without thinking about how it might sound. The first time he met me he said he could see why Carlos would like me."

"Of course he could," I say, not following.

"He said it was because my hair is the same color as enchilada sauce." Maggie says, rolling her eyes. "It may be true, but who says crap like that?"

"No feelters," Carlos repeats.

I look back down the hallway. "I don't think I can accuse anyone of not having filters after what I just said to Keith. I'm pretty sure he won't be speaking to me again."

Maggie leans against Carlos' enormous frame. "You rock," she tells me.

I take in the image of my best friend and my newest friend, and smile. These two are perfect for each other and will be so happy together.

"So, now that he's seen you, do you want to go get ready together? Learn how to share a bathroom?"

"No way! My dress is special, and he can't see it until the moment I walk down that aisle," Maggie says, standing on her tiptoes and reaching up to hold Carlos' face in her hands. His skin is like bronze next to her pasty Irish exterior, but I know that their

243

hearts are one and the same. Maggie puckers and Carlos leans down to meet her lips.

"In that case, then, I'll give you two a minute alone." I walk back into my room, pick up my lukewarm champagne, and gulp it down. I feel justified, relieved, and a little bit smug. "Take that, Keith," I mutter under my breath. "Orphan, my ass."

Maggie comes in and shuts the door behind her. "Nice speech, Luna. Now help me do something with this freaking enchilada sauce."

CHAPTER TWENTY-FOUR

There are no words to describe how I feel as I stand next to Maggie as she gets married. The overwhelming emotion is, without a doubt, joy. Maggie is beaming and I can honestly say that I have never seen her so happy.

I must admit that I am also experiencing some jealousy, not toward Carlos specifically, but I think toward the situation in general, because it is something that I feel is so far out of my own reach. Their passion for each other is evident, but so is the mutual respect and enjoyment they clearly find in each other's company.

I once thought I had this same combination of elements with Josh, and I can say that it was the most wonderful feeling in the world. That is, until the rug got pulled out from under me. So I hope with my whole heart that for Maggie and Carlos it lasts, because they are both too lovely to feel that kind of pain and disappointment. This hope mixes in with the joy and the jealousy, and it is an exhilarating sensation.

Fortunately, these emotions have taken the place of the far less appropriate amusement I felt earlier when Maggie first emerged from my hotel bathroom in her dress. She had referred to it as special, but has been handling this entire wedding thing in such a traditional fashion that I almost forgot that she is, indeed, still Maggie.

The dress is, without argument, special. It is unique. It is also unmistakably Mexican-inspired. Maggie's slight frame is completely engulfed by a poufy Pueblo blouse and voluminous tiered skirt. At first glance the dress is all white, but she lifts up the skirt to reveal more layers underneath in every color of the rainbow. It is horrific,

245

but I may have been able to contain myself if she hadn't added the hat.

On her head sits a humongous white sombrero with an attached veil. She looks like the Chiquita banana lady without the fruit on top. In the hotel room earlier, I nearly stabbed myself in the eye with my mascara wand, eventually dissolving into laughter on the floor of the bathroom.

God love her, she could have stripped me of my Maid of Honor duties right then and there as punishment for my convulsions, but instead she fell into a fit of giggles herself. "Isn't it fabulous?" she asked, twirling around so that the skirt went flying up in the air in a blur of color.

I managed to catch my breath and attempted to redeem myself. "I'm actually relieved," I began. "I was starting to worry you were going all mainstream on me, but the dress makes me feel much better."

"I know," she said, spinning around again like a technicolored tornado. "I looked for about five minutes for a dress, but I realized that it wasn't what I wanted."

"What do you mean? That is *definitely* a dress," I pointed out.

She sighed and smoothed the layers. "I know, but I felt like a total fraud trying on *gowns*. A tool in tulle." She flopped down on the bed in full wedding attire. "I decided that what I really wanted was a costume!" A wedding costume is quintessentially Maggie.

That was two hours ago, and I have banished my giggles and guffaws so that I can be the Maid of Honor Maggie deserves.

Now she stands on the altar of what might be the cheesiest wedding chapel in all of Las Vegas, in a *costume*. It is totally inappropriate for the average wedding, but in some bizarre, surreal, inexplicable way, it works. Maggie is truly one-of-a-kind, and only she can pull this off in a way that is anything but average.

I honestly think they could both be naked and it would go unnoticed next to the love and devotion that is so obvious on their faces, and the only disappointment is that the ceremony is largely unceremonious and over in less than fifteen minutes.

The post-wedding photo op is painful, so I am grateful when we all pile into vans headed for the reception. Keith waits until I climb into one van before quickly finding a seat in the other, and I make small talk with Carlos' older brother on the way. I feel bad about how I yelled at Keith earlier, and wish I had held my tongue. He is, after all, the only man who has looked at me twice in a very, very, long time. He is also a complete moron, I remind myself, pushing the regrets out of my mind.

The reception is at an authentic Mexican cantina, and Maggie looks right at home in her dress. I sit at the long, rectangular table, directly across from the bride and groom, and cannot remember ever having more fun. We are the loudest group in the restaurant, with laughter erupting from both ends of the table at regular intervals, but nobody seems to mind. We toast the newlyweds every five minutes, raising our margarita glasses and clinking them, and even throwing back a few tequila shots.

The food is spicy and delicious, and I get so lost in the festive atmosphere that when the wedding flan is brought to the table and quickly served to the guests, I cannot believe the time has gone by so quickly. I want to stay in this happy moment, celebrating my friends forever, but almost before I can process the thought, we are hugging each other and piling back into the vans.

I mow over a few people to make sure that I am in the same vehicle as Maggie and Carlos, and we salvage a few more precious minutes of revelry on our way back to the hotel. Once in the lobby, however, despite the fact that I am borderline drunk and feeling selfish, I realize that I have to let them go. It's their wedding night, for crying out loud.

I envelop my tiny, wonderful, sombrero-wearing friend in my arms and tell her how happy I am for her. A forced smile is plastered across my face, and while I am aware that it is insincere, I know it is also necessary. While Maggie hugs her new in-laws and Carlos shakes hands with Maggie's Dad, I flee to the elevators, where the tears stream freely down my cheeks. I am being silly, but I can't help it. I haven't lost Maggie, I tell myself. I have gained Carlos, which is a great thing, and he totally seems the type who would encourage Maggie to spend as much time with me as she wants to. I am just afraid that she *won't* want to.

Carlos is awesome and clearly makes her ecstatic when they are together without compromising who she is. Why on Earth wouldn't she want to spend every waking minute for the rest of her life feeling that way in his presence? Plus, per our conversation this afternoon, Maggie and I have spent a large part of our friendship bonding over our pathetic lives. Hers just got a whole lot less pathetic. Does this mean that we have less in common now?

When I reach my room, I slip my keycard into the slot and let myself in. I go straight into the bathroom to wash off the mascara that has now run all over my face. As I look at my swollen, red eyes I can't help but laugh. I am being truly ridiculous, and Maggie would be horrified if she knew I cried all the way up twenty-three floors in an elevator.

I run a bath and turn on the small TV in the bathroom. As I climb in and sink neck deep in the warm water, I start to feel punchy and drunk again. In an attempt to relax and settle down, I sink deeper so that the water covers my ears. The sound of the television becomes a muted, distant hum, and I let my mind replay the beautiful day I've had.

When the water is no longer warm, I climb out and notice my cell phone, which has been sitting on the counter top since I returned from my field trip to Krispy Kreme with Maggie. I wrap myself in a towel and pick up the phone, remembering in a moment of clarity to charge it. As I plug it in, the screen turns on and I realize I have a missed call from the Little's number. I dial voicemail and smile at the sound of Dory's voice imploring me to call with every colorful detail of the night. It's too late to call her back now, plus I'm tipsy from the three margaritas I drank at the reception, which I am afraid my aunt will sense immediately and disapprove of. I know I'll see Dory tomorrow, so I turn the phone off and look forward to telling her all about my weekend in person.

I snuggle into the folds of the warm, soft bed and either drift off or pass out, I can't be sure.

The following morning I brace myself for a brutal headache compliments of the tequila and emotional breakdown from the night before. Oddly but thankfully, I feel good. I feel rested and in great spirits, and my next thought is that I am excited to go home. Well, not *home*, but back to my family and the Little Inn.

My flight is not for another three hours, but I decide to shower, pack, and go on to the airport. I can grab a cup of coffee, a muffin, and a magazine to pass the time, and since there's no chance of me seeing Maggie this morning, there's no point in hanging around the hotel.

The taxi driver this time is friendly and pleasant, and seems very concerned with my opinion of Las Vegas upon my departure. I assure him that I've had a lovely time, and that I will definitely come back, even though I am not so sure. It's a little much for me, but I'm glad I came.

Although it's early in the day, the air is already oppressively hot and I break into a sweat just pulling my small suitcase from the taxi into the terminal. I check in at the counter and look for the security line, which I can't see because of a huge crowd of people standing in the middle of the airport. I get to the outskirts of the crowd and ask a woman wearing a visor and white Capri pants if she knows where security is.

"I hate to be the bearer of bad news, honey, but you're looking at it," she says. "I hope you're not in a hurry."

While grateful that I'm not, I can actually feel the stress radiating off of others in the throng who clearly are in a hurry. I remember the sad family from the last security line I had to wait in, so I take a deep breath and decide to block out the madness around me. I think instead about how happy Maggie and Carlos are going to be together, and how much fun spending time with them will be for me when I return to D.C. I think about my aunt, uncle, Neil Ray, Dory, and Sandra. I have missed them all, especially sweet Sandra. I wonder how many times today she's dusted her photographs, and whether or not anyone has played dominos with her since I left. I find myself smiling at the thought of my grumpy old grandfather sitting across from Sandra at her little table, playing dominos and getting his ass handed to him.

My mind wanders to the other people I have met in Mississippi, and I hope that Dolly is doing okay. I will definitely stop at the gas station on my way back to Pritchard and see if she's back. If not, then at least I can check in with Ginny and maybe get Dolly's phone number at home.

I wonder how Regina is doing and if her darling little boys are allowing her the rest she needs, and if she's sent her meddling mother home yet. Probably not, but at least Vernadeen means well.

I can't help but think about Darryl, too. He seems like a good man, and it pains me to think of all that he has lost. The woman he planned to spend his life with was taken from him without warning, and even though he has Lucy to take care of and distract him, I still think it would be terribly lonely. Maybe we have something in common after all: loneliness.

My positive attitude dissipates quickly when I notice how slowly the line is moving, and how close to me the man behind me is standing. He is almost rubbing up against me, and he must have a brief case or something on his shoulder, because every time he moves even slightly, it bumps into my lower back.

I attempt to make space by taking a small step closer to the lady in the visor, but this only succeeds in sandwiching me uncomfortably between them both, since the man takes this as his cue to move forward as well. I turn to make eye contact, as if to say 'Um, hello?' but he smiles and winks, completely oblivious to the message I am trying to send.

I turn a little sideways, so that at least I can push back at the bag when it swings, but he is so close that now my arm is dangerously close to his groin. Disgusted, I turn back and will myself the courage to ask him to please give me some personal space. Part of me is afraid that I will piss him off and still have to stand in front of him for another hour while this line creeps along, and part of me is just too chicken to speak up. As usual, I decide to wait it out, but when his cell phone vibrates in his pocket and I can feel it on my butt, I turn and say, "You going to answer that?"

Clearly embarrassed, he turns away from me and pulls the phone from his pocket to take the call, and for the duration of the security marathon, keeps his distance, for which I am extremely grateful. After what seems like an eternity, I make it through to my gate and have just enough time to run into a newsstand and grab a soda and candy bar before my plane starts to board.

As I exit the newsstand, an incredibly short man wearing a leather motorcycle jacket and dark sunglasses passes in front of me. I stop in my tracks when I read the script on the back of his jacket. *NOTORIOUS S.M.A.L.L.* Oh my God, he isn't an urban myth of Neil Ray's creation after all! I immediately feel bad for ever doubting the story.

"Notorious!" I call out after the man, unable to control myself. He half-turns and pumps a fist in the air, then disappears into the river of people moving down the terminal hallway.

I hear the boarding call for my flight and get on the plane, chuckling to myself and looking forward to getting back to Mississippi.

CHAPTER TWENTY-FIVE

I zone out on the flight back and am on the ground before I know it. I pull my suitcase out of the overhead bin and hurry toward the airport exit. I returned the Lincoln to the car rental company before I left, in an attempt to both save money and get a less ridiculous car when I got back, though I know Dory will be disappointed. I start looking for signs reminding me how to get to the rental car area, and am so focused on where I'm going that I almost don't hear my name being shouted. When it registers, I assume there is another Missi in the vicinity, because nobody here could possibly know me. I look around quickly but recognize no one, and the yelling stops.

I continue on and nearly scream when a hand comes down on my shoulder from behind. I whip around, and there stands Darryl. Beautiful, kind Darryl, with his dark, wavy hair and large, capable hands, is standing in front of me at the Jackson airport.

"God, you nearly gave me a heart attack!" I scold, but inside I have this weird, squishy feeling, and feel my face turn scarlet. He must have had the same ideas I did about us getting to know each other better. Should I jump into his arms? Kiss him on the cheek? Pinch myself? Surely I'm dreaming.

"Don't joke about a heart attack," he says, out of breath. "We've been trying to reach you on your cell phone all day."

Shit. I never turned it back on today. I could have been having a nice chat with Darryl in that horrendous security line in Las Vegas instead of being irritated by the space invader behind me.

"Well, I'm back now," I say cheerfully. Did he just say '*We've* been trying to reach you?' "Who is we?"

251

"Me, Little Dewayne, your aunt . . ." he stops and takes the handle of my suitcase from me. "Just come with me, okay?"

It dawns on me that this is not a romantic encounter at all. I follow closely behind, watching Darryl's long, determined strides. This is rapidly taking on the appearance of an emergency, but I can't make myself ask. I quicken my own steps to keep up and follow in silence until we reach Darryl's truck. He tosses my suitcase effortlessly into the truck bed, which ordinarily I'd have found attractive, but I am too numb to be impressed. He opens the passenger door for me, runs around to the other side, and in one fluid motion buckles his seat belt and starts the engine.

I can't imagine what's happened that would result in Darryl being dispatched all the way to the Jackson airport to wait for me to get off of a plane, but it must be bad. God knows this family doesn't need or deserve more pain. I finally manage to breathe and break my silence.

"Did someone die?"

"Your uncle . . ." Darryl begins, but is quickly interrupted by a strange, guttural sound from somewhere deep inside of me.

"Oh, no," I sob, and completely dissolve. The thought of Aunt Melba and my cousins losing Uncle Dewayne is unbearable. I don't realize that Darryl has pulled the truck over to the side of the road until I can feel both of his hands grasping my shoulders and hear him begging me to calm down.

"Your uncle is fine, Missi. Please listen to me. You need to stop and listen. Take a deep breath." He is calm and composed, and I have snot running from my nose.

I wipe my eyes and my nose and look Darryl in the eyes. "He's fine?"

"Big Dewayne is *fine*," he assures me. "What I was going to say is that your uncle was afraid you'd get back to the house and nobody would be there. Everyone is here in Jackson."

I immediately stop crying. "Here? Why? And why are you here, too? Where's Lucy?"

Darryl takes a deep breath and holds it for a few long seconds. He lets it out very slowly and squeezes my shoulders so tightly that it hurts. For the first time I am close enough to Darryl to pay attention to details. Like the deep creases at the corners of his eyes and across his forehead. He looks tired and sad.

"Lucy is at home with my mother. I am here because your aunt and uncle sent me to meet you when you arrived." He pauses and takes another long breath.

"And . . .?" I ask, feeling impatient now.

"Everyone else is here because of Sandra."

"Sandra? What happened to Sandra?"

"She had a heart attack," he says almost too softly to hear, but I do.

"Oh, God." My head starts to spin. I lean forward and put my head in my hands to try to make it stop, when suddenly clarity grabs hold of me. "Wait. She has a pacemaker, so it would stop a heart attack! Melba just took her Friday to have it checked," I proclaim.

"I know," Darryl says, still calm, but he turns the engine off. This simple act annoys me, and I snap.

"Why did you stop the car?" I bark.

"I need you to listen. I was hoping we could just get to the hospital and then I'd let Melba tell you, but maybe this is better." He takes his keys out of the ignition and sets them in his lap, as though he's afraid I will reach across and start the truck myself.

"Better than what?" I am beginning to feel uncontrollable agitation rising from within me, and know that it will all be misdirected at Darryl, but right now I don't care. I stare at the keys resting on his leg instead of looking at him.

"Better than walking into a room full of people who already know and who will fall apart all over again when you find out."

"Find out what?" I ask, hating the edge I hear in my own voice. "Tell me."

Darryl's voice is soft and steady. "Your grandfather went to check on her during the night. He said he can usually hear her breathing heavily from all the way in his room, but woke up to complete silence, which was strange. When he got to her bedside she wasn't breathing. He called your aunt and she called me."

I am confused. "But wouldn't a pacemaker, by definition, prevent a heart attack from happening in the first place?"

Darryl shakes his head. "Not this time. I called an ambulance on my way out to the farm, and they transported her here to Jackson, but she didn't make it. Missi, I'm so sorry."

At this I look up at him, and in his eyes I swear I can see clouds moving across a swirling blue sky. Sort of what heaven might look like, I think, but then realize that I have never believed in heaven before. Silent tears stream from my eyes.

"She's really gone?" I ask in disbelief. Darryl looks at me, his own eyes starting to tear up, and nods.

"I am so sorry." His sincerity is truly more than I can bear.

"Then let's go," I instruct.

Darryl starts to say something else, but changes his mind and restarts the truck. We drive in silence, and at one point he reaches over to hold my hand. I am sure he's just being supportive and sweet, until he says, "Stop picking at your cuticles. You're bleeding."

Sure enough, I look down and my fingertips are speckled with blood. I hadn't even realized what I was doing.

With one hand still on the steering wheel, Darryl reaches in front of me with the other, pops open the glove box, and pulls out a small box of antiseptic wipes. He tears a pouch open with his teeth, shakes out a wipe, and folds it gently around my raw fingers.

I sit there and stare out of the windshield, feeling no pain. I feel nothing at all.

We arrive at the University of Mississippi Medical Center and make our way through the lobby. In the waiting area sits Uncle Dewayne, Dory, Neil Ray, Stanley, and Little Dewayne. Everyone is red-eyed and clearly devastated, but they all rise to hug me when Darryl leads me in. Nobody says anything, but since I have no words for this occasion, I am grateful not to have to try.

"Baby Girl," comes a voice from behind me, and I turn to face Melba. She opens her arms to me and I fall into them, feeling the warmth and softness of her body surround mine. She strokes my hair and holds me tight, my tears dampening the front of her dress.

She loosens her hold on me and takes my chin in her hand. "Would you like to see her?"

I nod, and she leads me by the hand to a bank of elevators. I am numb to all details, but we eventually exit the elevator and walk down a corridor to the door of a dim, cold room. Inside, Sandra lays flat in a hospital bed, her arms at her sides and a serene expression on her face. Goosebumps rise on my arms and I want to pull a blanket over her to warm her, but know it would be pointless.

"She looks like she's sleeping," I observe.

"Well, she was," Melba says. "And for that we can thank God. She was never in any pain."

I stand over Sandra and drink in every detail for the last time. She looks so much smaller now, and her cheeks, which always seemed flushed with color, are now pale and chalky-looking. I take one of Sandra's pudgy hands in mine, expecting it to be warm and sweaty like usual, but it is cool and lifeless. I quickly let go, not wanting to erase my memories of what it felt like to hold my mother's hand.

"I wish I could see her smile one more time," I whisper, tears starting to wet my face again.

Melba nods and wraps an arm around my shoulders. "She did have a beautiful smile, didn't she? Contagious, I'd say. It was hard to see her smile and not smile back."

As she says it, I can picture Sandra in my mind in sort of a mental slide show. The day I met her, when she held my hands after the ants had their way with me, the times we played dominos and that day at Regina's house with the kids. Even when she just sat still, holding Missi the cat or with her feet in Dolly's pool, there was always the smile.

My chest begins to heave, and I bury my face in Melba's embrace, letting the weight of my emotions spill out. She cries along with me, and I feel almost selfish for it.

"I'm so sorry," I sob. "I have no right."

She gently pushes me to an arm's length and tips my chin so that our eyes meet. Hers are red and swollen, but warm and kind as always. "What could you possibly be sorry about?"

"You have already lost so much—your mother, your sons, and now both of your sisters—I cannot imagine how angry you are." I take a deep breath. "How incredibly sad you must feel to have another person taken away from you." My vision blurs as the tears continue and I realize that I am describing exactly how I feel. I too am angry and sad. I feel broken.

"You've lost people you've loved your whole life, and I just got here," I continue. "I have no right to take this moment and make it mine."

Melba shakes her head and lets go long enough to wipe her eyes and nose. "You have every right. She's yours, too. You spent your life not knowing the truth, and just when you find it out, it gets taken away again, and for good this time. It wasn't enough time for you, and I know it."

I look down at Sandra and can't help smiling through my tears. "I'll take the last couple of weeks over never knowing her at all," I say. "It's been the best time of my life, and I'll never forget how it felt to be around my mother."

"She was an angel on Earth," comes a gruff, scratchy voice from behind me. "Imagine what she'll be able to do in heaven."

I turn to find my grandfather standing in the doorway. I have no idea how long he's been there, but his face is blotchy and his eyes are moist.

I nod, not knowing what to say to him. The one thing I know for sure about my grandfather is that he lived and breathed for Sandra. She was his baby and he was her protector, and I cannot begin to imagine how her death will affect this already angry and distant man.

"I'm so sorry," I choke.

He looks at me, his eyes boring holes through mine. "I'm sorry for you, too. You being here has made her very happy." Tears begin to drip from his eyes, and for a moment I am too stunned to move. Finally, my legs carry me the few steps to the door and my arms reach out, knowing they may be brushed away.

I squeeze my grandfather tightly and he surprises me by squeezing back. It's stiff and I know we are both uncomfortable, so I let go quickly. He nods and walks out of the room, and I watch him retreat down the hallway, looking small and frail for the first time.

Melba and I stay with Sandra for a long time. I think neither one of us can bear to leave knowing that we'll never have her to ourselves like this again. From time to time I imagine that she is really just asleep, but before long the pain comes in waves that wash over me, fresh again, and I know that it is the kind of pain that a person feels only when they have lost a part of who they are.

I suppose that's why I felt so little emotion after Nina died. She wasn't really part of me. Maybe deep down somewhere I knew that she wasn't the real thing, even though I consciously never questioned it. I voice these thoughts to my aunt, and she listens quietly, accepting my train of thought for what it is; a coming to terms with the mind-numbing reality of the situation, but also an attempt to hang on to whatever I can of Sandra.

While Melba and I sit, she tells me stories about Sandra. She tells me about when Sandra was born and how she was the only thing that got them all through the death of my grandmother. How she was the world's happiest and most content baby, as if she knew that she needed to make life easy on everyone. She remembers how they would all fuss over her and compete for her attention, even Nina.

She reflects on Sandra as a child who knew no stranger and made all who encountered her smile, and as a pregnant adolescent, safely sheltered from the knowledge of what had happened to her, never questioning the growth of her belly or the pain she surely endured during my delivery. She tells me how Sandra was soothed by the responsibility of caring for her cats after I had been taken away, and I take sad comfort in knowing that she truly never felt the loss of me.

A long time passes while we talk, and there is a quiet tap on the doorjamb as a silver-haired doctor enters the room. He is an older man, and very small, so that when my aunt stands and goes to hug him, I worry that he may be lost forever or at the very least suffocate in her embrace.

Turning to me finally, Melba says, "Missi, I'd like you to meet Dr. Boudreaux. Richard, this is my niece, Missi Jennings."

I shake his hand and can see my own sadness reflected in his eyes. He obviously cared for Sandra a great deal, and I find myself attempting to comfort him.

"Thank you for taking such good care of my mother," I whisper.

The doctor's eyes widen, and I realize that I have given away a family secret. I look to Melba apologetically, but she squeezes my hand and grins sheepishly.

"It just never came up," she says to us both.

Dr. Boudreaux recovers quickly from this revelation. "Well, any kin of a Jenner or a Little is a friend of mine," he says kindly. Then more seriously, "Sandra was a very special person, and remarkable in a number of ways. I am truly sorry for all of our loss."

I nod my thanks, proud that one more person in this world knows who I am. "Do we need to leave now?" I ask, aware of the hours we have spent occupying this room and not knowing if any of the rest of the family is still waiting patiently downstairs for our return.

"You may stay with her a while longer," he answers. "I just came in to see if she was ready to be moved." He looks at me directly. "Do you have any questions for me before I go?"

I am temporarily stumped. I had so many questions earlier, but none of them come to mind now . . . except for one.

"Why?" I ask. "Why did she die? Her pacemaker was supposed to prevent that, wasn't it?"

Dr. Boudreaux looks at me so sympathetically that I almost start crying again. "She was a twiddler," he says simply.

"A what?" Is this some strange nickname for a person with Down syndrome? I am almost insulted by this silly remark until the doctor reaches up to scratch his chest. It is something I saw Sandra do many times, and I understand suddenly that he is illustrating his point.

"A twiddler is someone who unconsciously manipulates their pacemaker by rubbing or scratching the area of their chest directly outside where the pacemaker has been implanted. In Sandra's case, she loosened the pacing electrode, so that when she went into cardiac arrest, it couldn't help her." His eyes have never left mine, and when he finishes his explanation his hand is still on his chest. "When we tested the device last week it worked just fine, but this can happen."

My hand is on my chest, as well. "I've seen her do it," I say, "but I figured it was a nervous habit or something. I never realized it was something dangerous." I feel horrible, as if I should have known this and told her to stop.

Reading my thoughts, Melba wipes her eyes, which have filled with tears again. "If I had a nickel for every time I fussed at her about that I'd be sitting on a yacht somewhere instead of stirring slop for the fine people of Pritchard." She smiles through her tears. "Didn't do any good, though. She was like a child in that way; the more you fuss at them, the more they do the thing you're fussing at them about."

Dr. Boudreaux nods in agreement. "I almost think it made her more aware that there was something to fiddle with, as perceptive a gal as Sandra was."

We stand and sniffle together, Melba and I towering over the compact little doctor, until he finally says, "Shall we say a prayer before we take her down?"

"That would be lovely," my aunt replies, taking my hand and turning toward the restful form of my mother one final time. "Missi, will you do us the honor of the prayer?"

Instantaneously nervous, I shake my head profusely, and I know I must look like a child about to throw the mother of all tantrums. "I can't," I stammer. "I don't know how. I don't go to church . . ."

"Going to church doesn't make you good at praying any more than wearing a white coat makes you good at being a doctor," Dr. Boudreaux says kindly, stepping into line on the other side of me and taking hold of my free hand. "It's what's in your heart and your mind that matters, and praying is the very best place to begin. Start with 'Dear Lord' and then just say what comes to mind. I imagine you'll find out you're better at it than you think."

I look at Sandra, but the pallor of her skin just reminds me she is dead, so I close my eyes instead and my head fills with the image of her sitting across the dominos table from me, cheeks flushed and eyes smiling. This is better, and I begin my prayer.

"Dear Lord," I say timidly, "please take good care of Sandra. She was a warm, happy person who could light up a room with her smile, and even though everyone wanted to take care of her, I think Sandra was really the one who always took care of everyone else. So now it's her turn to be taken care of. I am not sure what heaven is like, but I feel sure now that there is one, so if you don't already have them, you'll need dominos and lots of cats for her to play with there. And if it's not too much to ask, please have some family pictures in

258

frames for her to look at. She likes to arrange them, and I also don't want her to forget what any of us look like."

I suddenly feel like a child with a wish list sitting on Santa's lap instead of a grown-up saying a prayer, but Melba nudges me. "Don't forget ice cream," she whispers.

I nod and continue. "Let her eat ice cream for breakfast, lunch, and dinner if she wants," I say, "and tell everyone up there how lucky they are that she is a part of their world now. They will love her." Though closed, my eyes are now streaming with tears, and I feel them roll down my cheeks and cling to my jaw line.

"Please make sure Sandra finds her mother that she never got to meet, and let them have their time together. She should get to know her mother. And one more thing—please make sure Sandra finds her sister Nina and thanks her for keeping me safe until I was ready to come back here. Make sure she tells Nina that I am happy. God, you can take her with you now, but we'll always love Sandra and keep her in our hearts. Thank you."

"Amen," my aunt and Dr. Boudreaux say in unison.

"I'd say that was just about the most beautiful prayer I have ever heard," the doctor says sincerely. "That's all you need to remember—say what you feel and it'll come out just right."

I lean down to hug this sweet man, and then the three of us leave the room together. Dr. Boudreaux pauses at the door and I am grateful when he decides to leave the light on. He pulls the door closed behind us and we walk slowly toward the elevators.

"Thank you for waiting for me," I tell my aunt. "And for trying so hard to track me down."

"Baby Girl, we'd have waited as long as we needed to, and I would have sent Darryl a lot farther than the airport if I had to." She brushes errant hairs out of her face and pats them down on her head. "I bet everyone else is waiting downstairs for you, too, wanting to be sure you're okay. You can be certain they all know how your heart is breaking."

"Then let's go show them we'll all be okay . . . together." We say goodbye to Dr. Boudreaux and ride the elevator down in silence, holding hands.

My family has not moved since we went up to see Sandra hours ago. They are exactly where we left them, and my grandfather sits alone in a chair in one corner of the room. Without speaking a word, long, tight hugs are exchanged and we move as one unit out of the hospital lobby, dividing into three groups for the journey home.

Little Dewayne and Darryl drive back together in Darryl's truck, and Neil Ray climbs in with Stanley for the trip home. I can't bear to be away from Melba right now, so I ride home in the back seat of her van, watching the profiles of Uncle Dewayne and Melba in the front and Dory and my grandfather in the row ahead of me. I study them all, noticing that they are all wearing their grief in the creases that now span their foreheads.

I turn and stare out the window at the sun setting in the distance. It is almost at the horizon, large and red, and just before the approaching trees obscure it from my view, a lone bird flies across the bright circle and disappears into the evening sky.

CHAPTER TWENTY-SIX

The next few days pass in a haze of sadness, but my family is mostly together, with the exception of my grandfather, who has firmly refused all invitations and is being given a wide berth. Melba has hung a sign on the door at the G 'n G explaining that they will be *closed in observance of a great loss*, and will reopen *when Melba feels like cooking again . . . probably in a week or so.*

Little Dewayne brings Regina and the kids to Melba's every day, and we set Regina up in Uncle Dewayne's recliner with her feet elevated and a pitcher of lemonade on a TV table beside her. From her throne she watches over her three boys while they play with Legos, Matchbox cars and puzzles, as the rest of the adults wander in and out, in search of something to distract them. Little Dewayne watches over Regina, as protective as a lion over his pride.

Lamar and Stanley hold down the fort at Little Land Clearing, but have cut out early every afternoon to see after their mother. I think they are also worried about me, which I find incredibly touching. Lamar's wife, Angie, drops in for an hour or so at a time, always bringing with her a plate of delicious cookies or lemon squares. She shyly joked that in times of sorrow she feels completely at a loss for words, so instead she expresses herself through baked goods, which is lucky for me.

Dory takes refuge in her bedroom with Bobbie Jean, whose parents have let her take a couple of days off from school to support her friend. Every now and then they come down and interact with the rest of us, but understandably we are not the most fun group to be around, so they eventually drift back upstairs to listen to music, paint their toenails, and talk about boys.

Neil Ray has been given the task of repairing a riding lawnmower out in the shed. I think he would rather be driving bulldozers or dump trucks with his brothers, but he seems to be the most concerned about Melba, so he stays close by. I spend quite a bit of time sitting in the shed with him, handing him tools and chatting about life. At nearly eleven years younger than me, Neil Ray is the cousin I somehow identify with the most. He tells me about how he sometimes feels like the odd man out in his family, but that, in his words "I am what I am and I ain't what I ain't." I suppose this is how I felt for a large part of my life. I tell him that every family needs some flavor, and that the Littles are lucky to have him to add spice to theirs.

"Sorbet certainly adds some flavor, too," I remark, treading lightly so as not to sound critical of his girlfriend.

"Yeah, well, she's spicy all right," he drawls, "but we're through, so I guess that's that."

"What happened?" I ask, trying to sound more concerned than relieved.

"She broke up with me because I told her I'd take her up to Jackson for a Faith Hill concert last night and didn't keep my promise." He looks up at me to gauge my reaction and quickly returns his attention to the small engine and the screwdriver in his hand.

"Um, she does know you had a *death* in the family?" Surely I misunderstand.

He raises his eyebrows. "Mm hm."

I understand completely. "Oh. Well. I'm sorry."

"Don't be," he says.

"Okay, then. I'm not," I reply, and as he looks at me from underneath his eyebrows a little smile escapes the corner of his mouth. "Stupid-ass-named-after-freaking-ice-cream-bitch," I mutter.

He doesn't look up this time, but I can see that the smile now goes from one side of Neil Ray's face to the other. "Mm hm," he says again, and I stride out of the shed and back into the house thinking that I would have made a decent older sister.

I enter the kitchen to find my aunt and uncle elbow deep in preserves. Apparently when Melba gets upset, she cans. Pickles, jellies, tomatoes, you name it, she tackles it head-on and puts it in a Mason jar. There are pots on every burner of the stove, some full of boiling water and empty jars, others bubbling with a thick, sweet-smelling orange substance.

Melba is barking out commands to Uncle Dewayne, and like an obedient puppy he does precisely what he is told. I watch for a few minutes, surprised at how adeptly he moves around the kitchen, tongs in hand, sterilizing, stirring, and every so often giving his wife an adoring peck on the cheek.

A timer goes off prompting Melba to rush to the stove. She turns the flames down underneath the jelly and then spins around, slamming into my uncle who is attempting to carry two full and very hot jars to the counter on the other side of the sink so they can cool. The jars fall to the linoleum and break, hot orange jelly going in every direction.

"Dewayne!" she yells, louder than I would have thought possible, and stomping her foot. "Oh, shoot! Shooty, shoot, *shoot!*" She covers her face with a dishtowel and falls into a chair, sobbing. I cannot move from where I stand.

Big Dewayne quickly sits in the chair beside her and rubs her heaving shoulders. "It's okay, love," he says softly into her ear. "There's plenty still good, though I know this isn't about the preserves."

She turns to him and buries her face in his shoulder. They sit that way for a long time, Melba completely letting go of her emotions while Dewayne silently holds her. I stand and watch, touched by the love and compassion between them, and while I am fairly sure they know I am in the room, I still begin to feel like a peeping Tom. Thankfully, Little Dewayne has heard the commotion and comes through the doorway behind me to check on things.

"Everyone okay in here?" he asks cautiously, seeing his parents entwined at the table and the mess on the floor.

Melba wipes her eyes and looks up at her oldest son. "I will be, baby, I've just wanted to cry real hard for a while now and decided now was a good time." She smiles and produces a sleeve-Kleenex to wipe her nose.

"I'll get the floor cleaned up," I volunteer, feeling utterly useless standing in the corner.

Melba holds her hand out to stop me on my way past. "No, Baby Girl, I'll do it. It's my fault anyway. These peaches weren't going to go bad overnight, I just felt like I needed to stay busy or I'd fall apart."

"Looks like you did both, Mama," Little Dewayne says gently. "You ought to go lay down instead. I'll help Missi, and we can get the rest of the jelly put up." He peers into one of the bubbling pots. "Looks done, anyway, and any old fool can spoon stuff into a jar."

Uncle Dewayne takes Melba by the hand and helps her to her feet. I find a roll of paper towels under the sink and as I get on my knees to start wiping up orange slime and glass, warm hands cup my chin and force me to look up. My aunt is bending over me, her eyes wet and bloodshot.

"Thank you, Missi. It helps so much to have you here." She leans down further and plants a kiss on my forehead.

I smile. "It helps me, too," I say. She straightens again and starts to walk out of the kitchen.

"Aunt Melba?" I call out, catching her just before she and my uncle head down the hall.

"Yes, angel?" she asks, turning around expectantly.

"'Shooty, shoot, shoot?'" I question.

She looks at me strangely. "I beg your pardon?"

"Just say '*shit,*'" I offer. "It feels much better."

Melba smiles and shakes her head. "Now that'll be the day," she says with a smirk, and takes Uncle Dewayne's hand again. They walk together out of the room and the kitchen is quiet again except for the sound of bubbling peaches.

Little Dewayne turns the burners off and sighs. "You know, it's okay for you to fall apart, too."

"Why do you say that?" I ask.

"Oh, I don't know. Maybe because you've lost two mothers in just a few months?" He starts taking empty jars out of the hot water with tongs and setting them on a dishtowel that is spread out on the counter.

I shrug and start wiping the floor again. "When you think about it, I haven't lost nearly as much as the rest of you have. Your mom lost her mother, a sister, a niece, two children, lost the first sister *again*, and now has lost her other sister, which I think is more like losing another child to her." I shake my head as my eyes fill, dripping tears onto the sticky linoleum.

"I lost one to gain all of you, and then I lost one more," I continue. "You lost two, gained *one*, and then lost another. I'm not exactly a fair trade." It is not lost on me that I have turned people dying into a math equation, but it's how I try to reconcile it all.

"'*To live in hearts we leave behind; Is not to die,*'" Little Dewayne says, not turning around, but I hear the break in his voice and I stop.

"That's beautiful. Did you make it up?" I ask, getting to my feet and stepping over to where he carefully ladles hot jelly into a jar.

"Lord no, Missi," he says ruefully. "It's from a poem by some guy named Thomas Campbell. It's something like two hundred years old, but Regina wrote it out for me when Clayton and Jerome died, and I've kept it ever since. I'm not big on poetry, but that stuck with me. If someone dies and you carry on like they never lived, then that person is gone forever. But if you live with a piece of them in your heart, then they're still sort of here, right?"

I nod, unable to speak around the lump in my throat, and set my hand on his broad shoulder. I never used to believe stuff like that, but I feel what I believe changing a little every day, and the more I get to know people like these, the more I understand that God exists, that he puts certain people in our lives for a reason, and that there must be a heaven for special people when they leave this earth.

Little Dewayne slops hot preserves onto the hand that holds the jar and winces in pain. He lets go and sucks the jelly off, then waves his hand around and blows on it.

"You okay?" I ask.

"I'm fine, Missi. We're all fine." He wraps me up in his huge arms and squeezes me tightly, then releases me and takes two spoons out of a nearby drawer. He scrapes some jelly from what remains in the pot on the stove and hands it to me. "This is good stuff," he says, taking another spoonful for himself and surveying the endless jars that line the counter. "It's a good thing, too, since we'll all be eating it on our biscuits for the next ten years."

I lick the sweet, smooth jam from the spoon and smile at the thought.

The house is too quiet now. Melba is still resting, and I think Uncle Dewayne is standing sentry to make sure she stays that way. Dory and Bobbie Jean are on the phone with some friends from school catching up on the gossip of the day, Little Dewayne and Regina are watching *Peter Pan* with Marcus while Daniel and Devon doze peacefully at separate ends of the couch, and Neil Ray has yet to emerge from the shed where he continues to tinker with the lawn mower.

I am restless, so I go in search of my car keys and realize that I never had a chance to rent another car. I hate to bother anyone, so I slip out the door with my purse and poke my head into the shed.

Afraid I'll startle him I clear my throat loudly, but he just looks up as though he was expecting me. "Do you think you might let me borrow your truck for a little while? The house is so quiet, and I'd like to stop in on a friend."

He grins at me. "You makin' friends here already, Missi?"

"Don't sound so surprised. I actually met her before I met you, on my way down here. She's been sick, and I want to see how she's doing." I watch as Neil Ray wipes his hands on a dirty towel and fishes his keys out of his pocket.

"She a friend I'd like to meet?" he asks with a twinkle in his eye, tossing me the keys.

I frown. "Yes, but don't get any ideas. She's older than your mother. I'll bring you back a Snickers bar. And a full tank of gas."

"Now that's a deal," he answers, shaking his head and turning back to the engine.

I make it to the gas station in no time, and am relieved to see Dolly's truck in the lot. The door of Neil Ray's truck squeaks as I push it open and wrestle it shut again. I walk into the food mart and call Dolly's name loudly. There is no response, which is odd, since the bell chimed when I came in, alerting her to a customer.

I decide to check the restrooms, thinking that she may be back there cleaning them, but when I open the ladies' room door, I nearly knock Ginny over and definitely surprise her.

"Ginny, I'm so sorry!" I say, grabbing her by the elbow to steady her.

"Good Lord! Oh, hey—you scared the bejeezus out of me, girl!" She sets a mop in a bucket of suds on the floor and wipes her forehead with the back of her arm. "It's good to see you. I left that note for Dolly, but when you didn't come on Monday like you said, she started to worry a little."

"Sorry about that. I . . . had an emergency." I am hesitant to share the details, remembering her sullen attitude the day we met.

"I'm sorry," she says sincerely, not at all like the sour girl from last week.

"Thanks," I reply. "I saw Dolly's truck out front. Is she here?"

"Yep. Bet she's in the back room. We got a delivery today, which is why she asked me to come help while she gets it unpacked. Go on back. She'll be happy to see you."

I thank Ginny and make my way to the door I'd seen Dolly emerge from the first time I ever set foot in this place. I knock before entering, afraid to startle someone else.

When I push the door open, Dolly looks up from a large carton and a wide smile appears on her face.

"There's my girl!" she yells, dropping a loaf of bread back into the box and stepping around several crates to reach me. She hugs me so tightly that I know I'll remember for the rest of the day that I've been hugged. "How are you, doll face?"

I squeeze back, but then hold her by her shoulders and put on my most stern expression. "More importantly, how are you?"

266

She waves away my concern. "Oh, darlin', I am fine. Now you know my big secret, but it's just something I try real hard to keep at bay, you know?"

I furrow my brow. "I would have thought that something like this would have come up in one of our chats." I just now realize how badly my feelings are hurt that Dolly never confided in me about her illness. We told each other so much, so why didn't I know she'd had cancer?

"Don't you be mad about this," she says, reaching up with one finger to smooth the creases between my eyebrows. "Relax that forehead, please." I can't help but laugh.

"I can tell you that it's honestly not something I think about all that often. All those other things we discussed, well, they were so much more important. Part of what makes us who we are, and things we struggle with daily." She stops rubbing, drops her hand, and looks me squarely in the eyes. "The cancer was so incidental in the grand scheme of things, and I was already exactly the woman who stands in front of you now before I got sick. You know, cancer has just been a little bit of an inconvenience."

I laugh and hug her back, wanting to give her one to last the day, too. We stand smiling and silent for a moment, until Dolly's face lights up. "Let's go take a dip. What do you say?"

"A dip sounds great," I say, and it's certainly what I'd been hoping for as I drove over here today.

"Snickers and a Coke?" she asks, holding the door back into the food mart open for me.

I grin and nod, happy to be here with a friend when I need one. I haven't bothered to call Maggie because she and Carlos are still on their honeymoon in Mexico, so I haven't been able to share the events of the past few days with anyone other than family members who are all just as sad as I am.

We settle ourselves with our feet in the pool and our Cokes balanced on the arms of our lawn chairs. I stash the Snickers bar inside my purse, good on my promise to take it back to Neil Ray, and take a long sip of the cold soda.

Dolly splashes her feet around before pulling out her pack of cigarettes and lighter. I eyeball her and clear my throat. "You really think you should be doing that?" I ask.

"Probably not," she says, looking down at what she holds in her hands.

"I'd say definitely not. I don't want to tell you what to do, you're a grown up and can make your own decisions. But I'd guess that someone who's already had cancer should not be taking part in any activities known to cause it." I worry for a moment that I have offended her, because she sits for a long time staring at the cigarettes.

"Dolly, I know it's none of my business, but the reason I am here right now is to make sure that you are okay." I set my Coke on the ground beside my chair and lean toward her. "I was so upset when Ginny told me you were at chemo last week. Even though she said it was maintenance to keep you in remission, it still scared me."

"You don't want me to smoke anymore?" She looks at me out of the corner of her eye.

"No, Dolly, I don't."

"Well, okay then." She gives the pack a good squeeze, crushing the contents, and drops it into the pool. "Guess I can't smoke them now." She tucks the lighter into her pocket. "Don't want to throw that in the water . . . I might can use it to light a candle or something sometime."

"That's it?" I ask, not sure if what just happened was just a show for my benefit. "You're not going to get more from your shop later on?"

"No, ma'am," she answers.

"How long have you been a smoker?" Surely it's not this easy to get a person to quit smoking.

Dolly looks up at the sun and squints. "Since I was fourteen."

I groan. "It may take a little more than that, then." I quip. "No offense, but decades of doing something are hard to undo. Maybe you can try the patch or gum or something."

"Nope," Dolly says, shaking her head slowly from side to side, her silver hair bouncing on the top of her head. "I've tried those things before, but they seem to make it harder for some reason, like I'm only half quitting. I don't need those gimmicks. When I say I'm quitting, I mean it. For good."

"But if you've tried to quit before and failed, what makes you think you can do it this time without any help at all?" I realize I am playing devil's advocate, but it just seems impossible that she could stop smoking today, based solely on a declaration of quitting.

"Because you want me to." She looks at the squashed pack of cigarettes floating on top of the water and then at me. "Nobody's ever asked me to stop before."

"Really?" I am shocked.

She looks sad for a split second, but the expression is soon replaced by one of gratitude. "My parents never knew I smoked. They would have pitched a fit! My husband certainly never cared much about my health, and I never had kids to worry about me, so

268

there goes that. But you're such a doll, and I know you genuinely care about me, so there it is. You want me to quit? I quit. I guess I like being your business."

"Good," I say, and I feel my eyes welling up.

"When did you get all motherly, anyway?" Dolly asks with a wink, turning the subject away from herself. "You were a mess when I first met you, but now you're so sure of yourself, bossing me around like this. And Ginny? Whew! That girl meets you one time and decides to change her juvenile delinquent ways and start saving money to go to the junior college!"

"She did?" I look back toward the store, remembering our conversation and the huge case of I-don't-give-a-shit she had at the time.

"She did!" Dolly crosses her arms, but looks pleased. "So maybe you've saved two of us from a life of misery and suffering, Missi."

I don't know what to say, so I shrug, and the tears start rolling. Dolly gets out of her chair and kneels in front of me, drenching her shorts but not seeming to care.

"Oh, baby, what's the matter?" she asks, the concern in her bright blue eyes unmistakable.

I finally unload my sadness on Dolly, starting with my surprise at finding Darryl at the airport waiting for me, and ending with Melba's meltdown in the kitchen earlier today.

"Oh, Missi, there are no words in the English language that can adequately convey how I feel," Dolly says finally. I have cried nonstop, and Dolly has cried with me. If my eyes look anything like her swollen and bloodshot ones, I will have a zinger of a headache later.

"My heart is broken for you, and for the rest of your family." She slides back into the water and stretches her legs. "Your poor grandfather. What do you think this will do to him?"

I shake my head. "I don't know, but it certainly can't make him any meaner than he already is," I say, instantly disliking how it sounds coming from my mouth.

Dolly sighs. "You know, I've thought a lot about your grandfather since you first told me about him, and I wonder if he isn't just a little misunderstood." She frowns and reaches into her pocket and fishes out the lighter she'd put there for safekeeping. "So much for that," she says, tossing it onto the grass beside the pool.

"Misunderstood? How do you mean?" I inquire. "I think I understand him completely—he's the grouchiest person I've ever met."

269

Dolly shakes her head. "Not grouchy, maybe, just terribly, terribly sad. Sadness can make a person seem like something they're not. It causes people to withdraw from those they love the most, and can mask all of their good qualities because the sadness is the thing that's most obvious."

I think for a minute, listening to the sound of the breeze high up in the trees and the bugs buzzing nearby. "I guess he's had a lot to be sad about in his life," I say finally.

"I know about sadness, Missi," she says softly. "Trust me when I say that the best parts of you all but disappear when you're sad like that."

"I've never thought about him that way," I admit to Dolly, "but let's say I give him the benefit of the doubt. How can anyone get past the sadness?"

"You need to give him something to smile about," she answers, standing to wrap her soaking wet arms around me. "You are so capable of doing it, and Lord knows you've done it for me."

"And you for me," I reply, standing shin-deep in the wading pool hugging my friend and, despite it all, smiling.

CHAPTER TWENTY-SEVEN

Sandra's funeral is a family-only affair, and I feel as though I've been granted membership to some amazing, highly selective club. Melba has made it clear to everyone that we are not to wear black, and that the brighter the color we wear, the better to celebrate the life of our "ray of light." I can't get past the "ray of light" image, and choose a sleeveless yellow dress I bought for my trip to Las Vegas. Walking into the kitchen, I find that I am not alone.

Melba is wearing a long white skirt and a yellow tunic, Uncle Dewayne has on black pants and a yellow button-down, and Dory sits at the table, which obscures all but a yellow cardigan hanging loosely over her shoulders. I stifle a giggle in an attempt to keep the somber nature of the day.

"Well, don't you look mighty pretty," Uncle Dewayne comments, pouring a cup of coffee and handing it to me.

Melba turns and smiles. "You sure do," she says cheerfully. She looks over to Dory and then to me. "My beautiful girls." Dory catches my eye and grins. I grin back and sit down across from her with my coffee.

There is a commotion as Neil Ray comes in the back door. "Mama, all the jelly's out in the smokehouse now, but you'd better hold off on the sweet pickles. There's no more shelf space out there." He stops a few steps into the room and starts laughing.

"What's so funny?" Dory frowns.

"Y'all look like a fleet of school buses," he cackles. "I imagine we'll be visible from outer space standing graveside today!"

The rest of us look around the room cautiously, but eventually let our guards down and laugh. The laughter is a relief. I am all cried out, and I think everyone else is, too. Maybe today we really can celebrate Sandra.

I have never felt as much a part of anything as I do today. It is a beautiful, sunny day, and the strong breeze makes it feel almost cool. The cemetery is completely empty except for us, and the sunlight and sound of leaves rattling gently in the trees make it feel more like a park than a place of eternal rest.

Sandra's casket is open for now, and she looks just as she had the last time I saw her—peaceful as though she were asleep. Today, however, she is pale and her face is covered in make-up, which she never wore before.

Beside us are tombstones bearing the names of my grandmother, Dorinda, and Clayton and Jerome Little. I hate for my family that they have lost so many so early, and I say a silent prayer that God goes easy on them for a long time. They need each other. *We* need each other.

The pastor from the Little's church has come to officiate, and it's clear that Reverend Dobbins knew Sandra for the bulk of her life. His words are poignant and kind, and capture Sandra's ability to make those around her feel happy and loved.

I look around at my family members, expecting tears and red noses, but I see smiles all around. I realize that I, too, am grinning at Reverend's Dobbins' account of the string of cats, one after the other, that Sandra took in and named Missi. Heads turn and acknowledge the Missi standing graveside, and I relish the thought that my mother had carried some small memory of me with her all these years.

When Reverend Dobbins finishes, we are all asked if we have brought a token that we'd like to put in Sandra's casket to be buried with her. Aunt Melba came up with this idea a couple of days ago, and after much thought I worked up the nerve to go by my grandfather's place and ask for access to Sandra's room. He stepped aside to let me in, but otherwise said nothing to me. Now I hold my token close to my chest and wait my turn.

Dory is first, and has brought a photograph of her as a young child sitting with Sandra on a swing under a tree. In the picture they are both grinning, and their hair is being blown by the motion of the swing.

Neil Ray adds an unopened bottle of A&W Root Beer, which I didn't know was Sandra's favorite. I like learning new things about her, even though she's gone.

Little Dewayne, Regina, and the kids step forward next and place a stuffed animal cat next to Sandra's arm. "To keep her company, plus she likes cats," Marcus says with a serious nod.

Stanley and Lamar together put in another picture, taken at a long-ago family picnic, and Uncle Dewayne lays a beautiful sunflower across her chest. Then it's my turn, so I approach the casket cautiously and add the Ziploc bag that now contains all of Sandra's four-leaf clovers. I will remember sitting in that grassy patch with her for the rest of my life.

Finally, Melba takes something from her pocket and holds it out for us to see. It is an engraved locket, and inside is a tiny photograph of their mother—my grandmother—who died while giving birth to Sandra. She opens the clasp and drapes it loosely around Sandra's neck. For the first time during the ceremony, I feel tears come to my eyes.

Just when I think we are finished, my grandfather clears his throat and steps forward. The rest of us move aside as he stands over his youngest child and takes her hand in his. I am not certain, but it looks like he tucks something small into her pale, stiff fingers before stepping away without a word.

To end the service, Dory sings the most amazing version of *Stand By Me* that I have ever heard. Without any accompaniment, her voice is clear and every note is perfect. When she finishes, I notice that for a few seconds there is no sound, as if even the birds have stopped chirping to listen. Eventually, they begin to sing again, and I stand in awe of my cousin. My grandfather has turned and started to walk toward the cars.

We return to the Little's, where Artie from Grits 'n Greens has shown up at some point and is setting out bowls and platters full of food on the kitchen table. Melba hugs him tightly, thanks him for feeding us today, and assures him that she will be back at work tomorrow. Artie leaves in a hurry to change the sign on the door at the restaurant, and says he'll be back later to clean up.

Before long, people start arriving. Friends of the family, Uncle Dewayne's brothers and their families, of course Bobbie Jean and her parents, and even Darryl and Lucy stop by to pay their respects and stuff themselves full of pork barbecue, cole slaw, potato salad, pasta salad, cucumber salad, and buttermilk biscuits. I have it on good authority that there is also banana pudding in the refrigerator, so I make sure to save room.

Our guests are so pleasant and friendly that I almost forget why we're all together until a familiar truck drives up the gravel path and I see Dolly climb out. I run over and wrap my arms around her, and she squeezes me so hard I almost can't breathe. I am so happy she's found her way here using my sketchy directions. Everyone else is wonderful, but it's nice to have a friend of my own in a sea of virtual strangers.

I make my way around the yard, introducing Dolly to my cousins and their families, and it's no surprise that she gets along beautifully with everyone. We head inside so she can meet my aunt and uncle, and Dolly and Melba hug each other as if they are long-lost friends. Their eyes well up as Dolly gives her most heartfelt condolences, and they cry tears of happiness as they share their stories of meeting me just weeks ago and how lucky they both are that I walked into their lives on that day. I stand by and cry along, happy that the two have finally met.

I eventually pry Dolly away from the kitchen and head down the hall to the family room, where I know Marcus, Daniel, and Devon to be. There is a pile of Legos in the middle of the floor, and the kids are happily playing alongside one another. They look up briefly when I introduce Dolly and acknowledge her politely, but quickly get back to their creations.

Across the room sit Regina and Darryl, Lucy tucked neatly between them on the couch holding onto a stuffed bear. Dolly shakes their hands, warmly congratulating Regina on the baby-to-be and telling them both how much she's heard about them. Normally I would be highly embarrassed at the suggestion that I had been talking about Darryl for any reason, but am temporarily distracted when I catch sight of my grandfather through the window, sitting alone out in the yard on a folding chair. I excuse myself, knowing Dolly will have a great chat with Regina at least, and head outside to confront Charles Jenner.

My feet crunch through grass that is in dire need of rain, and my grandfather looks up at the sound of my approach. As usual, he says nothing.

"How are you doing?" I ask, knowing the question is ridiculous, but not wanting to start the conversation negatively.

"Tired, I reckon," he answers, looking into the distance.

"Have you been having trouble sleeping?" I ask, wondering if for the first time in his life he's been the only one in that old house.

"You could say that," he says. I am afraid this is all I am going to get—these curt, abbreviated answers—but he surprises me. "As soon as I fall asleep I wake up listening for the sound of her breathing. It was so loud I could always hear it, even from my room, and when I don't hear it now, it reminds me of that night."

I swallow hard, hearing the agony in his voice. "You don't blame yourself, do you?"

He sighs. "I wish I could. I think being mad at myself might be easier."

"Easier than what?"

He finally looks me in the eyes. "Being mad at God."

I get it, I totally do, but there is something very important I need to say to my grandfather, and I need to say it now. I take a deep breath and sit down on the grass in front of him so that he has to keep looking at me.

"She was amazing. Everyone knew it. But there are others who are still here that are worth investing your time in." He opens his mouth to speak, but I talk quickly, not wanting my point shot down too quickly. "You have one daughter left, who is an incredibly warm and loving person, and does the nicest things for you without ever expecting or getting anything in return. Uncle Dewayne is a great guy, and their kids are some of the best people I have ever known. I have to admit, my jury is still out on Lamar, but the rest? You have five grandchildren and three and a half adorable, lively great-grandchildren. What's not to love?" I take a deep breath, but this time he stays quiet, his eyes intent on mine.

"You have the best family I have ever met. It is a dream family, and yet you don't seem to appreciate it. I realize I haven't known you for long, but you seem withdrawn from everyone except Sandra. And what is the deal with Dory?" I ask, really on a roll now. "You all but run from the room when she's around, and she's scared to death of you. She's beautiful, and sweet, and much smarter than she comes off, and she sings like an absolute angel!"

"That's the problem," my grandfather says, almost imperceptibly.

"What is?"

"Looking at her is like seeing a ghost." His face is pained, but I am hopeful that we are making progress. "She is, in every way, the spitting image of my wife."

"Dorinda?" I ask, remembering her name from the grave marker at the cemetery.

He winces. "Even her name . . ."

"Oh my goodness," I gasp, not having made the connection earlier, "Dory is short for Dorinda?"

My grandfather nods and grips the arms of the chair tightly. "But that's the tip of the iceberg. That girl looks exactly like her grandmother, sounds like her . . . and she sings just like her too." He

275

pauses and closes his eyes to the sun as though he is hearing something I can't.

"Right before she died," he continues, "just a little while after Sandra was born, Dorinda told me we'd see each other again, and that it would be sooner than I thought. For years I thought that meant I'd die young and find her in heaven, but then I realized that's no place I'll ever get one foot in the door, so I quit believing it. All those boys come along, and then that baby girl. From the minute she was born, I knew Dorinda had sent her."

"Isn't that a good thing, then?" I ask tentatively. "If Dory was a gift from her?"

He shakes his head and a single tear rolls down his cheek. "In some ways it feels like punishment. I look at that girl and see my dead wife, and I can't quite sort out how I feel about it."

My heart aches for my grandfather, and I think I may finally get him a little bit. Dolly was right when she suggested he is sad and misunderstood. I just wish he'd open his eyes to what's good around him, because he's already missed out on so much.

"Well, she's terrified of you," I inform him flatly, "and I doubt that was what Dorinda had in mind if she went to all the trouble of sending Dory to you." He frowns as though I have just pointed out that he is disappointing his deceased wife. Maybe that's what he needs to hear.

"If Dory was sent from heaven, then maybe you could try treating her like a gift instead of a punishment," I suggest. "She is your connection to Dorinda, and maybe you won't feel like you've lost so much if you can get some of it back." As I say this I feel sure he's not going to buy it, but for Dory's sake I wish he would. For his own, too. He just sits, not saying anything.

"Look," I go on. "I know what it's like to be unhappy, but more importantly, I know what it's like to become happy again after thinking it could never happen." I stand and place my hand gently on top of one of my grandfather's. "You can't beat it with a stick," I say, turning toward the house. After only a few steps I turn back.

"Can I ask you a question?"

"I reckon you're going to anyway," he says.

"At the funeral today, what did you put in Sandra's hand?"

He looks at me with such sadness. "My heart," he answers.

Four helpings of banana pudding later, the guests have departed except for a few and I am in the kitchen helping Melba cover the leftovers and stack containers for Artie to pick up.

276

"All things considered, today wasn't as horrible as I thought it would be," I remark, tearing off a sheet of aluminum foil.

"Amazing, isn't it?" Melba answers. "Something unthinkable can happen, but if you've got the right people around, you can end up a-okay."

I smile at my aunt. "You know, now that I'm motherless again, I could really use a parental figure in my life. Think you can help me out? I've been known to make pretty bad decisions if left to my own devices."

Melba sets a clean, dry bowl on the counter and winds an arm around my shoulders. "Missi, I started counting you as one of my own the day you stormed back into my life. It's not anything I meant to do, it just happened. That's how it works around here, I guess. I know the day is coming that you will leave us here and go back to your old life, but we'll always be here for you."

My old life. To think of it now, it doesn't sound too appealing. There wasn't much to it, with the one major exception being Maggie, and she's definitely not going back to *her* old life. She has a new one in which Carlos is the most important person, and I understandably will take a backseat to her new husband.

I hug my aunt tightly, not wanting to let go, until the back door opens and in walks Dolly with Darryl right behind her, Lucy sound asleep and limp in his arms. Her lips are parted, and there is a large wet spot on Darryl's shoulder where she has drooled on it. She is so small and beautiful, and looks so peaceful sleeping. It pains me to think again that this little girl will go through life without her mother, and how lucky I am to have gotten a second chance with mine.

"I best be on my way, darlin'," Dolly says, crossing the room to hug me. "He's just about the cutest, sweetest man I've ever met," she whispers in an attempt to be subtle.

I nearly swallow my tongue, subtlety not being one of my strengths. "I'm glad you came," I sputter, feeling my face turn scarlet. "I'll come by and see you soon."

Dolly hugs my aunt and gives Darryl an affectionate pat before she lets herself out. "She's lovely," Melba says after the door has closed. "I'm so grateful you found her that first day here. Who knows if you'd have found us otherwise?"

I smile at the memory. "It wasn't just the directions that helped. I left there with a whole lot of courage I hadn't brought along."

Darryl clears his throat. "She's really something," he says, "and she thinks the world of you, Missi."

If I don't stop blushing I am afraid my face will melt off, so I half-smile, turn away, and finish wrapping the leftovers in foil.

"Mrs. Little, thank you for including Lucy and me in your family gathering today. Sandra was a very special lady, and I know how much she's missed already." Behind me, I hear the sounds of my aunt hugging Darryl.

"You know you are as good as family to us, Darryl, and you and that sleeping beauty are welcome here anytime." There is a long pause, which I disrupt by tearing off another noisy sheet of aluminum foil. I cover the last dish, leaving me no reason to keep my back to Darryl.

"We've all been through a lot, haven't we?" Darryl asks as I face him again. I am surprised to see that he is looking right at me.

I grimace. "Not exactly the kind of thing you want to have in common with someone," I say, realizing too late how barbed it sounds.

"No," he answers, looking back at Melba, "but it's nice to know you're not alone." He smiles sadly and shifts Lucy to his other shoulder. She opens one eye, yawns, and goes back to sleep.

Melba reaches out to rub Lucy's tiny back. "Darryl Fortson, you will never be alone, and you best not forget that, you hear?" She gives him a motherly pinch on the cheek. "Now get that baby home and into her own bed."

Darryl smiles kindly and heads for the door.

"Missi, why don't you help Darryl get Lucy out to the truck?" Melba suggests.

I eye her suspiciously and she nods after him. "Sleeping children are dead weight," she adds, as if this should justify sending me out the door with Darryl when he obviously needs no help buckling a twenty-pound child into a car seat.

Still feeling bad about how bitchy my last comment sounded and worried that I have perhaps hurt Darryl's feelings, I walk to the back door and hold it open for him. He has to sidle out sideways to avoid rubbing up against me, and I pull the door closed behind us as we walk through the carport and out onto the gravel drive.

"Which side?" I ask as we approach the truck.

"Passenger," he answers, following me around. "If she's on that side I can turn just a little from the driver's seat and see her over my shoulder," he adds.

I open the back door of the extended cab pick-up and then quickly move out of the way so that Darryl can lift her into her seat. She is as limp as a rag doll as he buckles the harness tightly around her. I am taken by the fact that he has made a conscious choice about where to position Lucy's seat based on being able to see her easily while he drives. I wonder if it would have ever occurred to me to do this if I had a child of my own, or if I would have just flung open the nearest door and stuck the car seat there. I decide that your perspective must change when you are a parent in order to consider such things, and doubt seriously that I will ever see things from that perspective.

When Lucy is securely fastened inside the truck, Darryl gently closes the door and turns to me.

"When I said that it's nice to know you're not alone, I didn't mean to rub your recent tragedies in your face," he says apologetically.

"It's okay. I know you didn't mean it that way," I stammer, trying to find the right words. "I just got defensive for some strange reason. I think I tend to mistake compassion for pity." I look down at my feet and start shuffling rocks around with the toe of my sandal.

He chuckles and gestures back at the house. "If it makes you feel better, I don't pity you in the least. I've envied Little Dewayne since the third grade for being a part of this family. His mama and daddy are the most generous, kind people I have ever met, and every time I ever came out here I left feeling special and loved. I still do."

He pauses and looks out across the yard. "When they lost Clayton and Jerome, talk around town was that no family could ever get through something like that. But the Littles did, and maybe it's left its mark on each of them, but they stood together and made it. That's *your* family, Missi."

I squint into the setting sun. "Looks like the same can be said for you and Lucy," I say quietly.

He looks affectionately through the window of the truck. "You've got to have someone to make getting up each day worthwhile. Speaking of which, that little monkey has been waking up with the birds lately, so I'd better get her home and get some rest myself." He stands awkwardly for a second before issuing a shy wave and walking around to the driver's side of the truck.

"I really am sorry for all that you've been through, Missi," Darryl says as he pulls open the door, "but even though I don't know you well, I can say for certain that you'll be fine with this family around to support you." He waves again, slides into the cab, and starts the engine. I stand back as he slowly rolls down the path, kicking up dust in his wake and leaving me with my thoughts.

I think about what Darryl said and know that when I walk back into my aunt and uncle's house, I will be in the company of people who understand my loss because it is also theirs. What will happen

279

when I go home to Washington? Maggie will be devastated when she finds out about Sandra, but there is only so much even she can do for me. No one else there will even care. Who will be *my* person that makes getting up each day worthwhile?

As I start back toward the house in the waning daylight, I hear a familiar voice coming from around the side of the house. It's Dory's voice, I think, but instead of its usual bright, chirpy tone, it is subdued and shy. I am about to turn the corner and announce myself when I stop short and freeze at the sound of a second voice.

I hold my breath and strain to hear the conversation, even though I know I have no right to eavesdrop.

"You think you'll go on to college?" he asks, the question punctuated by the squeaking chains of the porch swing.

"I'd like to," Dory answers, "but I wouldn't want to go too far away. Plus, college is so expensive, I hate to put the strain on Mama and Daddy."

"Whatcha think you'd study?" he inquires.

There is a pause, but when Dory responds there is a strength and purpose in her voice that was not there a moment ago. "Music and education," she says definitively. "I want to keep singing, but I also want to teach. I used to think I wasn't smart enough to be a teacher, but you don't have to be a rocket scientologist to teach music to kids. You just have to love music and kids!"

There is a pause and a cough that may be disguising a chuckle, and then the swing creaks again. "That sounds mighty fine," my grandfather says, finally.

I feel like the smile on my face is so wide that my cheeks can be heard stretching, so I relinquish my post and tiptoe back to the kitchen door. When I step inside, I am met by the hustle and bustle of my aunt's kitchen. Covered containers are being re-stacked by Melba and Dewayne, and Neil Ray lifts the aluminum foil from one to forage for a snack.

"Neil Ray Little, you best hurry and get what you want," Melba fusses. "Artie will be here in five minutes to collect the rest. I told him he could take it home to feed those four youngins of his."

Neil Ray fishes out a biscuit and reseals the foil. "Thanks, Mama," he says sweetly.

Melba stops and scratches her head. "Your grandfather leave without saying goodbye?" she asks, genuinely concerned.

Neil Ray shrugs, but I know the answer. "He's still here," I say.

Melba looks relieved, then pained. "He still out in the yard by himself? I sure wish he'd come inside and eat. I fixed him a plate hours ago, but it's still in the refrigerator."

280

"He's on the porch swing."

Melba furrows her brow and reaches into the fridge for his plate. "Maybe I'll take this to him. Keep him company for a while."

"He's not alone," I disclose, the smile spreading on my face again.

"Who's he with?" she asks curiously, and three pairs of eyes look at me expectantly, news of my grandfather in the company of someone who is not Sandra almost inconceivable.

"Dory," I answer, and I am suddenly no longer the only one in the room who is smiling.

CHAPTER TWENTY-EIGHT

The next day arrives with wonderful normalcy. Melba's kitchen is a flurry of activity at dawn as everyone sets about the usual routine for the first time in a week. Eggs are frying, biscuits are baking, and five of us jockey for position at the coffee pot, the table, or the stove.

Cheer has been restored, and although I have no doubt that the rest of my family will carry the same ache in their hearts that I feel for a long time to come, it feels good to move forward again. Neil Ray and Dory banter, Uncle Dewayne fusses about the rain in the forecast that threatens to put his current project even further behind schedule, and Melba wonders aloud whether Artie remembered to place the fresh produce order for the restaurant.

"I'm sure he did," I reassure my aunt. "He seemed pretty on top of things yesterday."

Melba smiles at me gratefully. "You're right, Baby Girl. And even if he did forget, the world surely would not come to an end, now would it?"

"Ah, words of wisdom from Melba Little," Neil Ray says, planting a kiss on his mother's head. "I think I'm going to get on out to the site and see what I can get started on before that storm blows in."

Uncle Dewayne raises his eyebrows and grins. "Well, now, that sounds like a wonderful—and might I add, responsible—idea, Neil Ray."

"You know me," Neil Ray says with a wink, "wonderful and responsible are my middle names. Y'all have a good day, and I'll see you for dinner." He takes his sack lunch out of the refrigerator and heads out into the dim morning light.

"What got into him?" Dory asks, spooning honey onto a biscuit.

"I haven't a clue, but I like it," Uncle Dewayne responds. "I better get out there alongside him and support that ambition," he remarks, carrying his plate to the sink. He gets his own lunch from the refrigerator, kisses Melba, and turns to Dory and me. "Love you, girls," he says with bright eyes, and heads out the door.

I clean up the kitchen while Melba and Dory finish getting ready for work and school. The kitchen is so quiet it's deafening now, so I fill the silence with the sounds of pots and pans banging, water running, and thoughts about what in the world I am going to do today.

By six forty-five, the house is empty except for me, and it is clear that the sun is not coming out today. Besides doing some laundry—shocking that I am even considering this—I am at a complete loss about how to fill my day. Perhaps this is why I am contemplating doing laundry to begin with.

I finish tidying the kitchen, taking special care to make it shine so that when Melba returns from work there will be nothing for her to do. I go up to my room to gather clothes, tromp back down the stairs to start my first load, and return to my room to shower and dress for the day. Whatever that entails.

I take my time and actually blow my hair dry before I head back to the laundry room to put my clothes in the dryer. As I pass through the living room, I catch something out of the corner of my eye and jump. Sitting in Uncle Dewayne's recliner is my grandfather.

"Jesus!" I yelp, clutching my chest as if trying to keep my heart from bursting out of it. "When did you get here?"

"While ago," he says glumly. "The back door was unlocked and I let myself in. I thought everybody had gone."

My pulse is still racing, but I manage to catch my breath and sit down on the couch. "I know, it's quiet, isn't it?"

He nods. "Not nearly as quiet as my place. I couldn't stand being there another minute." He looks at his feet and then at me. "Didn't mean to scare you."

"No, you just surprised me. I was just thinking it was lonely here after so many people being around the last few days."

"That helped, didn't it? Distraction's always a good thing, but distraction usually gets back to routine pretty fast. I'm the one who takes longer to move on." He looks so sad it is truly heartbreaking.

"I think this is harder for you than for anyone else," I offer. "Sandra was your baby, and spent her entire life under your roof."

283

His eyes fill with tears. "Who am I going to take care of now?"

I swallow hard before answering. "Maybe it's your turn to be taken care of. Or just your turn to not worry about anyone for a while."

He wrings his hands in his lap. "That's all I know to do. I could always bush hog a field or slaughter a pig and worry at the same time. Now I don't have livestock anymore, and the only time I bush hog is when I can't see over top of the grass anymore. The worrying was my only constant. It made me feel like I had a purpose." He folds his hands together so tightly that I can see his knuckles turning white.

I think for a minute. "Well, if it helps, you can worry about me. I'm sure I'll give you plenty of reasons to once you get to know me better."

He looks at me and the corners of his mouth turn up just a bit. "Girl, I bet you're a fine mess, aren't you?"

"Without question," I answer. "You can worry about Regina, too. She's not sitting still nearly as much as her doctors have recommended, and they're afraid the baby will come too early."

He frowns and nods, so I continue on. "Dory's going to be dating soon if her brothers don't lock her away in a tower guarded by dragons first. Now *that* is something to worry about. Plus, Neil Ray may have broken up with that ridiculous Sorbet girl, but you better believe he's going to stir up some trouble with the next girl, so—"

"Good heavens, girl, I get the picture," my grandfather says, wide-eyed and holding his hands out to physically deflect my verbal barrage. "I s'pose my worrying days have just started, thanks to you."

Feeling very satisfied I soften my voice. "So you and Dory had a good talk yesterday?"

Another nod. "She's so much like your grandmother. It's strange, but I do feel like I've gotten her back a little. You were right about that. Thank you."

I feel the wall between us coming down, and my heart is light despite the rain that now comes down in sheets outside. My grandfather and I talk for a long while, mostly about what my life was like before Nina died and I came here.

I feel like I've helped give him another piece of his life back— some knowledge of who Nina was as an adult and what she was like. I don't sugarcoat the relationship I had with her, but I do try to focus on what a success she was which, strangely, comes as a surprise to him.

"You never saw her interviewed on television or listened to her radio program? Even out of morbid curiosity just because she was your daughter?" I am shocked.

"It was a whole lot easier to pretend she didn't exist than to acknowledge that she left with the intention of never speaking to us again." There is an unmistakable hurt in his eyes, and I recognize it as my own where Nina was once concerned. It is the kind of hurt that comes from feeling that you are not good enough.

"Her loss," I say, more deliberately than I intend, but it seems to relax my grandfather a little.

He shrugs and leans forward in the chair, resting his elbows on his knees. "I reckon so, but we lost plenty, too. When she left, we let you go, and at the time I thought our intentions were good. She convinced us that she could give you more than we could, and we thought Sandra would be better off if there wasn't a constant reminder of what happened to her."

"It's okay," I tell him. "I'm not mad about any of it. I know that you made a difficult decision during a time when you were scared and angry, and to be honest, I'm glad you chose to protect Sandra." He looks at me strangely, so I continue.

"She needed protecting. She couldn't do it herself. I took care of myself, and I think it got me farther than I ever realized."

"It got you back to us," my grandfather says, and for the first time ever I see his teeth when he smiles.

"Better late than never," I say.

Dory and Melba return to the house that afternoon, and couldn't be more surprised to find my grandfather and me sitting at the kitchen table, deeply involved in a cutthroat game of Backgammon.

"Daddy, what are you doin' here?" Melba asks, hanging her purse on a hook by the door.

"Too quiet at home, so I came to the noisiest place I could think of," he answers with a smirk.

"He was pretty disappointed to find just me here, though, so he took pity and taught me how to play Backgammon. I'm awesome at it already," I add, rolling the dice and moving a marker forward six spaces.

"Too bad you can't remember what damn color you are," he quips, moving the white piece back to where it started. "Try again."

I laugh and move a black one as Dory settles into the chair beside me. "I love this game," she says. "I get to play the winner."

Our grandfather smiles at her approvingly and takes his turn.

After dinner, it's evident that my grandfather has no intention of leaving anytime soon. Dory has gone upstairs to do homework, and the rest of us convene in the family room to watch television.

"Daddy," Melba begins, "I sure am glad you came by today. It sounds like you and Missi enjoyed your time together."

He nods. "It was a good distraction," he says. "I appreciate Missi wasting a day on an old man."

"Well, I appreciate you wasting *your* day on me. It would have been weird to be alone here all day." I flash him a sincere smile to let him know that I truly did enjoy spending time with him. "I'm glad to have gotten to know you better," I add.

He shifts uncomfortably in the recliner. "I suppose I better head on now," he says quietly. "Don't want to overstay my welcome any more than I already have."

Melba stands up quickly and walks over to where he sits. "I was just about to put on a pot of coffee and slice up some of the zucchini bread that Honey Woodward brought over yesterday. Why don't you stay a little while longer?"

He reaches out to squeeze her hand. "I'd like that, Baby Girl," he says.

Melba turns to leave the room, and I can see that she is smiling through tears. I think how sweet it is that he called her the same name that she so affectionately calls Dory and now me. I realize, too, for the first time, that Melba is the only immediate family he has left anymore, and how painful and sad that must be for them both. At least they live near one other and seem to have been brought a little closer together by the horrible circumstances of the past week.

"So, Missi," Neil Ray calls from across the room, interrupting my deep thoughts, "not that any of us are in a hurry to see you go, but you've got to be getting tired of this one horse town. When are you going to break our hearts and head north again?"

I swallow hard, having dreaded making this decision for a long time. "I guess soon," I say finally. "Everyone here is getting back to their usual routine now, and I can't sit around here all day while the rest of you are contributing to society, can I?"

I see my grandfather wince a little and realize I unintentionally hit a nerve. He has the same reservations about his future as I do.

"You've got Fergie and that big old farm to keep you busy," I remind him. "Maybe you could get some cows or something."

His face relaxes a bit. "I like cows," he says, "and chickens. Chickens need lots of attention. We had some a while back."

Uncle Dewayne is smiling from his perch on the end of the sofa. I think he's relieved that my grandfather is thinking about his farm again, rather than making the decision to move in here.

Melba returns with a plate of zucchini bread and some napkins. "Coffee's on, it'll be just a few minutes," she informs us.

She settles down next to Uncle Dewayne and he wraps an arm around her. "Your daddy's thinking about getting some cows or chickens," he tells his wife.

Her eyes get wide and a grin spreads across her full cheeks. "You're kiddin' me!" she exclaims. "There haven't been animals on that farm in years! I think that's a wonderful idea, Daddy."

My grandfather narrows his eyes at me. "All I said was that I *like* cows and chickens. I ain't going out to fetch a herd just yet."

"Sorry," I say meekly. "I got carried away."

"It wasn't a bad suggestion," he says apologetically, "but my farm needs a whole lot of work before it'd be ready for livestock. I got fences to mend, a barn to clear out . . ."

"Thank the good Lord," Melba says under her breath, but her words are not lost on her father, and I have a feeling that the still will be strategically relocated rather than disposed of.

"Our old chicken yard's been gone twenty years or more," my grandfather continues, "so I'd have to build a new one, and that'll take this old man a long time to do."

"I'd be happy to help out on weekends," Neil Ray jumps in. "I bet we could get it done in less time than you think. I got a buddy who works over at the lumber yard, and he's always got scraps he's happy to unload."

My grandfather and Neil Ray start discussing plans while Melba, Dewayne and I sit and listen with sincere interest in their joint project. Dory comes down before long and gets in on the action, telling our grandfather that she'll help whenever she's not working and can feed the chickens and vaccinate the cows like Bobbie Jean does at her place.

As the plans my family is making begin to take shape, so does a strange and very uncomfortable feeling in my chest. Their lives are already moving forward, but I have absolutely no clue what I am going to do with *my* life. I guess I'll call tomorrow and book a ticket back to D.C. and start making plans of my own. Get a job. Make some new friends, since Maggie will be busy being a married woman. Decide if I can handle living in Nina's big, expensive house with everything in it that needs taking care of. Make vacation plans to return to Mississippi to see my family. Thanksgiving isn't too far off.

Lost in my plans to make plans, I am unaware that the conversation in the room has ceased, and everyone is oddly quiet.

"Did I miss something?" I ask. "I'm sorry, I was daydreaming."

"Daddy just told us that as much as he'd like to do all of the things they've been talking about, it probably wouldn't be prudent to fix up a farm he might could lose anyway." Melba looks devastated.

"What? Lose the farm?" I turn to my grandfather. "Why would you lose the farm?"

"The 'f' word," Neil Ray explains. "Foreclosure."

"Foreclosure? What are you talking about? This farm has been in your family for what, a hundred years? How can you possibly get foreclosed on?" I'm sure this must be some misunderstanding.

My grandfather shakes his head in shame. "I took out a loan against the farm several years ago, and haven't been able to keep up with the payments."

"What was the loan for?" I ask, but before anyone answers, I know it was for Sandra's care.

"Farmers 'round here ain't got health insurance," he says. "I paid for Sandra's doctors out of pocket."

I am crushed, but I still don't understand. "What about the checks?" I ask.

"What checks?" Melba inquires.

"The checks Nina sent," I explain. "Her lawyer said the checks would keep coming every month. Surely that's enough."

Melba looks angrily at my grandfather. "She was sending checks?'

"Every month for as long as I can remember," he answers disdainfully.

"Well, what did you do with the money?" Melba asks, her voice getting louder.

"Nothing," he says. "I never cashed a one of them."

"What?" I yell. "Are you crazy? That would have saved you this whole headache!" And how is it, I wonder, that Nina's accountants failed to mention that decades of checks hadn't been cashed. I am pissed.

"I was not about to be paid off just to erase the guilt she felt after runnin' outa here," he retorts. "She was too good for us, so she went off and became a big deal and thought she'd send her pity money to her ignorant father and retarded sister? I didn't need it then and I most certainly don't need it now . . ." He trails off, and we sit in silence for a long time.

288

I am afraid to say anything, afraid that I will offend him or sound condescending in some way. The anger I felt a moment ago is gone, and I begin to understand and even admire the fact that he hadn't taken her money.

"So," he says finally, "I'll just go on now and let life take the road it's going to take." He leans over and kisses Melba on the cheek. "Thank you for dinner, darlin'."

"Anytime, Daddy, you know that," she says, forcing a smile up at him.

He shakes hands with Neil Ray and Uncle Dewayne and gives Dory a pat on the head before addressing me.

"You just got caught up in it all right from the start, and I'm glad you didn't know anything about it until you were old enough to make sense of it," he says to me. "I'm still not old enough."

"And it still doesn't make sense," I reply. "But I had a really nice time today."

"I reckon I did too," he says, and I hug him tightly. He is sturdy and strong, and I think what a shame it is that he won't have the chance to fix up the farm. He's got a lot of life left in him, and God knows what will happen to him if his home gets taken away. The shame alone may kill him.

I walk him out to his truck, but neither of us says a word. I stand and watch as his rusty old vehicle rattles down the drive and turns onto the main road, and I wonder if my grandfather will be okay.

CHAPTER TWENTY-NINE

The next day is utterly depressing. I toss and turn all night and then oversleep, which means that when I finally roll out of bed, everyone is gone and the coffee pot has even switched itself off. I eat some breakfast and make a fresh pot of coffee, hoping that my grandfather will show up like he did yesterday and keep me company, but by eleven o'clock it's clear that his pride is keeping him home today.

I make a big decision, one of the hardest I've ever had to make, and pick up the telephone to book an airline ticket back to Washington. I think that I should handle leaving like one would pull off a Band Aid. Just hurry up and rip. I can't get on a flight tomorrow, however, so at least I have a day and a half to say my goodbyes and find a ride back to Jackson.

More decisions face me now, such as where to begin my goodbyes. I start with the most important. Thankfully, Neil Ray rode to work with my uncle, and left his keys and truck for me.

Yesterday's rain is gone, and in its place is a sunny, clear, breezy day, similar to the one on which we buried Sandra. Her headstone is not in yet, but she is easy to find. The mound of dirt is wet, having been tamped down by the heavy storm, and the flowers have been blown around. I start by picking up errant blossoms and reorganize them to somewhat resemble the arrangement that was originally there. When I am satisfied, I sit on the damp grass and take in the sun.

I am not one to talk out loud to someone who is not actually there, but inside my head I think all of the things I would want Sandra to know. That I would not trade the short time during which I knew her for anything in the world, that I am sorry she was taken advantage of by that horrible man but not sorry to call her my mother, and that I will never, ever forget how good she made me feel when I spent time with her. I also think that even from far away, I will check in on our family every day and make sure there is nothing they ever need. I will do that for Sandra . . . and for myself, because I will need to know that everyone is fine.

As I sit there I can almost feel her presence. I turn my face up to the sun and try to imagine what heaven looks like, and when I finally look back to the ground my eyes settle on a patch of clovers. I lean forward and pluck one out of the ground. It has four leaves. I smile through my tears as I tuck it gently into my pocket, wipe my damp behind, and blow Sandra a kiss goodbye.

My next stop is Little Dewayne and Regina's. I know someone will be home since she is on her own version of bed rest, and Marcus should be getting back from school soon. I knock quietly in case anyone is resting, but I am quickly rewarded by the squeals of two little boys when the door opens and they see that it's me.

"Aunt Missi's here!" Daniel yells, jumping up and down. Devon is close behind and flashes me a toothy grin of recognition that melts my heart. I lean down and scoop them up before stepping into the foyer and shutting the door behind me.

"In the kitchen, Missi," Regina hollers, so I head that direction. She is sitting at the table surrounded by swatches of yellow fabric.

"What are you doing?" I inquire. "And where's Vernadeen?"

She looks at me and rolls her eyes. "Missi, I love my mother more than life itself, if for no other reason than because she is my mother. But good Lord, she was driving me up the wall, so I sent her back to my poor father who needs her far more than I do."

"What's the fabric for?" I ask. "It's pretty."

"Well, it finally occurred to me that since Little genes are involved in making my babies, I might have to squeeze out three additional little boys before a girl comes along, which I am not about to do. Dewayne and I have decided that no matter what, this baby is going to be our last, so we are going to enjoy every second of it, which means not finding out what it's going to be until the day he or she decides to grace us with his or her presence." She holds up a square of white material with yellow ducks parading across it.

"Ah," I say. "Yellow is the color, then."

"Yellow is the color," she echoes with a peaceful smile. "So to what do we owe the pleasure of your company today?"

"Just making rounds to see everyone before I head . . ." I am about to say *home*, but it doesn't sound right, so I quickly insert, "back north again."

"So soon?" Regina seems sincerely disappointed.

"I've been here for the better part of a month," I say, "and life moves along up there with or without me. I need to find a new job and figure out whether or not to keep Nina's house. It's going to waste sitting empty while I'm here."

She nods. "I completely understand, but we'll miss you. You are a wonderful addition to this family, and I think losing Sandra was a whole lot easier on everyone else with you here."

"That reminds me," I say, carefully extracting the clover from my pocket. "I found this today and want you to hang onto it. For luck."

Regina irons it out on top of the table with her fingertips. "Thank you, Missi," she says. "I'm not sure I could get any luckier, but it will remind me of you."

The little boys are getting antsy, so I lead them out to the yard to play until the bus drops Marcus off. From behind me, Daniel's voice goes from playful to serious.

"What happened, Aunt Missi?" he asks. I turn to see him pointing at my bottom, and my hand involuntarily reaches there. My pants are still damp from sitting on the ground at the cemetery.

"I just sat in some wet grass earlier," I explain.

"Oh," he says, furrowing his brow. "Looks like you peed."

I laugh and grab him underneath his arms. He giggles as I swing him around, and my wet pants are forgotten. We run and hide and chase until I am out of breath, and when Marcus comes home, we do it all over again. We are still outside when the light wanes and Little Dewayne returns from work, and after I help Regina get dinner ready, I hug this wonderful bunch of people and leave them to eat peacefully together.

I return to Melba's just as Uncle Dewayne and Neil Ray arrive. Melba and Dory are working the dinner shift at the G 'n G and won't be home until nine. The three of us dig through the refrigerator and make plates piled high with everything we can find. A quick warm-up in the microwave later, and we are devouring the leftovers.

We talk about our days, and Neil Ray proudly recounts how he successfully brought in a huge future project for Little Brothers Land Clearing. My uncle beams as he listens to a story he already knows, and it has clearly been a big day for them both.

"With the money I'll make on this one, I might afford a down payment on a house," Neil Ray says excitedly.

I look back to my uncle, whose face registers a mix of gratification and sadness at the thought. I wonder if the next time I visit, Neil Ray will have to come over to see me. Life is moving on.

"I'm going back to Washington the day after tomorrow," I blurt out. Uncle Dewayne and Neil Ray look at me, speechless. "It's time," I go on, "to let everything get back to normal. You all have lives that you led here before I came along, and I need to go back there and get a life of my own." I see Neil Ray shaking his head, so I attempt to drive my point home.

"You even told me once not to be late for the rest of my life," I say, pointing at him, "and while being here with all of you makes me happier than anything, I'm watching everyone else move forward, but I'm idling."

Uncle Dewayne covers the fist I hadn't realized I'd made with his enormous hand. "We're just being selfish," he says in a kind and soothing voice. "We'd love an excuse to have you here all the time."

Neil Ray murmurs in agreement. "You just fit in so well, it feels like you've been here all along."

Our easy chatter from earlier has fizzled, and the elephant in the room is almost visible sitting in the space between us. I am leaving. Soon.

We clean up the mess of food containers and dishes, and I make extra sure that the kitchen is spotless for Melba when she gets home. I join Uncle Dewayne and Neil Ray in the living room to watch some television, but it's hard to sit still knowing that tomorrow is my last day here.

"Neil Ray," I begin, and he turns his head to look at me, "I know you're pretty busy at work, but do you think your boss would let you take a half day off to get your cousin to the airport?

Before he can answer, my uncle interjects. "Actually, Missi, there's a heavy equipment company up in Jackson that I was going to check out before we buy a new grader, so Neil Ray can handle that for me after he drops you off." He looks at his son, whose face has lit up. "That sound okay to you?"

"Yes sir, it does, and I sure appreciate the opportunity to help like that." Neil Ray looks like a kid on Christmas morning, and gives me a wink. "I do believe I've got a good luck charm," he says excitedly.

Pleased that I have at least taken care of finding a ride to the airport, I settle back into the soft cushions of the sofa and enjoy the evening. I know tomorrow will be hard trying to squeeze in the last bit of family time that I can.

In the morning I make sure I am awake early to participate in the breakfast routine at the Little's. I sit at the table without saying much, and enjoy just watching the interaction between my family members. Even though I am a quiet observer, I feel very much a part of the moment, and when the house clears out and I am alone again, I remain at the table for a while, afraid that if I get up I will somehow forget this feeling.

When I finally pull myself away to prepare for my last full day in Mississippi, I try to organize my day. Melba instructed me to be at the G 'n G at 5:00 for a special family dinner, but I have lots of time to kill until then and want to make the most of it. I shower and dress, then sit on my bed and dial Maggie.

"Hola, chica!" she yells into the phone. I am at once startled by the sound and relieved that I have finally been able to reach her.

"Mags! How was your trip to Mexico?"

"Oh, Missi, it was so fantastic! I got to meet Carlos' *abuela*, and she is the most amazing woman. We made tamales together and tended to her chickens, and had long conversations—of course, she had no clue what I was saying and I had no clue what she was saying, but we seriously hit it off, and I can't wait to go back!" She is positively giddy, and I feel a rush of happiness for her.

"When did you get back?" I ask. "I've been trying to call you."

"Yesterday afternoon. When did you call last? Wait, are you home?"

"Not yet," I answer, "but I'm coming back tomorrow."

There is an unbelievable shriek from the other end of the line. "Oh, I can't wait to see you! You know, we've spent way too much time apart the past few weeks. I miss you!" She pauses, and then says more calmly, "I bet you're going to have a hard time leaving there, though."

"I am," I tell her, "but on normal days my aunt, uncle, and cousins are at work and Dory is at school, so I feel pretty useless."

"I hadn't thought about that, although I bet they'd much rather hang around with you. I take it that curmudgeon of a grandfather hasn't come around yet? He still making you feel like gum on the bottom of his shoe?"

I smile at the thought. "Actually, we've been getting along pretty well the last few days. I think I got through to him the day of the . . ." I trail off, having been about to say "funeral," but realizing that Maggie is not up to speed on the events that transpired after I returned from Las Vegas.

"Maggie, my mother died."

"I know, but you have your real one now, and I'm so happy to hear that you are getting along with your grandfather! I never thought *that* would happen."

"Not Nina, Mags. Sandra. Sandra died." I wait for a response, but there is total silence.

I tell Maggie about getting off the plane and finding Darryl waiting for me, and about going to the hospital, the long drive from Jackson back to Pritchard, and the sad days that followed. When I am finished, I can tell by the muffled sniffles that she has been crying, so I tell her about the beautiful service we held as a family, the friends and family gathered at my aunt's house, and about breaking through the concrete façade that my grandfather built around his heart to ward off painful memories.

I am emotionally drained when I finish, and am grateful that Maggie is the last person I will have to tell the story to. There is nobody else left in the world so important to me that it bears repeating again.

Maggie's voice is scratchy when she speaks now, and she sniffles through the receiver. "Wow, Missi, who would have ever thought this would happen?"

"Not me," I say, "but I am so grateful that I came when I did, because I really got to know her, and I think it helped my family to have me here. They helped me, too, but I really think I helped them."

"Of course you did," she says. "Gosh, they're so lucky to have you. After all they have been through, and all that you have been through, you finally got to go through something together."

I sigh.

"I feel guilty that I'm so excited to have you back here," she says. "I know how it will feel for them to miss you."

As usual my cell phone has not been charged in several days, and the low battery signal beeps in my ear. Before I hang up Maggie offers to meet me at the airport tomorrow and take me to Bangkok Bistro for dinner. Nothing could sound better to me right now.

I feel hopeful after talking to Maggie. At least I have something to look forward to. I have no clue where I will start looking for a job, but I do know it won't be at a law firm. I don't think I can stomach that again. My next stop on the Mississippi goodbye tour may have some insight, though, so I collect my things and head for Neil Ray's truck.

Dolly greets me with her usual enthusiasm when I walk into the gas station, and I am quickly rewarded with a hug so tight it takes my breath away and a sample from her latest purchase, a slushy machine.

"I've always wanted one," she tells me excitedly, "and it got so dang hot this summer that I finally shot the wad and ordered one! Whatcha think?"

I take a long sip through the straw and feel the icy granules travel the length of my esophagus, leaving a sharp pain in their wake. "It's delicious," I say. "I haven't had one of these in years."

"Well, mind the brain freeze, darlin', and head out to the pool. We've got some gossiping to do!"

She closes the door behind us and we settle into our usual places beside the plastic wading pool. We talk for a while before I share my news.

"You're leaving already?" she asks, her forehead wrinkling in confusion.

I nod. "I have to, Dolly. I know that the longer I stay here, the harder it's going to be to find a reason to leave. If I go now and get my life back together, I'll have a million reasons to come back and visit all the time!

She takes a deep breath and stretches her legs out in front of her before looking at me. "I wish I could tell you otherwise, but I know from my own experience that you're right. You've got to go and make your way, and then you can come back and show all of us what you've accomplished on your own." She taps the surface of the water with her feet. "You're going to make me so proud," she says.

"I want to," I tell her, "but I have no idea where to begin once I get back. I don't know what kind of job I want, much less what I'm qualified to do. I don't know where to look for help, and I don't even know where I want to live. Nina's house is beautiful, but it's a bit over the top to tell you the truth, and I feel silly living among the movers and shakers of Washington when I am incapable of moving *or* shaking!"

Dolly laughs out loud at this. "If they're moving and shaking, they're probably never home, so that's the last thing you ought to be concerned about. As far as a job goes, you are fortunate that while you decide what suits you, you'll still be able to pay the bills and put food in your mouth. If I remember correctly, Mama Nina left you quite a big inheritance. You can take all the time in the world finding a job, and you're not going to starve."

"I know myself well enough to know that that's not necessarily a good thing," I inform her. "I am the world's biggest procrastinator, and if I tell myself I have all the time in the world, I promise you I will never come back here, because I will be too embarrassed by the fact that weeks or months or years have gone by and I have nothing to show for it!"

"All I'm saying is that you have time, sweet pea. You don't have to settle. If you're looking for a new career, you could even go back to school and get yourself another degree. If I'm not mistaken, you recently gave someone else that same advice." She winks at me and I relax. "And if you have no interest in going back to school, you can use your extra time to volunteer. I imagine there are a lot of people hurting up in Washington. People who need feeding or clothing. While you're getting back on your own feet, you can help someone else get back on theirs, too."

Dolly is right. There are a thousand ways I can keep myself busy while I figure out what I am going to do. I can't wait for my path to magically appear in front of me. I have to lay the bricks on my own, one by one.

As I silently ponder my future, a police cruiser pulls into the lot, and I shrink into my lawn chair as Lowell Brown slides out from behind the wheel and swaggers toward us.

"Howdy, Miz Dolly," he says in a way that makes my skin crawl. "How's my favorite local businesswoman doin' today?"

"I *was* doing just fine until you showed up," she mutters under her breath, but then more audibly says, "I'm fine today, Deputy Brown, and you?"

"Oh, I'm dandy, thank you so much for asking." He stops a few feet short of the pool and I sneak a peek at him under my brow. Thankfully, he's not looking at me, and I'm not sure he'd recognize me even if he were. He's so caught up in himself that he could probably care less if the President of the United States were sitting here. "You got a cold beverage for a hard-working law enforcement officer?"

"You've been here often enough, you know where the drinks are. You just go on in there and help yourself. I'm a little tied up at the moment." I can tell by her tone that she is trying to be kinder than she feels, so evidently Lowell Brown hasn't just alienated himself from my family.

"Aw, Dolly, you ain't even gonna walk me in and ring me up?" he asks, oozing smarm and self-importance.

Dolly purses her lips before plastering a fake smile on her face. "God helps those who help themselves, Lowell," she says, and then adds, "but this one's on the house. Try out my new slushy machine."

"I think I will," he responds, tipping the brim of his trooper's hat and sauntering off.

Dolly shudders and shakes her head. "That man is a toad," she says, "and has no business whatsoever enforcing law."

"He's the one who pulled me over a few days ago!" I confess. "It's a good thing he didn't recognize me, because my aunt literally chased him off, and there's some bad blood between him and my family."

"I knew I liked your family," Dolly says with a grin. "What did he do?"

"Stole Stanley's girlfriend," I explain.

"That's one stupid girl, then," is Dolly's response, which makes me laugh again. "Tell that sweet boy *I'll* be his girlfriend. He was a handsome fella!"

We stop talking and giggling when Lowell emerges from the shop with a large slushy and a wrapped straw. He holds it up as if toasting us, and walks toward his cruiser.

"I should tell him to make sure that lid's on good and tight, but I just don't have the goodwill," she whispers, waving halfheartedly to him and leaning back in her chair. I watch as Lowell Brown juggles the cup while climbing into his car and hear the, "Aw, *shee-it,*" when he dumps a large cup of blue ice in his own lap. Rather than getting out and cleaning himself off, Lowell Brown and his giant ego slam the door shut and drive away. Dolly and I can't help but dissolve into laughter.

"What goes around . . ." I begin.

"Ends up all over your pants!" Dolly finishes. We howl until tears stream down our cheeks and our stomachs hurt.

" *'God helps those who help themselves, Lowell',*" I say, wiping my eyes and wrapping my arms around my abdomen. I have not laughed this hard in years.

"Well, it's true, Missi, He does," she says, suddenly serious again.

I look at my friend. "I've never really understood that before," I admit, "but I think you might be right. I've got to go figure this thing out on my own."

She squeezes my hand, and the sunlight makes her blue eyes and silver hair sparkle. "We all know what you're made of, girlfriend. We just can't decide what's going to be right for you in the long run. Only you can do that."

I nod and thank her for everything she's done for me. We talk for a little while longer, until I finally bring myself to say goodbye and let her get back to work.

"You know, Missi," she says, her deep voice clear and gentle, "you have done more for me than you can possibly know. You've brought a light and life to my world that I haven't had in a long time. I will miss you like crazy, but I know I'll see you soon, and in the meantime, you call me and keep me in the loop, you hear?"

We hug for a long time, standing in the pool that has been the venue for some of the most important discussions of my life, and eventually dry our feet and put our shoes back on. She stands in front of the life she created for herself after accidentally killing her abusive husband, and waves until I can no longer see her in my rearview mirror. I know that with Dolly as my inspiration I, too, can come back from tragedy and be happy. I smile as I drive towards my final destination for the day.

CHAPTER THIRTY

I don't know what I am expecting to find as I pull up the drive to my grandfather's house, but it's definitely not this. There is a pile of something in the field a few hundred feet from the barn, and it's blazing. I slam on the brakes and almost forget to turn the ignition off before I jump out of the truck and run toward the fire. My grandfather is standing close to it, watching it all go up in flames.

"What are you doing?" I holler, but he just stands there, entranced, and says nothing.

I shake him gently, but don't know how to address him. "Charles! Charles Jenner!" I say forcefully, but he does not respond. "Granddad!" I yell finally, and his eyes meet mine for the first time. I expect to see sadness, but what I see instead is surprise.

"You just call me *Granddad*?" he asks.

"Well, you were totally zoned out staring at the fire, and it freaked me out a little when you wouldn't answer me. Why, do you not like being called Granddad?"

"No, I like it fine," he says with a trace of a smile.

I turn back to the fire. The heat from it is almost unbearable. "What are you burning?" I ask him.

"Just some things I don't need anymore," he says matter-of-factly.

"You're not . . ." I begin carefully, "burning Sandra's things, are you?"

He looks at me sideways as if I've gone completely mad. "Gracious no, girl. I'm just clearing some things out of the barn that have been taking up space for years."

"Oh! Have you changed your mind about fixing it up and getting some cows?"

"No, I'm doing it so that when the bank takes this place away from me and sells it to someone new, nobody else has got to clean out all my old junk." He kicks some dirt with the toe of his boot.

My heart drops, and I stumble over an apology.

"You don't need to be sorry," he says. "I did this to my own self, and at least I hung on to it for long enough that my Baby Girl always had a home."

"But what about the money?" I ask.

"What money?" he asks back.

"The checks Nina sent that you never cashed," I explain excitedly. "That account still exists, and it was meant to go to you anyway! Better late than . . ."

"Never," he says, but not to finish my sentence. "I told you I'll never take that money, no matter how much time goes by. I don't need to be rescued yet again by my oldest child. Look where it got us the first time."

"But . . ." I say, trying to find the words to magically erase decades of pain knowing that I will come up short.

"Never," he says again, more firmly this time, but without the anger I had once come to expect from him. "Now, your Aunt Melba called here this morning to request my presence at your send-off supper, so I s'pose I know why you've come by. Let's go on in and I'll pour you some tea and you can go through your mother's things and see if there's anything you want to carry back north with you."

"I came to see *you*," I clarify, not wanting him to think I had come to claim any of Sandra's possessions. It is not lost on me, however, that he referred to Sandra as my mother for the first time.

"Well, all right," he responds, taking a last look at the burn pile before turning toward the house. "I just figured while you were here—if there's anything you'd like to have, I'd be happy for you to have it."

I match him stride for stride as we walk to the house, thinking that there actually *is* something I'd like to take with me.

We talk easily as we drink iced tea in his kitchen. It amazes me that the wall that once separated him from the rest of the world seems to have been knocked down. I think that in his mind he put it up to protect Sandra, but in the end he was the only one standing behind it. I have no doubt, though, that if he loses his home he will build it again, even higher and stronger.

When we enter Sandra's room, it is neat and tidy as usual, and Missi the cat lays curled up on the bed. I may be imagining the sad expression on her furry face, though I doubt it. She's gone a week without Sandra now, and even a cat, I would think, can recognize loss.

My grandfather stops at the door and goes no further into the room. I walk over to the bookshelf and pick up the photograph of Sandra and me from our first family dinner. Her face will be etched in my mind forever, but I want this picture so that it never loses its' clarity. I hold the *Best Friends* frame to my chest and skim the menagerie of other faces looking back at me from the shelf. My family. Nina and I never had a single framed photograph at our house growing up, and to this day I still don't.

"Would it be okay if I had the pictures?" I ask. "Unless you'd like to keep them here, of course."

"I think that'd be mighty fine," he says, leaning into the doorjamb. "Don't want you to go forgetting about us once you're back in the big city."

For a second I don't know what to say. "I couldn't forget if I tried," I assure him, "but it will make me happy to see their faces every day." I scan the photos again. "Are there any pictures of you?"

He shakes his head. "Not one for gettin' my picture taken. Might break the camera."

I laugh, but it occurs to me that when he's in a decent mood, my grandfather is quite a handsome man. He reminds me of someone. "What color was your hair when you were younger?" I ask.

He looks confused, but answers, "Reddish-brown, I suppose. Why?"

"Just trying to imagine what you would have looked like in all of those photos that were never taken," I say, but really I am thinking that Nina looked a lot like her father. Her eyes were green where his are blue, but the auburn hair, the facial structure, and stubborn, pointy chin are unmistakable. I keep these thoughts to myself, but wonder if he might be thinking the same thing.

"How 'bout a game of dominos?" he asks, breaking the brief silence.

"In here?" I ask.

"Naw, let's go back to the kitchen," he answers. "I don't want to disrupt the order in here."

"Okay," I say, stacking Sandra's photograph collection in my arms and following my granddad back down the hall. I grin at my newfound family heirlooms. I will display them proudly and keep them forever.

In true Jenner form, my grandfather creams me in four successive games of dominos. We don't talk much this time, but the silence is comfortable. When my grandfather ponders his next move, he taps his pinky finger on the table, and it makes me think about how Sandra would wrinkle up her nose when she planned her next play. There are so few similarities between the members of my family, and yet they . . . *we* are all linked by our relationship to this man.

"Thank you," I say quietly, not wanting to disrupt his train of thought.

"Do what?" he asks, looking up at me across the perpendicular lines of white tiles.

I clear my throat, suddenly wishing I'd stayed quiet. "Nothing, I just wanted to thank you."

He stops tapping his pinky finger. "That ain't nothing, but I've got no idea what you'd want to thank me for."

"All of it," I say, reaching out to straighten the line of play on the table. "You're ultimately responsible for all of it. For both people I ever knew as my mother, for the amazing group of people I now call my family," I stop for a moment to make sure he is still looking at me. "It all comes back to you."

He says nothing for a long time, and seems to be trying very hard to swallow before he finally responds. "I never thought about it that way. Your grandmother certainly had a lot to do with it, and I suppose it could be argued that your Uncle Dewayne and his mama and daddy had something to do with all those crazy cousins 'a yours. It's amazing when you think about how many people it takes to make one single person exactly who they are. But for what it's worth, what little part I did? You're welcome."

I am shocked, not only because I think that may be the most he's ever spoken at once, but also because it's one of the most introspective things I've ever heard. Every person I have ever spent any amount of time with has contributed to who I am, from Nina, Josh, Maggie, and even Richard, to Sandra, Melba, my grandfather, the rest of my family here, and Dolly. Each one of them has taught me something that has changed the person I was born as into the person I am now, and the person I am now is completely unlike any other human being on the planet. Oddly enough, I like who I am. I never used to think that I was particularly interesting or noteworthy, but I was wrong. I have a great story.

As if he can read my thoughts, my grandfather says, "You've got quite a story to tell back home."

Dinner at Grits 'n Greens is truly a memorable event. Marcus has brought a disposable camera along and has taken over Sandra's role of family photographer as he runs around snapping pictures of everyone while we stuff our faces full of pork barbecue, potato salad, okra and tomatoes, sweet corn muffins, and in my honor, banana pudding. I eat as though I am afraid I will never see food again, and revel in these last stolen minutes with my family.

We laugh and talk, and stories are told about things that happened long before I arrived in Mississippi. I drink it all in, wanting these memories to become mine also, to make up for all the years that my family time was shared with only one other person.

As the evening gets dark and my time left gets shorter, I make a point to touch every person who has touched me while I have been here. I hug them all and thank them for the privilege of being a part of this family. Even Lamar seems sorry to see me go, and he wishes me well until the next visit.

Marcus, Daniel, and Devon present me with sticky hugs and rolls of large paper. Unrolled, they are life-sized drawings of each boy. I hold the drawings to my chest and start bawling.

"You don't like them?" Daniel asks sadly. "Mama made us lay on the paper so she could trace us, but we did the faces and stuff. I don't draw too good."

"Daniel, I love them," I assure him. "I have been so upset about going home because I was afraid I would forget exactly what you look like, but these will help me remember! They're perfect." I sniffle loudly and bury my face in little boys.

When I have said a proper goodbye to everyone that does not live at Melba and Dewayne's, I roll up my drawings and head toward the door. This is every bit as hard as I thought it would be, and I am just postponing the inevitable heartbreak by prolonging the evening. When I reach the door, I almost knock down Darryl Fortson, who has just come in.

"Hi," I say. "Are you looking for Little Dewayne?" I point over my shoulder to where he and Regina are collecting their children to head home.

"Actually, no," he says. "I heard you were leaving, so I wanted to give you something."

I hold my breath as he hands me a brown paper bag. When I look inside, I realize it is a book.

"A little light reading for the flight home?" I ask, not understanding why my stomach feels the way it does when I am around him.

"Something like that," he answers as I extract the book and read the title. *First Aid and Safety for Dummies*. Nice. I can't believe I ever considered asking him to lunch. He would have laughed in my face.

"Thought you might need it," Darryl says with a smirk. "There's a section on insect stings."

I am not amused. "Is there a section on how to keep gerbils from eating their babies?"

"Sorry, the book store was out of *Rodent Childbirth for Dummies*." This elicits a small, involuntary grin from me, and he relaxes a little. "I know they're all sorry to see you go," he says, looking out at my family as they gather their things.

"Me too," I say. "Good luck to you and Lucy, and thanks for rescuing me once or twice."

"Glad to help," he responds. "I'd better be heading home. My mother's had Lucy all day, and if I'm not back for story time I'll get an earful from both of them."

"Thanks for the book," I say, considering whether a hug is appropriate. He seems to consider this too, but quickly turns and pushes though the door of the restaurant. I guess not.

"Was that Darryl Fortson I just saw?" Aunt Melba inquires coming up behind me.

"Yes," I answer, turning around. "He gave me a parting gift." I hold up the book.

"Isn't that sweet of him?" she remarks, looking out the door to see if he's still there.

"Or condescending," I reply.

She narrows her eyes at me as if scolding, but smiles again finally and pulls me into a big, soft, warm hug. "I'm going to miss you, Baby Girl."

The lump that used to make it's home in my throat has returned, and I choke back tears. "I'm going to miss you, too."

She gives me a final squeeze and wipes her eyes. "Let's get going. I think Artie's ready to be rid of us."

We head out into the night and drive home in silence. I think we all know that words are not enough right now. When we finally get back to the Little's, I go upstairs to pack so that I won't have to do it in the morning. Dory comes in and sits down on the bed opposite mine.

"Hey," she says quietly.

"Hey," I reply. "What's up?"

She sighs. "Nothing, I just wish you didn't have to go. My life would be so much better if you were here all the time."

I stop folding and sit down beside her. "I have to go," I tell her. "I have to go be an adult. I've never actually done that before. I had a crappy job and a horrible relationship with my—Nina. I basically floated by on my friendship with Maggie, and I have never done a remarkable thing in my life."

"But you *are* remarkable," she quickly interrupts. "You have brought back to my family some of what we thought we'd never have again. You make everyone around you feel happy, and you can make our grandfather smile. If that's not remarkable, I don't know what is."

"*You* make him smile," I counter. "He's really loved getting to know you, and you bring out feelings in him that he's locked away for a long time. I hope the two of you will keep getting to know each other."

Dory nods and lurches forward into my arms. "You're remarkable, too," I whisper into her golden hair. "Want to help me pack?" I ask, not actually needing help, but wanting to have her close by for a little while longer.

"I hate that you're packing at all, but I guess I'll help," she answers, and as I watch her start taking my clothes out of the bureau filled with her brothers' things, I think about how much Dory has changed in the short time I have known her. She is so much surer of herself, and has seemed to let go of all the things at school that were bothering her before. Like me, I think she's gotten more comfortable in her own skin. I think that happens when you make it through all that we have. You begin to realize how lucky you are to have what's left, and the rest doesn't matter nearly as much anymore.

I wake up with tears on my cheeks, and though I can't remember my dreams, I wonder if they were about leaving. I smell bacon frying, so I brush my teeth and head for the kitchen, trying to seem upbeat.

Melba is just setting a huge platter of pancakes, scrambled eggs, and bacon on the table. She looks up as I enter the room and smiles. "Good morning, sunshine," she says.

"Glad I didn't miss this," I say, sitting down next to Neil Ray. He scoops some food onto my plate before helping himself, and I can't help but giggle. "So chivalrous," I declare, pouring syrup onto my plate.

"Gotta practice, you know," he responds, shaking Tabasco sauce onto his eggs. "I've got to get back out into the wild world of dating so I'll have stuff to talk to you about on the phone."

306

"You won't have a problem," I insist, "but try to avoid girls with ridiculous names."

"Uh, we're in the Deep South, remember? Strange names are kinda hard to avoid, Mississippi Moon." He winks and shoves a huge forkful into his mouth.

Everyone in the room erupts into laughter, and we fall into our normal routine of easy chatter and clanking dishes. I think about how tomorrow I'll be eating breakfast alone, which makes it hard to swallow, but I manage to finish my food and plaster an artificial smile on my face for the remainder of the meal.

When the time comes for Dory to head out the door to catch her bus, her eyes fill up with tears as she hugs me for what seems like minutes. She finally hoists her backpack onto her shoulder and walks down the gravel drive, turning to wave at least half a dozen times along the way.

Melba closes the door and we return to the kitchen to clean up breakfast dishes. Uncle Dewayne and Neil Ray are still at the table, discussing the big visit to the construction equipment place in Jackson today. My uncle is giving advice on how to negotiate a price on the machinery, and Neil Ray listens intently.

When they finish strategizing, Big Dewayne takes his bag lunch from the refrigerator and kisses Melba on the cheek. He gives Nail Ray a hefty pat on the back and wishes him luck, and then stands in front of me with one hand on my shoulder.

"I'm going to miss you, sweet girl," he says, his voice cracking a little. "You come back and see us soon, you hear?"

I nod and start crying in earnest, no longer able to be strong. He wraps his arms around me and holds me until I collect myself and pull away to wipe my nose. "Thank you for being like a father to me," I tell him. "I've never known what that felt like."

"Thank *you* for being like another daughter to me," he says. "You are a wonderful addition to our family." He leans forward and kisses my forehead. "Be safe, Missi, and call us when you get home."

"I will," I assure him, and the idea that someone might be thinking of me and worrying about me when I am gone fills me with joy and relief.

Saying goodbye to Melba is something entirely different. She looks at me as if I am on my way to save the world. She tells me how proud of me she is, how much she believes in me, and how lucky my future employer, coworkers, and boyfriend will be to have me. It is a tough nut to swallow, considering that I have no clue where to start. Square one, I suppose.

Melba hugs me fiercely and cries openly, but there is such hope for me in her eyes that I can almost believe it myself. I am so sad to leave this wonderful, caring, gracious, unselfish woman, because I feel there is so much more I can learn from her about who I want to become.

Neil Ray comes in the door from loading my bags in the back of his truck. "Break it up, ladies," he says kindly. "You'll see each other before you know it."

We sniffle and snort and nod our heads, but I can't help thinking that after I'm gone, life will go back to normal here and I'll be . . . well, not forgotten, but thought of less and less frequently. Isn't that how it usually works? Out of sight, out of mind.

I have to pry myself away from my aunt's embrace and we walk out to the truck. Neil Ray opens and closes the door for me, kisses his mother, and hops into the driver's seat.

Fortunately, Neil Ray is so nervous about his meeting today that I don't have much time to mope about leaving. I basically conduct a two-hour pep talk on the way to Jackson, and without realizing it end up lifting my own spirits with my words of support.

"You'll do great," I say finally, and in my head I think, *I'll do great, too.*

When we pull up to the terminal, Neil Ray gets out and hefts my bags out of the truck bed. He sets them on the curb and smiles widely at me before giving me a hug.

"You're fun to have in the family, Missi," he says. "Come back soon."

I hug him back and promise we'll talk soon. "I want to hear all about today, and then detailed descriptions of the new girls you date."

"Will do, Cuz. You be careful, now."

I sling one bag over my shoulder and extend the handle of my rolling suitcase. I wave to my cousin as he gets back in his truck and drives off, and then I walk with purpose into the airport.

Today the security lines are short, my flight is on time, and as the plane leaves the ground I am hopeful.

CHAPTER THIRTY-ONE

Hopefulness lasts all of three days. I hate Nina's house. It's beautiful, but it's so formal and stuffy after I'd gotten used to country comfy at my aunt's. Now I am afraid to break something or get the oriental rugs dirty. I still don't think of any of this as mine, even though there was no one else to leave it to.

I contemplate selling the furniture in an estate sale and buying more casual stuff, but I know it will be completely out of place in this old, historic townhome. The crown molding alone is pretentious.

I have not seen Rosa since I returned, so I call her. She explains that in my absence she's been temporarily cooking and cleaning for the couple next door, whom I've never even laid eyes on. She says that of course she'll tell them she has to come back to me now that I'm home, but I let her off the hook. I don't need a full-time housekeeper to clean up after just me, and I am pretty handy with a microwave, so surely I won't starve. I miss my aunt's food terribly.

I have spoken to Aunt Melba and Uncle Dewayne every day since I got back. I put on a show of excitement about the eleven resumes I have posted, but don't tell them that I highly doubt I'll get a call. My resume is not all that impressive.

They tell me that things are good there. Neil Ray got on the phone one evening to tell me he successfully made the purchase of the grader for Little Brothers Land Clearing. He sounded buoyant, and I know that making his father proud makes him happier than dating the prettiest girl in Mississippi.

I ask after Dory and my grandfather. Apparently, Dory went over to the farm to pitch more ideas for the new barn and hen house but my grandfather turned her down. He is convinced he's going to lose the farm. Dory is heartbroken, and I wonder if Charles Jenner

309

will crawl back into perpetual sadness.

Maggie is coming for dinner tonight, which is the only thing I have looked forward to all day. Carlos is working the night security shift at the National Gallery of Art, so we are getting Chinese takeout, opening a bottle of wine, and laying around on Nina's expensive white sofas while we talk.

Maggie picked me up from the airport the other day and we went straight to Bangkok Bistro. Carlos met us there, and while I adore his wonderful, charming personality, I felt like a third wheel. He and Maggie didn't make me feel that way—I just let the new dynamic get to me. I am really excited to have her to myself tonight.

When she arrives, the house seems instantly warmer somehow. Her lively ways and all of the bright colors that make Maggie who she is—from her hair to her eyes to her fuchsia t-shirt dress and purple sandals—fill the empty house with spirit and life. She breezes in the door with a brown paper sack tucked under one arm, and reveals a bottle of expensive tequila and a bag of limes.

I call in our food order after Maggie painstakingly picks out six entrees from the take-out menu, and we settle on Nina's pristine, white couch with the strongest margaritas I have ever had.

"Margaritas and Chinese?" I ask.

"I'm multicultural now," she says, throwing back the rest of her drink and pouring another from the crystal pitcher on the coffee table.

I laugh. "You certainly are, Margaret O'Leary Ortega."

"My initials spell MOO!" she shouts, then dissolves into tipsy giggles. I need to get food in her tiny body before she gets completely smashed.

I watch her smile disappear as she sets her glass down on the table. "Maggie, are you okay?"

She slides closer to me and takes my hands in hers. "I don't know how to tell you this," she begins, and I hold my breath. I know exactly where this is going. I nod to urge her on.

"Carlos and I are thinking seriously about moving to his hometown in Mexico." Her voice is quiet but resolved, and I know immediately that she is not being forced into this, but that it is what she wants, too.

"Carlos has been away from his family for ten years," she goes on, "and our visit there after the wedding was so wonderful that it made him even more homesick. He has a dozen aunts and uncles there, and cousins that are like brothers and sisters to him. I think it would be a great place to raise a family."

She looks at me as if pleading for my understanding, but what she doesn't realize is that she already has it. "Mags, it's okay," I assure her. "I get it. I finally know how good it feels to be surrounded by family and unconditional love. Carlos' family will be so lucky to have you in their lives." I hold tightly to her hands and look her in the eyes.

"I wish I could be so lucky," I mutter, and am saved from Maggie's tearful sympathy by the doorbell. I pay the deliveryman, kick the door closed behind me, and hold up the enormous bags of food. "Let's eat," I say, leading the way into the kitchen.

We talk about a hundred different things while we eat, but my mind keeps coming back to the elephant in the room. Maggie is probably leaving, and I will have absolutely nothing left here if she does. No job, no family, and no friends I can count on the way I have always counted on her.

"Why can't you just go back?" Maggie asks as she polishes off her plate of sesame chicken and fried rice. She picks up an eggroll and takes a huge bite.

"What do you mean?" I inquire, knowing full well what she means, but wanting her to say it out loud for me.

"Go back to Mississippi, Mississippi," she says with her mouth full. I still cannot wrap my brain around the idea that my given name is Mississippi Moon.

"I can't," I say, clicking my chopsticks together nervously. "I haven't done anything yet."

"Done *what*?"

"Gotten a job, made new friends, found a boyfriend, helped the homeless." I am rambling, and have clearly confused Maggie.

"The homeless?" she asks, raising her eyebrows. "Since when are you philanthropic?"

"I'm not," I sigh. "That's the point. I came back here to do something with myself. I feel like going back there would somehow continue a lifetime of riding on the coattails of other people, like you. You are singly responsible for any sort of social life I've had as an adult. I have to learn to rely on myself and to make decisions on my own."

She stops chewing long enough to ask, "So where do the homeless factor in here?"

I tell her about my last poolside chat with Dolly, and the whole bit about God helping those who help themselves. "She said that while I was getting back on my feet, I could help someone else get back on theirs."

"But you can still do that," Maggie pleads, "just not here. I think what she meant is that you need to look outside your own world and share yourself. You have so much to give."

"What, so I sell this place and everything in it, and head back to Pritchard, Mississippi to help the homeless there?" I ask flippantly.

She shrugs, as if to say *Why not?* "I just think you deserve to be around your family. You were truly deprived of it for thirty-three years, and I know you'll end up miserable here. I can tell you already are."

"It was my idea to come back," I assert. "I made that decision for myself."

"Only because you felt like you had to," she says, and I know immediately that she is right. "Maybe all you really need to do is tie up loose ends."

"So what do I do?" I ask, snapping open a fortune cookie. It reads, *The time is right to make a change.* I slide it across the table so Maggie can see it.

She grins. "You have to decide for yourself, remember? I'd say that's an omen, though."

She unwraps a fortune cookie and breaks it to reveal her own. "*Look for new outlets for your creative ability,*" she reads, frowning. "What the hell does that mean?"

"Maybe you can design jewelry or something in Mexico," I suggest. "Didn't you say Carlos is from a silver mining town?"

"When am I going to have time for that? Carlos' *abuela* predicted that we are going to have five kids! Maybe I am going to get creative in the sack!" I cover my ears and yell as she cackles and leaves the kitchen to retrieve the pitcher of margaritas. I start collecting empty containers to throw away, and find one extra fortune cookie lying on the table. I break it apart and almost throw the fortune away before deciding to read it. *As the purse is emptied, the heart is filled.*

I look around the vast kitchen with its stainless steel appliances and high, coffered ceilings. I don't need all of this, I think to myself. It's beautiful and would make a lot of people happy, but I'm not one of those people. I know without a doubt now that I need to sell the house. I wonder if technically the fortune cookie has decided *for* me, but clearly this decision-making crap is not my strong point. I know deep in my heart what will make me happy.

312

It's as if this was all in some divine plan. I have started to believe that there is such a thing, and on a daily basis I find reason to support my belief.

I call Thomas Anderson first thing the following morning and tell him that I plan to sell Nina's house. While definitely not surprised, I don't think he was expecting to hear from me this quickly.

"You shouldn't have any trouble selling it, Missi," he advises. "Old Town sells no matter what the rest of the market is doing. Matter of fact, my wife has been looking at some places there now that our kids are out of the house. She wants less space to keep up with, and frankly, it would cut my commute by more than half."

"Do you think she might want to look at Nina's?" I ask. "It's immaculate. I haven't had time to mess it up yet," I add with a laugh.

"Oh, Missi, we couldn't," Thomas quickly responds. "I am sure it's a conflict of interest in some way, and if you list it with an agent, you could get top dollar."

"And have to pay a six-percent fee," I interject. "It almost makes more sense to sell it on my own."

It takes a little nudging on my end, but Thomas agrees to send his wife over to look. She arrives in less than an hour.

"I hope I don't seem too eager," Candace Anderson says as we shake hands and she enters the foyer. "I am so sorry about your mother."

I have met Candace once before and she is exactly as I remember her, very attractive and impeccably dressed, just like Nina. She is exactly the sort of person who would fit in this house and truly appreciate it.

"I'm glad you're eager," I say, hoping to make her feel at ease. "I would really like to sell the house quickly before any maintenance is needed. It's too much for me."

I give her a tour and then suggest that she walk around on her own and take her time looking at closets and storage space. I sit in the kitchen nervously drinking a glass of sweet tea. I don't make it nearly as well as my aunt, but far better than my grandfather. It makes me think of my family as I sip it, and I lose myself in thought until Candace breezes quietly into the room, her eyes lit up.

"It's positively gorgeous," she gushes, but it sounds sincere. "May I ask what you are planning to list it for?"

"Actually, I haven't gotten that far," I admit. "I'm hoping not to list it at all. Your husband said you had looked at some places nearby. What is the going rate around here?" I sound like an idiot, but it's not as if I am pretending to be a real estate mogul. I just have a house to sell.

"Grab your keys," she tells me, and we head out the front door. We walk down the block to another townhome that is for sale. She takes a flyer from the plexiglass container by the front walk. "$995,000," she reads, and continues on. I nearly pass out. *A million dollars for a house?*

I walk with her for a few more blocks, and she tells to me about her children, twin boys, who are just out of college and starting jobs in New York and Boston, respectively. She is obviously a loving and devoted mother, but seems to respect her sons as the adults they now are and acknowledges that she is excited to see them succeed on their chosen paths, even though they have decided to do it at a distance. How is it that I never got to that point with Nina?

After some more walking, we find three more homes of similar size and location. Two have the same realtor's number listed on a fancy sign, but no flyer or price listed. Candace writes the telephone number on a monogrammed notepad she pulls from her purse. The third has a flyer, which she extracts with a flourish.

"One-point-two," Candace says aloud with a smile. "I think we've got something to go on now. Let's go back to your place and call this agent to get her pricing. I'm sure we can come up with a good number."

"Okay," I stutter, "like average them or something?"

"Oh, don't be silly, Missi," Candace answers, almost sounding offended. "Your mother's home is far superior to any of those. It even has the original woodwork and that lovely garden in back! Nothing like it is even on the market right now, I simply wanted to know what the going rate for average is on your block."

Ha, average! I follow Candace back to the house with my mouth hanging open like a cocker spaniel's.

It's sold. I can't believe it. All parties involved are tickled, but I feel like I have pulled off the heist of the century. One-point-six million dollars for something that was never even really mine? Thomas and Candace act as though they've stolen it from me, but what they've done is given me freedom. The purse has not exactly been emptied, but my heart is full with what I am free to do now. My definition of helping the homeless might not be exactly what Dolly was thinking, but I know without a doubt what I have to do.

Thomas has a real estate lawyer that he knows working on expediting the closing, but there are no contingencies. No inspection, no they-must-sell-their-current-home-first, nothing. Candace even wants to purchase a good bit of Nina's furniture and two oriental rugs, which is fine by me. The rest will be consigned at a local antiques shop thanks to Nancy, Nina's former assistant. The Andersons will love the house, and the house will be all the more spectacular with a lovely couple like them to fill it with life.

I spend my last days in Washington packing my few worldly belongings into cardboard boxes to ship. I decide to keep Nina's collection of Southern literature, which I pack carefully into small boxes so they aren't too heavy. Maybe I will read them, probably I won't, but I still want to have them.

I also spend several hours at Thomas Anderson's office, making arrangements for my accounts to remain in Washington even though I will no longer be here. I can access them from anywhere and transfer funds to open a local bank account at my leisure. Nina's accountants, Harry and Nick, stop by with some tax paperwork, and oddly Nick is not nearly as good-looking as I remembered. He's a little too slick and polished for my taste these days.

Maggie spends much of this time with me, and we are being very grown up about the whole thing. She and Carlos are going to end up moving to Mexico, where they will propagate the species and no doubt live in bliss together, so I would have to get on an airplane to go see her anyway. Airports are easy to come by.

I have also made arrangements for when I arrive. My mind races with hopefulness and anxiety, but I know I am doing the right thing. I'm just not a hundred percent sure that a certain person is going to feel the same way . . . at first. I plan to be very persuasive, however, and am not above getting downright pushy, if necessary.

CHAPTER THIRTY-TWO

When my flight lands I am suddenly seized by doubt. I remain in my seat until every other passenger has gotten off, and still it takes irritated looks from the flight crew to get me moving. Melba's the only one that knows I'm coming back, and she'll be waiting for me inside the terminal. She said she's not one for driving around in circles.

I plod slowly, asking myself why I am back. *Really* why. Is it because I failed to be happy in Washington the first time and didn't give it a chance the second? Is it because I can't be there without Maggie to guide me through the motions of every day life? Am I looking for someone new to lead me?

When I get right down to it, though, I know those aren't the reasons and I am grateful for the realization. I am not chickening out. I am making a bold choice to be a part of something I have not had until recently, and which makes me immensely happy.

I did not choose to be left out of my family—someone chose that for me. *I* am choosing to participate, and not just on holidays and vacations. I am so much more sure of who I am when I am here than at any other time or place, so it just makes sense. I have told my aunt that I will stay with her only until I find myself a cute little house nearby—but not too near. I do not want my family to feel as though I am depending on them to shelter, feed or entertain me, and I have every intention of finding a job that is fulfilling and that keeps me busy.

I simply don't want to miss out anymore. I don't want to hear about Neil Ray's girlfriends over the phone and never get to give them my stamp of disapproval. I don't want Dory to call and excitedly tell me what colleges she's going to apply to and not also see the look of sheer wonder on her face when she gets her acceptance letters. I don't want to come home to a voicemail letting me know that Little Dewayne and Regina's new baby has been born.

I want to be in the thick of things. I want to help Melba at the G 'n G when she is short on staff. I want to babysit Marcus, Daniel and Devon and their baby brother or sister while their parents spend time alone going out to dinner or to the movies. I want to hear Dory sing as often as possible, and I want to sit at a table full of people who are my family and listen to the stories of how they became who they are.

Most of all, I want to help my grandfather. I have seen the man that he can be when he feels hopeful, and there is no reason he can't be that man all the time. He's given away everything he ever had to take care of others. It's his turn to receive. If he even knows how.

I pick up my pace through the airport and start looking ahead for my aunt. She should be easy to spot, even in the large crowd standing beyond the security checkpoint, but I don't see her. Maybe she's running late. I pull out my cell phone to check for messages, but there are none.

I checked two suitcases this trip, so I head down the escalator to baggage claim, certain she'll find me there. As I descend in a clump of fellow passengers, I hear my name called and nearly fall down the moving staircase trying to figure out where the voice came from. Whoever called me obviously saw me going down, so I wait at the bottom of the escalator for them to catch up. It did not sound like my aunt.

As I scan the few faces now coming down the escalator toward me, I finally recognize one. *Oh, shit.*

"Who died this time?" I ask wearily as Darryl Fortson gets off at the bottom and approaches me. I wait for his answer before I allow the tears to flow freely.

"Nobody," he says, clearly tickled by the question. "Is that what you associate me with? The perpetual bearer of bad news?"

"Well, you can't blame me," I admonish. "You've been known to spring some pretty shocking stuff on me."

"One time!" he pleads. "Only once! And that was not my choice. I got the short end of the stick for sure on that one." He looks around at the flight numbers posted at the baggage carousel. "Can we just get your bags and go? Melba Little is fit to be tied waiting for you to get home."

Home. It sounds so good. "I thought she was going to pick me up."

"Well as it happens, I was over at the G 'n G with my mother and Lucy for supper last night. Melba was dying to tell someone

317

about you coming back, but wanted to keep it a surprise for the rest of the family." He stops and grins. "She said she was driving up to Jackson today to fetch you, but I offered to do it for her."

"You did? Why?" I ask, sounding surprised and more than a little ungrateful.

He shrugs. "I thought I'd save your aunt the trouble, and, well, it would be nice to get to know you a little better."

I must be staring at him with some blank expression on my face—disbelief, maybe—so he throws his hands up in the air. "If you'd rather wait for Melba, I can be on my way now . . ."

"No!" I shout. "I wouldn't rather wait. It'll be two more hours before she'd get up here, and . . . I'd like to get to know you better, too. You can give me some tips about living in the Deep South, such as what other insects or small mammals I should avoid."

He smiles again, and we retrieve my bags and walk out into the bright afternoon. It's a short walk to his truck, where he opens the passenger door for me and gently lifts my bags into the bed. I can't help but remember the last time this happened, but this feels much different.

I look behind me and see Lucy's car seat strapped tightly in the back. I need to be careful, I know, because this man has a child and a longer history with my family than I do. I watch Darryl from the corner of my eye as he buckles his seat belt and starts the truck. He is extremely handsome in a rugged, tired sort of way, but when he turns to look at me he smiles, and for the first time he doesn't look so sad.

We talk easily on the long drive to Pritchard, and by the time we arrive I know that at the very least I have a friend in Darryl Fortson. He loves my family as much as I do, so I can't help but like him. He is smart and can be quite funny, and when he talks about Lucy his whole face lights up.

Darryl takes me directly to Grits 'n Greens, having mentioned that my aunt was afraid Dory would go into cardiac arrest if she got home from school and found me at the house. As if my return could generate such a response.

I have become positively giddy by the time we park on the street in front of the restaurant. Darryl sends me in the door while he unloads my suitcases and brings them inside. The place has just cleared out from the lunch rush, so I have to go into the kitchen to find Melba. She stands with her back to me as she ladles country gravy into a storage container. Artie winks at me and goes back to washing the dishes, and I sidle up next to my aunt, trying not to startle her.

318

"Can I help?" I ask, folding my arm around her wide shoulders.

Without missing a beat, she answers. "You just did, Baby Girl." She wipes her hands on her apron and wraps me up in a massive embrace. "Oh, how I've missed you."

"I've only been gone a few weeks!" I say, but the tightness with which I cling to my aunt betrays my words.

"I didn't want you to go to begin with," she admits. "It just wasn't my place to say it."

"Well, I'm back," I announce to nobody that doesn't already know.

"Thank the good Lord," Melba says joyfully. "Maybe your cousin will quit sulking around the house in your absence."

"Dory's been that sad?"

"Well, Dory, too. You know that girl misses you like crazy, but I was talking about Neil Ray. He's been positively depressed! You'd think he lost his best friend or something."

I laugh at the image in my mind, but am also truly touched. It is amazing to know that I have been missed anywhere near as much as I have missed all of them.

"Where's Darryl?" my aunt inquires, looking over my head and back out into the restaurant.

I walk through the restaurant and see my suitcases sitting neatly inside the door, but there is no sign of Darryl. "I guess he had to run," I say, narrowing my eyes at her. "That was pretty sneaky of you."

"Baby Girl, I had nothing at all to do with it. I was about to come undone keeping your coming back a secret. He just gave me an outlet, is all, and he was very quick to offer to pick you up himself." She purses her lips as if suppressing a laugh. "It would have crushed him if I'd turned down such a sweet offer."

"Hmph," I mutter, not at all sure what just transpired.

I wash my hands, put on an apron, and help Melba and Artie put away the rest of the food.

"Have the guys from the post office been here lately?" I ask, remembering my first day here.

Melba chuckles deeply. "Where else do you think they're going to eat?"

I fold the towel I'd been using and set it down on the counter. The kitchen is immaculate, which I know is the only way my aunt will have it.

"Ready for the challenge of your life?" she asks me with a twinkle in her eye.

"Absolutely not," I say, "but let's go anyway."

319

We pull into my grandfather's gravel drive, half-expecting to find Fergie gone and chugging around out in the field. Instead, she sits in her usual place under the carport, looking as if she hasn't been driven in ages. I bet he won't take her out again for as long as he thinks he's going to lose his farm.

It's reassuring, then, when he emerges from the house before we have even finished parking the car.

"Thank the Lord," Melba says under her breath, "he's not in the bed."

He stands by the door wearing a navy blue jumpsuit that makes him look like an auto mechanic. When I climb out of my aunt's van, he breaks into a grin and holds both hands to his face in disbelief. He laughs out loud as I approach him.

"My lands, girl, you must've missed us bad!"

I fold my arms around his broad shoulders and feel him pat me lightly on my back. "You have no idea," I tell him. When I let go he is shaking. "Are you okay, Granddad?"

"I'm fine, I reckon," he says. "Just surprised to see you. Why don't y'all come on inside and have a glass of tea. Hey, sugar," he greets my aunt with an affectionate nod.

"Hi, Daddy," Melba says, holding the door as we make our way inside. Her smile is so big it dominates her entire face. We are partners in crime today.

My grandfather pours tea into three glasses and we settle at the kitchen table. "So, what brings you back so soon, and how long you plannin' to stay?"

"Everything, and as long as you'll all have me," I answer, and watch his face while this registers.

"You're back for good?" he asks, his eyes wide and disbelieving. I nod, and his eyes brim with tears.

"Is that okay?" I carefully inquire. Perhaps this is too soon. Perhaps I bring with me painful memories that are more easily kept at bay when he doesn't have to see my face that often.

He takes a deep breath and wipes his eyes with a handkerchief. "Oh I reckon it's more than okay. I've just gotten used to losing people, I s'pose." He blows his nose loudly and looks from me to Melba and then back to me. "I couldn't be happier," he says finally, and I know those aren't words my grandfather has said in a long time. I take this as my opening.

"There's one condition, though," I start to explain. He narrows his eyes then and folds his arms across his chest like a defiant child.

"Your aunt ever tell you I ain't one for conditions?"

320

"Yes," I say firmly, "yes, she has. But I'm only willing to stay if I know that everyone in my family is taken care of. I can't be here and watch people I love suffer."

He is still quiet and listening, but his head has started to almost imperceptibly shake from side to side, as if letting me know he has made up his mind and would rather me leave than listen to my condition.

"Let me finish before you decide anything," I demand. I look at my aunt who is uncharacteristically silent. She nods at me in encouragement. I know she will jump in if I need her to.

I inhale and hold my breath to the count of five before letting it go slowly and presenting my plan. "I want you to take the money Nina put aside for you that you never took from her and pay off your farm."

I expect him to turn red and for steam to shoot from his ears, but instead his shoulders droop and he seems to shrink into the chair. "I can't do that any more than I can bring my Baby Girl back from the grave."

"Why not?" I ask, not willing to drop the issue *ever*. "If you think about it, she wasn't really giving the money to you, she was giving it to you *for* Sandra. It technically wasn't yours to ignore. So imagine that Nina had been putting the money into an account for Sandra where it would have collected interest instead of sending you a check to tear up every month. Sandra would have accumulated a lot of money, which would more than have paid for her health care, and you never would have had to take a second mortgage out on your home."

"So then it's Sandra's money," my grandfather counters, "and still not mine to take."

"Of course it is, Daddy," Melba chimes in gently. "You were her next of kin. When a person passes away without a will, everything they have rightfully goes to the next of kin."

"Wouldn't Missi be her true next of kin?" he asks, defiant. "The money would still be yours."

"She didn't know me," I point out. "Not until a few weeks ago. Nobody bequeaths anything to someone they just met. *Please,* Granddad. It's yours.

"It *ain't*, though, darlin', no matter how you try to twist it. It was never mine to take. I made my choice and if I had it to do again, I'd make the same one." He looks at me sadly, and I know in this moment that he'll never change his mind about this.

"Daddy, you can't lose this place," Melba pleads. "This house holds every memory I have of Mama, and I can't allow you to let it be taken away from the rest of us when there is an alternative. I am not a selfish woman, but I will dig my heels in on this one. Our family started here."

"Our family isn't going to come to an end just because of a house," my grandfather calmly counters. "If I lose the house, life will go on. At some point I'm going to die and the house will go to someone else, and I assure you that life will go on then, too. This house does not define our family. The people in it do, and as long as we have each other, who cares what my address is?"

I begin to panic, because his arguments start to sound more convincing than mine. I came here determined to make him take the money, and he's thrown a curveball of logic our way. Of course a house doesn't define a family, but I still can't let this happen.

"I'll buy it!" I shout, startling everyone, including myself. Melba and my grandfather stare at me as though I have just taken my shirt off.

"What?" they ask in unison.

"The money isn't mine, either. I wasn't even very nice to Nina, and the only reason it got left to me is because she didn't have anyone else. If she'd had a cat, the cat would be loaded." I pause for effect, but they keep staring, so I continue. "But she didn't have a cat, so *I'm* loaded, and I don't want the money. I just sold her house for a million and a half dollars, for crying out loud!"

My aunt starts choking, and my grandfather looks horrified. It's too much information, I know, but I am desperate.

"You are officially the wealthiest person I know," Melba says. "You can't spend that kind of money in a lifetime down here."

"I know!" I yell, thinking this is just what I need to keep my argument afloat. "What am I going to do with it all? It's not as if I'm never going to earn another cent in my lifetime. I mean, I can't exactly retire at thirty-three! I still plan on doing something with my life, but right now I can buy twenty houses with what I have, so please," I look at my grandfather beseechingly. "Let me do this for you, for our family. If you won't take the money, then let me buy the farm."

He says nothing, but the defiance is gone from his face. I look for a sign to keep going but find none, so I shut up. I look at Aunt Melba again for guidance, but she is leaning back in her chair, satisfied that we have done all we can. I can hear the sounds of birds chirping outside, which makes the silence in the kitchen all the more deafening.

After what seems like an eternity, Charles Jenner clears his throat. "So you'd be what—my landlord?"

"What? No," I say, certain I have just screwed this entire thing up beyond repair. "That's not at all . . ."

"Would I pay you rent or something?"

"Of course not," I stammer, "why would you pay rent for something that you own outright?"

"You mean that *you* own outright," he corrects.

I try to calm the swirling feeling in my head long enough to process everything. "So you'll let me?"

"Let you what?" he asks.

"Let me buy the farm?" I clarify, wondering if we are still on the same subject anymore.

"The women in this family don't wait for people to *let* them do anything," he says. "Seems to me, you want to do something you're going to do it, regardless of whether or not anyone lets you. Guess you got yourself a squatter, then."

A squeal comes from my aunt and I realize I'm triumphant. "Well, now that that's settled," Melba says happily, "let's go surprise your cousins. Daddy, you coming?

"I reckon I am," my grandfather affirms, and all is right in the world again.

My homecoming, as my aunt has started calling it, is the single most perfect day of my life. Dory completely freaks out when she arrives home from school to find me here. She starts screaming and jumping around, then smothers me with hugs and soaks me with tears of joy. When she calms down, she heads to the phone and proceeds to call the rest of the family to share the news.

"They're all coming," she declares coming back into the kitchen later and wrapping her bony arms around me.

"Who all?"

"Everyone. Regina, the kids, and Angie are on their way, and Daddy, Little Dewayne, Stanley and Lamar are cutting out early and coming straight here. Daddy's not going to tell Neil Ray. We all want to watch him flip out," Dory giggles. "You know, he's been groping around here since you left."

I have to suppress a laugh, but the image sticks. "I heard," I say, the intended meaning still coming through and surprising me once more. I was so sure that after I left everyone would go back to old routines and, maybe not forget me, but think about me less. The fact that there has been actual moping is pretty awesome.

It feels so good to be sitting in Melba's kitchen again. It feels like home. We sit and talk for a little while until the roar of engines

323

alerts us to the fleet of vehicles driving toward the house. "Three pick-'em-ups, a minivan, and a Corolla," my grandfather calls out from where he stands by the window.

"Are you kidding?" I ask, running for the door.

"It's like a dang parade," he chuckles.

There is a cloud of dust swirling around in the yard, but I can hear the voices of people who are happy to see me.

"You're back!"

"Aunt Missi, Aunt Missi!"

"Are you really staying this time?"

"Welcome home, girl."

I stand and accept hugs for the longest time, and my face hurts from smiling. It is so good to see everyone, and I can hardly believe that they have all come running just to see me. That and the promise of a good meal, I'm sure. In the short time I've been gone, I swear the kids have grown, and Regina's belly definitely shows more obvious signs of its contents.

The kids start a game of wiffle baseball, and their great-grandfather pitches. I have never seen him interact with them before, but they are not the least bit thrown by it, and he seems to be having a great time.

As I stand surrounded by family and drink it all in, another truck pulls up and Neil Ray climbs out with a large brown paper sack in his arms. "Why on earth does Mama need four dozen eggs?" he asks, "And what's everyone doing here? Did I forget someone's birthday? It sure ain't mine . . ."

As I emerge from the crowd of relatives, the sack falls to the ground and Neil Ray transforms into a whooping maniac as he runs to me and lifts me off the ground.

"You're going to hurt yourself!" I holler, but he starts spinning me around and continues to shout.

"You're back, and nobody died!" he yells, and then quickly sets me down and looks around. "Did they?"

"No, baby," his mother clarifies. "Your best friend is back to stay. Washington no longer suited her."

"Hot damn!" Neil Ray exclaims, and hugs me once more. "Sorry," he says, suddenly embarrassed.

"Don't apologize to me," I say, basking in the enthusiasm with which I have been welcomed back, "but I think the eggs are toast." The sack sits in a crooked heap on the ground.

"It's okay," Dory pipes up. "We didn't really need eggs. Daddy just wanted to make sure he was the last one home." This elicits a

324

light punch in the arm from her brother, followed by a squeeze around her shoulders.

"It's okay, little sister," Neil Ray says. "It's totally worth it to have big sister back." The smile on his face is priceless.

One more truck pulls up the lane then, and I watch with surprise as Darryl gets out of it and fetches Lucy from the back seat. She is uncharacteristically smiley as they walk toward the large group of us, and when they get within earshot, I hear Darryl say, "Tell them what we've brought, sweet pea."

"Pizzi!" she yells, and I swear it's the cutest thing I've ever heard even though I have no idea what she just said.

"*Pizza?*" Marcus and Daniel scream in unison, clearly smarter than I am. "No way! We never get to eat pizza!"

"You went four towns over to get pizza?" Regina asks.

"I've got six of 'em in my truck that smell so good you're lucky we didn't eat them on the way here! Anyone want to give me a hand? We've got some celebrating to do." He winks at me, and it's all I can do not to throw up or pass out, I feel so nervous all of a sudden.

"He's diggin' you," Dory says quietly over my shoulder.

"Oh, hush, Dory," I say, but silently wonder if she could be right. I feel like my feet aren't touching the ground as I follow several of my family members to Darryl's truck.

"Can I carry anything?" I ask once there.

"How about this?" Darryl says, passing Lucy into my arms. She smells like apple juice and graham crackers, and looks me sternly in the eyes.

"What your name?" she asks in a whisper.

"Missi," I say quietly.

Lucy touches my nose with the tip of her tiny finger and looks at me for a moment. "Pizzi!" she finally calls out again as the boxes are unloaded and carried toward the house. We follow, and I take a mental snapshot of this moment to tuck away in my memory forever.

CHAPTER THIRTY-THREE

The sun went down an hour ago, but everyone is still going strong. The lights from inside the house cast a glow on the yard where the kids are playing an endless game of tag fueled by pizza and Hawaiian Punch. I sit on the tailgate of Little Dewayne's truck sipping sweet tea and thinking that there is no other place in the world I would rather be.

Several times tonight I have watched Darryl from a distance, and on two or three occasions he's caught me looking. I feel like an idiot, but I am completely out of practice where men are concerned. I locked up that part of myself when Josh came out of the closet, and honestly I'm more than a little scared of dusting it off again. Rejection hurts.

Neil Ray walks up and leans against the tailgate. He is openly drinking a beer in front of his parents, and nobody seems to mind. I take the can from him and take a swig, thinking of the day he took me fishing and told me, basically, to get a life. "Thought this was a forbidden," I say snidely.

"A hardworking guy deserves to relax every now and then," he answers. "I guess more than one of us is making grown-up decisions now."

"I guess so."

"Heard my rich cousin is buying the Jenner farm with her gazillions."

"They're really not my gazillions," I say uncomfortably, wondering if I'll ever come to terms with what Nina left me. "A lot of it should have gone to him years ago."

He takes a long drink. "Well, he's in there with Daddy and Dory throwing around plans for the barn and chicken house again, so

I'd say you've done something pretty amazing. I'm going to collect that lumber from my buddy this weekend and get it over there so we can get started before he changes his mind again." He looks across the yard peacefully and sighs. "You going to go out with Darryl Fortson?"

This catches me off guard, even though it's been on my mind all evening. "If he asks me I will," I say thoughtfully. "But he's got a lot to consider with Lucy and all. He might not be ready. Besides, I'm not sure he'd ever be ready for me."

"Oh, he's ready alright," Neil Ray says seductively. "He's even asked permission to ask you out!"

I nearly spit out my second sip of beer. "He did? Who did he ask, your parents?"

"Daddy, Mama, me, your friend Dolly . . ."

I freeze. "He asked Dolly? And all of you?" My head is spinning. "Well, what did you say?"

He snatches his beer back from my hand. "Well, I think we all wanted to say he's not good enough for you, but the truth is he's a great guy and you two'd make a nice couple."

My eyes water and I am about to throw my arms around my cousin until he adds, "Even though you're *much* older than him."

"Do what?" I exclaim, clamping my hand over my mouth as quickly as the words come out.

Neil Ray chuckles. "You know he's only thirty-one, cradle robber."

"Neil Ray!" I shout, slapping him playfully on the arm, causing beer to slosh around inside the can.

"Hey, watch the brew, sister," he teases. "Do you have any idea how hard these are to come by around here?"

I think about how hard it was to come by happy moments like this in my former life, but how they wash over me now like waves on a beach, one after the other. I hope that I never take for granted how it feels to love and be loved. I look through the darkness into the lit windows of the house and feel as if I am looking into the future, or maybe into my soul. Either way, I know that I have finally come home.

327

ACKNOWLEDGEMENTS

A special note of gratitude goes to my sister, Cori, whose intimate knowledge of heart diseases and the devices that treat them made sweet Sandra real.

I am forever grateful to the many that took time to read this book throughout all its stages. Your feedback and encouragement mean the world to me, as do your friendships.

Made in the USA
Middletown, DE
25 October 2017